FEVER 42

CHRISTOPHER FAHY

FEVER 42

CHRISTOPHER FAHY

OVERLOOK CONNECTION PRESS
2006

FEVER 42
©2002 by Christopher Fahy

Dust Jacket illustration © 2002 by Neal McPheeters

Published by
Overlook Connection Press
PO Box 1934, Hiram, Georgia 30141
www.overlookconnection.com
overlookcn@aol.com

Also Available in Trade Hardcover
ISBN: 1892950464

Trade Paperback
ISBN: 1892950332

Book Design & Typesetting:
David G. Barnett/Fat Cat Design

To:
Dave Hinchberger

1 • T.S. Eliot's Need

Ted Wharton came out of the dream with a raging erection. Which was nothing unusual; dreams always had that effect. Dreams about airplane rides or teaching Walt Whitman or watching World Series games all ended like that because that, for better or worse, was how he was made. Even nightmares would shock him awake to lie disoriented, dazed—and stiff. Why *stiff?* he wondered. Was he using it to defend himself in those battles and sweat-drenched flights? As a club or spear? As a magic wand? Why *stiff?* It was a mystery.

But this dream wasn't any mystery, this dream was one of *those*. It had been about Joy Dollinger, a kid in his honors psychology class. She had been on a bed, a bed in a field, a bed that was draped with a giant American flag. She'd been sitting right smack in this bed's dead center—noontime sun high up in blue—and was naked except for her underpants. It was shockingly hot and bright on the bed, but she smiled in the heat, cheeks flushed, her dark blond hair cascading across her breasts. He saw her firm flat stomach, navel, saw those white bikini underpants, askew, her sex exposed. He stared at her, at her curious smile, stared at her body shining in sun, then was quickly awake—to pale blue bedroom light, his member tight and throbbing, stiff as it had ever been in his life. He sighed, heard June, his wife, snore softly, snort, turn away from him under the sheet. He shifted, winced, and pushed himself out of the bed.

He feared that one of the kids would be up and about and catch him groggily staggering with his stupid bulge. Brad, thirteen, no doubt had bulges of his own by now that amounted to something. Still, to observe his old man in such a state. Kim, eleven—well God forbid she came upon him now. He maneuvered into the hallway carefully. The sun through the window crowned the horizon with red. All quiet on the eastern front.

In the bathroom he closed the door, sat down, and his penis touched the cold slick inside of the bowl. Oh *God* he hated that, but sitting was the only way to take care of erections like these. He sighed again and closed his eyes and the trickle of urine slowly came, the sentinels of muscle wavered, slowly the shaft went slack. The sex ache faded but didn't die. How long had it been since he and June...? Two weeks? It was on a Saturday (as usual), he remembered that, but...when?

Good God, he thought, forty-two years old and I'm horny as a high school kid. As horny as one of my goddamn students. "*Students,*" he mumbled. Except for Joy and a handful of others, *pupils*. Students, wouldn't it be nice.

He passed some gas, stood up, pulled up his pajamas and looked at himself in the mirror: forty-two years and five days old. Don't feel it inside, but the glass doesn't lie. He didn't really look *bad* for his age, he was only a *little* heavy, no belly to speak of, his neck hadn't started to wrinkle... But he'd always had a roundish, boyish face, and now a hollowness was capturing his cheeks, a sunken quality he didn't like, reminder of the skeleton below. More gray than he'd realized in that floppy bearlike bush of hair, and the crown...*was* getting thin. That puffiness under his eyes, that slackness below his ribs. *And at my back I always hear/ Time's winged chariot...*He turned the light on, which made things quite a bit worse, ran steaming water into the sink and lathered his graying beard.

• • • • •

His penis gave him another nice twinge as he slipped his jockey shorts on.

"What are you doing up so *early*?" June said from beneath the covers.

"Nightmares," Ted said.

"I *told* you to do that income tax."

I *told* you... *Jesus* he hated that tone in her voice. "The nightmares weren't about the tax."

"That's what caused them, though."

"You sure of that?"

"I'm positive."

"Great." He silently passed more gas as he zipped up his pants. "What's your schedule today?"

"I won't finish till six."

"I cook tonight?" He was sitting on the edge of the bed now, tying his shoes.

"Don't you always cook Thursdays?"

"Yeah."

"Then why did you ask if you cook?"

"I don't know, forget it." He pulled the shoelace tight and tied it forcefully. "What's in the freezer?"

"You do the shopping, you ought to know better than I do."

"Yeah." He stood. "Christ, Brad has the orthodontist."

"When?"

"Three thirty."

"I can't get away from the agency then."

"I know, I know, I'll take him."

"It's not such a great big deal."

"No, not for you, you never take him."

"Let's not start *that* again."

"Whatever you say." He looked at himself in the full length mirror that hung on the bedroom door. His face looked tired, sallow, drawn. Damn stupid dreams, they wrecked your sleep, what good did they do? Wish fulfillment. That asshole Freud. He thought of psychology class again, Joy Dollinger... And what would he teach them about today? Motivation. Moti-fucking-vation. I could use some, he thought. I could use a ton.

• • • • •

The *Courier-News* was lying outside in brittle springtime sun. He read it as he drank his coffee, ate his toast, and his mind kept wandering off to her hair, that shiny honey-colored hair. He saw her as she'd looked in class—when? Yesterday? The day before? In green. Green sweater? He remembered the dream...

He was faculty advisor to the *Whitman Bard*, the yearbook, and Joy was one of its editors. The other was Rick Castle, a bright, athletic, serious, hard-headed kid that Ted didn't like. Twice a week Joy and Rick worked together, twice a week they worked alone—across the hall from Ted's classroom in the audiovisual (A-V) room, the home of overhead, film strip, slide and video equipment. A long broad table of birch-grain formica took up one wall of that horrible room, and now it was covered with photos and typewritten copy and sketches with headings like, "Class Artists," "Senior Athletes," "The Student Council," etc.

Ted, now in his sixteenth year in the English department at Walt Whitman High School, Somerside, New Jersey, was yearbook advisor for the fourth time, surely a record. He hated the job; it was tedious, heightened his compulsive tendencies, and the corniness and sentimentality the project aroused in his students made him want to puke. And the room, that goddamn claustrophobic A-V room with no windows, stuffy as hell no matter what the season, even with air-conditioning, was the worst. Sometimes one of the editors showed some wit, like that Rodgers kid who had laid out pages called "Class Morons" and "Most Likely to be Incarcerated," but the kids he had this time…

Rick Castle—trim haircut, square jaw, accepted at Brown, a nascent broker or tax attorney—had no sense of humor at all. To Rick, the yearbook was serious business—*deadly* serious. It would be his gift to the ages, the only shrine most of his classmates would ever have, and it had to be right. He'd fiddled with the "Senior Athletes" page so often Ted wanted to choke him.

Joy Dollinger was totally different from Rick: offhanded about the yearbook, impatient, impulsive, creative. Ted couldn't quite figure her out, but he liked her; found himself looking forward to sessions where she was involved. She was bright—remarkably so—and attractive: five-six, dark blond and well proportioned, high cheekboned, her eyes a cool blue-gray. It wasn't her looks or brains that got him, though, it was her manner, that smile of hers. That skeptical, almost superior?—yes, *superior*—air.

He'd had her the first half of sophomore English, and even then, as a braces-faced reed, she'd seemed special somehow. Now, in the rarefied atmosphere of honors psychology, her uniqueness was unmistakable. She laughed at things that nobody else found funny, and then when the others cracked up, she sat deadpan. She never volunteered answers to easy questions, but waited till everyone else was stumped, then hit the bullseye. She knew so much about psychology Ted wondered if maybe her parents were in the field, so he looked them up in the records, and no, her father worked in insurance and her mother was a "housewife."

The way she looked at him in class disturbed him, but he couldn't say why. It wasn't a seductive look—or at least not your typical kind of seductive look; there was something odd, off-centered about it. That tiny gap between her front teeth when she smiled—why was it so attractive? Most teenage girls repelled him; they were too raw, too fresh, too milkily well-fed, but Joy was different. There was something quirky and angular there, something more mature. And now this dream of his, this fiction of subliminal design, had doubled her appeal.

Yesterday during sophomore English, his last class of the afternoon, he had given his "students" an open book test and helped Rick and Joy in the A-V room. Rick was once again shifting the photos around on the "Senior Athletes" page, and Ted was helping Joy decide what drawing to use to preface the senior class—most were mawkish, baroque—when Joy stood up, reached out and picked up a yearbook from another school, thumbed through it, then placed it in front of Ted. She leaned over his shoulder and said, "This is more what I had in mind. Subtle and clever. All the ideas we have so far are so *childish*."

As she said the word "childish," a wisp of her long blond hair brushed his cheek. A rich deep thrill went down his chest and he felt a bit hypnotized.

Throughout his adult life he'd had the feeling that somewhere inside him, quite close to his heart, there lived a tiny version of himself, a tiny Ted. This Little Man cowered and whined and laughed and wept and screamed and did all the other things big Ted might want to do but wouldn't dare. The Little Man had often made his presence known in these times with Joy, and now he was doing a cartwheel as big Ted's eyes looked down at the book in her hands. The picture she liked was nothing great, but it sure was better than what the "class artists" had drawn; it had *life*.

His voice sounded funny as he said, "Well, show this page to Arlene and Danny. They can do something this good."

Joy smiled her charming gap-toothed smile, stood straight again, and brushed back the wayward hank of hair. "How delightful to work with an optimist," she said.

• • • • •

Ted remembered this scene as Brad and Kim came charging into the kitchen with T.S. Eliot, whose eyes, as usual, were wide with amazement. Kim opened the door for the beast (white and furry, like a mutant sheep), who bounced across the lawn (*Mere anarchy is loosed upon the world*) and barked his way to the graveyard adjoining the land of those who dwelled on Harmony Lane's west side. Brad reached the refrigerator first, took out the milk and orange juice, and poured himself some of the latter. "Well what are you putting it back for?" Kim said testily. "You know I want some too."

"Here it is, here it is," Brad said, his croaky adam's apple voice still phlegmy with sleep. He put it on the counter so hard some juice sloshed out of its top.

"Thanks a lot, you're a big help, jeez."

Ted thought: And thus begins another episode in the drama of Ted Wharton, optimist.

Brad sat at the table; poured cereal, milk; started reading the cereal box. A year ago he was a kid, then the glands woke up, and now—The Incredible Hulk! He chewed with smacking sounds, engrossed in the crap on the box, and some milk squirted out of his lips.

"Oh gross, disgusting!" Kim said with a horrified face.

"Just shut your mouth," Brad said. His braces shone like armor in the sun that poured through the picture window.

"You shut *yours*," Kim said, "so you don't *drool* like a dog."

Ted ground his teeth together. Every goddamn morning, another fight. The words burst out: "When the hell are you going to learn that it's so much *easier*, so much more *pleasant* to be civil to one another? You *look* for trouble, you *look* for ways to pick each other apart. I'm so damn *tired* of it."

Brad started to read the cereal box again. Kim pouted and said, "Pass the milk, *please*."

Brad complied automatically, not looking up.

Ted folded the paper, laid it down, stood up; slipped his sportscoat on. As Brad grabbed the comics and avidly scanned them, Ted looked through the picture window—at T.S. Eliot, sniffing among the graves. That dog! When in, it wanted out; when out, it wanted in. If not barking, it was pissing; if not pissing, jumping. It had knocked people flat with its leaps; Ted was lucky he hadn't been sued. (If *he* could jump like that he'd be an NBA All-Star—even at forty-two.) It also had a habit of

CHRISTOPHER FAHY

rolling, squirming, writhing in anything putrid. Why? The vet had suggested a primitive hunting instinct; the dog was acquiring the scent of the thing it was going to track. If that was true, T.S. Eliot's ancestors must have tracked shit, since that's what it rolled in most.

Right now he was pissing; watering R.P. Wentworth, late head of the Haddonwood Bank. Ah well, Ted thought, *The paths of glory lead...* I'll pick you up outside of school at three," he said to Brad.

His eyes on the comics, Brad replied, "Uh-huh."

"Did you hear what I said? I'll come at three, so be on the corner."

"I heard you."

"Okay, have a good day at school."

"You too," Kim said.

"What's for supper?" Brad asked, mouth full.

"Christ, supper," Ted said. "London broil, I forgot to take it out." He started toward the refrigerator.

"I can't eat London broil when I have my braces tightened," Brad said.

Ted stopped. "That's right. Okay, spaghetti, then."

"But we had spaghetti on *Monday*," Kim wailed.

"Yeah, I know, but what can I do, he can't chew meat when he's had his braces tightened."

"He fakes it," Kim said. "It doesn't hurt that much, he just makes a big deal out of it."

Brad gave her a killer glare. "How would *you* know?" he said. Wait'll *you* have braces and it hurts, and I'll laugh at *you*."

"I'm not gonna *need* braces," Kim said, and Ted could have choked them both. "Shut *up!*" he said. "That's it! You'll have spaghetti! And I don't give a damn who likes it and who doesn't—you, your mother, me, *any* of us, that's *it!*"

Steaming, he left the kitchen and went to the living room, where his briefcase sat; picked it up, came back, went out through the garage. Snow clumps and a cold damp wind, the gifts of March. As he opened the Plymouth station wagon's door he looked at Waughbach Cemetery, and there in the sunstruck muck was T.S. Eliot, hard at work, his hairy haunches high on the butt of a sleek Irish setter.

The Bonanzas' dog, Ted thought. Good God, the Bonanzas' dog! "T.S.! You cut that out! Cut it out! Do you understand English? Get over here, *now*, or I'm sticking you in the bank!"

T.S. hated "the bank"—his doghouse—but the threat went unheeded. The frizzy white fool was locked in tight, oblivious. Ted picked up a stone and heaved, but it fell far short. He stood there watching, cursing, then got in the car and drove off.

The Bonanzas' dog! He hoped to God they hadn't seen the rape; he'd never gotten along with those people. Actually, he'd never gotten along with any of his neighbors, but then, except for the Bonanzas, he'd never *not* gotten along with them either. When he'd moved to Westdale eight years ago, a few of those boneheads had tendered him offers of "fun"; invitations to join the racquetball club, the swim club, the golf club, etc. He'd turned them down, though June had objected and joined the swim club without him "for the kids," and ever since then he'd been looked upon as an oddball.

He didn't even know the names of most of the people who lived on his street, and with June and the kids, he didn't bother to use the few names he knew. Since the neighbors all identified so strongly with their jobs—indeed, were appendages of their jobs—he referred to them by their line of work. Thus the guy who ran the auto agency was Mr. Chrysler, there were Mr. and Mrs. RCA, Mr. and Mrs. Monsanto (across the street), and the 7-Elevens (next door). Bores, one and all. "T.S. Eliot," Mrs. Chrysler had said, "such a cute name, it sounds so *English*." And she claimed to have gone to college.

The only guy he'd ever had angry words with—over T.S. Eliot's trespassing—was the Bonanza Steak House manager. And now whose dog was the fool beast humping? Of course.

As Whitman High came into view he thought of Joy and remembered his dream again. The power began to rise in his groin and he said to himself, My God, what would people think? The parents of these kids, my colleagues, June, what would they *think*? Joy Dollinger, how old is she, seventeen? Four years older than *Brad*? Well, asshole Freud was smack on the nose when it came to that stuff; where the glands were concerned, "right" didn't exist, the slippery bastards would fill you with juice and make you dream all *kinds* of things.

As he turned into the parking lot he thought he would take June's advice and finish the tax this weekend. He had enough problems without these wackadoo dreams.

· · · · ·

The staff room was filled with its morning bustle, everyone checking the mailboxes next to the door.

In and out went Elmer Crutch, the woodshop teacher, crusty, half deaf, with tufts of gray hair in his ears; Hank Springer, the peppy and trim and depressingly upbeat gym teacher past retirement age, who talked with his hands on his hips; Dawn Schwimmer, Spanish, with shocking pink nails, whose name made Ted think of that favorite painting of summer cottage owners, "September Morn"; and one of the math teachers, Murray Sheinstein, a dapper bowtied fellow, bald down the middle, with curls of black fuzz like the Stooge named Larry. "Good morning, Ted." (Hi, Larry. How's Curly? How's Moe?) "Morning, Murray, how's it going?"

On a sagging, cracking, plastic couch (evidence of the school district's spendthrift habits) sat Sara Kellogg, home economics; frog-like Esther Craven, biology; Joyce James, English, thin and weak-eyed, author of indecipherable memos; and Madge Nader, chemistry, president of the Teachers' Association. They sipped at their styrofoam coffees and chatted inanely. Allen ("The Jerk") Burk, head of the English department and Ted's immediate superior, stood talking to Gordon Hoover, history, one of those boobs enamored of high technology. A fitting fate for Hoover, Ted thought, would be heart-lung-liver-spleen-kidney transplant and all its attendant horrors.

What a rotten mood I'm in for a Thursday, he said to himself as he checked his "Dailygram," the list of the day's events. But how many members of this staff were competent—or even sane? Six? Eight? Maybe ten at the very most. Two of the sanest stood in the south wall sun, and Ted went over to them.

George Frangelli, history, had been teaching at Whitman for almost as long as Ted, and was Ted's only faculty friend. Marty Zeller, math, had been on board for only two years. He'd come from a South Philadelphia school and considered Whitman a piece of cake, but this morning he looked perturbed. With a squint and a little laugh he said, "Well, Ted, you see the purple people?"

"Who?"

That slow, tight Zeller smile. He was only about Ted's age, but looked years older; thin, drawn, dark, with slicked-down hair and hollows below his eyes. "The purple people, pal, the purple people."

Ted raised his eyebrows and said to George, "Translation?"

George—roundish, bald, with heavy tortoise-shell glasses—grinned. "A few of the kids shaved the tops of their heads and dyed their remaining hair purple. They have also seen fit to apply purple lipstick and purple nail polish, and stick purple rings in their noses and ears.

"Terrific. Girls, I hope."

"Two of them are," Marty said.

"Who are they?"

"Ginny Grayson, Gloria Wilks, Bob Ramsey, Eddie— What's that kid's last name?"

"Morrison," George said.

"I don't know them," Ted said.

"Lucky you," Marty said. "Only twenty more years to retirement, and now *this*. If it spreads, if it catches on, saints preserve us. Spending your life with adolescents, little did I know." His expression was sad and weary.

Ted laughed. "Hey, I have one at *home*."

"You poor, poor fellow," Marty said. "With braces? Pimples?"

"Braces, yes. No pimples yet."

"I pity you," Marty said. (He and Edith, his wife, didn't have any kids.) "But he'll grow out of it, it'll *end*. Here it *never* ends, they just keep coming *at* you. Lord!"

Ted chuckled. "Well, as you said, only twenty more years."

Marty groaned. "I have the purple people *now*, first period—and have to *ignore* them, act like they look like everyone else, or I'm doomed." He checked his watch. "Oh Christ, it's time. All right then, into the valley of death!"

Ted left the staff room with Marty and George behind shocking-pink-fingered Dawn Schwimmer (the rosy-fingered Dawn). In the hallway crush—the juking and jiving, the macho bravado, the flirting and giggling, the loud flood of faces familiar and foreign—the dream came back. He pressed it down. He would get into Poe this morning. Good old madman dope fiend Poe, who'd married his thirteen year old cousin. The kids would love it. He entered his room.

The dream kept replaying itself in his mind. By the time third period—honors psych—arrived, he was actually apprehensive, and when Joy came into the room he could feel himself flush. The dream had been so *vivid*: that giant bed, that blazing sun... But this was the real Joy, her hair not nearly so long as the hair of the Joy in the dream, and she said, "Hi, Mr. Wharton," blandly, smiled her curious tempting smile (those teeth!), and Ted felt weird as he said, "Hi, Joy. It's tomorrow we work on the yearbook, isn't it?"

"Yeah."

"I didn't think it was today."

He kept the class active, kept asking them questions, kept challenging them in order to fight off the dream. But his eyes kept going to Joy; and with time running out and a smartass junior, Terry Blaustein, yakking about rewards, the image of the bed came back so strong he began to grow firm. He nodded thoughtfully, as if weighing what Blaustein was blabbing about, and eased himself into the chair at his desk. When

Blaustein finished, Ted said, "Very perceptive. Good work. To explore the subject further, everybody read pages 205 to 209, and we'll continue with this tomorrow."

He looked up from the book, his organ aching, and again his eyes wandered to Joy. She was smiling at him now and his mouth went dry. He wet his lips and said, "Another topic I'd like you to read about starts on page 156..." That restlessness, that tension down below—he didn't like it at all.

· · · · ·

The tightening at the orthodontist's was more traumatic than usual. Brad nursed his spaghetti, sucking it rather than chewing, and making horrendous noise. He was still at the table when June came home. It was almost seven o'clock.

"Spaghetti," she said.

"Brad's teeth," Ted said. "I know we had it Monday, but it's all he can eat."

"I had lasagna for lunch."

"You want me to make you a western?"

"No, it's okay."

Brad got up from the table, a strand of spaghetti still dangling out of his mouth. He sucked it, *slurp*, and it vanished. He went to the family room to watch TV, and the argument started with Kim.

"Jesus," Ted said, "those *kids*. They do nothing but pick on each other."

June sat at the table. In the overhead light her face looked greasy, gray.

Ted went to the colander, dished out a bowl of spaghetti. "I've *had* it with kids," he said. "*All* kids. Christ, a bunch of them chopped up their hair and then dyed it purple. You should've seen them, they looked like freaks."

"I guess that's the point," June said.

He set the bowl in front of her. "I guess it is. I'd like to work in a world where everyone's over twenty-five for a change. I put up with those dodos all day at school and then I come home to *these* two."

"Send them up to their rooms."

"They've calmed down now."

The spaghetti steamed up to the light. June stared at the bowl. Ted looked at her face and his tiredness deepened.

The day had been rough. During lunchroom duty the kids had pushed into the hallway ahead of the bell and he'd bullied them back. The clowns with the purple hair had cavorted outside, making hash out of sophomore English. That goddamn dream, the orthodontist, making dinner—and he still had his papers to grade. To June he said, "You look bushed. Do you want some wine?"

"Please."

He went to a cabinet for cabernet and glasses; came back, sat down, and poured.

June sipped her wine. She picked at her salad and said, "I'm bushed, all right. Everyone wants to go to Disney World."

"Everyone *always* wants to go to Disney World."

"But today was just madness. The airlines keep changing their prices..."

"You're due for a raise."

"Yeah, I guess, but I can't complain. I get such a good deal on travel."

"You can't eat travel."

She smiled, fork stuck in her food. "What a typical Ted remark."

He swallowed the wine in his mouth; put his glass on the table again. "Hey June, it's nice you like to travel, but the basic reason for working is money, right?"

She ate a bite of spaghetti, drank some wine. She looked at him and said, "The job is stimulating. I get to go all over the world dirt cheap." Her hair—short, frosted, blond—looked artificial. "I like seeing new places and doing new things, that's why I work for a travel agency, not just for the money. I don't want to stagnate, Ted. I don't want to do the same things over and over, day after day, I'm not happy that way."

He looked at her still quite pretty face, the bags below her eyes, and said, "Do you think I'm happy that way?"

"You seem to be." She frowned at her bowl. "Did you put any salt in this sauce?"

He gave her the shaker. His stomach hurt. He had eaten too much, one of his common failings. He sipped his wine. June salted her sauce as he said, "June, somebody's got to man the ship. I know you like to travel. I know you like your job, but if you're doing that, *somebody's* got to take the kids to the dentist."

"Not the martyr bit."

"It isn't any martyr bit, it's a *fact*." He drank some wine. He stared at the glass, at the shimmer of light on the cabernet's dark red surface, and suddenly the dream came back again. He said, "Let's forget this crap. You busy tonight?"

"Meaning?"

"What do you think?"

"I'm exhausted, Ted."

"So am I. But you want to know something? You know how often we make it? Once a month. Twelve times a year. That's ridiculous, June."

"We're busy people."

"Too busy. We've just got to find more time for ourselves."

"I'd love to, but how?"

"Let's take showers and hit the sack early."

She pushed her half-full bowl away and oh, did he hate that gesture. It simply meant she wasn't hungry, but always seemed to imply much more: a rejection of his cooking—a rejection of *him*. "I'm really worn out," she said.

"Come on." Jesus Christ, did he have to beg?

She cupped her hand over her mouth, closed her eyes, and sneezed. Ted waited till she sneezed again. She always sneezed twice, never more, never less. As she blinked and twitched her nose he said, "So what do you say?"

She sighed. "Oh, all right. I need a shower anyway, that damn office was hot."

• • • • •

The shower refreshed him, but soon he was tired again. He had drunk two more glasses of wine while grading the papers, and now, as they went to their room, he was flushed and warm.

Kim was in bed and asleep, but Brad was still watching TV. As Ted slowly ascended the stairs he heard the announcer say, "As long as you are between the ages of forty-five and seventy-five, the National Association of Senior Citizens guarantees you…" Forty-five! Ted said to himself. That's obscene!

June yawned and removed her robe. The lamp near the bed drew dark shadows below her limp breasts, threw highlights on the stretch marks on her bulging abdomen. In his sleepy wine-induced high, Ted thought: *Too fast! Life is going too fast!* How lovely she'd been such a short time ago, with her round-jawed beauty queen face, blond hair, green eyes, smooth skin. Short time? They'd been married for seventeen years! And these last few years had fled like thieves, and terrible changes had taken place, and now she was thirty-eight, he was forty-two. A loss of luster in the skin, that wrinkled stuff at the eyes... Their youth was gone!

But I don't *feel* old, he told himself as he slipped into bed beside her. He kissed her neck mechanically, thinking: How am I different now from when I was nineteen or twenty? He pecked at her ear. I'm tired, that's how I'm different. God, when I was nineteen...

He stroked her buttocks and a terrible sluggishness hit him. The wine. Why the hell had he drunk all that wine? She kissed him without any passion. He reached below. He rubbed his finger this way, that way, kissed her neck and rubbed harder. Felt her cringe. Hurting her, too rough.

He eased off. Her eyes were closed and he reintroduced his hand. It went easier now. The dream returned with sudden force and he found himself starting to grow. He rubbed his organ against June's thigh. She spread her legs—reluctantly, he thought.

At last he was hard with the image: Joy Dollinger on the red-white-blue striped bed, and his fingers were working smoothly now and June was breathing heavily. It's still there, I've still got it, he thought. It takes longer, okay, but at least it's still *there*. When her eyes were shut, her mouth drawn back as if in pain, he knew she was ready—or ready enough—and he entered.

And let Joy's image carry him off as he held his wife of seventeen years and worked quickly, quickly, forcing the feeling to rise. But then when it did, a horrible wash of dread shot through him, Joy's image died, and what he saw was T.S. Eliot humping the Irish setter. He was suddenly left with himself, with the heat of himself and the wine, June's flaccid breasts, too real in the light, his undigested dinner in his gut.

He worked harder, broke into a sweat. He tried to recover the image of Joy but it wouldn't come clear; it was distant, blurred, mixed up with T.S. Eliot, he felt the slosh of food in his stomach, the slick cold sweat on his skin; could feel June's interest wane, knew she wanted it finished. "Hey," she said, "you asked for this, what happened, is it too much for you?"

That did it; cut him dead. Nothing left but to fake it. He groaned and collapsed on her in his sweat, his heart beating fast and hard in his ears, his stomach slightly sick.

"Did you make it?" she asked.

He was slimy, as slick as a snail. "Yes," he lied, out of breath, his heart beating fast, too fast. As he groped for the tissues, he pictured himself dropping dead of a heart attack. He rolled onto his side, gave her tissues, and wiped himself. "Hand me my underpants," she said. He did. She slipped them on, stuffed tissues inside them. "Well, better than nothing," she said.

"Yeah," he said, his heart starting to fall. He belched acid, went into the bathroom.

He urinated, his penis ragged, insignificant, then looked in the mirror. I'm old, he thought. I'm fucking *old*. He stared at the slivers of gray in his hair, the slack at his hips, and then—deep sadness struck. *The goddamn wine*, he thought, *I drank too much*. He heard Brad close the door downstairs and click off the light, and he hurried back to his room.

June was already snoring. He lay there in darkness, listening. She had never snored until four years ago. She couldn't help it, of course, but it drove him wild. He poked the bed. "What!" she said with alarm in her voice. "Turn over, you're snoring," he said. She did. The snoring stopped for a minute then started again.

He lay there, shaft throbbing with thwarted desire and listened to June's loud snores. Then they stopped and the house was still. Dead still. He felt buried, he felt like a corpse. In his mind he saw Waughbach Cemetery, those gravestones waiting there at the edge of his land. He thought of the day's events, the purple kids, that dream again…

June's snoring resumed. He felt sick to his heart. With Joy in his mind and his eyes squeezed shut, he desperately masturbated.

2 • THE LITTLE MAN WIDE AWAKE

June's snoring kept waking him all night long. He'd lie there tensely, staring at darkness, then finally he'd touch her shoulder, making her jerk and say, "What!" "You're snoring," he'd say, and she'd fall back to sleep, and a few minutes later start sawing the lumber again.

A horrendous affliction with no sure cure. Modern medicine's whiz kids could transplant hearts, but were stumped by the common snore. What a boon nose transplants would be! Till then he'd have to live with the racket—or sleep in the study, which June would surely perceive as a lessening of affection.

Each time a snort woke him up he remembered Joy: saw her there in psychology class; in the A-V room as she worked on the yearbook, her legs on the rungs of the stool; on that huge red-white-blue bed in her underpants. The last of these images kept him alert for an hour.

The alarm played music at his foggy brain and he moaned and told himself: Friday. Keep thinking that. It's Friday.

The paper was there, the kids, the dog, June rushing out early. The kids in their morning battle. The paper, the kids and June, the dog, the thoughts of school, paper kids, June dog, school thoughts, the old routine. I don't want to stagnate, June had said, I don't want to do the same things over and over, I'm not happy that way. Do you think I'm happy that way? he had said. But damn it, society had its structure. School started at nine and stopped at two-thirty, you had to be in by eight and leave no sooner than three. There were seven days in a week, and mortgages and VISA cards, and kids with schedules of their own, so what could you do? Break it up now and then with a flight to Tahiti or Maui or Munich or some other place that was so Americanized it might as well be Cleveland? Maybe that did the trick for June, but it left him cold and exhausted, and even more broke than before.

June loved those trips. And the garbage she bought at those duty-free shops! She was expert at spending; in fact, it was her greatest strength. The money she earned at Happy Trails Travel didn't half cover her appetites, and Ted had to work every summer to make ends meet.

So what would he do this year? Teach summer school? Tend bar? Check servicemen's cars before they were shipped overseas as he'd done two years ago, employment compliments of the Colonel, June's father, to whom he was supposed to be grateful for the rest of his life? It paid good money and was better than slaving through syntax with teenage imbeciles or mixing drinks for older imbeciles who'd forgotten syntax and everything else they had learned in school, but lord, if it took a good word from the Colonel to work there again…

Mr. Monsanto was there when Ted went outside, inspecting a bush for signs of early bloom. Inadvertantly, he cast his glance Ted's way. The distance between them—the width of the street—was a bit too skimpy for them to ignore each other, so they nodded and said hello. Monsanto had two weeks vacation a year. One reason Ted had gone into teaching was to avoid that two week deal, and now, with his summer jobs, he was lucky if he got a week.

He got into the Plymouth and drove away. A summer free, how nice it would be. Loaf around, read those books he had meant to read, maybe swim some, go fishing. He hadn't gone fishing in years, since Brad gave it up, and he asked himself: Do I *like* to fish anymore? What *do* I like to do?

Years ago he'd had tons of interests, and now? He was almost as bad as Brad, whose only delight seemed to come from those cursed video games. Quarter after quarter down the slot, while the country couldn't house its poor or rehabilitate its handicapped or pay its teachers decent wages. Ted's brother, Frank, no whiz at school, had spurned a college education and become an electrical contractor. Now he made twice as much as Ted and took six weeks' vacation, four in August and two—in Aruba—in February.

Oh well, Ted thought as he pulled away from the traffic light, too late to change things now. What else could he *do* but teach? What else did he *want* to do? Maybe Frank would take him on as a helper? The job held no appeal, but at least he'd be making money. Working for his baby brother, wouldn't that be something? Moving back to Maryland, to Epitaph, the old home town? Admitting that Frank, the one who hadn't gone to college, had been right? Too embarrassing, no, he could never do it. Anyway, he'd probably hook up some wires wrong and electrocute himself. If that should happen, what a loss to the world. Shelley, Keats, the Crane boys, Thomas Wolfe, Ted Wharton, gone before their prime. How sad. My *prime*, he thought. He belched a sour belch and thought of the end of the day and The Spouting Whale.

· · · · ·

In the staff room, some of the same cast of clowns: Hank Springer, his hands, as usual, on his hips; Murray Sheinstein ("Good morning, Ted." "Good morning, Murray."); and a few who hadn't been present this same time yesterday: Paul Whiteside, earth science, one of the few black faculty members; Morty Price, who taught business and looked like a floorwalker; Dixie Tower, who taught French and looked like a streetwalker; Maddy Bisbee, art, red-cheeked and Rubenesque; and next to Ted as he looked in his box, Dora Rosen, librarian—petite and thirtyish, frowning as she checked the Dailygram. One of those fringe folks who never did front line battle, Dora had only been with the system a year and a half, and Ted didn't know her well. "Hi, Dora." "Hi, Ted." Librarian? he thought. Perhaps that was more his speed. He was always taking courses anyway, so why not in library science? He went through his mail, began tossing it into the trash.

Burk the Jerk was with Gordon Hoover again. Ted ignored them. Marty Zeller came up, his tired dark eyes squinting.

"So how'd the purple people eaters treat you?" Ted asked.

Marty grunted. "Twenty more years," he said. "Pretty soon we'll need cops in the hallways even out *here*, in the *country*."

Ted laughed. "It's hardly country."

"Compared to South Philly, it's country," Marty said. He reached in his mailbox as Ted tossed the last of his junk away. "All I ask is a little peace and quiet," Marty said as he looked at the crap. "I promise not to take up a lot of space, just give me a room and a little stipend, my brandy at night and my golf on the weekends, I promise not to kill anybody or run for office..." Opening his fingers wide, he dropped his mail in the trash can on top of Ted's. And suddenly Burk was there, saying, "Ted, may I see you a minute?"

Ted followed him to a spot to the left of the bulletin board thinking, Christ, now what?

"I've been talking with Howard," Burk said in that prissy way of his that drove Ted wild. Howard was Howard Grimsley, the superintendent, and Ted thought, Uh-oh, trouble. Burk said, "Howard wants to organize a Media Review Committee, and I think you'd be an ideal choice to serve on it." He smiled a prim, coercive smile.

Jesus, just what I need, Ted thought. He said, "A Media Review Committee? What's it going to do, watch TV shows?"

Burk pursed his lips. "Set library book selection policy, that sort of thing."

"I thought the library *had* a policy."

Burk said, "You know how Miss Page was."

Ted did indeed. Miss Page had been the school librarian for ages. In her dotage she'd taken to hiding new library books in her house. "Well what about Mrs. Rosen?"

"*Ms.* Rosen has a policy of *sorts*," Burk said, but Howard feels too much is left to her individual discretion—a carryover from the Page administration." He stood there, ramrod straight, diminutive, his wingtips sparkling. "Think about it," he said. "I'm sure you'll do an *excellent* job," and he bustled off. Everybody left the staff room, and Ted's heart sank.

As he entered the hallway chaos he thought, The Jerk had to pull this on a Friday, didn't he? Goddamn it, I ought to say no! I ought to say no right out!

"Hi, Ted, how's tricks?"

Looking up at the sound of the drawling deep voice and internally cringing, he saw the principal, Big Marvin LeMaster, loping along beside him. LeMaster was about 6-6, two hundred and forty pounds, pear-shaped, hound-faced, with huge black-stockinged calves. He was quite a bit younger than Ted, but horrendously weighty and pompous.

He huffed and puffed as he walked along. "Allen speak to you yet about the proposed committee?" He said it with eyebrows raised, eyes wide, hoping, of course, that Burk *hadn't* said anything so that *he* could drop the bomb.

"He just mentioned it to me," Ted said.

"Good," LeMaster said, not quite hiding his disappointment. "Well, we better get cracking. I'll call the first meeting in a week or two."

Oh no, Ted thought, not Marvelous *Marv* as chairman! Well sure, the principal had to be on the committee, so why not put him in charge? Phil Shuck, vice-principal, would also be appointed, but he was no problem, a guaranteed no-show. Lord, what a pair they were! Without Grimsley, the superintendent, a real tough nut, and Warren Volstead, the semi-literate ex-marine in charge of student discipline, the place would fall apart. In a system riddled from top to bottom with boobs, LeMaster was the biggest boob of all—and many of the staff routinely added a suffix to his name that led to his being known as The Big Jerk *Off*, as opposed to the simple Jerk of Allen Burk.

LeMasterbator loped and wheezed. "I'll check my calendar and get back to you soon," he said.

Ted said, "Terrific," hoping the sarcasm wasn't apparent. He stopped at his room and watched the Marvel amble down the hall. Why didn't I just say no? he thought. Goddamn it, no spine, no *spine*. Belching, he went through his door to face senior English.

He was depressed all morning because of LeMaster and Burk. Because he hadn't said *no* to LeMaster and Burk. What a pushover. Always had been, always would be. And he was tired, exhausted, distracted, something would have to be done about June's snoring, but Jesus, *what?* Laser? How could he broach the subject without all hell breaking loose?

First period, the seniors and more Poe. All agreed he was cool. Opium, booze, that thirteen year old cousin, yes, he was quite a guy. In a way there was something to be said for living your life flat out like that. But the pain, the *pain*. You had to be a genuine lunatic to make it work, not suburbanite sane and teacher tame, and Christ this would be a long day.

He practically slept through second period, junior English. He desperately needed a boost, and so, third period, psychology, he decided to jump head first into asshole Freud. It would wake everybody up, including himself, it always did. They might not go for rats in mazes, Thorndike, Hull and Skinner, but Freud brought them back from the dead.

The ego, id and superego, Ted explained, were the mind's Three Stooges: Moe, the hard-headed director, was ego; Curly, with his appetite, was id; and Larry (Ted thought of Murray Sheinstein as he spoke) was superego—conscience-stricken scaredy-cat. The kids, as always, lapped it up. And the thing of it was, as a teaching device, it worked. No one had ever yet failed his test on Freud's personality theory.

Joy Dollinger watched Ted's act with a subdued, bemused expression. Does she like this or not? he kept asking himself, and damn it, the dream came back *again*. He lectured with increased animation, drawing on the board (the iceberg/unconscious diagram), and pacing back and forth. Much laughter from most of his fans, but no more than a puzzled smile from Joy. By the time the period ended, though, his mood was ten times brighter.

Study hall duty, lunch, and then sixth period, sophomore English. He taught half the session, then gave an assignment and went across the hall to the A-V room. What he saw when he went through the door made him catch his breath.

Joy worked on the yearbook without Rick Castle on Fridays, and there she was at the phony birch table, her feet on the middle rungs of her stool, her skirt high up on her thighs. Ted stood there a minute just looking, then closed the door.

Joy gave no hint that she knew he was there. He went to her, keeping his eyes off those glorious thighs. "So how are things working out?" he asked.

"Sssh," she said, unstartled.

Ted smiled, fascinated by her single-mindedness. She moved some type, replaced one photo with another. "There," she said with a shake of her head, her blond hair flicking. "Rick will kill me, but this is the way I like it."

"It looks better that way," Ted said. Furtive glance at her knees. "Did the band photos come?"

"Not yet."

"You better call Keebler. We don't have much time left."

"I called yesterday. He promised they'd be here Monday."

"Good." That muscled indentation in her thigh. The Little Man was gawking now with beady eyes.

She moved on the stool, exposing her legs still more. She was wearing a gauzy pale blue blouse with the top three buttons undone, and her shift in position revealed the high curve of her breast. The Little Man gaped. Ted quickly looked at the layout, feeling heat rise to his face. Her scent, that flowery perfume; an artificial smell, between realities, but very, very nice.

She said, "I have something to show you," reached for a manila envelope, peeked into it, and brought out a bunch of snapshots, most of them curled and worn. Shots of babies and little kids. "'When We Were Very Young,'" she said. She grinned an adorable "isn't that corny" grin and held out a photo. "Look at this little sweetie."

Ted laughed. A toddler in a baseball cap, holding a tiny bat; the cap crooked, the shorts falling down.

"Jim O'Connell," Joy said. "Would you believe a hairy ape like that once looked like *this*? What was it the old song said? 'Money can make you funny, but time will wipe you *out*.'"

"How true," Ted said. He felt a twinge of sadness, stifled it and looked at Joy's next selection: A smiling, ruddy cherub with a watering can in her fist.

"Who's that?"

"Three guesses."

"I'm afraid I have no idea."

"That," Joy said with a laugh, "is Judy Brannigan."

"You're kidding."

"Judy 'The Blimp' Brannigan, age two. Who could ever predict that a cutie like this would grow into the fearsome blubberball we know and despise today?"

Ted sidestepped this remark with, "Are her parents heavy?"

"I never laid eyes on them," Joy said, laughing again. That gap in her teeth, that delicate pale blond fuzz on her upper lip. "Good God these are funny." She rifled through them, shrugged and said, "We can't use them all, though, there's not enough room, so somebody's feelings are going to be hurt. Here's the picture of me," and she handed it over.

A slender little blond-haired girl, nude, stared quizzically into the lens. Ted looked at the slit at the top of her little pudenda and felt himself blush. "Yes, I think this is one that you'd better not use," he said.

She wore that same questioning, eyebrow-bent gaze from back then in toddler time. "You don't think I'm cute?"

"Adorable," he said. "But I don't think the *Whitman Bard* is ready for centerfolds."

Joy laughed, took the photo back, sat scrutinizing it. "My hair was so *blond* back then," she said. "It was light like that until I was seven or eight, then it started to change. I liked it better the other way." She flashed her smile; his heart took a quick bright leap. "Quite a dynamite body, don't you think?"

"Yeah, you were a knockout."

"Were?"

Ted's throat seemed to catch for a second. "I'm afraid we won't be able to use that shot," he said evasively. "Don't you have one that's less controversial?"

She smiled coyly. "Why Mr. Wharton, I do believe you're embarrassed."

He ignored that, too, feeling strangely disorganized, and looked at the layout again.

"Well, don't worry," she said as she stuffed the photos back in the envelope, "there won't be any pictures of baby Joy in the *Whitman Sampler*" (her facetious term for the *Bard*). "There's been grumbling from certain quarters that I'm already taking up too much precious space. Student council, honor society, this committee, that committee, literary magazine… As if anyone cared if they had their picture in some stupid thing that will sit in the top of a closet for fifty years. A lot of these jokers see this as the peak. This! Whitman High! And it probably *will* be the peak for some of them. These hotshot jocks are big heroes now, but once they graduate, then what? They'll look backward at this all their lives. My God, can you imagine that? I want to look forward, always forward, I want to keep trying new things for ever and ever."

Ted found himself slightly mesmerized again. The Little Man, however, was wide awake; and as Ted stared down at Joy's mouth, at that top tooth gap more appealing to him than perfection, the Little Man was bending closer, closer—and kissing Joy's cheek!

Clearing his throat decisively, Ted said, "This discussion is interesting, Joy, but it isn't getting the yearbook done. How do you plan to handle this student council page?"

She shifted on the stool again and said, "I thought I'd put the logo center left and have the officers around it in a wheel."

Ted pushed the logo into position. "Okay, you've got this here. Now…"

"No, down this way more," Joy said.

As she reached for the logo, her hand grazed his. When it did, it froze, just stayed there, touching him, and neither of them moved.

A shock flashed up Ted's arm and struck his chest; he felt weak in his center, dazed. Time disappeared. There was nothing except this hand of hers, this smooth and magical construction hot and soft on his startled skin. "Oh…here," he said.

She looked at him, eyes bright and bold. "No, here," she said in a soft voice, moving the logo down. She smiled. "Well, what do you think?"

Bright puffs inside him blew apart; the Little Man felt faint. "And then the officers go around it."

"Like this," Joy said, distributing the photographs. "The one of me is atrocious, isn't it?"

Ted's tongue was stiff. "It looks fine," he said. "The whole arrangement looks fine. Then the group picture—"

"Goes right here, at the bottom, centered. And Miss Spoonfeather goes on the right."

"Looks great," Ted said. The bell rang in the hall, reminding him of his roomful of sophomores, certainly out of control by now. He said, "Looks good, real good. Well, I've got to get back to my class. Just set that aside and I'll see what Rick thinks of it Monday. Maybe we'll have the band photos by then."

"I hope so," Joy said.

"See you later," Ted said.

The corridor was cool, disorienting. He hurried across to his class feeling guilty—about what?—and…naked, transparent.

He calmed the disorder, collected the papers, gave homework and stood at the door till the last of his "students" was gone. Then he sat at his desk thinking—what?—with a frown. Again, in the hallway, the bell, forlorn and hollow now. Was it a vision or a waking dream? Fled was that music: Did he wake or sleep?

● ● ● ● ●

In The Spouting Whale he wasn't tired at all, just agitated, irritable, thinking about Joy's hand on top of his. He drank his beers, he listened to the talk, he watched the patrons laugh and gesture, come and go—and he felt old.

He'd been coming to The Spouting Whale on Friday afternoons for sixteen years. It was a ritual with many of the Whitman faculty—male faculty, primarily, though an occasional intrepid female staff member sometimes wandered in. Ted had seen the tavern change from "The Submarine" to "The Captain's Cabin" to its current appellation, and lord, the changes in the faculty in all that time. He and George—and Burk the Jerk—were the only old-timers left. Old-timers. Old. As Marty Zeller talked, Ted felt antique.

The purple people had raised some hell in Marty's class and he'd had to get Volstead to haul them out. As he leaned on the table, smoking, he looked exhausted. "Years ago, I actually wanted to *teach* kids something," he said. "No joke, I really *did*." He was into his fourth beer and starting to get a bit maudlin. "I wanted to give them the *feel* of numbers, show them that math is *exciting*."

"I wish somebody would show *me* that," Ted said, disturbed by his thoughts of Joy, but trying to cheer things up.

"I could do it," said Marty. "Christ, I could teach math by having the kids play darts, do you realize that?" He was watching the dart players down by the mensroom door. He smoked, eyes distant, sad, and looked at George. "But Jesus was I naive. To think that the kids would care. To think that the administration... Stimulation is the *last* thing those assholes want. Every principal I ever worked for was just like LeMasterbator. Never gave a good goddamn about a thing except appearances. If the kids were quiet and the shades were drawn and the doors were shut at the end of the day, they were happy. I learned. You learn or you don't survive." He smoked; he looked at the dart game again. George Frangelli, raising his stubby eyebrows, sipped his beer.

Ted felt sorry for Marty. The guy was a born teacher, no doubt about it, and now he was plain burnt out. Ted had never had Marty's zeal. He had gone into education to avoid the draft, have summers off, and because it seemed like a fairly harmless way to make a living, not because of any burning desire to teach. Once in it, though, he'd found that he liked it, liked most of the kids, and was actually pretty good. But the years had taken their toll on him, too; he'd just had too damn much of Whitman; its high-pressure parents, its wiseguys and toughguys, its faculty meetings, its Marvin LeMasters and Grimsleys and all the rest. The routine. Too much of the goddamn routine.

"Ideals," Marty sniffed. "You know what it all boils down to? A choice of ways to prostitute yourself. I don't care what line of work you choose, it always comes down to that."

George said, "Marty, you need more beer." He raised his hand like a student to signal the waitress, who came and took the order.

Marty smoked with a faded smile. His eyes seemed focused on something beyond the room. "I have this cabin in Pennsylvania," he said. "It's back a dirt road on a little pond. Edith and I spend two weeks a year at that cabin. She reads, I fish, I loaf around, I watch the birds. I love that place. If I had the money I'd move there tomorrow and never be heard from again. I'd plant my garden there." He looked at Ted. "You've seen the garden I have in my yard down here? I'd have one twice as big up there. A garden keeps you sane, it really does."

The waitress came back with the beer. Marty stared at the glass, then lifted it slowly and sipped at the foam. "It is necessary to cultivate one's garden. Candide, right, Ted?"

Now Ted *was* tired. The lack of sleep from the night before, the excitement of Joy, the beer and Marty's gloom had suddenly hit him. "Right," he said.

"I don't have any dreams, all I want is that cabin and garden," Marty said. "Teaching? Maybe in China or Japan or Israel or some other place where they value education instead of degrees. You see those pictures of Japanese students *bowing* to their teachers. Jesus." He stared at his beer.

Ted and George exchanged glances. George raised his glass. "Well, here's to twenty more years," he said.

"To twenty more years," Marty said with a tired grin.

They all drank.

3 • MALLED

Saturday morning, Ted worked on the income tax, distracted by bloom on the forsythia, that scraggly untrimmed yellow band between his land and the cemetery.

When Ted had considered buying this house, so long ago, the realtor had said to him, "You got quiet neighbors out back. *Real* quiet," and Ted had never guessed how much time he would spend in this study trying to work but finding himself instead staring out at those graves.

It would seem to make sense to purchase a plot in Waughbach; he wouldn't have far to go when he kicked the bucket. But no, they would cart him off somewhere and do things to him, then bring him back here, so, from the travel angle, Waughbach held no firm advantage over any other place. And since he seemed doomed to live out the rest of his days in good old Westdale, it might be nice to spend eternity somewhere totally different. California, maybe, or Maine, Hawaii...

Typical income tax-induced thoughts. And this morning a further distraction, of course—Joy Dollinger: that moment when their hands reached out and touched. He hadn't moved away—not instantly, as he always had during similar accidents with other girls—and that was pretty scary.

For what happened when their fingers touched, what happened that time when her hair brushed his cheek, was: chills. Yes, genuine *chills*, a sensation he hadn't felt in years. In his youth he'd had plenty of chills: from certain landscapes, cloud formations, music, movies, plays; from poetry, mere sequences of sounds and words; and of course, most of all, from girls.

One time right before their engagement, he and June had spent thirteen straight hours necking. Brief food and bathroom breaks, then back to the couch and their arms, lips, tongues. Thirteen straight hours! He couldn't conceive of that now. Thirteen hours of *anything* would bore him stiff.

For years now he'd had the notion that life as he lived it was merely a temporary situation, a transitional stage to something far better. But that far better stage never came. When was the last time he'd had real chills—till these touches of Joy's? Back when Brad was a baby? That long ago? Good God, it was true! He thought of Brad's birth and those wonderful first three years. He'd been such a neat kid and they'd had such great fun on the bed or the grass or splashing around on the beach. Watching his son discover the world had affected him deeply, and chills? You bet. By the time Kim arrived, he'd been through the process once and it didn't have nearly the edge. Not nearly as many chills with her, but *some.*

Now the kids never gave him chills. He loved them and was curious about them, fascinated by them, but they didn't thrill him. It was fun to watch Brad play ball, to watch Kim at gymnastics, but not *thrilling.* To be honest, *nothing* was thrilling, *nothing* had any edge, it was all *deja vu.* He didn't want to go places, meet anyone new, because they weren't new, they were clones who all talked about money and sports and politics, crap that put him to sleep. It was easy enough to put him to sleep, because he was always tired. Where the hell had his energy gone, his enthusiasm? It seemed as if a veil had dropped over the world. Why? Brain cells rotting? Nerve endings dying? Was this what it meant to get old? *But yet I know, where'er I go, That there hath past away a glory from the earth.*

Old Wordsworth *knew,* Ted thought as he stared out the window at the graves. The "light of common day" kept coming at you till it blinded you, and he'd felt it coming for years. Worried and restless, he'd gone with June to Europe, trying to revive his flagging spirits. But what he yearned for wasn't to be found in any place or happening, he knew that now. What he yearned for belonged to a *time*—a time that was gone, that had vanished for good. *Nothing can bring back the hour of splendor in the grass...* And yet that feeling when Joy's hand touched his...

He thought of the yearbook and all those kids, so young, their lives ahead of them. What a treasure they held in their grasp, but how many knew it? Few of them seemed to have any idea of their own potential. He tried to think back to when he was young like that, a zillion years ago. What had he felt? Anxiety, probably. Uncertainty, certainly. What had his hopes for the future been? To make a name for himself, no doubt. Nothing wrong with that, that's what had sparked old Freud. Not the greatest of aspirations, but it was *something.* Most of today's kids seemed like drones, TV or otherwise-drugged zombies. Didn't they have any goals? Any dreams?

To be fair, his own high school class had had its supply of ciphers, and he thought of one kid in particular, Victor Ruff, whose mind had been an academic blank, but who, amazingly enough, had the batting average and pitching record of every major league player on the tip of his lisping tongue. Weird Vic had gone into the world and done *something,* Ted assumed. —Had become a statistician, maybe, maybe an accountant. (Why didn't he get an accountant to do this tax?)

But what about these super kids like Joy Dollinger? The brilliant, sensitive kids, what would happen to them? Would the "light of common day" kill the gleam in their eyes? Would the world turn them into Vic Ruffs? He thought of poor Marty Zeller. Good teacher, good man, and look at him. All those years of pulling shades and locking doors and meeting absurd demands, and the guy was a husk. As a kid he had probably been a superstar—like Joy, Bill Hartman, a few of those others.

God, life was hard, much harder than he'd ever dreamed it was going to be back when he was young. And it went so fast! Twenty years until he retired—and was that his goal? Some goal. Retirement was endless worry: what kind of illness would you get, how bad would inflation be, would you outlive your money? His father had worked for Zeus Electric for thirty-five years, then died a year after he quit. His mother died three years later, when Brad was two. The grandmom and grandpop who never were. Too bad, they would have been great.

He shifted to one of his favorite topics: other lines of work. Morty Price sold insurance in the evenings, Gordon Hoover was a weekend minister. God, weren't there any *decent* jobs? Librarian? Had he ever known a truly happy librarian? Dora Rosen seemed okay, but he didn't know her, it could be an act.

He looked out at the graves again and thought: Okay, so I stick with teaching, it's not so bad. What I really need more than a different job is a real good friend. Just one. Is that too much to ask? George Frangelli was a friend, but not a *good* friend. He was funny and bright and compassionate, but somehow…deficient, not someone that Ted could be close to—*really* close to. Was it George's fault—or his own?

Years ago, June had been his good friend, the kind of friend he felt he needed now. But instead of becoming closer, they'd drifted apart. It had happened gradually over the years, with each misunderstanding, each argument with the kids, each fight with her parents (her goddamn father, the Colonel!), each VISA bill. Years ago they had liked the same movies and music and books, had looked at the world through one pair of eyes, and now—they hardly knew each other. Now they were leading parallel lives that barely touched—like the rest of the couples in Westdale. It just happened somewhere along the line—with everybody. The only couple he'd known who'd had it together all the way were his mother and father, which was pretty pathetic. They might *still* have a good thing going if they hadn't smoked. His mother had quit (too late) but his father hadn't believed that smoking was really bad for you, even when it got to the point where it took all his strength to breathe. Loyal to the end to Zeus Electric, he swore nuclear power was safe. He thought Nixon had been a fine president. Good old Dad. Ted pictured him now, on his death bed, too weak to light up, and having his wife do it for him. They killed him good, like cigarettes should. His boozing hadn't helped any either, of course.

Ted tore himself away from the window and looked at his desk again. He had to stop daydreaming, get this shit done. He had promised to go to the mall with June and the kids later on.

Why? What did they need at the mall? Not a thing, as far as he was concerned, they already had more crap than they could use. But June always wanted to do "family" stuff, and the mall was something both she and the kids adored.

Of course, she would find something there that she wanted. She wanted so much! There was always something a little wrong with whatever she already had. She could use a new toaster, iron, blender, teapot, coffee maker, stove, refrigerator, dishwasher, food processor, kitchen sink, vacuum cleaner, bathroom sink, towels, pillows, bedspreads, sheets, venetian blinds, TV, pocketbook, wallet, jacuzzi, sauna, gazebo, car, family room, refinished basement, pool… It was endless, endless…

Nobody in this family is *satisfied,* Ted thought—including me. We're all like T.S. Eliot: if out, we want to be in; if in…

He looked through the folder marked "June." Where the hell were the rest of her records? Every year there was something missing—and something superfluous. Why had she saved these receipts? He shuffled through scraps of paper, furious; opened the door and called into the hall. "June?" Nothing. "June!" No answer. Back he went to his desk, in a snit.

A few minutes later, her voice at the foot of the stairs said, "Ted, are you finished yet? Are you ready to go to the mall?"

"June, what are these receipts?"

Tense silence, then: "Do you think I can see them from down here, Ted?"

And thus it went.

• • • • •

Shopping was a disease with June, and the kids were infected too. At the mall Ted wandered aimlessly as Brad and Kim bought tapes and CDs, June bought blouses, underwear, a skirt—on sale, which was very good. For her to come home with nothing was dreadful, a crushing defeat, while to get things on sale was a triumph, a glorious coup. To June, to *buy* was to *live*.

Ted was glad for this break from the tax. He and June had had quite a flareup about her receipts, had stewed for a while, then agreed to act like adults and go malling as they had planned. Dizzy with computations he'd eaten a bagel, staring across the lawn at the forsythia. June told him again he should get an accountant. He pretended not to hear.

And now, as he ate a vanilla fudge cone and drifted along with the throng, he wondered what Joy might be doing on such a fine day. Probably shopping at some other mall. It was spring outside, flowers were blooming, and ninety percent of the U.S. population was walking around in climate-controlled environments filled with stores. The mall was America's chief entertainment and form of socialization, a plastic substitute for the village green and Main Street. What was the purpose of education? Ted thought as he slurped wayward fudge from his finger. —To train better shoppers? America: the land of consumers seeking the ultimate bargain, the land where the good is the same as what sells.

Consumer. He hated that word. It always brought to mind a gigantic insect, something out of a nature film enlarged a thousand times, its serrated jaws relentlessly chomping on everything in its path. Sometimes he pictured his fellow mallers as merely a vast collection of bugs with claws full of credit cards.

He crunched up the last of his cone, chomp, chomp, and browsed and didn't buy. By the time they got back home, he was totally beat.

June wanted to go to a movie. He didn't, he wanted to finish the tax. Why had he gone to the mall, she asked, if he hadn't finished the tax? For a break, he had needed a break—and besides that, she'd asked him to go. Another argument (she worked all week and needed *her* break too, a movie), and she fumed while he slaved in the study.

At the dinner table she said to him, "I *told* Brad to clean up his room, but he hasn't done it." He said, "Well tell him again, don't tell *me*," and finished his meal in silence.

In the study again he thought of how terribly changeable people were. He'd be getting along with June one minute, and then she would make a remark, he'd respond—and all at once, just like that, they despised each other. A short while later they'd be on good terms again. How little it took to throw things off! What hope could there be for peace in the world when human feelings were so finely tuned?

He worked till eleven, the sound of the TV bubbling up through the floor in quick bursts, and then quit, still not done.

She snored; he couldn't sleep. Columns of militant meaningless figures marched through his weary mind, and he thought of Waughbach cemetery, all those finished lives outside his window; lay there under its dark rectangular weight.

• • • • •

It took him till noon the next day to wrap up the tax. The weather was warm and sunny and soft, and Brad had cut the grass for the first time this year. Ted had watched for a while from his study window, amazed by how strong and competent Brad had become. He'd be fourteen by summer's end, almost a man. Too soon, too soon.

When he finally finished and went down for lunch, June was reading the Sunday paper at the kitchen table. A mosquito—the first of the year—had lit on her neck and was busily sucking away. Without thinking, he hit it.

She jumped. "Jesus Christ!"

He held up his blood-smeared index finger. "Mosquito," he said. "It was making a meal out of you."

"God, you scared me to death."

"Just trying to help."

"Well don't."

He made a sandwich and ate in the dining room. When he finished, he went out back.

A row of daffodils in bloom, and the smell of the freshly cut grass. Not a very strong smell, and he leaned down, gathered some clippings, held them up to his nose. Not as strong as they used to be, and surely the fault was his. Just a part of the general fading, that haze, that veil.

What had happened to spring? It went so fast these days, and once it was past...no big deal. In his youth he had reveled in spring; all the world had been fragrant and bright. Now the sharpness was gone. For a while he'd thought it was air pollution dimming things, but he gradually realized the dimming was in himself. Had he lost the capacity to respond, or merely suppressed it? That spark he had felt with Joy made him lean toward suppression. If he *bothered* to see, if he *bothered* to smell, weren't things the same? He had felt those chills, and that was a pretty good clue. It was odd that strong sensations like those persisted; they *should* be reserved for the young. What good did it do a man of his age to feel chills? It could even be *dangerous.*

The hour of splendor in the grass, the goddamn grass. He sniffed it again. Did it smell the same as it had years ago, or not? Shrugging, he tossed the clippings down. Maybe yes and maybe no, but one thing for sure—no chills anymore with June. Even after she'd been away for a week on one of her trips, no chills when she returned. He'd always hoped they'd come back, along with her, but no, they were gone for good. Well, what did he expect? How could a person you'd lived with for seventeen years give you chills? A person had to be new, unknown, so you could fill in the blanks, the trouble spots, with fantasies. —Fill them with magic that couldn't exist, romantic crap. June, Jesus, she always sneezed twice, he knew in advance every move she was going to make. How could he have that knowledge and still expect chills?

At this point in his ruminations (should he *chew* on the grass? Would it yield its essence *then?*), T.S. Eliot, fuzzy white wool-covered fool, came sheepishly out of Waughbach Cemetery, toting a substantial bone. It was always a bit unnerving when he did that. (Alas, poor Yorick.) The dog sat down on the bare patch under the maple and crunched away.

Ted looked past the dog at his house, at a trouble spot. Goddamn. "His" house, the property of the Westdale Savings Bank, was brick on the first floor, and cream-colored clapboard up top. It was boring as hell but comfortable, and didn't require much upkeep, but now he could see that a section of roof needed work; the shingles around the chimney were curling, cracked, and he'd have to get after them soon, or hire somebody. He didn't know which was worse. It was always a hassle to hire somebody, but to do it himself...

Ted hated to work with tools. Anything physical made him feel lousy, even so-called "play." Racquetball and the rest were fine for the neighbors, but give him a book anytime.

Was this healthy, though? The popular press said no, you needed exercise, and maybe, he thought, this was part of his problem. Exercise, activity, he ought to give it a try. Fishing (*did* he like it anymore?) or gardening, something gentle like that. Marty Zeller was lucky to have his garden, it *could* keep you sane. Ted had tried his hand at it once, had dug a small plot near the property line, but all that had sprouted were cucumber vines, and the fruits were round, with wicked-looking spikes all over them, like miniature maces. Terrifying. Maybe he should try again, ask Marty what to plant.

T.S. Eliot's teeth made a horrible noise on his bone. Ted looked at the dog and saw Mr. 7-Eleven across the way, behind his house, twisting a wire around the neck of a black plastic garbage bag. Mr. 7-Eleven looked up, saw Ted, gave a nod, which Ted returned. Mr. 7-Eleven went back in his house. Ted passed some gas.

This gas of his! June snored and he was flatulent. They were falling apart at opposite ends. It wasn't just mind over matter, no, it was *time,* time wiping you out.

He looked at the grass with a frown, then picked up a couple of blades and nibbled on them. Ugh. He spit them out, went into the house and watched TV with Brad.

He had a drowning dream that night. He was out in a rowboat with June and the kids, Brad caught a fish, Ted cut off its head and tail then decided that it was too small. To everyone's protest he put the fish back in the water. Matter-of-factly enough it started to swim, dark blood shooting out of both ends, then suddenly it went white, chalk-white, turned belly up and wriggled slowly, falling.

Then Ted was the fish. He was headless, alone in the boat and the boat was sinking, the motor was pulling it down, he was thrashing and screaming without any legs or head, he couldn't swim—

He woke to cornets and trumpets; clicked the radio off and lay there, staring at the window, square of gray, his heartbeat heavy in his neck.

It was pouring out. Monday morning rain, the worst, the worst. And over in the corner, where the chimney went up through the cracked, curled shingles, he heard: drip, drip.

4 • DEAD ON THE GREEN

The typical Monday school chaos with everything moving too fast. As Ted went through his mailbox, he thought: First period quiz, then check on the band photographs, see the head of the prom committee, see Marty about that bindery he mentioned... Gordon Hoover and Dora Rosen, Madge Nader and Morty Price. George Frangelli.

"George, how's it going?"

"Well, Ted, all things considered..."

This was trash and that was trash. He dropped it in the can. "You seen Marty around?"

George said, "You haven't heard."

"Heard what?" —And a rising sense of disaster.

"Marty had a heart attack. He's dead."

A thousand tiny arrows of panic shot into Ted's chest. He said, "Jesus Christ"; felt the blood draining out of his jaw.

"He was playing golf and collapsed. By the time they got him to the hospital, it was too late."

Ted said nothing. He was drowning, felt faint.

"He'd had heart trouble for a while," George said.

"I didn't know that."

"Yeah. Edith could never get him to give up smoking, though."

"He smoked like a fiend," Ted said. The swirl of people, and in it, his dream: no head, no legs, in the boat, going down.

"Forty-four years old."

Murray Sheinstein was there. "Hi, Ted." His stoogey smile. "Murray, hi." Murray looked through his mailbox.

Ted said, "When's the funeral?"

"No funeral. Edith's starting a fund in his memory, you can donate to that if you want."

"Okay." Ted's breath was a hard, dark weight. He dropped the rest of his mail in the trash.

"Talk to you later," George said. "The show must go on."

"The show must go on," Ted said. He went into the hallway with George, feeling dizzy. He stood near the wall till the feeling passed, then went to his room.

He gave the senior English class its quiz, then went to the window and stared outside.

Marty Zeller was dead. —Of natural causes, at the age of forty-four. Two more years, he thought, and *I'll* be forty-four.

The rain had not let up. He looked past the wide, dark manicured lawn to the flat South Jersey scene: two gas stations, Shell and Exxon, lighted in the gloom, and wedged between them a mini-mall with a dry cleaner, liquor store, flower shop, and the pizza place where the kids hung out at lunch and after school. He stood there, staring, thinking on a level deeper than words and feeling incredibly sad.

After a while he turned away and sat down at his desk. He thought of what Marty had said on Friday about his place in the country, his garden. Everyone ought to be granted a couple of years in his prime to do what he wanted and nothing else, or what was the point of it all? Marty should've had the chance to live in that cabin a couple of years and fish and garden and watch the birds; it was only right.

He managed to get through the rest of his morning classes somehow, and at lunch they all talked about Marty. He signed the card they were sending to Edith and took her address so he could mail a check to the fund she was setting up.

By the time sixth period came he felt fairly normal (though very wiped out); gave the sophomore class an assignment, and went to see what Rick Castle had done on the yearbook. He dreaded the thought of complacent Rick and that claustrophobic A-V room, but as George had said, the show must go on. Maybe those damn band pictures had come.

He was startled to see Joy Dollinger there on the stool. She was frowning down at the table, her chin in her hand. She heard him; turned; her bluegray eyes looked blurred. The fluorescents shed a pinkish cast on her shoulders and golden hair. "Oh what's the use?" she said looking down again, "I just can't *concentrate* on this crap."

Her manner jolted him. He said, "I expected to find Rick here."

"He's sick. I asked Mrs. Nader if I could take his place."

Then he saw she was shaking. He frowned. "Did those band pictures come?" It seemed foolish to say it. He looked at her hand, that tremor; remembered that accidental touch of a few days before.

She gave him an envelope.

He glanced at the pictures and said, "Good." He looked at her downcast face, feeling edgy, unsettled.

Abruptly, earnestly, she stared at him and said, "Why did it have to be *him?*" There were tears in her eyes.

"Mr. Zeller," he said.

Her quivering had increased. "He was one of the good ones, one of the ones who cared."

"It's a terrible loss," Ted said. "I've felt awful all day."

Joy looked at the floor. "When I was a freshman, algebra gave me fits," she said. "I don't know, I just couldn't get it, I was into a goddamn *thing* about it, and you know what he did? He spent two hours with me, hours he could have spent making up tests or marking papers or working on lesson plans, and it straightened me out. Those two hours made everything clear. He did that for lots of kids. Kids who couldn't make change when they came to his classes *loved* math by the time they were through." Her eyes were bright and wet, intense. "He acted like he didn't care, but he did, and we knew it, *everyone* knew it. There isn't another teacher the kids like more"—those crystal eyes on his—"unless it's you."

Taken aback, Ted said, "Really."

She laughed, and a tear fell down her cheek. "Sure, all the kids love you. You care, you're funny, you're fair, you don't pull any tricks like Burk or Hoover or some of those others, you're one of the *good* ones, Mr. Wharton—so don't die!"

She was shivering violently now. It frightened him, and he said, "Joy, listen, are you okay? Maybe you ought to see the nurse."

"I don't need any *nurse,*" she said. Her face was contorted, pale. "I need—"

Then suddenly she fell at him, threw her arms around him, pressed her head to his chest and started to cry.

He was petrified, electrified. What he thought was: the door. It locked automatically when it closed, but he wasn't the only one with a key, there was one in the office for all to use, and what if somebody came in? "Joy…" His lips were numb.

"Don't talk," she said, her voice in his shirt, her heat and vibration against his chest. "Just hold me. *Please.*"

He did; put his arm on her shoulder and patted her like a dad. But his feelings were not father feelings; he raced inside. That rich perfume and the warmth of her shoulder, her sweater softness, the wisp of blond hair at her ear—sweet teenage secrets forgotten for such a long time, all back again. He flushed; he felt prickly and hot. The room was suffocating, charged with energy. "Joy…let me get the nurse."

"No," she said, shaking her head. "No, I'm all right now." Her crying had stopped. She let him go and sat up straight; brushed her hair back and wiped her eyes. "I'm sorry. Please, I'm sorry, I was just…scared."

Her shaking was subsiding. "It's okay," he said, and felt an immense relief at the space between them, that cool two feet. "I understand."

She smiled sadly. "I know you do." She pressed her tongue against those gapped front teeth and said, "I had an older brother, Skip, he died two years ago. He was only nineteen, just two years older than I am now."

Her body's imprint lingered on his chest. He said, "That's terrible, Joy. I don't remember him. I guess I never had him in class."

She was looking away, looking down. "He didn't go to Whitman," she said. "He went to military school."

"Oh." He stared at her knees.

She looked at him sharply, frowning, her blue eyes stunningly bright. "You see, what I mean is, Mr. Zeller smoked, and it's bad for your heart, that's probably why he died, but Skip didn't smoke or drink, his health was perfect, he was killed in an accident."

"That's awful."

She shifted her gaze to the table again, the scatter of photos there, and said, "I don't know what to do."

"About what?" he said, confused.

With a tremulous mouth she said, "We could die this minute—all of us! The air is poisoned, the water is poisoned, we're born with missiles aimed at our heads, what do people expect? Plans? Goals? You need a future to have plans and goals, and nobody *has* a future anymore!"

Ted was afraid she was going to start that terrible shaking again. He said, "Why don't you ask the nurse if you can leave early? There's only one more period."

She wiped her eyes again and slid off the stool and stood in front of him. "Okay," she said, "I guess that's a good idea."

She was almost his height and very close; he felt her body radiating heat. She pressed her lips together in that way she had and said, "Do I make any sense? It's all just kid talk, that's what you're thinking, right?"

"No, Joy, it makes sense."

She smiled then, her eyes on his. "You know why you're such a good teacher?" she said.

That hypnotized feeling again. He tried to fight it, lighten it with laughter. "Why?" he said.

"Because you're part kid yourself. Some part of you never grew up."

He knew he should turn away, become abrupt, excuse himself, do anything to break the growing spell. But he just kept standing there and said, "You think so?"

"I know so," she said.

Without any warning her hand was on top of his shoulder. Stunned sparks ran over his arm. The Little Man was wild with delight, but Ted was paralyzed. "There's adventure in you," she said staring into his eyes. "You know what's important to kids because you still feel it. Christ, ninety-five percent of these teachers might as well be dead!"

Her hand seared into his jacket, his flesh. The right thing to do was to forcibly take it away. No fooling around, just reach out, grab her wrist and take that hand away. But her eyes were filling with tears again, her mouth was quivering again, and he just couldn't do it.

She held him with those sad, clear eyes and said:

"It is in truth iniquity on high
To cheat our sentenced souls of aught they crave,
And mar the merriment as you and I
Fare on our long fool's-errand to the grave."

He stared at her dumbly. She said, "You taught me that."

"I did?" he said. His voice was weak. He cleared his throat.

"You quoted it in class."

Her hand was still there on his shoulder. Was he going to stay like this forever? "Joy—"

"In psychology class."

"Housman in psychology?" he said with a feeble laugh. "I must have forgotten what class I was teaching."

"We all get a little confused at times," she said, and her eyes were closer, her mouth was closer, he stared at her mouth without moving. Her lips were very, very close, he saw delicate fuzz on her chin, felt her breath on his cheek, and then as the Little Man watched with incredulous eyes, her lips met his.

The kiss was tentative, tender, and burned like flame. She broke it, looked at him.

He could feel it all falling apart, feel all of the pieces just falling away. He said, "Joy…"

She touched her finger to his lips; it felt delicious. The Little Man was beside himself with a mighty desire to open his mouth, take that finger inside.

Ted finally acted; took her arm, removed her hand; felt the smooth, smooth skin of her wrist. "Joy, listen, we'll have to talk." He let her arm go, checked his watch. "Look, I have to get back to my class."

She kept staring at him.

"It's okay, it's all right, we'll talk about it. Tomorrow." He went to the door and opened it. "Are you coming?"

She centered her tongue in that gap in her teeth and nodded thoughtfully. She came up close and he smelled her scent. He held the door; her heat flowed by. In the hallway he said, "We'll talk about it tomorrow."

"Tomorrow," she said.

He crossed the hallway and entered his classroom just as the bell went off. Yes, this was his room and these were his sophomores and this was Whitman High. A question about the homework from Doris Grubb. It took him a minute to zero in. He answered as best he could. They all went out.

During study hall he sat at the desk with a frown on his face, tapping the blotter absently with his pen. Deep thoughts. But when study hall ended, his mind was no less confused. All he knew was, he'd talk to Joy. Tomorrow. But tomorrow she worked on the yearbook with Rick. Well maybe he'd still be sick. He hoped so, he had to see her alone, had to straighten this out.

Have to straighten what out? he thought. One innocent little kiss? Forget it, pretend that it never happened, let sleeping dogs lie.

He drove home in a stew of emotions, thinking about Marty Zeller, his cabin, his garden; imagined him lying there dead on the green. Forty-four years old. *It is in truth iniquity on high…* He remembered Joy's eyes as she recited that. June wouldn't be able to quote a line of Housman if her life depended on it, she'd been a home economics major—and couldn't even cook anymore. He wondered how he'd feel when he saw her tonight. Would she sense anything? Would it show? Good God, one innocent little kiss! How did men cheat on their wives and not have them find out? Cheat, Jesus, he'd never be able to do it. One friendly accidental peck and he was ready to confess.

As he started down Freedom Drive, he pictured Joy on the stool, skirt up; her firm, delicious thighs. He saw her mouth coming closer, closer, felt the warmth of her kiss again. When he parked in front of the house, he was hot and hard.

• • • • •

By the time June got home he had marked some papers, mediated several sibling squabbles, made the dinner, thought about Marty a dozen times—and the incident with Joy had lost most of its charge.

"I've asked you to call if you're going to be late," he said as June entered the kitchen. "The souffle's wrecked, it's a limp piece of crap."

"I'm not hungry," she said. Her skin had a pasty look. "I ate a late lunch, I'll make myself something later."

He took a deep breath and said, "Marty Zeller died. Heart attack."

June set her briefcase beside her chair and sat down, frowning. "God," she said, "how old was he?"

"Forty-four. It hit me hard, I really liked the guy."

"How terrible. Marty Zeller. Did he have any kids?"

"No."

She looked at the flat souffle sitting there on the trivet. "Forty-four. Six more years and *I'll* be forty-four. He smoked prettily heavily, didn't he?"

"Two packs a day."

"Well I gave that up, at least. Why is it you have to quit what you like so you don't drop dead?"

"It's a lousy deal," Ted said. "It is in truth iniquity on high to cheat our sentenced souls of aught they crave, and mar the merriment as you and I fare on our long fool's-errand to the grave."

"God, how depressing. Who wrote that?"

"A.E. Housman."

"I never liked his stuff. That reminds me—I'm thinking of going to England in a couple of weeks, why don't you come along?"

He shrugged. "I've been to England."

"Not *all* of England."

"Did I tell you I have to chaperone the senior prom?"

"Well what does that have to do with England? The prom's not in April, is it?"

"It's May fifteenth."

"Then why did you bring it up?"

"I don't know."

June looked at her plate—clean, untouched, shining, its border of blue fleur-de-lis. "You never want to do *anything*," she said. "A guy your age just dies, and even *that* doesn't make you want to do anything."

Ted rubbed his forehead and frowned at her shiny plate. "That isn't true," he said. "It's just that travel doesn't interest me."

"Well what *does* interest you?"

"Hey June, enough, okay? It's been a rough day, I don't want to get into this kind of crap."

She sighed. "So where are the kids?"

"Getting their TV brainwash."

"How's Kim's finger?"

"What's wrong with her finger?"

"She cut it opening a can a pears last night, didn't you know that?"

"No."

June got up from the table. "I'll see how it's doing." She looked at him. "Are you sure you don't want to go to England?"

"I'm sure."

"You only live once."

"If that," Ted said.

• • • • •

He sat in the family room, June ensconced on the couch with the *Courier-News* and Brad and Kim lost in TV, and kept wondering what to do. Talk it over with Joy? —Or pretend it had never happened? Tomorrow she worked on the yearbook with Rick, so how could he see her alone? Maybe best to forget it. Christ, how to decide?

As he mulled this over, T.S. Eliot stared mournfully, accusingly, from his spot on the red shag rug; just stared with those huge expectant eyes. Why the hell did that stupid animal do that, what did it want from him? What did any of them want from him? Trips to England? Trips to malls? For God's sake, *what?*

The dog continued to stare at him. Did it think that if he wanted to, he could give it the gift of speech? Unnerved, Ted left the room and went upstairs. The TV said, "It's filled with vitamins, but how does it taste?" "Like shit," Ted muttered to himself.

In the study he wrote Edith Zeller a note, enclosing a hundred dollar check for the Zeller scholarship fund. June would kill him if she knew he was sending that much, but he'd really liked Marty, and it was the right thing to do.

In bed he remembered the kiss and he couldn't sleep. That jolt when her lips touched his had worked magic: the years between adolescence and middle age had instantly disappeared. Just like that, he'd turned seventeen again. An *incredible* feeling. Chills, real *chills.*

It had frightened him and he'd loved it: her hand on his shoulder, those tender lips, her heat pulsing through him... Wonderful, wonderful, dangerous, crazy. He'd have to talk to her, yes, tomorrow, and straighten things out. In the darkness, June snoring, tears came to his eyes and he didn't know why. He thought of Marty Zeller. Cultivate your garden... Long fool's-errand to the grave...

He lay awake into the deep quiet hours, thoughts ripping and dancing, loins aching with need. June snored the entire time, and at last he went down to the kitchen and poured two shots of Red & Black scotch and sat staring at nothing, thinking, thinking, reliving the A-V room till the liquor took hold. Then he went back to bed (June's snoring had finally stopped, thank God), and fell into a fitful sleep.

5 • INIQUITY ON HIGH

Though he'd had a terrible night, he wasn't tired. His mind was focused, intense, alive, arrowed toward his afternoon meeting with Joy. He saw Rick Castle in the hall, but Rick or no Rick he would manage to talk to Joy alone, this business had to be settled.

During psychology class he didn't call on her when she raised her hand, afraid that the sound of her voice might break his resolve. Then a lucky distraction ate time and his preoccupation: a beautiful girl named Allison Walker threw up on her desk, splashing puke on the pants of Freddie Wilkinson, a loquacious and natty black kid who appeared to be on the verge of barfing too and was quickly excused. Allison, red with humiliation, was hustled off to the nurse. The stench was so wicked that Ted had the class stand outside in the hall while the janitor, Mr. Stanley (or was his first name Stanley?) mopped up. By the time the job was finished, the bell had rung.

The minutes passed in an odd, fast-slow suspension: that agony that swells before your operation or your wedding or your first child's birth. Ted taught without spirit, mechanically, aching for each period to end. He ate no lunch. At last he gave his sophomores their busy work and started across the hall. He would have to tell Rick to go back to his class, and alone with Joy he would square things away. His hand shook as he opened the door.

She was there on the stool, one foot on a high rung, one on a low rung, skirt above her knees. A shot of desire jarred Ted as the door hissed shut. No Rick. With a curt nod he said, "Hello, Joy." Good: firm and businesslike.

She stared at him, face serious. "Hi."

"Where's Rick?"

"I told him to get lost. You and I have to talk."

He sat on a stool across from her, his heartbeat quick in his neck. "Joy, I'm glad we're alone." Christ! That wasn't the right thing to say! "What I mean is—"

"I know," she said, her eyes bright and hard on his, "you don't have to tell me. You hate me."

Shaking his head, he said, "No, I don't hate you, things happen, that's all. I know Mr. Zeller's death affected you deeply. I know—"

"Do you know I love you?"

A shock traveled over his shoulders and arms. "Joy—"

"I do, you know. I've loved you for months. Could you tell?"

"Joy, look..." And his voice was thin, and everything seemed to be spinning away from his center, flying away into space.

She stared at him with those earnest blue eyes. "I'll prove it to you," she said. And she slid off the stool, her skirt stretching higher, and put her arms over his shoulders. She looked straight at him, then closed her eyes and kissed him hard on the mouth.

Her taste, her teeth, her hands on his back, her firm bright body against him. She broke the kiss and stared again. He fought the wonderful feeling and lost; fell into the light of her eyes. In a soft, delicious whisper she said: "It is in truth iniquity on high to cheat our sentenced souls of aught they crave," and her lips were there and closed off his words and her mouth was rich and hot.

And (No! Oh no!) the Little Man took control: the dam suddenly broke and his hands were moving across her back, around her blouse, met no resistance, felt her breasts, he was lost in the heat and the flow of her mouth, she had her hand between his thighs, he was instantly hard as stone. A thousand thoughts flashed into his brain and fled. His hand was up inside her skirt, felt the silky sheen of her underwear, the stool scraped backward as he stood...

I'm finished! he thought. I'm done for, dead! and even that thought dissolved and she held him tight, her chin in his shoulder as she worked his fly. She kissed him again, all liquid, tongue, they sank to the floor, the Little Man pulled her fabric aside, Ted's hand was in her heat. And then he was magically on her and "Yes!" she said, teeth clenched, eyes closed. "I've had all my tests and I'm perfectly clean, yes, yes!"

Her hot breath steamed his face in the tiny room. A stool went crash, he didn't care, he animaled into her fluid, she said, "Oh yes! It's right, it's right!" He was flat on top with his face in her breasts and his mind was crying Oh Jesus, Oh God. She shivered and bit her lip, he burst, he thought of his class across the hall, the key to the A-V room in the office, Rick Castle, his sophomores.

They held each other, panting. Dazzled and half insane, he took out his handkerchief as she said, "It's all right, it's good, it's fine. Don't worry, it's fine."

He breathed the gigantic breath of a man on the gallows; stood up, dizzy, wiping the sweat off his face with his quivering hand. Her smell on his fingers. His body shook to its bones.

She touched her finger to his cheek. "You were wonderful, beautiful. Don't worry, please. Just take care of your class now, everything's fine."

He brushed himself off, tucked his shirt back in, ran his hand across his hair. The eyes of the photos on the fake birch table stared. He checked his fly. She smiled. He left the room.

He hurried to the mensroom; urinated, shivery. Looked down at his penis, confined to one woman for seventeen years, now damp with the juice of Joy, a seventeen year old girl. Some girl! he thought. Wow! Girl? The thrill began to rise again. He remembered his first real sexual encounter, when he was nineteen, with that hooker in Montreal. He'd gotten himself so excited he'd climaxed in thirty seconds without penetration, then didn't know what to do with the rest of the night. The whore kicked him out of her room and he found his buddies, also finished, also expelled, waiting out in the sad, tattered hall. They loaded the car with food and beer and laughed the whole ride back to Burlington, secretly praying they hadn't contracted something.

Good God, having Joy had been more exciting than Montreal! He zipped his fly, washed up, and combed his hair. The flush hadn't left his face. Couldn't wait for that, had to get to his class. He left the mensroom, went down the empty hall; passed the A-V room, saw himself on the floor with Joy, shoved the image back down. Breathed deeply, went in to his sophomores.

Two kids in a minor scuffle there in the rear. "Fogle! Schultheis! Get in your seats!" The class shuffling papers, pretending to work. He half expected them to point their fingers, laugh in accusation. How could his crime not show? The bell went off.

"All right, if you didn't finish, complete the assignment at home." Some groans. "Read the story on page 43, 'The Most Dangerous Game.'" More groans. "You'll like it, I promise."

"I bet," a boy named McConkey said from his seat near the door.

"Guaranteed," Ted said, and the kids went out. He smiled at them like a normal person as little explosions of fear and excitement caromed inside his veins. He saw her, felt her, smelled her all over again. He was lost. Changed forever. Doomed. He quickly got his stuff together, pulled the shades down, turned the lights off, locked the frigging door.

•••••

At home he took a shower, soaped himself three times, let the water run hard and long. He dried himself briskly, threw his shirt and underwear in the washer, threw his pants in the bag of stuff for the cleaners.

It was Tuesday, the day of his course. He had taken a course every fall and spring since he'd graduated from college. He had gotten his master's and then, bored with English, had switched to counseling and psych. He got his master's plus 30 and kept on going, but wasn't exactly sure why, as it didn't mean any more pay. It made him look loyal, committed, though, and that was a big, big plus. Not to take courses made superintendents suspect that you thought you had outgrown your need for instruction. Oh, perish the traitorous thought! As he didn't have anything better to do and the school district picked up the tab, he kept going, and who could say? In the future he might just bag a "terminal degree." Dr. Wharton. Had a real nice ring, and he might just give it a shot.

As June worked in the kitchen (she cooked on Tuesdays, Fridays and weekends, that was the deal), Ted sat in the study and tried to catch up on his reading. The course he was taking this spring was called, "Treatment Modalities For The Behaviorally Challenged" ("What To Do With Your Wackadoo Kids"). The teacher, a Dr. Zahara, fifty-five or so, was adenoidal, pale, myopic, and dry as desert sand. He had probably never set foot in a high school class since his own graduation, would probably be as much help as a fart in a gale when it came to dealing with purple people or similar yahoos, but none of that mattered to Ted. Years ago he'd relinquished all hope of learning anything in these classes, and was perfectly happy to put in his time and collect his credits, his "proof of professional growth." (How Grimsley, the superintendent, loved that crap!)

He looked at the textbook and tried to read, but his mind was consumed with Joy. At the dinner table, lost in thought, he snapped at both children for minor offenses and gulped the meal, a hamburg casserole, hardly chewing, not tasting a bite.

He damn near ran over a cat on Washburn Avenue, and in class, with Zahara rambling on, he saw the madness again and again, in stop-action detail—and savored each sinful frame.

Electric energy infused his cells; the world was fractured, prismed. Where to now? She adored him, and he could do anything with her. No, no, he couldn't, good God, was he totally mad? Another shock of power in his groin, then the flash of his inner eye: on the floor with her, those long blond thighs, those heels in his back, pressing down. Good God what a ride it had been! The way she had shuddered, that animal jolt. Had it ever been feral like that with June? She was so *controlled*, she was always *thinking*, but this swift girl had lost her mind, become nothing but flesh. For him. And he'd loved every second of it.

Oh God, he wanted more. But Jesus, no, just let her run the show with Rick, he'd stay out of the A-V room just as much as he could, avoid it completely when she worked alone. He must. He would. Zahara slogged on under pebbled fluorescence. Ted dreamed.

He stopped at a tavern after class and had three beers. June was sleeping when he got back home. Joy again, again Joy, "It's all right, it's fine," and he stroked himself to the rhythm of June's snoring till release made him quiver to his toes.

Two orgasms in one day. Two *good* orgasms in one day. When was the last time *that* had happened? When he was nineteen? He lay there, thrilled, depleted, confused, amazed with his awesome new life.

6 • FIRST NAME BASIS

In class the next day she was cool as could be, as if nothing had happened, as if dreams could never come true.

When he went to the A-V room, heart thrilling with dread and desire, she was fighting with Rick over which illustration should preface the senior class. Her "Hi, Mr. Wharton," as he came through the door was totally neutral and bland, and he found this intensely arousing; felt heat in his groin.

"Which do *you* think is best, Mr. Wharton?" she asked. A quick smile, bright flash in her eye. He saw himself on her again, on this floor. He bent over and looked at the drawings. From her perch on the stool she threw warmth like a stove; his hot skin glowed.

He rubbed his chin as if finding it hard to decide. "This one here," he said.

She tossed her head triumphantly. "Of course! Come on, Castle, wake up, this other thing's crap."

"Let's try to hold the invective," Ted said.

Rick sulked. "So. Two against one."

"It's just my opinion," Ted said. "It's your yearbook."

"Yeah." Rick crumpled up his selection and tossed it into the trash can under the table.

"What a sport," Joy said. She winked at Ted. He felt effervescent, ecstatic, pained. He said, "We ought to have galleys of the will and prophecy by next week. We'll make up a dummy page for the class trip and rough out the copy, then after you go on the trip you can fill in the actual details."

Joy turned to Rick; plaid skirt, smooth knees. "You want to do the copy?"

"I don't care."

"Fine, I'll do the layout."

"I might want to do that too."

Joy rolled her eyes at Ted and said, "We'll work on it together."

"Yeah, okay," Rick said. He swiveled on his stool. "I've got to get going. You be ready to work on the honor society Friday?"

"I don't see why not."

"Great," Rick said morosely. He slid off the stool, picked up the illustration that Ted had liked, shook his head, put the drawing back down on the table and went to the door. "See you later."

They both said, "See you, Rick." The door sighed shut behind him.

Ted, with a sudden sharp stomach pain, said, "Well, back to my class."

Joy smiled; that gap in her upper incisors. "Before you go, I have a question," she said.

Heart pounding, he said, "What's that?"

She stared at him, her tongue on the edge of those parted, imperfect teeth. "How'd you like your hot cock in my mouth?"

He stood there, his mind shooting blanks. A frantic excitement bloomed in his groin and his legs began to melt. And suddenly Joy was down on her knees with her hands at his fly, the zipper fell, she groped inside, and his penis, stiffening fast, banged into the light. He was shocked by its size and hue, that darkening red. She held it, put it against her teeth, surrounded it with her lips. A white expansion filled Ted's brain and he thought he was going to faint.

Back and forth she went, back-forth, back-forth, and the Little Man went bananas. Ted stood transfixed; he'd never had this before, always wondered what it was like, and now—here it was! It felt more comforting than sensual, wasn't really all that great, but my God, the total *gestalt!*

Joy unbuttoned her blouse, placed his hand on her breast. He pictured the door behind him opening: screams and the end of his life. He rubbed her stiff nipple; the tight room swam. The gleam on his shaft, those lipsticked lips, her golden hair, its perfect part... With her hand she magically worked his foreskin and wham he was suddenly hot as July, his power scrambled up the ladder and smashed its way free.

—Through the gap in her teeth. She swallowed it, licked it, tongued his too tender knob, his hand still at her breast. She laughed, sat straight, wiped her mouth with her hand and fastened her blouse. Said: "I figured we wouldn't be able to see each other till Friday, so I'd better take care of you now. You wouldn't want to have to go without for another two whole *days.*"

With fresh terror supplanting his shock, he took out his handkerchief, wiped himself, and tucked himself away; zipped up, his knees quaking and weak.

"Right, Mr. Wharton?" That gap, those lips. "Two days is such a long time."

He looked at her stupidly, dizzily, numb. When finally he found his voice again, he mumbled, "I guess you can call me Ted."

• • • • •

The degeneracy of it! The sheer deceit! Sitting here at the table with June and the children as if he were still the same, still one of the family, the dutiful husband and father, still honest and clean. The guilt of Macbeth oozed out of his every pore; at any moment a gory ghost would appear at the sink or stove and expose his sins. He picked at the meal he had made, roast chicken (overcooked, dry), leaving most of it on his plate.

After dinner he went to his study and marked test papers. Watching the dying light on the graves and picturing Joy's ministrations, his hot astonishment banged through his body again. Her expertise! How long had she been in training? God! And how many other "students" of his were equally as skilled? His touchy tube throbbed and grew rigid yet one more time.

He drank two shots of Red & Black before bed but they didn't slow down his whirl, just curdled his stomach. As June snored away he lay staring at darkness, his heartbeat hard. Then it started to hurt, each pulse of it sending a stab through his upper chest.

He would die. If he kept it up with Joy he would die, have a heart attack. He wasn't a kid anymore, he was forty-two, an affair would kill him.

The pain banged into his sternum and out through his ribs. Oh God have mercy, he thought. All he wanted to do was forget, all he wanted to do was sleep. But her lips, her lipstick smeared on his shaft, and suddenly he was hard again. Those teeth! That gap! June snored.

7 • BEAR ON THE GRASS

In psychology class the next day she was silent, just watching with quiet eyes. But Friday, at the end of the period, she said, "In your personal opinion, Mr. Wharton, is Freud's extreme emphasis on sexual motivation justified?"

A murmur from some of the boys in the back and a snicker. Game time, Ted thought; she was already playing games. They awaited his answer intently. He suddenly pictured them naked—all of them—doing unspeakable things.

"Freud lived in a highly repressed society," he said. "In those days, some people actually thought the legs of pianos were lewd, and put covers over them." Much laughter. "It's true. With the radical change in attitudes since then, we've come to understand that a much smaller part of behavior is sexually motivated than Freud believed."

"Yeah? Prove it," grinned Joel Parker, tall, blond, baseball player-wiseguy.

Ted ignored him. Luckily, the bell went off. "We've done enough on Freud for now, we'll discuss him again later on. For Monday I'd like you to read the section that starts on page 253, 'Development of the Individual.' Read the first twenty pages."

In the rustle and mutter he saw Joy staring, smiling. —And he wanted to do it again, right there on the floor. Sixth period steamed at him like a train.

• • • • •

She was there on the stool, alone, absorbed in her work. He closed the door behind him, burning, bright in every cell. In the back of his mind he kept telling himself this was it, he would end it right now—and his pocket was stuffed with tissues.

She turned. Put her feet on the highest rung of the stool, her right foot first, her left foot next, and spread her legs apart. She wore no underpants.

"Pretty stuffy in here, don't you think?" she said with a smile.

His heart in his throat, his palate dry and he ached all through.

"Hey, Ted, come over here."

He obeyed. Heard a rustling sound in his head, sniffed a wry laugh, dying.

"Oh, Mr. Wharton," she said. She inched her skirt up higher, exposing her all to the light. "Now tell me, do you really believe that stuff you just said about Freud?"

"You might be able to convince me otherwise," Ted said through the beat of his blood. Her legs and crotch were rich, delicious, a feast.

"If you were to bury your face in my muff," she said, "do you think it might change your mind?"

He stood there, her heat enveloping him, then slowly he sank to his knees. She put both hands on his head, grabbed his hair.

"If you were to touch my bud with your tongue—do you think it might sway your opinion?"

His sick heart blasted. He'd never done this, never even come close. He was terrified, thrilled. She drew him near and he leaned to her pinkness, her flap. Stuck his tongue out tentatively, gingerly.

Not bad. He kind of liked it. All he could smell was perfume, powder, that flowery scent of hers. Lilies of the valley? Roses? Both? She rubbed his hair. "Oh good, go on, go on."

He pressed the width of his tongue on her damp as he held her hips. Licked avidly. Her hairs were gleaming with his wet, her wet, she tossed her head back, shuddered, laughed. "Theory and practice"—she caught her breath—"are two different things, right, Ted?"

He was drowned in her softness and warmth, all thoughts were gone. His world was her hot loose center, his breath was her heat. He felt her bud turn spongy, plump, and caught it with his tongue. A shiver coursed down her thighs. He did it again, and again she shuddered. Sharp intake of breath and her hand on his head gently urging him on.

"Oh, Teddy, good. Oh Teddy Bear, it's so good."

On fire, he reached for his fly. She held his hand, restrained him, bit her lip. That gap; a quick head shake. "No, later, after school," she said. "Then we can do it right."

He was gasping, steaming. "Okay," he said. "Yeah, after school." He took out the wad of tissues and wiped his face. His testicles felt as large as soccer balls.

He stood up and brushed himself off; she pulled down her skirt. "I'll meet you at Pikesboro Plaza—you know where that is?"

"Yeah."

"Five o'clock, under the 'J' in the parking lot. I have a red Honda Accord."

"Under the 'J.' Five o'clock." He looked at his watch. "I'd better get back."

She grinned. "See you there, Teddy Bear."

In the hallway he felt like a rat flushed out of its hole. He went to the fountain against the wall and washed his mouth out, flooding it, his mind hot and reeling with what he'd just done.

He had never so much as mentioned that subject to June, knowing full well she would find it disgusting. Beyond disgusting, *baffling*. Her compulsive logic would force her to ask herself: Why does he want to do *this*? What sense does it make to put his mouth down *there*?

Good old June. She didn't want to be stuck in a rut, so she traveled to England and France and Japan, but she hadn't tried anything new in the sack since that time they'd first done it doggie style fifteen years ago.

He stood outside his classroom door, his mind aflame; heard the sophomores carrying on in there. She'd called him "Teddy Bear." Good God! Esther Craven (biology), hugging her briefcase (full of embalmed frogs?), shambled past. Squat, dumpy, piano-legged Esther. As he nodded hello, he wondered if Esther engaged in oral high jinks with Mr. Craven. He tried to imagine it, failed, and went in to his Visigoths.

• • • • •

In The Spouting Whale he sipped his beer and watched time ooze away. It was already 4:25, and a rising excitement spread through his stomach and groin.

A most excellent day for a tryst. June never expected him home before seven on Fridays, his afternoon out with the "boys." Often he came in closer to eight, a bit woozy with booze, to half-consciously pick at whatever she'd cooked that night. (It was usually macaroni and cheese, dried out, lukewarm.) He could do it with Joy for an hour or two and still have time to spare.

Tuesday nights would be perfect too. He'd play hooky on Dr. Zahara and screw instead. He might also be able to work out some other time on a flexible basis. That committee LeMaster had spoken about—that media review affair—would give him a fine excuse. He could see a lot of its meetings on the horizon, yes indeed.

He drank, and looked, and listened. This was the first time the "boys" had gathered since Marty Zeller's death, and the stories were flying. Remember how Marty did this or did that? Remember when he told LeMaster, "Marv, you know what your problem is? You're culturally deprived." Yes, good old Marty, they'd miss him terribly, but his early demise wouldn't change them a bit. They'd do everything just the same as before: moan about teaching, depend on the union to fight their battles, stay with their wives if they loved them or not, read the papers and watch TV. No one was more predictable than a teacher; more middle class, spineless, and boring. He listened to them ramble on: about the brand new baseball season, their home repair projects, their lawns...

Teaching! What a profession! It wasn't a profession, it was voluntary servitude, and what in the world made them stick with it year after year? The fear that they couldn't do anything else? Their mad concern for tenure, status and security had never meant a thing to him, but all of them seemed so threatened that there had to be something to it. June was threatened: the thought of him losing his job scared her silly. He had no other skills, so why didn't it scare *him* silly? Did he have more faith in himself than these others? Less understanding of reality? He listened to them talk about their money market funds and wanted to tear his hair.

He had never *really* been one of them, not in his heart, and now he was totally different, an outlaw, a renegade. Let them moan, let them think that they had to submit to fate, he was going to *live*. Why not? Who'd ever know? He looked at George, whose round cheeks were glowing with beer, and felt sorry for him. Not a touch of adventure in the man, not the tiniest spark of daring. Wally Blood, Big Wally, jolly, purple-faced, huge boozer—so predictable. Marty had been different, but Marty was dead.

He checked the clock above the bar: 4:42. Almost time. Morty Price and Dave Waterman laughed and drank, and what would they think if they knew about Joy? That he was a sicko? Degenerate? Before this had happened, that's exactly what he would have thought. Had *happened*, yes, that was the truth of the situation. He hadn't planned it, hadn't even *wanted* it, it had simply *happened*. He drank his beer and thought: Right. Tell me another one, Wharton.

It was time to go. He drained his mug and stood and said, "Well guys, I've got to be on my way. June's working late, I have to cook." He tossed a tip on the tabletop.

"Already?" George said. "Come on, have another beer."

"I'd love to, George, but I can't."

Tony Troxell, aging jock gym teacher and baseball coach, said, "I thought you and June had a deal."

"We're flexible," Ted said.

"You're henpecked," Tony said with a rosy grin. "Alice is *trained*. She knows this time is *mine*. I bust my nuts with these savages all week long and *deserve* to get sloshed on Fridays."

"I gotta go."

Tony clucked like a chicken and said, "Come on, have another beer."

"I really can't."

"Henpecked."

Ted laughed. "I'll see you guys Monday."

• • • • •

The station wagon was stuffy and hot, and he rolled the window down, then flatulated audibly.

Come on, he told himself, get that under control! To paraphrase Dorothy Parker: Gals seldom make passes/ at guys who are gaseous.

His throat was hard and his stomach was pleasantly sick. He felt almost the same as he'd felt when he'd gone to his first burlesque show years and years ago—at seventeen! Joy's age! Those feelings weren't extinct, no way, they had merely been stifled all this time, and now they were free again, all their power restored. All their power restoring *him.* He wheeled out of the parking lot, slightly high from the beer, and drove down the street.

He thought about George and the rest of them back in the tavern, there in the dark with the Millers sign turning, throwing its slow repetitive rainbow onto the stucco wall. Joy was right, they were dead. From now on, all would be sameness, over and over, until they retired. And once they retired, then what would they do? Watch more television, read more papers, shop for their gravestones? He thought of Marty, dead on the golf course, his father, dead in the hospital bed. Screw that, sports fans, he was going to *live.*

• • • • •

The red Accord was sitting there under the 'J.' Ted pulled into a space, got out, and walked across the asphalt, scared someone might recognize him. Highly unlikely, as Pikesboro Plaza was half an hour and half a dozen shopping centers away from Westdale, but you never knew.

Joy smiled at him from the driver's seat. She was wearing a summer dress cut low in front; the slanting rays of the sun shot gold bands through her hair. "Hi, Teddy Bear, ready to roll? Want to drive this little peach?"

Ted laughed, a quick tang in his heart, and said, "Sure." He opened the door, she slid across into the passenger seat, he got inside. The interior of the Honda—black and chrome—was precise as a watch. He started the engine, put the car in reverse. "Where to?"

"Thunderbird Motel. It's a ten minute drive, I'll show you the way."

He went out of the lot feeling happy and light and free. The cars, the surface of the road, the traffic lights, the stores were vivid in every detail, and he suddenly realized: the veil that had covered his eyes for so long was now gone, he could see again! The world was childhood sharp and new. Why? An increase in hormones, in corticosteroids? A "strictly psychological" change (whatever that meant)? Who cared, as long as it was a fact? As the Honda zipped along, as the air from the sunroof whipped his cheeks, he remembered the Jersey shore from years ago, when he was in college— his first car, the Chevy, that bright exhilaration as he drove it along Dune Drive.

Joy pressed a button on the dash; rock music blared:

Feel the heat, feel the heat,
Put your hand on the meat...

Put your hand on the *meat?* Ted thought. Good God! Joy grinned, fished around in her purse, came out with a slim cigarette, punched the lighter, waited.

You know that I'm a big shot, baby,
*Look out, here it comes...*the tape sang on. Did that mean what he thought it meant? He said, "Is this your car?"

"Sure is, Bear."

"Nice."

"I'm glad you like it." She bent to the lighter's bullseye, took a long deep drag and held it, teeth together, lips slightly parted, her nostrils flared, then pushed the lighter back in the dash and held out the cigarette.

He was ready to say he didn't smoke when it dawned on him what this was. He'd seen it smoked at parties, but June disapproved so strongly he'd never dared touch it. He felt nervous, but thought: What the hell? If you're going, go all the way.

He took the joint, dragged deeply, inhaled. Years ago, before his father's emphysema, he had smoked Pall Malls. It surprised him how gentle this was, how easy it was on his throat. He held the smoke in as he'd seen her do, gave the cigarette back. He felt nothing but lingering mild effects of his beer. He wondered how long it would take to work. Would he still be able to drive?

The Honda floated down the road in his happy, effortless hands. The Dollingers, he thought, must have some dough to be able to buy a car like this for their kid. Most Whitman families did have dough, a lot more dough than any teacher had. He could use a new car, the station wagon was acting weird, but he couldn't afford one now.

The joint came back and he sucked it again. "Turn right at the light," Joy said. He did; felt gravity and a surge in his eager groin. He saw himself in the A-V room, her skirt up, his head in her lap.

You know what I say
When they say I'm too hot?
I say it's better to burn
Than to rot.

They were driving down General Haze Boulevard now, that six lane strip of sleaze that rocketed out of Camden. Liquor stores, gas stations, and tacky motels. ADULT BOOKS! PEEP SHOW! GIRLS! OPEN 24 HOURS!

"Okay, up ahead on the right," Joy said. "You see it?"

A sign with a garish squared-off hawk or eagle: Thunderbird Motel. He was actually going to stop on General Haze Boulevard? Looked that way. He turned into the parking lot. "Is it safer to park out back?"

"Safer? What do you mean?"

"Get your car out of sight of the highway."

She smiled. "Who's going to recognize my car? And who cares if they do? Come on, let's go."

The end of the music, a dying sun, his feet a bit soft as they walked across to the office. What name to use? Pay cash, of course.

The clerk was tall and tufted, with a beaky nose and folds of skin at his neck. The Thunderbird in the flesh? Ted found himself trying to keep from laughing. He took the registration card and signed it "Dewey Cum," and found the pun wildly funny. He reached for his wallet and Joy said, "Forget it, I'll use my VISA."

He stood there and watched her pay, his heart banging hard. He remembered his honeymoon trip with June. The first place they'd stopped, he had signed the card "Theodore Wharton." The clerk had looked at it indignantly and said, "Mr. and Mrs., if you please," and had made him change it and asked for his driver's license. Now a phony name, a VISA card in a different name, and nobody batted an eye.

The Thunderbird gave Ted the key, attached to turquoise plastic; said, "The key to your room, Mr. Cum." He made "Cum" rhyme with "room," creating a comical couplet. As they left the office, it was all so outrageously funny Ted's eyes filled with tears. He started to giggle, and soon he was laughing his head off.

"Good grass, huh?" Joy said. "I pay top dollar for it, it damn well ought to be good. Where the fuck is this room?"

They walked through a grimy passageway, Ted still with a silly grin pasted over his face. He stopped to stare at the ice machine, which he found intensely amusing. "Come on," she said, and pulled his hand, and they floated up the stairs.

He stumbled across the threshold and fell on the bed, convulsed with laughter.

Joy laughed too. "Jesus, Bear, you act like you never smoked before."

He giggled, tears flooding his eyes. "I never did."

She sat beside him. "*Never?* You have to be kidding. My God, I've been smoking since I was *twelve.* Three fourths of the kids in your classes are out of their skulls, they get stoned on the bus or out in the park before they come into school, and you've never *done* it?"

He couldn't stop laughing. "Never. No." Good Christ, what a riot this was! "Three *fourths?* You're exaggerating."

"Like hell I am."

He laughed. She smiled and ran her fingers through his hair. "Oh silly, silly Bear."

The way she said it made him think of that Winnie-the-Pooh book he'd read to Brad and Kim when they were small. How did the poem go?

Isn't it funny
How a bear likes honey?
Buzz! Buzz! Buzz!
I wonder why he does?

My God, that was *hysterical*—yet so profound! He used to read it to Brad, The Incredible Hulk. How quickly the years had flown! Soon Kim would be as old as— Joy!

He grinned at her and said, "If I'm Bear, you must be Honey."

"Suits me fine," she said.

Then all at once the silliness drained away. He felt stuffy and hot, aware of the stale motel-room smell. He stood, brisk crackles in his ears, and turned the air-conditioner on.

The sound of it was jarring, huge. He watched Joy under the crooked lamplight as she reached behind her, undid buttons, smoothly stepped out of her dress. A pale beige bra, her nipples visible through it, and off it came. Then her panties, black-edged bronze, were peeled off nonchalantly and she stood there naked and bold. His heart was in high gear. Would it burst? Did he care?

"You ready for your shower, Teddy Bear?"

The air-conditioner hissed at his skin as he took off his clothes. He followed her into hospital brightness, stepped into the steaming wet, he was soaping her breasts, she was down on her knees in the streaming flow and licking, licking, they held each other and slithered and rubbed, their breaths hot mist in the lush rain forest of lust.

On the bed he was lost in the loose wet heat of her thighs, he was spun to fantastic colors, went down, down, down. He was on his back, she was over him, facing him, spreading her heat, he plunged his tongue, tasted vinegar tang, he was thick with her lathery musk. All thoughts had dissolved in her liquid, all morals, all fears, all restraints, there was only the succulent goodness of flesh, there was only *now*.

Buzz! Buzz! Buzz! Then she sat on him slick and he slid right in. Up and down, up and down she drove, a galloping cowgirl, her fingers pressed into his shoulders so hard that it hurt. "Ride a cock horse to Banbury Cross!" she cried, eyes closed, and shuddered and gasped and shivered along her spine as he sucked in breath and blasted, hugging her close as he followed the burst to its end.

They lay there, sweating, on fire, one flesh, and she covered his mouth with her mouth and tongued his tongue. "It was good, Teddy Bear. You're good, sweet Bear." Her breasts were warm and soft on his chest and his mind knew the blankness of heaven.

Snapping sounds in his head and the lamplight was splinters of glass. He wanted to live in this dream forever, he wanted it never to end. But the thoughts came creeping back, came marching back.

June was probably home by now and wondering what she could throw together for dinner. Boy had her cooking declined since she started to work. That macaroni and cheese of hers was so *hard*. He had broken a tooth on it once.

Joy kissed his cheek. He wondered if she could cook. She said, "Forever and ever not knowing you'll be, forever not knowing you were."

He looked at her eyes, feeling suddenly sad. "Who wrote that?" he said.

"I did," she said. "I wrote it when I was fifteen, after Skip was killed. It's corny, I know, but still, it's true. All those millions of years before you're born, when you have no idea that you'll ever exist, and then, all at once, you're here! Then you die and spend eternity—the same eternity you spent before your birth—not knowing you ever existed. And that's why I live for now, sweet Bear."

The noise in Ted's head was starting to fade. "How was your brother killed?" he asked. "What kind of an accident?"

"War training maneuvers. My father was a marine, and all that macho shit rubbed off on Skip. He felt he had to prove something, I guess, so he enlisted, they had this mock battle and something exploded. On Parris Island. The bastards, I'll never forgive them."

"Who?" Ted said. He could feel the dream seeping away. His genitals felt neutral, calm.

"All of them," Joy said. She laughed a bitter laugh and said, "You want another smoke?"

"I better not," Ted said. He checked his watch. "It's past six thirty, I ought to be home by eight."

"By eight? Shit, we still have plenty of time," and she kissed his chest, moved over his stomach, took his organ into her mouth.

To his utter surprise and delight it stood tall as a little marine. And soon he was at it again, on top, working slowly with quiet passion, and managed to finish. It was muted this time around, but he actually *finished*. Twice in less than an hour! Amazing!

"Can we do it tomorrow?" she asked.

"I doubt it, weekends are tough. I take a class on Tuesday night, we can do it then."

She pouted. "And what will my poor little pussy do until Tuesday, Bear?"

"Prepare," he said. "Get ready for the fucking of its life!"

She shrieked, delighted. "What shocking language! What would dear old Miss Spoonfeather say?"

Miss Spoonfeather, head of the guidance department, was pallid, arthritic, antique. Her grammar was Victorian; she even said, "somebody's else."

"Fuck Miss Spoonfeather," Ted said, smooth with dope.

"What an image," Joy said. "Spoonfeather in bed. Do you think she knows how to give head?"

• • • • •

His family was there in the family room watching TV. As he set his briefcase down on the foyer floor he felt like an evil intruder, a Star Trek heavy, a villain from outer space. He was struck by a sudden Raskolnikov urge to confess, to fall on his knees and whimper and beg their forgiveness. He was not of this world, not earthling Ted Wharton, the Daddy who'd changed these kids' diapers and wiped their chins and sat up long nights with their fevers. "There's macaroni and cheese in the oven," June said without turning around. She was flat on the couch, laid out, surrounded by *Courier-News*. Kim laughed at some crap on TV and Brad scowled. "The kids were hungry, so we ate."

"Okay," Ted said, and his voice sounded alien, thick with guilt. How could they fail to hear it? He expected them to turn around with shocked wide eyes and point their fingers, cry out, *J'accuse!,* but no, they stayed transfixed by print and tube. T.S. Eliot, on the other hand, was highly curious, and sniffed at him relentlessly. *He* knew what the story was, all right. If wives had the noses of dogs, what an interesting world it would be. He went to the kitchen, took the casserole out of the oven, and chewed it while thinking of Joy.

The *smoothness,* that's what got him—the way they had merged with each other. It had taken him years of blunder with June before they had even come *close* to that, and here in one brief afternoon—nirvana! Buzz! Buzz! Buzz! the memory hummed in his dying high, which here in the dull constraints of home had somehow flared up again. He wondered where he was going and where it would end, and didn't really care. His mind drifted down through layered words, he kicked T.S. Eliot, private eye, as the animal nosed his shoe, he chewed the overly crispy casserole, and mused.

He had always identified with those oddballs who walked off their jobs with no warning and disappeared; faked their deaths, perhaps, by driving their car off a bridge; then surfaced somewhere with another name, another face, to earn their bread in a new, invigorating way. Sherwood Anderson leaving his paint plant and running away to Chicago, that sort of thing. Absurdly romantic, but what the hell? If that's what it took to feel alive, why not?

Now *he* was one of those oddball outsiders. His teacher and daddy roles were a sham; his real self was dark and mysterious, shadowed in rented rooms. As he ate the macaroni and cheese by himself, he felt shut out, an interloper in somebody else's home. He felt like a secret agent, a spy ("T.S.! Get out of here! Bad dog!"). He was not just a middle-aged high school teacher entrenched in bland suburbia now, but a *dangerous* man, a *powerful* man, a man attractive to seventeen year old girls!

"Ow! Damn!" Pain rocked his jaw as he felt in his mouth. The tooth hadn't broken, but Jesus this crap was hard! He set the remainder on the floor, where T.S. Eliot, built by God to demolish bone, took care of it in a flash.

He went to his study, briefcase in hand, and sat down at his desk. So what did he think of this girl? What was it he actually felt for her? Unbridled lust. Was that wicked? A deadly sin? Quite possibly, but he *needed* her, damn it, he'd never really *indulged* his lust before. Ah yes, that favorite copout, need. Well, after all, we *did* have needs, old Freud and the rest...

He marked a few freshman grammar papers and thought: Cunnilingus and marijuana! Two discoveries like that in one day! It was almost too much to assimilate, and which did he like the most? He could hear canned laughter, canned life, on the downstairs TV; felt his family's dull presence below the floor. He tried to get on with his grading, but couldn't; his mind was a runaway movie screen—the A-V room with Joy on the stool, the red Honda Accord, the bright shower, dim bed, the rapturous dream of their flesh—and he went downstairs and had two shots of scotch to knock himself out.

• • • • •

In the night's quiet center he bolted straight up in the dark.

In the dream he had been in a train station. Where? Paris? Washington? Montreal? He was there to meet June and the kids but they weren't in sight, there were mobs of strangers, he fought his way through them and craned his neck, staring. Sweat ran down his face.

Trains stood like dragons on the tracks, aglow, the people inside them smoking and reading, wrapped up in themselves, and he ran down the platform, fighting the crowd, old students of his, he realized now, and then he saw June.

She was sitting up front in a car on track 12, with the kids in the seat behind her. All three of them seemed to be crying. He ran to them in the yellow light, feeling sick to his heart, and the train started pulling away. The announcer's voice was echoey, thick, too loud. It said, "Track 12, Chicago, Chicago..."

Ted was running and shouting and waving his arms. "No! Wait! I've changed my mind! June, wait!" But the train was steadily moving off without them seeing, without them hearing or looking up, and then they were lost down the dark night tunnel and only the taillights remained, red dots, and soon those too were gone.

Ted sat there, his breathing quick and shallow, his heart beating horribly fast. His ears rang and hissed in the dark. His skin was hot and he thought: I'll die. Good God, I'm going to die!

He got up and went into the bathroom. In the mirror his face was tragic, old, but his cheeks were as pink as a babe's. His heart raced on and he took his pulse. One hundred and sixty-five! He panicked, broke into a sweat. He couldn't die, he just couldn't, he wasn't prepared!

He had never made out his will. He'd thought he was still too young for that, and he also thought—as quite a few others did—that drawing one up would somehow hasten his end. And now he was going to die for sure, his body could certainly not take a pounding like this and survive.

He went downstairs in the dark. In the kitchen in horrid fluorescent light he poured himself another drink, some brandy this time. It felt soothing and good; burned pleasantly. He drank a second shot and his heart calmed down.

His ears still rang but his heart was fine, behaving sensibly again. He stared at his hand on the glass and thought: I'm forty-two years old, I've got to watch myself! He poured more brandy and thought of Lolita, La Dolce Vita, old Aschenbach and his sweetie boy. I've got to stop, he told himself, it's suicide. Not only that, I'm making a fool of myself.

In bed he thought of the dream, the train, the kids and June fading away, and he felt a softness toward them, a sadness for them. Then June started snoring again. He lay there, waiting, waiting, his patience dissolving, the snoring expanding, filling the room with sound. He poked her.

"What?"

"You're snoring."

"Oh."

8 • SHAPING UP

The dope was to blame for his racing pulse. He looked it up in the morning while everyone else was still sleeping (still riding that train?). Flushed feeling and tachycardia, common side effects in those not accustomed to it, said *The Medical Home Companion.* So that's all it had been—the marijuana. In the cheerful Saturday morning sun his panic seemed absurd.

Yet precautions were surely in order. He *was* forty-two, and sedentary, and if he was going to fool around he would have to prepare himself.

Prepare himself! For God's sake, no, he had to just end it, it was absurd, obscene!

Back in his college days, when he was a counselor at Camp Geronimo in upstate New York, the camp director's husband had run away with a seventeen year old girl. The girl had been beautiful, blond and slim, while Mickey Stumm had been short, fat, pasty, bald and vile, always smoking cigars and laughing at his own foul jokes with a pigeyed squeal. The affair had baffled and sickened Ted, and now here he was neck-deep in the very same thing.

No, no, this was different, totally different! For one thing, he wasn't fat or bald and didn't smoke, and for another…well, it was *different,* that's all.

No denying it, though, it was madness. Yet the thought of it ending made him die a little inside. Just a few more times, another week or two, and then… Then what? Oh God, he was lost! To paraphrase Pascal, the cock has its reasons, of which reason is ignorant. And even if reason knew *that,* it didn't help.

Okay, he was committed—for another week or two if not for the long haul—and had to prepare himself. Get his heart in shape, that was job number one.

He finished the glass of orange juice he'd been sipping during these ruminations, and went up and dressed in his sweatshirt, old khakis, and sneaks.

By the time he had jogged to the end of Harmony Lane—one block—his heart was already protesting. Up Washburn Avenue, along the cemetery, had to stop and walk, he was breathing so hard. He felt like a fool. If any of the neighbors were watching, Christ. Next thing he knew, he would start going barefoot to work, get a tan, buy a motorcycle. No, no, just increase his endurance, nothing wrong with that. He started to jog again. It felt awful. He gasped his way to Freedom Drive, then walked back home.

He was still out of breath when he went inside, and June was there in the kitchen. Looking alarmed, she said, "What's the matter? Are you okay?"

"Sure, fine," he said yanking his sweatshirt off, slumping into a chair, his chest heaving, a wicked stitch stabbing his bottom right rib. "Just doing a little jogging."

Her face turned incredulous. "Jogging? *You?*"

He fought for breath. "I've been feeling a little rusty," he said, "out of shape. You get to be forty you have to start watching yourself."

"Uh-huh," June said.

"If Marty had jogged, he might still be alive."

"If Marty hadn't *smoked* he might still be alive."

"Agreed, but exercise is important too. I think I'll join the jogging group at school."

"The jogging group? I never knew there was a jogging group."

The pain in his side was sharp and nasty. He took a deep breath. "They meet three times a week."

June raised her eyebrows. "Are you sure this is a good idea? You've never been very physical, it just doesn't seem like you."

And did she suspect? he wondered. God, how could she *not* suspect? Wasn't his crime apparent? Didn't it show in his face, his eyes, his voice? "You don't get any exercise," he said, "your arteries get hard. You're prone to not just heart attacks but strokes—and premature senility."

"I think it may already be too late," June said.

Brad came into the kitchen; regarded his father's perspiring face, amused. "Did you say you were *jogging?*"

"That's right."

Brad grinned. "In *sneakers?*"

"What's the matter with sneakers?"

"They'll kill your feet. If you're serious, you better get running shoes. Those things don't have any cushion, the shape's all wrong."

"Oh," Ted said. The pain in his side was not getting better. He went to the sink, ran a glass of water, drank it, sat down again.

"My father called while you were getting in shape," June said. "They're coming next weekend."

"Jesus," Ted said, and Brad snickered.

"Why do you always have to comment?" June said.

His reaction had been so automatic, he'd scarcely been aware of it. "What?"

"That comment, 'Jesus,'" June said.

He sighed. "June, why should I pretend? I can take your mother, as numb as she is, but the Colonel..."

"We *know* your feelings by this time, Ted. Why do you always feel compelled to express them?"

Brad chuckled and got out the Wheaties. In the family room, the TV was selling some thrilling trash to toddlers. Ted suddenly thought of Joy. He shrugged, stood up, said, "Sorry, I'll try to control myself," and went upstairs to shower.

• • • • •

On sunny weekends like this, June always wanted the house improved in some way. Her list was substantial: the gutters and downspouts needed cleaning, the trim needed painting, how long was he going to let that roof leak go? The garage should be reorganized. Etcetera.

He decided to start on the trim out back. It was quiet there, nobody would watch him (he hated to have his work observed by his competent handyman neighbors), and scraping old paint was a mindless chore that would let his thoughts roam free.

And roam they did, all over his week with Joy. The A-V room, the Thunderbird Motel... By ten o'clock he was horny again and went to his study and masturbated.

His feelings about this libidinal recrudescence were sharply divided. It was good to know he still had the old fire, but it disturbed him, too. He'd thought he'd matured, had put that frantic stuff behind him. Wrong, totally wrong.He still didn't know himself—at forty-two! My God, how long would it take?

When he went outside again, a burial was in progress in Waughbach Cemetery. For whatever reasons, it was rare to see anyone buried there, especially nearby, and this one was very close. Too close: it was in the zone that T.S. Eliot saw as his private preserve, and the mangy moron was standing beside the grave and barking his scruffy head off.

Under his breath Ted cursed the dog and went back to scraping the trim. No use trying to collar the fool, if he went over there it would think he was showing support and would carry on all the more. He scraped and thought of Joy; the dog kept barking; the burial finally ended and the mourners left. T.S. Eliot watered the new gravesite, was hollered at and kicked in the rump by somebody over there, and then it was lunchtime, then time for the mall.

$$\bullet \bullet \bullet \bullet \bullet$$

As he drove, he thought of Joy and read the bumperstickers: Skiers Make Better Lovers. Truckers Make Better Lovers. Virginians, Fishermen, Plumbers Make Better Lovers. Just what were these banners proclaiming? Did they really mean Better *Screwers?* He considered the plumber bumpersticker: power augers, plumber's friends, pipe wrenches—kinky—and a Volvo cut into his lane. DON'T POSTPONE JOY! its bumper commanded. Exactly!

At the mall Brad helped him pick out some jogging shoes. He felt funny about it, as if Brad were helping him cheat.

When they got back home, he took a nap. They were going to see the Phillipses, and he needed to rest up for that.

The Phillipses were typical of the handful of couples with whom they were friendly: overly-groomed, dull, sociable, and quasi-literate in a way peculiar to the college-educated. ("Hopefully, Fred and myself will be able to lie this issue to rest." —Alice Phillips.) Fred Phillips was a pharmacist, which was a boring, paranoid profession consisting of counting pills into bottles and screening out junkies. (That long-haired guy who'd ordered terpinhydrate with codeine—why wasn't he coughing?) Ted had actually fallen asleep after one of their dinners, had conked right out in the rocking chair as Fred had babbled on about some sort of FDA crap, and June had chewed him out for it all the way home. That's why the nap. No more lapses like that would be tolerated.

Boy did he ever need that one good friend! Back in college he'd actually thought he would find him someday: a guy he would hit it off great with, who liked what he liked, had the same sense of humor, whose life was different from his but *interesting.* No way. American men were so messed up with cowboy fantasies, CB fantasies, athlete fantasies and faggot fears that they couldn't even see each other. The only hope was with women.

June *had* been his good friend, hadn't she? Years ago? Or had he been kidding himself? If only he'd kept a diary, taken notes, so he'd *know.* He only knew now that he had a June who wasn't the friend he needed, and Fred and Alice Phillips and two other equally deadly couples, the Grays and the Sleepers, out of all the people in the world.

He dreaded the thought of going to Fred and Alice's. He wanted to nap right through the night, but of course that was out of the question. June wouldn't allow it.

• • • • •

They were having martinis in the living room, which had plump white two-seater couches, an oyster-white rug, a piano, a chrome-and-glass coffee table. "Well that's what she said to Fred and I," Alice Phillips insisted to June, as Fred gave Ted the inside scoop on his latest retirement fund. Ted scarfed his martini imprudently fast and nodded, blinking, trying to keep his lids from shutting down.

The doorbell donged and the Phillipses' daughter, Eileen, came down the stairs. Ted saw her in school every once in a while, but only now did he realize how much she'd grown. Her girlhood was gone; she was now a young woman—a very attractive one, too. She answered the door and a tall, good-looking, blond-haired kid with a cocky grin stuck his face inside; said, "Hi, Mr. and Mrs. Phillips."

Ted knew the guy. His name was Rod Rheingold.

Rod did a double take when he recognized Ted. "Hey! Mr. Wharton!"

Feeling incriminated by his drink, Ted nodded and said, "Hi, Rod." He'd had the kid for tenth grade English; recognized him as a wiseass jock who worked just enough to get by. In his alcohol glaze he imagined a series of Eileen-Rod obscenities. These were quickly replaced by an image that made him frown.

"Hey, don't get sloshed now, Mr. W.," Rod said. "See you later, folks." He flashed his smug confident grin again as Eileen went out. The door closed.

Fred said, "You know Rod?"

Frowning into his empty glass, Ted said, "Yeah, I had him in English once."

"Have a refill?"

"Don't mind if I do, Fred, don't mind if I do," Ted replied, because that was how pharmacists liked you to talk. Jesus, why did they always wear ripple-soled shoes?

As Fred fixed the drinks, Ted scowled at the floor and wondered why the sight of Rod had triggered that image of Joy.

"Rod's a good kid," said Fred, giving Ted his martini. "Got a real good head on his shoulders."

And a real good cock in his pants, too, I'll wager, Ted thought. You're drunk, he thought, and thought, Damn right, and drank. Rod and Joy? Fred went on with his fund. Rod and *Joy?*

The connection put him in a grouchy mood, and at dinner he said, "Would you pass I the meat please, Alice?"

They stared at him as he took the plate, Fred grinning a simple grin. Phuck pharmacists, Ted thought. As he chewed the beef he wondered what stage Eileen and Rod had reached by now. And again that disquieting thought: Rod and *Joy?*

9 • HEARTBURN

Tuesday night they parked in a pine-lined lane beside a golf course (Marty Zeller's old golf course?) and did it in the station wagon.

June hadn't wanted to cook on Sunday so they'd gone to McDonald's. Kim had finished her shake in the car, had left her container on the floor, and as Ted now positioned himself, he gave it a boot.

He had smoked half a joint and was floating, but still, the Plymouth put a definite damper on things: to use family property in this way seemed traitorous. As he crushed Kim's empty cup with his shoe, he worried that the car would smell of dope tomorrow—or possibly longer.

He had never done it in a car before, and didn't like it at all. His movements were delineated by the steering wheel, the shift lever, the transmission hump. He banged his funnybone on the turn signal lever and twisted his back. Trying to avoid a cramp, he popped out at the start of climax, but managed to slip back in in the nick of time.

On top of him, her pressure killing his shoulder, she said, "I like it when guys come outside of me, too, I like to see it spurt. The other way is good because you get the jolt, but you don't see anything."

Guys? Ted thought in his cannabis daze. How *many* guys? What kinds of guys?

"That stuff they say about feeling it shoot up inside you is crap. All you feel is the jerking around, you don't feel it shoot."

Ted was happy to know that. He'd always wondered about it, but had never dared ask June.

"And the taste? It sure isn't great, but it isn't bad, and it's high in protein, right?"

"I don't really know," Ted said, something fluffy and warm in his ears. He thought of the class about wackadoo kids in that room with the blue fluorescent lights; of Dr. Zahara droning on. That class was almost over now.

They disengaged themselves, and his shoulder felt better. Joy lit a fresh joint, held it out.

"No thanks," Ted said, "I'm fine." He'd read somewhere that that's what you said when you didn't want any more.

"You sure?"

"I'm sure."

He leaned against the door and watched her smoke. Seventeen years old. It had always seemed incongruous to him that youth could catch up to age. That some rookie could pitch to—and strike out—a star who'd been in the majors when the rookie was still on a potty chair. Ted had been twenty-five when Joy was born. She'd come into the world the year of his marriage, and how he'd have laughed back then at the thought that an infant would threaten his life with his wonderful new bride, June.

He watched her smoke. Through the open window he smelled the dark scent of the evergreen trees and the piney earth, and began to feel sad. There was something out of his past in that smell—of Camp Geronimo? Where the fat bald camp director's husband had run away with that girl? He watched Joy's full and perfect lips caress the joint; its orange glow.

She smiled a little and said, "What's wrong? Feeling guilty?"

"Maybe," he said.

She shook her head. "Well don't. Life's too damn short to waste on guilt. After Skip died I said, Fuck guilt. I mean people punish themselves, and for what? God gave us our equipment, right? He gave it to us so we could enjoy it, and that's what I'm going to do."

She sucked the joint and held it out, and once again he declined. Extracting the last puff of smoke from the roach and dropping it out the window, she said, "There isn't any *time* for guilt. The big corporations have poisoned the planet, and *I'm* supposed to feel guilty? Let the bastards who ruined the earth feel guilty. We talk about cleaning things up, what a joke, it'll never happen, we're far too evil and dumb— thanks to God, who made us that way. —And gave us sex to drown our misery and breed more misery. No, Bear, no guilt, no guilt."

She was shaking the way she had in the A-V room after Marty Zeller had died, but not as hard. "Fuck guilt," she said. "Just fuck it." Biting her lip, she said, "Put your arms around me, Bear," and she leaned against him, suddenly brittle and frail.

It was almost like holding Kim: no sex, just softness, warmth, the delicious smell of her hair. She said, "My father and other old people just can't understand. They're still afraid of *Communists*. They still think bombs will keep us safe. The air is killing us, no place is safe, we're probably parked on a hazardous waste site right this very minute." Biting her lip, she abruptly sat up with a laugh. "Good Christ, that dope can make you paranoid, you were smart not to smoke any more."

He didn't say anything for a minute, then his curiosity got the best of him and he asked her about Rod Rheingold.

"Oh God, let's not talk about *him*," she said.

"I just wondered."

"Yeah, I went with the creep. Just because he's hung like a horse, he thinks he's hot shit."

A sudden unpleasant twinge hit Ted's gut.

Joy laughed. "Well, he was good practice," she said. "If you've handled that baseball bat of his, you can handle anything. Christ, I'm starving to death, let's find something to eat."

Diminished, Ted started the car.

They went to an ice cream place in Parkview Plaza. Parkview Plaza was far from Westdale, but still, Ted was deathly afraid he'd be spotted with Joy. He ate the sundae, rich syrupy glop, too fast, eager to get back to the car, get back to its anonymity, and his stomach felt sour and sick.

He got home at 11:35, much later than he usually did on Zahara nights, and the house was still.

As he lay beside June wide awake, indigestion burning, he felt like a total stranger. Seventeen years together and now they had nothing. He listened to her horrendous snoring, Joy's juices on his genitals, and wondered again where their life had begun to go wrong. Imperceptible shifts to the flashover point, where everything had soured; less laughter, more indigestion, a flabbiness of the palate; a million minor disagreements, the hassles with the kids; her diminishing softness, her growing efficiency (Christ, she would rather straighten the house than make love!).

He felt sad for June as on and on she snored. Did she realize how bad things were? Was she totally unaware? If they talked about it, maybe they'd still have a chance. But where to begin? ("Say, June, I have an idea. Suppose I put my mouth on your...") No. Impossible.

And so was sleep. Because of June's snoring, his indigestion, his thoughts—especially his thoughts of Rod Rheingold. Okay, the kid had slept with her, but had he *savored* her? Hell no, he'd had her the way T.S. Eliot ate his dinner: generic nuggets or sirloin steak, it was gulped in a flash. Letting Rod have Joy was like letting a three-year-old eat Godiva chocolates. But it bothered him greatly to think about it; he just couldn't let it go.

Before she had driven away in her Honda, she'd slipped him a joint. Now he eased out of bed, took the joint from his jacket pocket, locked himself in the study and finished the whole damn thing. Then he went to the family room; watched TV without sound. A singer had an incredibly funny wide mouth...

10 • SUNRISE, SUNSET

In the morning, all he remembered about the TV was that singer's mouth. He had fallen asleep on the couch. The dog woke him early with another of its charming habits—banging the wall with its tail and rump—which wouldn't stop till you let it outside. Ted did, poured coffee from the white machine that had brewed it while he dreamed. As he drank at the kitchen table, his mind on Joy, Kim sat down with a bowl of Cheerios. She stared at him.

"What's the matter?" he said, her gaze making him guilty.

"There's a hair growing out of your teeth," she said with a puzzled, disgusted expression.

Ted stood, nearly toppling his chair. In the powder room mirror he checked Kim's assertion, and saw, between his upper incisors, a gleaming blond pubic kink!

Before they'd parted the night before, Joy had begged him for still more mouth-work. The request had turned him on all over again. In spite of his indigestion, he'd feasted with the blind blood thirst of a mosquito.

He plucked the hair, examined it briefly, then washed it down the drain. Good God, what a fool he'd been! From now on he'd shower and brush his teeth just as soon as he got back home, no matter how late it was. He must reek of her scent (a clue: the dog had nudged his nuts as he'd opened the door), and he'd have to shower right away, now, before June came down!

Back in the kitchen he said, "A piece of thread. It must've come off the sheets or something."

Kim's piercing eyes—so much like her mother's. "It looked like hair," she said.

"Yes, it certainly did," Ted said. With a frown he continued, "You left your shoes on the family room floor last night and I almost broke my neck on them. Try not to do it again, okay?"

She scowled. "Okay."

Ted swallowed the rest of his coffee and went upstairs. He scrubbed his teeth and showered intensely, soaping himself three times. As he dressed, June muttered, "What time is it?" "Time to get up," he said, then went outside and sat in the Plymouth with the windows closed. It smelled okay—he thought. But whose candy wrapper was that on the floor? Brad's? Kim's? June's? Joy's? He snatched it up, along with Kim's flattened milkshake cup. Christ, his brain was too soft for this kind of intrigue, he'd get caught!

· · · · ·

Joy and Rick worked together today, and Ted was glad. The stuff in school would have to stop, it was absolutely insane.

Halfway through sixth period, he went to the A-V room. When Rick turned away to check some drawings, Joy cupped her hand on Ted's crotch. Instantly firm, he left the room, astounded again by the depth of the passion that she could arouse in him. He thought about her all afternoon, all evening, all night.

There wasn't any yearbook work Thursdays, and during psychology class, Joy was quiet. He glanced at her from time to time and pictured himself in the A-V room, the station wagon, the Thunderbird Motel. He remembered the last time he'd fished with Brad, that bass that had swallowed the hook, the way he had mangled its mouth and stomach while trying to set it free. He was a lot like that fish now, hooked, hooked bad. Of course, he could free himself if he wanted to, but free himself for what? There was nothing he wanted more than to be with Joy. —Hooked *bad*.

• • • • •

Friday morning, at the staff room mailbox, Tony Troxell said, "I hear the Walker girl's knocked up."

"You mean Allison Walker?" Ted said.

"Yeah. I thought she was getting a little soft at the edges."

"She doesn't seem like the type. Good student."

"Good at other stuff too," Tony grinned.

"Yeah, I guess," Ted said, breaking into a quick, cold sweat. Good Christ, he had never even asked, he had just assumed... Well of course she was on the pill, she had to be.

In the A-V room she said, "I'll meet you at five o'clock, under the 'J.'"

He said, "Right," and wanted to tell her: "We can't do it here anymore," and ask: "Are you on the pill?" But before he could say anything, she raised her skirt.

—To reveal a diaphanous blue bikini. Her equipment was fully visible through it, and all his resolve dissolved. He would crawl on his knees if she asked him to and do anything, anything, right in this room, right now. "Five o'clock at the 'J,'" he said, and, burning, he went out the door.

• • • • •

The Blue Note Motel, Joy's selection again, was only about a hundred yards from the Thunderbird. The name Ted used this time had an Asian flavor: E. Rex Chun. Again, she paid with her VISA.

In the room—a faded baby blue, with a blue fluorescent bulb above the sink—he said, "You should have let me pay."

"No problem," Joy said. "I get a couple of hundred bucks a week from my old man."

"Wow," Ted replied. Brad got ten dollars a week and Kim got five.

She shrugged. "It doesn't go that far with clothes, gas, car repairs..."

"Well let me pay next time."

"We'll see. If I can afford it, I'll do it."

She smiled then, and raised her skirt. Those marvelous thighs, that thin blue underwear. "Undress me," she said.

He went to her, groin aching, mouth bone-dry. His hands were shaking as he took off her skirt and blouse (what a chore this would be with June). A matching sheer blue bra. His erection was bursting against his briefs as he fell on the bed with her, kissed her hard, slipped his finger around and under that flimsy bikini.

He fingered her as she lit a joint, she zipped his fly down, pulled him out, they smoked, she licked, he pulled the top of her bra down and kissed her breasts. Nirvana!

They showered and went at each other hungrily, doing it hard and long. She stopped him, turned, got up on her knees, inviting him in again. As he sank into heat he was startled to see the tattoo—about half dollar size—on her upper left cheek. A yellow sun with blood-red rays above three bands of blue—the sea?—and centered in the sun, in green, was: JOY!

"Faster!" she said. "Faster, Bear, use your finger!" She guided his hand to her button; he rubbed it, kept pistoning hard. "Come outside me this time," she said, her voice breathy and rough. "In my crack! On my spine!"

Her request excited him unbearably. With June there would surely be a substantial penalty for early withdrawal, but Joy was a whole different animal! *Now!* her tattoo, and *now!* her backbone, *Joy, Joy, all over Joy!* (Walt Whitman). Against his will, he thought of Rod Rheingold again. Rod probably had three times as much, was probably a goddamn fire hose. A typical teenage American male, he was fifty percent dork, forty percent stomach, ten percent brain. —And that was being generous on the brain's behalf.

They lay naked beside each other and smoked more dope. He was sated, depleted, content as a cat. He wanted to sit here the rest of his life on this paid anonymous bed with this marvelous nymph. But he'd have to go home soon. He couldn't afford to be late tonight, the Colonel was coming. Why was contentment always so brief? (*And Joy, whose hand is ever at his lips, bidding adieu...*)

He savored the moment. The ring of cheap light from the lamp with the pale blue shade circumscribed his world. Home, family, work, war, the goddamn Colonel, taxes—all part of the shadowland beyond. He looked at Joy's wonderful body and smoked; felt crisply melting thoughts. He grinned. "I like your tattoo."

She laughed. "I like it too—amazingly enough. I did it on a dare." She rolled her eyes. "*Rod* bet me I wouldn't, so of course I did. Some lady in Camden, a Puerto Rican, she did a nice job, no pain. Paid for with Daddy's allowance money, wouldn't he simply die?"

Ted sniffed. Rod's name had soured him again. It seemed that the shadows beyond the light were starting to advance. Then he asked for more trouble; why couldn't he let things slide? "Your father works in insurance, right? I saw it in your records."

"Right. He's president of Colonial Safeguard Company." Smoke left her nose in a rush as she gave him the joint. "What a scam."

Ted took a last drag, his mind drifting down. "Why scam?"

Joy greedily sucked at the roach. "Life insurance for old folks," she said. "You have to be over fifty-five. No health exam, that kind of thing." Dropping the roach in the ashtray, she snorted a laugh. "Who needs life insurance *then?* That's for when you have kids, when you're *young.*"

Ted thought of June and Brad and Kim; of his mortgage. The thoughts began to crystallize, turn slowly in his mind.

"They offer all these deals—well, you've probably seen the ads on TV, they were my father's idea. TV validates our world, right, Bear? I mean for most people—especially older people—it makes things real, and my father understands that. At least he understands *something.*" Her gaze seemed to rest in her thighs, her nest. "You should see the brochures. Endorsements from the Association of Retired Physicists, the Association of Retired Pharmacists... Christ, there *aren't* any such organizations."

And thank God for that, Ted thought. Could you imagine a whole association of old retired Fred Phillipses?

"Nobody's ever challenged them, and they've made a mint. The sad thing is, my father can't even *enjoy* his money, he just likes *making* it. He's so fucking obsessed, he's so— Oh, let's not talk about him anymore."

"Okay, let's not," Ted said. His mind was filled with colored cellophane. He said, "I hear Allison Walker is pregnant."

Joy laughed. "Well is that supposed to be news or something? Didn't you realize that when she tossed her cookies in psych?"

Ted stared at her beautiful eyes. "No, I didn't," he said.

"Yeah, she has wicked morning sickness. Serves her right to get caught, the little bitch, pretending she's so damn holy, like she doesn't even have a cunt. She should've used her head."

"It was pretty dumb."

Joy grinned. "I don't mean used her head *that* way, I mean *this* way." She bent down, rimmed him with her tongue. With a will of its own, his organ began to rise, and she laughed, sat up again.

"Where'd you learn this stuff?" he asked. He was thinking of Rod again. First Joy, and now Eileen, little Eileen Phillips, with whom he had played Monopoly a couple of years ago.

"You want to make your boyfriend happy but you don't want kids, so you learn to give head. But a lot of girls have a funny idea about it, some hardly consider it sex—they convince themselves they're still *virgins*. Some of the little fools think they're safe from diseases that way. There are nasty surprises every so often, but *everybody* gives head."

"Everybody?" Ted said. "Even Mary Willis?" Mary Willis was dumpy, hairy, smelly, played the cello.

Joy laughed. "Okay, there are some exceptions. But *she* probably doesn't do *any-thing*—unless it's with groundhogs or toads or something." She smiled. "I wonder how Rick's going to handle all this."

"All what?" Ted said.

"The pregnancy, of course."

"Rick Castle? You mean…Allison?"

"Sure, didn't you know?"

"Hell, I can't keep tabs on who's going with whom. Jesus Christ, Rick Castle."

"Oh sure, the All-American couple, Mr. and Mrs. Clean as a Bean, the pair all youth looks up to, winners of the Rotary-Lions-Kiwanis Award for Exemplary Youth. No abortion, can you believe it? She probably didn't know she was pregnant till her bathing suit didn't fit."

"Rick Castle," Ted said again.

"You thought he was constipated before, just wait'll you see him now."

Stray pieces of panic were floating around in Ted's high. He said, "I'm sure you…naturally you take precautions."

Her smile again; that gap in her teeth. "So *that's* why all the concern about Allison Walker. Really, Bear, do you think I'm that stupid? I've been on the pill since I made my decision two years ago. My decision to *live*."

Ted breathed. "Fantastic," he said.

"Hey, Bear, you think I'd mess you up? Or mess *myself* up? Jesus, that's all I need, a *baby*." She shrugged. "Of course, if I did get pregnant, I'd have an abortion. God, Allison is dumb."

"She's an excellent student."

"Well that doesn't mean you're *smart,* all you need to do well in school is a decent *memory*." She laughed. "Rick Castle, I think it's great, he had his entire life planned, down to the smallest detail. Mr. Know-It-All got his tight ass kicked—but good."

Ted looked at her beautiful face, at the post-coital blush on her cheeks, and felt time seeping away through the seive of his high. The Friday afternoon gang at The Spouting Whale would be finishing up about now. They were drinking their final drafts of oblivion, ending their moaning and groaning for one more week, heading home to their kids and wives. Which was what *he* had to do, as the goddamn Colonel was certainly there by now. He said, "I've got to get going."

Joy licked her lips seductively, leaned back and spread her thighs. "Hey, not quite yet, I want you to taste my honey."

"Joy, really, I can't…" A soft blue halo floated behind his eyes.

She touched herself. "It's time for your honey, Bear."

Hell, what was the sense of fighting it? He sniffed a laugh and lowered himself to her musk.

• • • • •

Before leaving the Blue Note he rinsed out his mouth and obsessively checked his teeth. Under the sad blue bulb the mirror was gray and his image was covered with film; he kept telling himself to concentrate on the way he looked, but his eyes wouldn't open wide enough, admit enough light.

She drove him back to the parking lot, to his Plymouth; they kissed and she said, "I'll see you on Monday, Bear," and was gone.

He drove home, melancholy, thoughts detached, a thin tune tinkling in his ears. When he walked through the door he saw the leather bag in the foyer, heard the whine of the Colonel's aide-de-camp, June's mother, Mabel—and he wanted to sneak up the stairs and crawl into bed and hide and go to sleep. Instead, he slipped into the powder room and thoroughly checked himself again, threw water on his face to try to stop the jukebox in his head, then went to the far-too-bright kitchen where all of them were.

"Ted!" the Colonel boomed as he thrust out his hand. "How are you, just talking about you!"

Ted's knuckles crunched in the Colonel's fierce grip. "I'm fine, Tom. How are you?"

"Terrific, couldn't be better!"

"Hi, Mabel."

June's mother, powdered and painted and dry as an autumn flower, tenderly took his bruised paw. "So good to see you, Ted. You're looking well."

"Thanks, Mabel, you're looking fantastic," he lied. —And June's getting to look more like you every day.

"We haven't eaten yet," June said in an accusatory tone. "We decided to wait for you."

"Well, here I am," Ted grinned, thinking: Here I am *where?* Who are these strangers I've known for so long? Who am *I*? "Beer, Tom? Mabel, how about some wine?" and he thought, Where the hell is the flag? His head was still pleasantly muddled; the tune played on. Who the hell was in charge back there, the Little Man? He didn't especially like the song but he liked marijuana, it floated you past all kinds of gruesome shit.

The meal was exquisite, the best June had made in months—since the last time her parents had come, as a matter of fact. June adored her father, this snow-headed martinet, this military parody, nothing was ever too good for her dear old dad, and tonight it was juicy prime rib, mashed potatoes, fresh peas, corn, white onions in sauce. Ted ate with marijuana lust, nodding at the Colonel's bullshit about the American Presence. The Colonel had never seemed more like a cartoon figure with his snappiness, his brushy trimness. He and Springer, the track coach/phys ed teacher, were two of a kind: they always seemed to have just stepped out of an ice-cold shower. Lunatics were reputed to have this bright unflagging energy. It usually unsettled Ted, but tonight he was merely amused. The table tableau seemed false as opera. He felt as if he could finish dessert, get up and say, Thank you, nice seeing you all, and never ever come back.

Kim cleared the table and June and her mother cleaned up in the kitchen, duties the Colonel expected of females. In the living room, Ted and his father-in-law had brandy and cigars. That's what you did when the Colonel came. That and listen to combat stories from World War Two, when the Colonel had been a lieutenant. Brad loved these tales, but they terrified Ted, who swore he would blow up the Pentagon to keep Brad from going to war.

June and Mabel and Kim came in; the Colonel blasted on; Ted drank. The dope had retreated and the booze took over, sending him Lethe-wards. He nodded off twice during some of Bastogne's worst fighting, had brief shocking flashes of Joy, and finally, the living room lamps looking five times as bright as they usually did, he excused himself.

"Ted! Calling it quits so soon? I was just getting started!"

"I had a big day, Tom."

"Well, up bright and early, tomorrow's a big day too."

Ted thought: The flag-raising. Jesus.

June frowned. "Can't you stay up a little later, Ted? Mother and Daddy visit so seldom."

"I'd like to, June, but it really has been a long day." He thought once again of the Blue Note Motel: Joy's naked body on the bed, that sunny tattoo on her tail. His family stared. "Well"—he nodded—"goodnight."

Before he went up, he looked in the hallway closet. Yes, there was the flag, untouched since the last time the Colonel had come, tucked away on the highest shelf.

In bedroom darkness he heard their faint voices, the sounds of the lives that were bound to his life by memory, paper, and blood. He remembered the dream of them moving away on that train. In spite of the booze and fatigue, his heart speeded up. He had a few joints in his jacket, but didn't dare smoke one now.

The flag, his jumbled mind thought, the goddamn flag. I don't want to get up at the crack of dawn. Well maybe he would be lucky and it would rain.

11 • ROUTING THE COLONEL

But the day was sunny, and he woke to: "Out of the rack, troops, we raise the colors at oh seven hundred! Ted! Where's the flag?"

"Hall closet, Tom."

He lay there, mouth furry and bitter, and stared at the ceiling. June was already out of bed, he could hear the kids, it was time for the goddamn flag charade again. Was he doomed to repeat this ritual all his life? Till the Colonel *died?*

Twenty minutes later he was out on the lawn. He held the flag, Brad clipped it to the rope, then pulled it sharply up the pole as they stood at attention, saluting.

As always, Ted wondered what his neighbors could possibly make of all this. Why did the Wharton family turn fervently patriotic once or twice a year? During one of the Colonel's visits a while back, the Monsantos installed a pole in their own front yard. Their flag-raising lasted two weeks, finally petering out when they realized the Whartons' ceremonies had ceased. Months later the Colonel came back, the flag went up, and so did the Monsantos' flag. Ted wondered if they thought he had the inside dope on some obscure, chic, patriotic holidays, and were bound and determined not to be excluded.

Before the Colonel departed last time, he'd succeeded in drawing forth two other flags from closets where they'd lain neglected for God only knew how long. As Ted used his salute to shield his bloodshot eyes from the brilliant sun, he thought: If the Colonel really put his mind to it, he could probably start his own country.

Ted looked at him as the flag reached the top of the staff. There were actually tears in the old man's eyes. He raised the flag every day that it didn't rain, yet the act still made him cry. For what broken ideal did he weep? Was he really that moved by this land of supermarkets, freeways and TV? He was, of course, for he loved that plastic shopping mall life, he was a real *American.*

As Ted stood there with sun in his eyes, he thought, Forty-two years old and I still put up with this. I actually stand here on the lawn of my very own home and submit to this crap. I put up the flagpole for *him.* Why? It was the easy thing to do, that's why. Just as going to classes on wackado kids was easy, staying in education was easy, shopping on Saturday afternoons at the mall was easy. Easy death versus rigorous life? In Ted's case, no contest.

"Excellent, Brad," the Colonel said, "that's how to raise it, nice and brisk." He grinned and said, "Let's chow down, troops, big day ahead, we're going to need some rations in our guts."

•••••

Before the flag was lowered that evening, the Colonel ran their asses off. Each one of his days was a part of the Campaign of Life, and he planned it with the thoroughness of an invasion. He made Ted drive to Brandywine, then recounted the battle in every detail, pacing over the site as if he were Washington risen from the grave. Each time he visited, they had to go to Brandywine or Valley Forge or Independence Hall or some other place where, as the Colonel put it, "The cradle of liberty was kindled."

Ted had always put up with the Colonel's outings with little or no complaint. The kids seemed to like them, June claimed to like them even if she didn't, there was really no point to making a great big deal out of things. But now it was different; now he was changed, awake; and he went through the motions sourly, feeling his life blood seeping away to time as surely as if he'd been wounded. As the Colonel tramped over the battleground, Ted thought of something Joy had said : "I hate wars, Bear. I hate the very thought of wars. I like it warm and soft and loving, with lots and lots of sex." And he wanted to be with her now in illicit release, away from responsibility, away from the chains of the past.

•••••

"Breakdown in the moral fiber, Ted! Breakdown in the moral fiber of our youth!"

The Colonel was livid in the living room, really worked up. Ted drank, and before he knew it, he'd knocked down three martinis. His ears were hissing loudly and the wallpaper seemed to be closing in, to be squeezing the oxygen out of his lungs. Where was Joy right now? Driving around in her Honda, no doubt, while he was shackled, mired in this domestic tar pit with this lunatic jingoist father-in-law, with a wife who was barely aware he existed, with kids who would sooner get rid of *him* than get rid of their TV sets.

From the kitchen, cries of consternation. The dog had groveled in something unspeakably vile, the house was reeking, and oh, it would spoil the meal. "A bath?" Ted said. "Now? Right before dinner? Why don't we just tie him up outside?" But June insisted, and Ted gave in. Why the hell did he always give in?

With Brad he dragged the beast outside and hosed him, soaped him, hosed him again, Mr. 7-Eleven observing the whole charade. T.S. Eliot shivered and shook, soaking Ted, and he went inside and showered and changed his clothes in martini fatigue. When he sat on the bed to put on his shoes, he felt like going to sleep.

Another dinner fit for royalty—ham, scalloped potatoes, baby carrots in butter, green salad—and his mind was with Joy in her Honda, smoking dope and listening to her tapes:

Makin' love to a stranger,
Makin' love to a stranger,
Batman, Superman,
The Lone Ranger.

Brad and Kim started arguing over the salt. Kim claimed that she'd had it first and that Brad had snatched it away. Ted mediated, wild inside, a lion in a cage. The Colonel ignored the whole skirmish, enmeshed in the U.S. presence in Latin America again. His gin-reddened cheeks stressed his passion as June and her mother dissected the Bloomingdales sale.

T.S. Eliot, fragrant and famished below the table, started a high frantic barking. Sulking Kim, possessing the shaker now, sprayed spiteful salt on her ham. Dry Mabel smiled venomous sweetness at Ted as he passed her the carrots.

My baggage, Ted thought. This is what I've collected in seventeen years. The dog barked on.

"A dictatorship?" the Colonel said, his glittering eyes on Ted. "I agree, it's a dictatorship—but it isn't soft on Communism. 'You support a dictatorship,' people say. Well you know what I say to them? 'You think Stalin wasn't a dictator? You think Mao wasn't a dictator? And what about Castro, what do you say about *him?*'"

The kids were in another hassle, this time over the milk. T.S. Eliot's barking increased. Ted's face was hot and flushed; his mind was wild. What the hell was he *doing* here? Who *were* these people? Lunatics, crazies, this place was a raving *madhouse.*

"Our presence in Latin America—"

Ted booted the dog in the rump. It yelped in pain. All faces turned.

Ted looked at his father-in-law. In the hissing white silence he said, "To be perfectly honest, I don't really give a good goddamn about our presence in Latin America."

The Colonel stopped chewing, his right cheek bulging with food. He scowled and said, "You don't." Then he started to chew again.

T.S. Eliot, scruffy cur, slunk into the kitchen. Bright rivers flowed over Ted's ears. "No, I don't," he said. "And you want to know why? Because our presence in

Latin America has nothing to do with me. The people involved in decisions down there have nothing to do with me. The people involved in decisions down there are millionaires who want to protect their investments. They're killers prepared to sacrifice as many young lives as they have to in order to do it."

With difficulty, the Colonel swallowed his food. He said, "I find that absolutely shocking, Ted. You can't be serious. The Communist threat will always be with us, no matter what—"

Ted threw down his fork; it clattered against his plate, flipped onto the tablecloth. "Communism is dead!" he said, "It's dead and gone! You sound like your brain went to sleep in the nineteen fifties and never woke up!"

The Colonel sputtered; his wife put her hand on his arm. June said, "Ted! That was totally uncalled for, Ted!"

"Oh, was it?" Ted shouted. He crushed his napkin into a ball and threw it onto his plate; it sat, expanding, on his ham. "I think it was totally *called* for!"

He was dimly aware of the fear on the faces of Brad and Kim as he jumped up out of his chair. He went to the hallway closet and snatched up the carefully folded flag. Took it into the family room. Threw it into the fireplace. Winding a sheet of newspaper into a torch and lighting it, he touched it to the flag's right edge. The stripes caught merrily, turning brown. June yelled, "Ted!" from the archway. Kim started to cry.

Ted shouted, "A guaranteed first for Harmony Lane!" He looked at the Colonel, his teeth on edge, and said, "This is what I think of your goddamn U.S. presence in Latin America!"

The flames began to flicker, diminish, and smoke poured into the room. He'd forgotten to open the damper. Coughing, pointing at the Colonel, eyes now watering, he said, "You talk about the breakdown of morality! People like you are the immoral ones! It's people like you who bulldoze the rainforests, ruin the ozone, hang onto nuclear weapons! You make morality impossible! The food on this table is riddled with cancer from nuclear tests of years ago! The whole world's sick! The future's dead! Is it moral to rob our youth of its future? How can people without any future be moral?"

He saw Brad's startled face, Kim's tears. "I'm just sick of this crap!" he said. "Do you understand? I'm goddamn *sick* of it!" He hurtled quickly past them and mounted the stairs.

In the bedroom he heard the commotion; heard the Colonel assume command and extinguish the fire and rescue his precious flag. Kim continued to cry. Ted lay on the bed and felt bad for her, breathing fast, heart pounding. June came into the room, demanding that he apologize. He refused. "You bastard!" she said, going out again with a vicious slam of the door.

They were packing. They were going back home to Sellerstown, PA. He heard June's protests, heard his mother-in-law say, "June, it's better this way. No, no, we'll come for another visit soon, but for now it's best…" Half an hour later, the house was quiet.

Ted couldn't believe it. He had routed the Colonel! For the first time in seventeen years, he had routed the Colonel!

June came back, her face hurt, hard. She went to her bureau and got her pajamas. "Well," she said, "are you satisfied? Are you proud of yourself?"

"No," he said.

Snatching her pillow off the bed, she said, "I'm sleeping downstairs tonight." She glared at him, her mouth a line. "Do you know how you've made them feel?" she said. "Do you know how you've made the *children* feel? There's something wrong with you, Ted. You're sick. You need a therapist."

The hell I do, Ted thought. I know what I need, and I'm getting it.

When she went downstairs he locked himself in his study and smoked a whole joint.

• • • • •

As he ran the next morning he felt both good and bad.

He had finally asserted himself, but Jesus, they were the kids' grandparents, their *only* grandparents, the kids adored them, was it fair to have acted that way? As he ran, he thought of his own dead mother and father, sad that his children had never known them. His shoes were still not broken in and he rubbed the skin off his heels. He came limping back into the kitchen.

They were wary of him. He tried to act normal, setting to work on the trim again. He scraped till his arms were aching. As he scraped, Brad mowed the lawn.

The dog had rolled in shit again and he gave it another bath, this time without complaint. He praised June's dinner, retreads from the tragic night before. They got in bed together silently; she turned away.

He wondered: What did she make of his total indifference to sex? Did she think that his urge had died? Had she even noticed?

Sore-armed, sore-heeled, he thought of Joy. His penis grew instantly hard; aimed itself toward June's back like a gun.

12 • LIBIDO-METER

When he saw her there in psychology class he longed for her deep in his teeth, in the root of his tongue. He saw her calves, her perfect knees, recalled the liquifaction of her thighs. Liquifaction! What a word!

When as in silks my Julia goes,
Then, then (me thinks) how sweetly flows
That liquifaction of her clothes.

Next, when I cast mine eyes and see
That brave Vibration each way free;
O how that glittering taketh me!

But no more stuff in the A-V room, he'd have to wait till tomorrow night for that brave Vibration. He'd neglected to tell her they couldn't do things in school, but he'd tell her tomorrow. Tomorrow for sure. Today he was free from that worry—Rick Castle would be in the A-V room alone.

• • • • •

He was motionless on the stool, staring down at the table. Ted almost felt sorry for him.

Rick looked at him with beaten, hangdog eyes. "I want to quit the yearbook," he said. "I want to resign."

With teacherly false concern Ted said, "Resign? But Rick, you can't, we only have six weeks left, Joy and I can't do it alone." He thought: But we sure can do it together!

"I don't have any heart for it anymore," Rick said. "It doesn't seem to matter anymore."

Ted sat on the stool beside him and thought of Ed Michaels, a former colleague of his who'd been married at seventeen. The kid who had caused the marriage was in his twenties now, a physician. Ed's second son was in graduate school and Ed himself was a teacher, so things had worked out in the end. But God, what a brutal row he'd been forced to hoe: Eight years as a part-time undergraduate, five as a part-time graduate student, daytime work in a liquor store, nighttime work in a supermarket, never any vacations. Brutal indeed, but he'd done it.

Ted said, "Rick, I'm counting on you."

Rick shook his head. "Things are different," he said. "Things have changed."

Ted feigned ignorance; it was part of the game. He said, "Miss Spoonfeather might be able to help if you're having problems."

Rick sniffed. "I doubt it."

He was probably right, Ted thought. Miss Spoonfeather probably could just about tie her own shoes. He said, "Rick, you made a commitment—and you seem like the kind of person who honors commitments."

That ought to get him, he thought. In his mind he saw Allison Walker. Bright, very bright, but Jesus she must be naive. Kept naive, no doubt, by parents who wished to preserve her innocence. But it wouldn't work, you couldn't do it, the glands would eventually win.

"Yeah, I made a commitment," Rick said, "but I didn't know things would turn out the way they've turned out, that's all."

"Nobody ever knows how things are going to turn out when they make a commitment."

"Yeah." He looked sick.

Ted *did* feel sorry for him now. "Okay, forget the yearbook today, but think about what I said. I really need your help. I think you're man enough to stick it out no matter how tough things get." (My God! He sounded like the Colonel!)

Rick gritted his teeth. "I hope so," he said. He got up from the stool. "Okay, I'll think about it. It's just that my heart's not in it. I don't feel like part of the class anymore."

Ted wanted him out before—God forbid—a confession came. He had a conflicting urge to help the kid, but that was Spoonfeather's job. "Well just go back to class and take it easy."

"Right," Rick said sardonically. At the door he turned and said, "Oh. Here. I almost forgot. Joy asked me to give this to you."

The envelope was sealed. Ted said, "I hope she's not thinking of quitting too."

"No way," Rick said, and closed the door behind him.

Ted didn't like the tone of that "no way." Did Rick suspect? Frowning, he opened the envelope and unfolded the paper—scented, blue—and read in Joy's bold hand:

Dear Bear,

When I saw you in class this morning I got all damp. It was all I could do to keep from fingering myself right there in my seat. I kept imagining your good stiff cock and how it would taste in my mouth. Tomorrow night I'm going to suck your weekend load right out of you. In the meantime, why don't you pick up some lit? Something we can enjoy together. Can't wait to feel your soft balls in the palm of my hand.

Love,
Honey

Ted stared at the paper. Jesus Christ, was she nuts? To trust Rick Castle with this! He'd almost walked out of the room with it! My God, if he'd opened it up, if someone had gotten their hands on it... One little mistake like that, and...Jesus Christ! It was terrifying to think about, and made him feel...alive!

He read the steamy note again, then put it away in his jacket pocket, a thrill coursing over his spine.

Some "lit." Donne? Marvell? Pope? That probably wasn't what she had in mind...

• • • • •

"*The Joy of Love?*" she said as she finished the joint. "I didn't mean this kind of crap, I meant something *good.*"

Ted (alias Dick Harder) sat on the motel bed (the Sierra Motel) in his blue bikini shorts (brand new—his first non-white shorts ever), feeling foolish. He had gone through a lot of emotional turmoil to acquire this book, and all for naught. He'd prowled around the department store for half an hour before he had mustered nerve enough to touch the damn thing, make his fingers lift it, take it to the counter—to the (of course) female clerk.

"*I'm* the Joy of love. *The* Joy." She riffled through the pages. "Drawings," she said, "how quaint. Jeez, Bear, I thought you'd come up with the hard stuff."

He shrugged. "I just didn't have time."

She cocked an eyebrow, smiling her funny smile. "Well, maybe by Friday. There's a whole bunch of places along this strip, you ought to be able to find something really great."

There was, it seemed, a porno store for every motel on the boulevard, and there were a lot of motels: the Thunderbird, Blue Note, and Monaco; the Silver Bubble, Riviera, Catnap and Belaire—none of which were listed in Ted's *Tourist Guide to South Jersey.* The *Catnap* Motel. Had anyone actually ever *slept* there? ("Hey Honey, hey kids, here's a good place to stop, the Catnap Motel, right next to...Sutton's Sex Shop?")

He looked at the gentle uplift of Joy's young breasts and said, "I'll try to do better," leaned forward and tongued her right nipple, his body aflame. She laughed, stroked his hair and lay back on the bed, legs wide. "Make a meal out of me, Bear."

He did, and discovered something fantastic: if he covered his lower teeth with his lip and used that hard ridge on her after he used his tongue, she went bonkers. Again and again he dipped down, nuzzling in. That little thump when he hit the spot, and

71

she wriggled and writhed and moaned. A new technique! The Wharton Method! Wow!

A couple of weeks ago, he'd have thought this behavior bizarre if not downright perverted. But Jesus, her warmth and her shivering flesh on his face, the way she went Oh and Oh, it was heaven, all worry was banished, all time was banished, he loved it, loved it, loved it. He was nothing but mouth and groin: down-up, down-up, her heat and...Keats! ...*Whose strenuous tongue/Can burst Joy's grape against his palate fine*... Joy's grape! Oh he'd pop it, all right!

Her tongue tucked into her cheek, eyes closed, she made him stop, then wet him with her mouth. He entered her slick and quick and hot and she moaned and sucked in breath. Her legs were high as she said, "Slap against me. Yes! I love it when you slap, now give me slaps!"

He banged his mound against her, bone to bone. "Oh my God!" she said, and dug her heels into his back and thrust and thrust till he couldn't hold out anymore. When he broke he saw showers of stars.

They lay in the tawdry light and shared a joint. There were layers of graywhite smoke in the orange glow as she said, "Wow, how would you rate *that* performance?"

"On a scale of one to a hundred?"

She laughed and said, "I was reading Freud and I had this fantasy. About a machine that would measure pleasure, sexual satisfaction. It's called a libido-meter. You plug yourself into it during the act. When you're finished, you get a readout."

High from the dope, Ted chuckled and said, "Who would want to do that?"

She smoked. "Well Jesus, Bear, we can say we loved it, but after all, people can lie—even to themselves. We have to be scientific about these things or we might just fake ourselves out. Remember Wilhelm Reich?"

"Sure. Mad as a hatter."

"Remember his cosmic orgone detector? The libido-meter would be a device like that, all these wires and buttons and stuff. We could sell them to sex researchers. Weird? I bet those fools would buy them!"

As they finished the joint and lay there together, Ted tried to recall if he'd ever felt such contentment, such peace, with June. After sex with her, he instantly started to think about other things. Had it always been that way?

He kissed Joy's nipple and said, "I hate to bring this up, but about that note."

"Did you like it, Bear?"

"I loved it. But Jesus, you can't take chances like that, it could ruin us."

"Nothing can ruin us, Bear."

"Joy, really—it's foolish. And so is doing things in school, we'll have to stop."

"But it's so *exciting*."

"And so *crazy*."

She frowned. "Well I *have* to leave you notes." She kissed his cheek; his groin instantly surged. "Please, Bear?"

"Okay," he said, "but we'll find a hiding place for them, don't give them to Rick."

She laughed. "I thought it was kind of appropriate."

"Did he tell you he wants to quit the yearbook?"

"*What?* That creep, he better not, we have shit to *do*."

"You're telling me."

"One little setback and he falls apart."

"It's not exactly a *little* setback."

72

She tossed her head. "These jokers who plan their own lives to the last detail just crack me up." She was quiet a minute, a thoughtful look on her face, then said, "How come you got into teaching?"

"What brought that up?"

"Just curious."

He shrugged. "I guess I thought that I'd do a good job."

"Well you do, but how can you stand it? Those idiot kids, your idiot colleagues, no money... I'd think you'd be sick of it by now."

"I am."

"Then why not quit?"

"And do what? I'm not trained to do anything else. I have an investment, as they say. It's security."

She made a face. "Security. There ain't no such animal, Bear. And Jesus, there must be *something* else you could do that would bring in some bucks."

"You have any ideas?"

"Sure. Be a gigolo for rich old twats whose husbands have croaked."

"Sounds great."

"There must be *something*."

"Maybe so, but I haven't found it."

She faked a shudder. "Teenagers, ugh. I gotta give you credit."

"Hey, they're not all bad."

She laughed, then pressed her lips together and said, "Am I the first? The first student you've made it with?"

"Yes."

"In how many years of teaching?"

"Sixteen."

"Amazing. How could you resist for all that time?"

"I don't know." He wished she'd stop asking him questions.

She fondled her pubic hair. "Can you resist me now?" She kissed his ear, she kissed his chest, she kissed his sex. Once again, he grew firm.

"Want to help this teenager build her libido-meter?"

"Absolutely."

"That's the spirit. Now the first thing we have to do is some basic research..."

• • • • •

This time his mood was entirely different; he felt giddy and disconnected. As he worked away from behind he kept seeing the yellow sun, red rays, blue sea, that JOY! in green, and what ran through his head was not erotic, not romantic, but just plain dumb, a silly song he'd heard when he was a kid about years flying by, it was later than you thought, you better enjoy yourself today, right now. As he pistoned behind the tattoo he kept thinking, Enjoy yourself! Enjoy yourself with Joy, Joy, JOY!

13 • SEXSUPERETTES

The scene with Rick on Wednesday was total gloom. Zombie-like, he moped and sulked. Joy gave him the finger behind his back, and when he departed early, she took his photo out of the yearbook pile, laid it out on a page and wrote underneath it, *Poor pussy-whipped fucker.* "Wouldn't it be great to do a *real* yearbook?" she said. "To tell the *truth* about these cruds? Jesus, we'd have a bestseller!"

Where the top and a leg of the birch formica table joined, she discovered a gap— a perfect place to hide her notes. "Check it out every day," she said, "I never know when the urge to create will strike."

Neither Joy nor Rick worked on the yearbook on Thursdays, but Ted went into the A-V room, reached under the table, and there, sure enough, was an envelope. He felt the way he used to feel as a kid when the tooth fairy came.

There wasn't any note inside. Instead there was hair—pubic hair, bright golden curls. Lady Caroline Lamb had sent Byron a lock of her snatch when he published *Childe Harold.* Ted held Joy's swatch between thumb and finger, his member stiffening fast with delight at this fine literary allusion. Good God did she know how to get him!

As soon as school ended that afternoon he drove to General Haze Boulevard. (Who *was* this long-gone general, anyway? The person hazing had been named for? The Colonel, bless his heart, would surely know.) Ted wondered how Haze would feel if he came back now and saw his name attached to this potholed slash of asphalt lined with smut. He'd probably resign his commission on the spot.

He parked on a side street and walked to a squat pink cinderblock bunker with yard-high letters proclaiming: BOOKS XXX FILMS XXX WE NEVER CLOSE!

He had shed his jacket and tie and had donned sunglasses. His heart was pounding and his stomach was vaguely sick. It was summer in April, hot humid and bright, and sweat trickled over his forehead. At the door to the pit, that gaping maw, he faltered and almost lost his nerve, then plunged inside.

Racks and racks of the stuff; he was overwhelmed. At the rear, a hallway that led to the movie machines. Four customers, all of them men about his age, in business suits.

The register next to the door was manned by a monster of thirty or so with a scruffy black beard, long oily hair, huge biceps with purple and green tattoos. He stood on a platform behind a display case crammed with devices constructed of flesh-covered plastic. Most mimicked the tumid male member, while some were total mysteries: tubed, convoluted—to serve what dark perversions? Parts, perhaps, for Joy's libido-meter?

The monster lifted a stack of thick magazines, then hammered the edges hard on the countertop, scowling at Ted. Overcome by a wash of shame and trying his best to seem nonchalant, Ted looked at the racks.

—At a photograph of a beautiful woman with heavy makeup and piles of bleach-blond hair. She was squatting down, and below her raised skirt, through a slit in her ruffled panties, hung—male organs! Ted looked at the magazine's title: *Juicy Fruits.* The sign at the top of the rack said, TRANSVESTITE-GAY. Quickly he moved down the line.

Hundreds of color photos of people doing it. The stuff assaulted him; he reeled. Times change, okay, but lord, he'd had no idea. He thought of the very first issue of *Playboy,* that centerfold of Marilyn that seemed so innocent now. Today, *Cosmopolitan* outdid that. Today there was *Playgirl,* displaying the naked dongs of ballplayers, actors, and similar overpaid crooks. The next thing you knew, the frigging *president* would be waving his dork between those covers. He thought of the fuss over Errol Flynn and some fifteen year old girl. Today, that was *nothing.*

A trickle of sweat coursed over his cheek as he thought, Nothing? Really? For movie stars it was nothing, but for *him?* Sure, movie stars could do anything, but teachers? God forbid! The pay was low, low, low, but the standards were high, high, high. Athletes and artists would be forgiven, laborers would be forgiven, but teachers? Never. Suppose one of the school board members or maybe a parent of one of his "students" should catch him leaving this place. Would it be nothing?

A clothing merchant in Somerside tried to burn down his store to collect the insurance and damn near blew up the block. So what happened? After three months in jail it was business as usual. This year he was Kiwanis president! Forgiven. But a teacher? Caught diddling around with a student? Siberia! He fantasized a teacher scandal sheet, a *National Enquirer* of education: "At Jersey's Whitman High, the word is out: Ted Wharton has the hots for seventeen year old Joy Dollinger!" Seventeen, he thought. Jesus Christ, seventeen was terrible, he was almost as bad as degenerate Errol Flynn!

A patron came into the store and a ripple of fear hit Ted's chest. He glanced at the newcomer sideways; nobody he knew. But he couldn't take this anymore, it was just too risky. He scanned the racks, impulsively snatched up a rag called *Do It!*, and went with it to the counter.

I'm supporting the Mafia, he thought as the monster-man taped *Do It!* into a not-quite-opaque-enough bag and rang up the sale. But is that my fault? Do I have to feel guilty about that, too? "Thanks a lot," the guy said in a squeaky high voice. Ted frowned. Did the mob favor eunuchs for their porno outlets?

He slipped the dynamite into his briefcase, wedging it into the sophomore themes. As he drove, he could feel it burning, leaking, giving off deadly rays. As he carried the briefcase into the house, it felt as transparent and fragile as glass. He shoved it into the closet and closed the door, afraid it might start ticking like a bomb.

• • • • •

Do It! went with him to school the following day; sat there in briefcased blackness beside his desk. In psychology class he felt it radiate its heat to Joy, who wore a stunning, V-necked, pale blue blouse that made him ache all through.

When he went to the A-V room she was working alone at the table. "Hey Bear, come over here and look at this. See? The moment of truth."

She had pasted some head shot photos—cutouts—on a sheet of paper, and was sketching bodies under them. The drawing of Bob Whippet, captain of the football team, had been finished—and was obscene. It showed powerful shoulders, a hairy chest, and a monstrous penis extending below the knee. She had captioned it "Best Hung Jock."

The sketch was excellently drawn. "So you're an artist, too," Ted said.

"I'm a woman of many talents," Joy said. "Did you think I could only fuck?"

An instant current of lust shot into Ted's thighs. He nodded at the drawing. "Don't you think that's a slight exaggeration?"

"Jealous, Bear?"

"A little."

She laughed. "Well, rumors are often false, of course, you'd have to ask Dee Andrews to know for sure."

"Dee and Bob get it on?"

"Oh, only about ten times a week."

"Have you seen Dee naked?"

"Sure, in the showers, after gym."

Another libidinous rush as he asked, "So what does she look like ?"

"She's cute," Joy said. "Good little tits, blond pussy hair. Like this," and she sketched a figure.

"I see. And what style of cunt?"

"Compact, shipshape. Even with all the screwing she does with superdong, she hasn't turned inside out."

He gave her the picture of Mary Willis, the cello player. "What about Mary?" he said with a grin.

"Oh Jesus," Joy said as she pasted the photo down, "she doesn't even know what it's *for*. —Though the cello *is* a common substitute for the human body."

He laughed. "Are you sure?"

"Hey, ask your man Freud." Her pencil went to work under Mary's head. "A blob, an absolute blob, and her snatch? It's fat, like this, sort of pudgy around the sides, with little scrawny tufts of mousey hair."

"It figures," Ted said. Under her photo he printed: VIRGIN FOR LIFE. "And Andrea?" he asked.

Andrea Johnson was slender and cool, with deep green eyes.

"She's very shy," Joy said. "She seems embarrassed to take off her clothes, then she gets in the shower real fast so that no one can see her. But I *have* seen her, and is she built! One of those with the slender but well-shaped thighs, a perfect flat stomach, good breasts—firm, high, good nipples, bright pink—she's a knockout."

"Well who does she make it with?" Ted asked. He found this extremely exciting; his genitals throbbed.

"I don't know. She's the mystery woman. I think she goes with some older guy, some college guy or something. She doesn't have much to do with us; she's a loner."

"Like you."

"Oh, worse. Much worse. She doesn't even play the game. I go through the motions, at least."

"You sure do."

"Oh Bear, I didn't mean *those* motions. What a dirty mind you have."

She turned to him, leaning forward. He could see down her braless blouse, glimpse a nipple's pink rim. "Susan Merry," he said, his mouth dry. "What about Susan Merry?"

Joy sketched. "Very interesting cunt," she said. "She has the kind that comes all the way up in front—like a change purse. Like this."

"Intriguing."

"Oh, isn't it, though?" She turned again and fixed him with those grayblue eyes and said, "Did you like the note I left you yesterday?"

"You bet."

She stood and leaned over the table, spreading her legs. "It took lots of research to come up with that, and I think you should check my sources."

He had sworn he would never do things in school again, but he was wild, mad. With the Little Man fervently urging him on, he raised her skirt and licked at her from behind.

$$\bullet\ \bullet\ \bullet\ \bullet\ \bullet$$

The image of that act came back again and again as he sat in The Spouting Whale. George, Tony, and Morty Price were moaning about LeMaster and Grimsley, as usual. Same old grievances, same old lives.

"Leaving early *again?*" Tony said. "Jesus, Ted, it's time to show June who's boss."

"I know it, Tony, I know it."

In the air-conditioned dusty metal cool of the motel, his passion burned white hot. They were naked, finishing the dope, when she said, "Let's see what you bought, Teddy Bear."

He tore open the brown paper bag. She laughed at the cover and flipped through the pages; stopped a moment and read. "Good God, who writes this stuff? 'Swapped spit.' 'They swapped spit,' is that *sexy? The Whitman Bard* could do better than *that.*" She examined a picture, turning the magazine around, and then moved on. She looked at him and said, "Well, Bear, it's a vast improvement, but there's no cum shots."

"Oh," he said.

"I like to see it shooting and running down. This way they could be faking it, it might look hard but really be soft. The other way, you *know*—unless they use Elmer's glue, and I sure wouldn't put it past them." She frowned at the magazine. "Go get another one, okay?"

On fire, he wanted to take her this minute. "What?"

She looked at him. "Get one with good cum shots. —One where you see it shoot into the air, they can't fake that, that's genuine. I have to know it's genuine."

"You mean you want me to put on my clothes and go out and buy something *now?*"

"Please, Bear? I'll make it worth your while."

He sighed, little marijuana crackles in his ears. His shoe looked distorted as he tied the lace, something wrong with the shape of the toe…

After the dark of the motel room, the day was explosively bright. As he crossed to the snowwhite porno store, he thought of June making him wash the dog before dinner on Saturday night. What was it with women? Why did they always put you to work at the most inconvenient times? They seemed to have an innate knack for that. And why did men always give in?

He went to the closest store, not the one that he'd gone to before. This one was manned by a bloated dwarf, also thickly tattooed, also up on a platform. Ted hustled up to the racks, wondering about the psychology behind this platform business; slid by the "Male," "Bondage," "Breast Fetish," and "Transvestite" sections and stopped at the "Explicit Hetero" department.

They had what she wanted, all right—ejaculate on every surface: pubic, anal, dorsal, abdominal, buccal, lingual, gingival. Goggle-eyed, Ted tried to remain objective. American culture thought it revolting to dine on roaches and grubs, while certain other cultures considered such crawlies gourmet fare. Objectively, was semen any more disgusting than, say, raw egg whites? It was probably *less* disgusting. A lot of these eager eaters here would probably turn six shades of green if they had to consume a raw egg.

But good heavens, look at it all! Who *were* these nymphs and satyrs? What did they do with the rest of their time, what were their mothers and fathers like, how were their apartments decorated? He stared at the taut, athletic bodies. *Golden lads and girls all must/ As chimney sweepers, come to dust.* With a sudden depression infusing his lust, he selected a publication entitled *Spurts Illustrated,* paid the gnome, and hurried back into the sun.

On the boulevard the cars whizzed by, hauling mommies and daddies home from a hard day's work. Was it possible that he knew not a single one of these thousands who traveled this open road out of Camden, Whitman's deathplace? He certainly hoped it was!

"Oh, much, much better," Joy said. Eyes wide, she said, "What action wow, this stud shot across the *room!*"

Ted stared at the photo, thinking it must have been faked. The jet was fully two feet long. He had never had thrust like that, even way back when.

"Hey, look at this! Black leather gloves! How *elegant,* I'll get to have a pair!"

The gloves were holding a streaming organ below red lipsticked lips. What was happening here? Was the mouth replacing nature's prime target? Was the reproductive function becoming vestigial, expendable? Oral, oral, oral, four-fifths of the the book was oral, and what would asshole Freud have to say about that? A snail's reproductive organs were in its head. In the dim past, had man's been too? This oral emphasis seemed wrong, and not only wrong, but...*dirty.* Yes, love *had* built its mansion in the place of excrement, but the mouth was the organ of eating and drinking, the place of nourishment. Wasn't there something...*debasing* about using it in this way?

No, no, he'd seen *animals* do it. He distinctly remembered T.S. Eliot lapping away at the flanks of a springer spaniel and having a grand old time, and if *they* could do it...

I think I could turn and live with animals,
     they are so placid and self-contain'd,
I stand and look at them long and long.
They do not sweat and whine about their
     condition,
They do not lie awake in the dark and weep
     for their sins,
They do not make me sick discussing their
     duty to God,
Not one is dissatisfied, not one is demented
     with the mania of owning things,
Not one kneels to another, nor to his kind
     that lived thousands of years ago,
Not one is respectable or unhappy over the
     whole earth...

Well, maybe, Ted thought. If Whitman had known T.S. Eliot, he might have changed his tune about the whining part; that animal's plaintive squeal could drive you bats. But respectable? No, not one, and Ted dived in, ran his tongue from her knee to her thigh in that marvelous light, the squalid lambency of cheap lampshades. What the hell was the name of this place again? The Rendevous? Without the "z"? The apogee of sleaze.

"Bear, wait, I want to show you something, something I drew."

Wait? Wait some more? She swung her legs away from him and went to her pocketbook. "You drew something?" he said. His tongue ached for her spot.

She came back to the bed. "Yeah, see? Libido-meter plans."

He looked: at a sketch of a couple standing nude, with all sorts of labels, arrows, lines. Still buzzing with dope, he laughed.

"See, subject A (that's me) stands next to subject B (that's you). Wire A goes from subject A's left breast to subject B's right fingertip, wire B goes from A's right tit to B's left hand. Wire C leads straight from A's tongue to B's glans, wire D runs from B's soft tongue to A's juicy button. Wire E over here, also hooked to A's clit, crosses wire A on its way to the shaft of B's cock. Here's the asshole to asshole wire, the labia to testicle connection, here's the dong to vagina hookup." She smiled at him. "You like it, Bear?"

"It's a work of genius," he said. His erection throbbed; he leaned forward.

"Wait a second, hold on, I have to explain the instrumentation first. This gadget here's the semen-meter, which gauges amount of load; this thing's the prostate-meter, which registers force of shot; here's the all-important clitty-meter, which tracks clit swelling and contraction; and last (and least) the nipple-meter, which measures titty hardness. Put them together and whatta ya got? The libido-meter! And here's the scale that charts the total score. If the mercury hits the red zone, bells go off." She looked at his eyes. "You ready to try it, Bear?"

"Am I *ready?*"

She laughed. "Okay, let's do it then, let's send it right over the top!"

In sweet oblivion, they pumped and rocked. His eruption sent him soaring with pleasure, and then they were into the pictures again, she was mouthing him, they were smoking more dope, he was lost in her legs, they were lying there perfectly sated, drained dry.

"I guess we showed that libido-meter a thing or two," Joy said as she thumbed through the magazine still one more time. "Jesus, we almost broke the sucker." She closed *Spurts Illustrated*, looked at his eyes and said, "This is good stuff, Bear, but know what I think? Next time, we should make our own."

• • • • •

They used her new Polaroid camera. He'd bought her a pair of black leather elbow-length gloves and black see-through panties to match at a lingerie place not far from the porno stores. Again and again they set the timer; used every position of body and mouth; tried closeups and longshots, and watched as the blurred orange squares took on faithful crisp hues.

And the camera was great! Through some trick of its lens, it distorted him to advantage—he looked gigantic! "A libido-meter maximum score," Joy said as they littered the bed with photos. "A one hundred plus. Look at this one, Bear, the way you're smiling, isn't it just too cute? We make a damn attractive couple, no doubt about it."

"No doubt at all," Ted said from the depths of his sensual Sargasso Sea. He had never felt happier, never felt more alive.

14 • LUCINDA'S WICKED DREAMS

For God's sake hold your tongue, and let me love,
* Or chide my palsy, or my gout,*
My five gray hairs, or ruin'd fortune flout,
* With wealth your state, your mind with arts improve,*
*   Take you a course, get you a place,*
*   Observe his honor, or his grace,*
Or the King's real, or his stamped face
*   Contemplate; what you will, approve,*
*   So you will let me love.*

Everything outside of his times with Joy was murky irritable blundering. His classes, faculty meetings, domestic duties, car to shop, Brad to orthodontist, Kim to gym, himself to dentist (Was bridgework imminent? Would it change Joy's image of him?), having "friends" over, going over to "friends'" (oh boring, death)—all salt in the open wound of his false existence. He'd come down with a fever that wouldn't relent. Oh sure, an obstreperous bastard in class, a preposterous bill of June's, a near accident in the Plymouth (dreaming of Joy!) would make him touch earth for a moment, but most of the time he was flying.

Alas, alas, who's injured by my love?

That, he'd just as soon not think about. And *was* it love? Of course not, it was sheer carnality. The sight of her in honors psych drove him wild with anticipation; those notes she left under the table made him damn near drool. Rick had called it quits, the A-V room belonged to them, and in spite of Ted's terror they did it there all the time. She would lean on the table and lift her skirt, he'd enter her from behind as he looked at the seniors' photos scattered about and ask her: What does this one look like naked? Who does she do it with? She'd tell him as he pumped in fear and exhilaration, certain the door would open wide and his staid, respectable teacher's life would explode in disgrace and ruin. The thought of that horrible possibility, far from making him stop, only sharpened his lust. As Oscar Wilde said about his trysts with stableboys: "It was like feasting with panthers. The danger was half the excitement."

His energy level astounded him; he'd tapped an inexhaustible well of power, or so it seemed. It had happened before in his life, when the kids were small and he'd had to be up with them all night long with their illnesses; he'd been able to go for days with almost no sleep, to be brightly alert in an instant at three A.M. if he heard them cry. That burst had faded years ago, he'd been slogging along in the muck for ages, but now the old zip was back!

He was constantly racing inside, his throttle wide open. Was it dangerous? It didn't feel dangerous, it felt great! He was jogging five days a week and felt strong as a bear (a bear!), stronger than he'd felt when he was in college. He had even stopped all that farting!

In class he was android Ted, the teaching robot, the robot with X-ray eyes.

Thanks to Joy's information, he felt he could see through his female students' clothes, and while they were answering questions he'd picture their nipples (blunt, sharp, rosy, brown), their buttocks (unblemished or pimpled), their crotches (dense, sparse, smooth, kinky), and hear not a word they said.

He was Ted the accomplished criminal. No more lying awake in the dark weeping over his sins, no more pains in the chest—that foolishness was long gone now. Cut out enough hearts, shoot enough kids, you get used to it. Psychopathic liar Ted told June he had meetings—meetings of the Media Review Committee. It was very, very important for him to attend, and attend he did, without fail.

When he paid, they went to the plush motels in Apple Heights; when she footed the bill, they went back to the strip. Sleaze fascinated her, and he bought her more tacky lingerie, more raunchy "lit." Her favorite magazine concerned a teacher and one of his students. Again and again they would act it out. ("Miss Dollinger, come up to my desk. Kneel down, Miss Dollinger.")

His family was a set of faded cutouts, gray silhouettes. Ever since the Colonel fiasco they hadn't been after him much, and he moved among them as a guerilla moves among peasants, functioning in a separate space: marking papers, doing the laundry, making his lackluster meals.

Apparently (and fortunately) June's libido had radically ebbed. Ted wondered: had he always been the instigator? Had she simply given in to him, regarding it as her duty? Didn't she find it strange that he never pestered her anymore? Did she think he was dangerous? Out of his mind? He tried to act pleasant and normal, but ghost in a dead past that he was, it was next to impossible.

He used to like watching the kids at their sports, but no more. He didn't like watching the kids or hearing the kids or even thinking about them. They drove him nuts, especially with their radios, that music that was *Joy's*, a music that was linked to specific locations, positions, and smells, and he screamed at them to turn it down so he could concentrate. On what? On dreams: of the A-V room (the S-X room), her car, motels, a field near a worn-out orchard ("I love to do it here Bear, it's so open, so sunny, so...pastoral."). Then back again to reality, his two-tone house with wall-to-wall rugs and peeling trim and leaky roof and insurance and mortgage and wife and kids... Good God, they were going to kill him, but what could he do?

• • • • •

"These potato pancakes are too *thin* or something," Kim said sulkily.

Ted felt like dumping the batter over her head. He poured another ladleful onto the griddle, chafing, glancing at his watch. It said ten after five. They were eating early because he had a meeting of the Media Review Committee—or so he'd told June.

"Yeah, they *are* too thin," Brad said. "It's like they're made out of applesauce."

"You kept them on pulverize too long," June said with a disparaging look at what hung on the end of her fork. "Two cycles is all they need."

"I only *did* two cycles," Ted said.

June shook her head. "They wouldn't be this thin if you did, you must've done three or four."

"I did *two*," Ted insisted. He had no idea how many he'd done, but if they didn't like it they could make their own goddamn meals.

"Texture is the critical thing with potato pancakes," June said. "If they're mushy, forget it."

"I'd love to," Ted said—and pictured Joy in her Honda Accord, waiting beside the "J" in the parking lot.

"Oh don't be so damn sensitive," June said. She chewed the piece of potato pancake, muttering, "mushy" under her breath. Ted wanted to pop her one. "Your cooking was getting better," she said, "but these last few weeks it's fallen off drastically."

Ted gritted his teeth. "Well damn it," he said, "I work hard all day and have to come home and get a meal together and who appreciates it? Nobody! Half the time you're reading the *mail* while you eat! I ought to just buy TV dinners, that's what I ought to do!"

Kim made a face and—gesture of her mother's—pushed her plate away. "I'm finished," she said.

"Me too," Brad said in his husky baritone, plopping his crumpled napkin next to his plate. They both went into the family room and turned the TV on.

A pancake sizzled in the grease, its periphery turning to hard brown lace. Ted, appetite extinguished, yanked the griddle's plug out of the wall.

June frowned at him and said, "What's happening to you?"

A nick of alarm arrowed into his heart. "What do you mean, what's happening?"

"You're just so *touchy*. That disgraceful display when my father was here, and…you're so *distracted*. You're off in a world of your own all the time. I don't think you even *care* about your family anymore."

A sadness seeped into Ted's anger. "That isn't true," he said. The grease in the griddle continued to sputter and dance.

"I get the feeling"—her mouth quivered slightly; she caught her breath—"that you don't love me anymore."

Ted looked at the batter-stained placemat and shook his head; ran his hand through his hair. "I *do* love you," he said—and he really believed it. In spite of all his frustration with June, he *did* still love her. —Or wanted to, wanted to desperately.

She touched his hand. He felt like pulling it away. Why? If he loved her, *why?*

"I'm going away soon," she said. (To the Netherlands, not to England, she'd changed her plans.) "I wonder if you'll even miss me."

"Of course I will."

"I wonder."

Keeping her hand on top of his, she looked at his eyes and said, "Come with us. Please?" (She was taking Kim, but Brad was staying home.) "I can still work it out—for you *and* Brad."

Ted looked at his plastic placemat again. "June, trips aren't the answer. Europe isn't the answer."

"Well, what *is* the answer, then?" She took her hand away.

He sighed and said, "I've been working too hard, that's all, I've got a lot on my mind. The yearbook, this Media Review Committee…"

The TV chortled away in the family room, filling the silence between them. "Well quit those things," she said. "Don't tie yourself up like that." She picked at a piece of dried food on her placemat. "We haven't touched each other in ages, Ted."

So she *had* been aware of that after all. He suddenly felt very sorry for her, for himself, for both of them. He felt stranded, marooned on a desert island, lost in the heat and glare. He didn't know what to do or say, he only wished that time would reverse itself and make things right again.

The doorbell rang, smashing his mood. "Who the hell can that be?" he said.

June jumped to her feet. "Oh God, I forgot, it's Joe Bishop."

"Joe *Bishop?*" Ted said. Joe Bishop had taught with him at Whitman, special ed. His job had been eliminated a year ago, and Ted hadn't seen him since.

"He came by the agency today," June said, heading into the foyer. "He sells vacuum cleaners, Electrakweens. I said I might be interested, and he told me he'd stop by tonight."

It was five twenty-five. "Tonight!" Ted said, walking after her. "I have to put up with Joe Bishop *tonight? I* have a committee meeting!"

The doorbell rang again. June stopped and looked at him. "You see?" she said. "That's just what I'm talking about, you jump on every little thing."

"*Little* thing?" Ted said. "You don't even tell me he's coming until the goddamn doorbell rings!" It rang again. "I have a committee meeting," he said, "and when it's time to leave, I'm *leaving!*"

"You do that, Ted." She went to the door and opened it.

Ted heard Joe Bishop's high-pitched voice, and there he was, with machine, hose, suitcase. "Ted! How's it going?"

"Hi Joe, how are you?" Big smile, fake smile, was his whole life a lie?

Joe's handshake was businesslike, firm. "So how goes it at Whitman?"

"Good. Things are fine."

They walked into the living room.

"Big Marvin treating you all right?"

Fake laugh. "Well, you know big Marv."

Joe's squeaky chuckle. "I sure do."

Joe looked good. He was sporting a thick, trim beard and had put on some weight. He was wearing a classy gray pinstriped suit, a blue pearl-buttoned shirt, a luxurious tie. He sat on the couch and chatted, smiling, vacuum cleaner and suitcase next to his glossy black wingtipped shoes. How were Tony and George? Wally Blood? Yes, he'd heard about Marty's death, it had shocked him deeply, then down to brass tacks, he snapped open the suitcase, the kids came in from the family room to see what was going on. Joe asked to see their current vacuum, and Brad hustled off to get it. Ted checked his watch. It said twenty of six. He hoped to God this nonsense didn't take long.

With a conjurer's flair, Joe Bishop placed four gleaming stainless steel balls on the living room rug. The old cleaner (they'd bought it right after their marriage—seventeen years ago!) could only suck one ball and feebly retain it, while the new Electrakween could suck up all four balls and hold them firmly in its grasp. Ted had to admit it was very impressive. The patter went on as Joe ran the Electrakween over the rug June had vacuumed this morning before heading off to work, and all gasped at the dirt, the deep down hidden dirt which had lurked beyond their old cleaner's power. They were told how this deep-down dirt would destroy the fibers, leading to rug disintegration, on and on, and it was damn near six fifteen.

Ted was astounded—not by the vacuum cleaner, but by Joe himself. At school he had always seemed a bumbling sort, inhibited, hesitant, self-effacing, and suddenly he was a master showman, clicking attachments and crawling around on the carpet as if he'd been born for the job. He charmed the children; countered June's embarrassment over the lurking dirt; displayed the attachments with polished skill; gently, almost offhandedly, brought up the delicate matter of price. Time payments, the warranty, the virtues of the mighty Electrakween Corporation, etc. (it was six thirty-five!), and June took the bait.

Ted sat there, stewing, as papers were signed, and thought of Joy. She might already be at the shopping center, why didn't he leave? He wondered: Would Joy someday be reduced to this, be trapped and standardized and fleeced like this? Of course she would, she would age and give in, and time would wipe her out the same as it had wiped him out and had wiped Joe Bishop and Marty Zeller and everyone else he knew out. Time and suburbia had beaten Kerouac, a true blue lunatic, so surely they wouldn't spare Joy.

As Joe was packing up with a cheerful grin, Ted said, "Joe, look, I don't mean to be rude, but you make any money at this?"

Joe's grin turned expansive. "Oh, only about three times as much as I made my last year at Whitman."

Joe had been at the top of the scale, had a master's plus thirty. For him to be making three times *that*... Ted said, "You're kidding."

"I know it sounds incredible," Joe said, "but it's the truth."

Ted hoped his envy wouldn't show. "Hey, that's terrific, Joe, I thought it would be a real struggle. I mean how many people buy vacuum cleaners?"

"You'd be surprised," Joe said with a knowing smile. "You'd be *amazed*. As a matter of fact, we're doing so well around here that we're thinking of starting a Somerside office. "So" (the demo machine in his hand, suitcase under his arm) "if you ever decide to leave teaching and make some money, just let me know. You'd be great. You've got good presence, good speech, an attractive appearance... Think about it." He grinned again. "Losing my job at Whitman was the best thing that ever happened to me. I never *knew* there was so much money in the world. Not only that," he said with a wink at Brad, "you don't have to put up with kids."

Brad booed; Joe laughed. "Hey, you're not bad one at a time, but en masse... Well thanks, June, see you, Ted, I'm off to another customer..."

Good God, it was quarter of seven! Ted watched as Joe got in his car and pulled away, then stared at the alien presence on the spotless rug: its beige enamel, bright chrome bumpers, that zipaway cord June adored.

"Now what?" she said with a slight twinge of guilt in her voice.

"Oh, nothing, I guess. I just hope the damn thing's worth it, it'll cost us an arm and a leg."

The TV started up again in the family room. June rolled her eyes. "Oh, not *again*," she said. "Every time I buy anything, I've got to hear this crap. As if I live in the lap of luxury. We got that other vacuum seventeen *years* ago, Ted. And it isn't *us* it's going to cost, it's *me*. It's my money, I've earned it, and I'll spend it the way I want."

"Okay, okay," Ted said. "But a stupid *vacuum* cleaner. We're going to need a new car soon, the Plymouth's a wreck. And to buy the thing from Bishop, he's just so...*sleazy*."

"Sleazy? What's sleazy about him?"

"I don't know, it just doesn't seem right somehow. He was a *teacher*. Teaching used to be...a profession, a commitment."

"Oh, good grief," June said, "what is it, some kind of disgrace to quit teaching and make some money? I can think of lots more disgraceful things than that."

"Me too," Ted said, and thought of Joy under the "J", waiting, growing impatient, leaving. "Now I'm going to be late for my meeting," he said. The TV spewed its jolly trash in the family room. He said, "He makes three times as much as he made as a teacher. So what does America value more—clean rugs or education?"

"Oh for God's sakes, Ted."

He shrugged. "I'll be late," he said.

He went through the kitchen in time to catch T.S. Eliot stealing the cold potato pancake that sat in the griddle. He whacked the startled beast on the rump and hurried out the door.

• • • • •

"Good God, where *were* you?" Joy said.

Ted slid into the passenger seat, saying, "Sorry, I got held up."

She was coppery, summery, wearing white; her arms were bronze and gold. "It makes me nervous when people are late," she said. "I always think something's happened to them." She started the engine, pulled out of the space, sped off.

"Remember Joe Bishop?" Ted said. "Mr. Bishop?"

"Who taught the retarded kids?"

"Yeah. I just bought a vacuum cleaner from him, that's why I was late."

"I wondered what happened to him."

"He was good as a teacher. Really cared about kids, and now he sells vacuum cleaners."

"Good for him," Joy said. The action of her skirt and thighs as she drove made his testicles ache.

"I guess it's good, but...I don't know, all he cares about now is how many balls his Electrakweens can suck."

"So you bought one to take my place when I'm out of town?"

He laughed.

She said, "I bet he makes pretty good money."

"About three times as much as he made at Whitman," Ted said. He hadn't accepted it yet; it gnawed at him.

"Well great," Joy said. "I mean teaching is fine, I guess, but to do it your whole *life*... Especially with that bunch of airheads he had. I couldn't stand that, I think too fast, I move too fast. After college I'm going to New York, where the action is. I want to edit a women's magazine, like *Cosmopolitan* or *Vogue*. Not that I give two shits about *Cosmo* or *Vogue*, but I'd like the work, I'd have money, meet people... I'd have a ball."

He felt a twinge of jealousy, remembering what it was like to be young like that, to believe in a future of endless possibilities like that. She would leave for college soon and be out of his life, and it made him sad. "Big dreams," he said.

"Hey, you have to have dreams," she said.

"'In dreams begin responsibilities,'" he said. "What poet was that, Miss Dollinger?"

She frowned, one eyebrow cocked. "Uh...Yeats?"

Disappointed that she'd answered correctly, he said, "Very good. And who else?"

"Who else? I don't know, who else?"

"Delmore Schwartz—who died a derelict, surrounded by his manuscripts, in a filthy hole in...New York."

"Tough luck," Joy said. "Well, none of that tragedy stuff for me, I'll edit *Mademoiselle*."

Ted admired her confidence—and her thighs, which showed below her snowwhite skirt, but his jealousy made him say, "What makes you so sure you'll succeed in a job like that?"

She smiled. "Don't worry, Bear, I'll make it, I know how to play the game."

The Honda zipped. The ominous nerve-wracking blinding beam of a motorcycle jittered past. "*Rod* used to take me biking," she said. "Big thrill."

Ted didn't want to think about Rod—or college, or work, or anything else that was real. He said, "Where the hell are we going?" This wasn't the route that she usually took to the strip.

"To the drive-in, Bear."

"The *drive*-in? I thought it was out of business."

"Not yet, it's still hanging on by a thread, thanks to specialization."

"You want to go see a movie?"

She laughed. "Not a movie, a *movie*."

She flipped the directional signal on and turned right. The tires crunched on gravel; headed toward the drive-in's ticket booth. On the billboard it said:

LUCINDA'S WICKED DREAMS
plus
OVERSIZE LOAD
Seven Dollars Per Car Pack 'em In!
XXX XXX

"Lucinda's wicked dreams," Joy said. "In dreams begin realities, right?"

"Responsibilities," Ted said, his heart suddenly hot.

"Oh, yuk, I like my version better."

He insisted on paying. She drove inside. The screen displayed a clock that said: 9 MINUTES TO SHOWTIME.

"Oh good," she said, "I thought we'd be late." She parked in a slot and Ted reached for the speaker; hooked it over his window.

He had been to this drive-in once, with the family, years ago, for a Disney film. He'd merrily gone to the snack bar for popcorn and drinks, but tonight you wouldn't pry him out of this car for a million bucks. He wondered about the projectionists, the snack bar vendors, the cops who patrolled. The same gang who'd worked those Disney shows?

It was dreadful to be here. The drive-in belonged to the past, and Joy belonged to the future. Why was the future dragging him into the past? "I don't get it," he said. "Why would anyone come here when they could just rent a tape?"

Joy tossed her head. "Well, sex in a car is fabulous. And sex in a car at a drive-in is the best! And of course lots of people would never show porn flicks at home. Do you?"

"With two young kids in the house?"

"Exactly. And June wouldn't go for it either, I bet."

June. As if she had met her, was one of her friends. He didn't like that. "No," he said.

"I thought not. So when does she leave?"

"Sunday night."

"I can't wait. What a week we'll have."

She was tilted back in the seat and her skirt was up; he could catch a thin glimpse of her underpants; they looked blue. Those blue transparent ones? He felt weak in the mouth. He glanced at the magical point of light in the concrete box where the images lived, watched the clock on the screen eat time, breathed the soft spring air and Joy's perfume, and he wanted to crush himself into her belly and thighs and devour her whole.

This movie, he wondered, suddenly anxious, what was it going to be like? A million years ago, back in college, he'd gone to a smoker at Thi Delta Pi. The film had been jumpy and out of focus, a loathsome amateur job. Jammed in the sweaty back of the room, all he'd seen was some vague jerky streaks and he'd sneaked away; declared the next day that he'd had a fine time, the film had been great; and he'd never joined a frat. The books Joy had urged him to buy had propelled him into the present, nothing he saw tonight would shock him, but just being here, just seeing all these cars filled with…whom? Solid and shady citizens, plenty of teens, of course, maybe some of his "students"? The thought made him shudder.

His mind was a Mexican jumping bean. Rigidly, as if caught in a vise, he sneaked looks at other vehicles. It was hard to see, but in front of them—long hair, a carload full. Its owners had followed the billboard's advice to "pack 'em in," and he wondered how they could stand it. When things got hot, would they do it together? Had it come to that? Of course it had. It had come to that thousands of years ago in Sodom, Gomorrah, and Rome. Even so, it was hard to accept. He'd check the hydra's hairy head again when the film was on to see how it functioned.

In the car to his left, past Joy, a snow-headed couple stared at the screen, faces solemn and blank. This persistence of biology, what did it mean? —That reproduction was merely an adjunct of passion? To spend your life's savings, your pension, on *this*. Old Grandpa and Grandma, still looking for action. It was truly depressing.

Show Time! the screen proclaimed with dancing lights, and Ted's stomach felt queasy and tight. He glanced to his right to see what brand of deviant was lurking there—and damn near died.

He slid down in the seat below window level, his knees on the dash.

Joy, freshly rolled joint in her hand, said, "What are you doing down *there?*"

He broke into a sweat. "It's Bisbee," he said in a whisper, jerking his thumb to the right.

"*Mrs.* Bisbee?" she said.

"Yeah, Maddy Bisbee. Let's get out of here!"

Joy smiled her sardonic smile. With a mock southern accent she said, "Well, well, I do declare. And is that *Mr.* Bisbee with her, or do we have a scandal on our hands?" She pulled the cigarette lighter out of the dash.

"For Christ's sake, don't light that!" Ted said. "Let's go!"

She looked at him, amused. "Go? Why?"

"Why? You think I want her to *see* me here?"

Joy shrugged. "So what if she does? If she has something on *you*, you have something on *her*."

Sweat flooded Ted's face. "The difference is," he said, "they're husband and wife and we're teacher and student—and believe me, that's a *difference*."

Joy lit the joint. Defiantly blowing smoke, she said, "She's not going to tell anyone, because people will ask how she knew. What's she going to say?"

That sounded right, and Ted calmed down a bit. "Okay," he said, "but listen, we have to move. I can't do anything next to Maddy Bisbee."

Joy laughed. "Oh Bear, you look so comical down there. Here, have some, relax," and she held out the joint.

"Joy, *please*. You shouldn't smoke that stuff in a public place, you'll get caught!"

"And I'll pay the fine, big deal."

"Joy…"

"Okay, okay, put the speaker back and we'll go."

Ted looked at the chipped gray box above his head. It was saying, "My cousin Lucinda was the wild type…" Slowly he rolled the window down, still crouching out of the Bisbees' sight, and slipped the speaker off; it burned his hand, felt lethal as a grenade. He peered above the window's rim, saw the cinema-frozen Bisbee faces, and slowly, with horrible quivering strain, slid the speaker out onto its rack. Pulled his arm in quickly and slumped again, his heart banging hard in his throat.

Joy sucked the joint and said, "Oh Jesus, Bear. Here, have some before you die."

He took the joint and smoked as she started the car, backed up. She cruised down the lane, turned left, traversed another lane, turned left again, drove back behind the box where the projector's beam knifed darkness, pulled into a space way off to the right, cut the engine and parking lights. "Okay?" she said.

Ted nervously glanced around. Nobody he knew. He hooked the speaker onto the window and let out a sigh. "What rotten luck," he said. "Maddy Bisbee, here. All the way out *here*."

Maddy Bisbee taught art. "She'll go to the ends of the earth in pursuit of culture," Joy said. "Let me have that joint. Oh, you let it go out." She lit it again, sucked deeply, gave it back.

While they had been moving from Bisbee to back row, Lucinda had taken a husband: a short but attractive guy with a full head of dark brown hair and a bushy moustache. Lucinda herself was blond, a bit on the chunky side, rather thick at the waist, but cute in a cheap sort of way. And eager, oh my! She really went at it, and soon Pete (the husband) was extricating himself.

To judge from those magazines he'd bought, *coitus interruptus* was de rigueur in porn. What effect was this having on youth? Did they think it was normal? Could it be that this stuff was propaganda, part of a plot to reduce population? Joy still had him do it that way sometimes, and now that the novelty was gone, he didn't like it. It was lonely, detached, unfulfilling, too…*airy*. But if all you knew was porn, you'd think staying *inside* was perverted.

Now Lucinda was hard at work again, but not with Pete, with another guy, the chauffeur or handyman (Pete had money). It seemed she was the victim of an unfortunate quirk, apparently metabolic, that made her require gratification around the clock, on the hour. She did it with the oil man, the newspaper boy (same guy who played the chauffeur), a vacuum salesman (a vacuum salesman!), a local politician campaigning from door to door. Under the movie's casual flippancy lay deep hostilities toward motherhood, religion, family, faithfulness. It turned Ted off at the cortical level, but down in the glands, oh boy!

Lucinda, desperate, hied herself to a shrink. His therapy? More sex, of course, with himself (same guy who'd played the politician), his theory being that excess would purge the urge. Joy got a real bang out of this scenario. She smoked the second joint and watched the screen and slowly rubbed Ted's crotch. When the therapist made his deposit (between Lucinda's breasts), she said, "I'm sure there's more than that in those agates of yours," and then they were off and running.

Fingers, tongues, lips, teeth, saliva, sweat. The car steamed up, he was lost in the greenhouse, the tropical jungle of passion. The windows cataracted with their wet, the tinny gray speaker panted and moaned, the air was lubricated with her musk. He wondered: What are the Bisbees doing now? What do the Bisbees *do?* Good God, if Maddy Bisbee watches porno movies, *everybody* does. Ethel Spoonfeather? Well, not *everybody*.

They finished and lay in each others' arms and the windows began to unfog. They watched the film in thick, dulled silence. Sex was a drug. A wonder drug, absolutely, no doubt about it.

They watched old Pete, the husband, come back on the scene—and he *was* old Pete; his hair and moustache had turned white. A Dorian Gray effect was operating here: each time Lucinda cheated, it put a few years on Pete, and now he was a doddering old man. Joy was furious. "Look at this crap!" she said. "Do they think that's *sexy?* What kind of an idiot thinks up garbage like this?" She started the engine and snapped on the lights. Ted barely had time to unhook the speaker before she backed up and pulled out.

Her attitude baffled him. In silence he watched her determined and angry face as she raced to the highway, sped into the stream. "Everything was just great and they had to spoil it," she said. "They had to ruin it for us, didn't they? To bring *age* into it like that. To bring *time* into it like that. The purpose of sex is to *murder* time, to *banish* it!"

Ted was dizzy with marijuana, confused, unable to grasp her shift in mood. With a nonchalant laugh, he said, "'Time is the school in which we learn, time is the fire in which we burn.'"

She looked at him with startled eyes. The Honda swerved. "What?"

"Delmore Schwartz."

"That's horrible," she said. "It's dreadful!" She pulled to the side of the road, slowed down, stopped, turned the engine off. She sat there, shaking, her hands on the steering wheel.

The week before, she had gone through a shaky spell in the A-V room. She was having her period, asked him to do it and he had refused. (He had come a long way, but he still wasn't ready for *that*.) She had started to tremble. Her period, she said. It made her that way sometimes. Soon she'd regained her composure and worked on him orally. This time the shaking was worse, much worse.

"Joy, what is it? What's wrong?" That fatherly feeling had hit him again, and he pictured old Pete in the film.

On the roadway, the cars flashed by. Looking down at the steering wheel, she said, "There's no *time*. School ends in a few more weeks, there's just no *time*."

His mind was scrambled, lost. He wished to God he hadn't smoked so much. He said, "You're seventeen, you have all the time in the world."

She turned her face to him, eyes wet. "Do I?" she said. "That's probably what my brother thought, he had all the time in the world." A tear fell down each cheek and her face broke up. She said, "Hold me. Hold me, *please*."

It was like the first day they had touched, weeks ago, after Marty Zeller had died; but no chills this time, just sadness, sadness. He smoothed her hair as she softly cried on his chest.

Streaming headlights; the whoosh of tires. She sat up again, took a tissue out of her pocketbook, wiped her eyes. "Oh Jesus, what a fool I am. Forgive me, Bear."

"It's all right."

"Sometimes the dope...I swear, I ought to give it up. I *will* give it up. But it's not only that, it's...I never got over it. Skip, I mean. The only thing that helps is meditation. My shrink didn't go for meditation, he wanted to dig and dig. Dig into my pants is what he *really* wanted, he didn't help at *all*."

"So...you meditate."

"Yeah. What's good is to kick it off with a hit on a joint, then just drift. But sometimes, when I smoke too much, it's terrible. It brings it on. Like now. I never know when it's going to happen. That stupid, stupid film!"

She started the car, looked into the traffic, pulled out. She was quiet awhile, then said, "I'll be glad when this yearbook is finished. I don't feel connected to those kids, I'm not one of them. Why do I feel that way?"

"I'm sure a lot of kids feel that way," he said. "That's how I felt too, when I was in school."

"You did?"

"Sure. I still feel that way. You know—different."

"That's good to hear. Sometimes I think there's something wrong with me. That shrink...well, I don't want to talk about *that* lunatic."

By the time they reached the shopping center parking lot she seemed fine again and was laughing about the film. "Good God, what imbeciles! To screw it up that way! *We* could make better movies than that, we really could. Which gives me an idea..."

15 • BIG IS BEAUTIFUL

The video camera and tripod and tapes had been purchased with public funds (your tax dollars at work). Their first attempts were worse than that college smoker Ted had gone to way back when: amorphous blobs of light, but after a while they mastered the focus and ripped off some pretty good ten minute tales called *The Joy of Sucking, Mastering the Art of Fresh Nookie,* and *Let's Eat Right To Stay Hot.*

The latter was a treatise on the Wharton Method, which Ted had down to a science: that slide of chin and ridge of lip, that bump of button, her sigh of delight—it drove them both berserk. *The Joy of Sucking* was, as the title implied, her show. In *Mastering the Art*—the most successful of the tapes esthetically—they co-starred equally.

The entire week that June and Kim were abroad—that season of heartbreaking maple bloom, collapse of tulips, cherry blossoms stripping away in the wind—they taped every day in the A-V room as the sophomores taught themselves English, then watched their creations, erased them with deep regret, relived them at night in their motel rooms, their cars, that field beside the orchard. Ted told Brad he was tied up with meetings, and gave him McDonald's money.

The A-V room absorbed their lust, emitted a torrid aroma. In the warming weather the room turned sticky, its laughable fan ineffective, and during the taping sessions Ted dripped with sweat. Toward the end of the week his orgasms changed: had a peppery, stinging component. It took longer to get in the spirit of things, get it up, get it on. Well, after all, he *was* forty-two years old.

They were watching the replay of *Big is Beautiful*, Ted on a stool with Joy astride, her skirt hiked high, her groin locked wetly into his, when—a knock on the door and a singsong voice: "Mr. Wharton? Is Joy with you?"

Ethel Spoonfeather, guidance counselor! Ted felt the color drain out of his face, and his pelvis instantly froze. He looked at Joy, who continued to rock, her heels on the rungs of the stool. Eyes closed and lips drawn back she said, "Don't answer, Bear. Just do it, do it, big is beautiful!"

He watched himself explode on tape, felt his orgasm gathering once again as Joy pumped. "Just a second, Miss Spoonfeather, be right there, I'm up to my elbows in glue."

Joy said, "I need your glue, let me have all the glue you've got," and that did it, he gushed, felt a tang in his rectum, a sharp bright twinge, withdrew all glistening, tucked himself in, they were off the stool, cut the VCR, and he opened the door on the scene of complete decorum.

Miss Spoonfeather's leathery, prunelike face. "Joy, the scholarship interview's Thursday at nine-fifteen. They just telephoned me."

Yearbook editor Joy, on the stool once again and intent on her work, looked up from her layouts and galleys and said, "Thanks, Miss Spoonfeather. Here, let me write that down," and she whipped an appointment book out of her purse. Ted thought she probably *would* work for *Cosmo* or *Vogue* someday.

"Here's the location," Miss Spoonfeather said, "Miller building, room 43," and Ted noticed the drip, his drip, leaking down Joy's calf. A slight panic, a rush of desire, a hot tingling taste in his mouth. He glanced at the VCR. If he switched it on, what would happen to Ethel Spoonfeather? Death on the spot? Not a bad murder mystery plot—how to do the old lady in.

When she left, they both burst out laughing. "Give me your handkerchief, you creep," Joy said. She wiped her leg with it and said, "Look over there, in the corner."

Her panties. Rolled up in a ball where she'd tossed them.

"Good God," Ted said. He felt prickles of bracing fire all over his skin. "Joy, Jesus, we're crazy to do things here."

Her eyes were shining. "But isn't it great when you almost get caught? Don't you feel so *alive?*"

He looked at her and remembered Brussels, that old world Baltimore, and the time he'd convinced June to lie with him naked outside their twelfth floor room. The balcony was walled with concrete east and west. "Nobody can see," he said, "what the hell are you worried about?" They had just gotten started when June leaped up as if she'd been stung by a bee. Scared, furious, she whispered from the doorway: "Somebody's looking down at us—from there!"—the balcony above—and Ted saw the head withdraw. The *thought* of being caught had given the act an edge, but the *reality* was horrible. And if being caught with your wife by a stranger in Brussels was horrible...

"Joy, this is serious."

She shrugged and slipped her panties on. "What's the worst that could happen, Bear? You'd quit and sell Electrakweens and make three times what you're making now, would that be so hard to take? 'Good morning, ma'am, here's my machine. This thing is my power nozzle. Spread out on the couch over there and I'll demonstrate.' Not a bad job, Bear, you'd like it."

• • • • •

He was back in his room with the sophomores—those strangers—explaining tomorrow's assignment, his mind fragmented, when—holy Christ! In the fluster of Ethel Spoonfeather's visit, they'd forgotten the tape! It was still in the VCR!

The bell went off. He sped into the hall—and there was jolly Wally Blood at the A-V room's wide open door, with the stand that held the VCR and monitor.

On the verge of cardiac collapse, Ted said, "Wally, hold on a second, I left a tape in there."

Grinning and sliding his hand down under the monitor, Wally came up with the fatal cassette. "I was going to turn it in to the office," he said. "No label on it."

Oh my God! "I always forget to put one on…"

"I wound it back," said Wally, handing it over, and Ted in a frantic flash saw all he had done with Joy occurring in high speed reverse: watched his rigid urethra vacuuming sperm and depositing it in his sac, watched his rod fall slack. Had Wally seen…? That grin! My *God*.

"The wonderful thing about World War Two is, there's so much *footage*," Wally said, his round fat cheeks magenta. "And the kids never tire of Hitler. Never. It's great."

Ted gripped the blazing tape in his clammy hand. And what would he do with it? Where would he hide it?

Wrinkling his bulbous nose, Wally said, "This room smells weird."

"You think so?"

"Don't you smell it?"

"No."

"You must have a cold or something." He rolled the equipment into the hallway

Ted's legs felt weak. "Sorry to hold you up," he said.

"No problem, Ted." Another grin, and Wally reached into his jacket pocket. "Before you go, take a look at this. I found it on the floor in there."

Ted took the note. It said:

Dear Bear,

All I can think about is your luscious cock. I sit in class and look at you and dream of what we'll do together later. I taste your taste, I smell your smell, I see your stuff squirting out of your tube and all I want is to do it with you, keep doing it and doing it, forever and ever and ever.

Honey

Ted's fingers felt anesthetized. Around him, kids headed to class.

"Which of these yahoos are Bear and Honey?" Wally asked, his grin obscene.

Little whistling sounds sailed through Ted's ears. "I have no idea," he said.

"You think they're doing it in school? Right here in the building?"

"Hard to believe."

Plucking the note out of Ted's hot hand, Wally said, "Pretty wild, huh? They'll love it in The Spouting Whale." Face florid, he tucked the note into his pocket. "Maybe they do it in there," he said with a jerk of his head toward the A-V room. "Maybe that's why it smells so weird."

Big is Beautiful gouged Ted's palm. Forcing himself to laugh, he said, "You have quite an imagination."

Wally giggled. "Stranger things have happened, Ted." Still grinning, he trundled off.

Shaking, Ted went to his room.

• • • • •

He had finished his shower, was drying himself, when the telephone rang. Before he could answer it there in the bedroom, Brad got it downstairs. He heard Brad's muffled voice, then silence.

He went to the door of the bedroom, rubbing his thigh with the towel. "Who was it, Brad?"

"Wrong number," Brad said. "They wanted some guy named Bear."

Cool numbness spread into Ted's chest. "Oh," he said. He went back and sat down on the bed, the towel limp in his hand. He looked at *Big is Beautiful*, which sat, encased in plastic, on June's dresser; remembered the note, prize possession of Wally Blood.

Ten minutes after Brad left for McDonald's, the telephone rang again.

"Hi, Bear. I do have Bear this time?"

"Joy, what the hell are you doing?"

"Your kid sounds just like you, it's really amazing."

"Don't call me here, Joy."

"Hey, take it easy, *please*. Nothing'll happen, I'm just having fun."

"It doesn't pay to do crazy things like this."

"Oh Bear, no, that's where you're wrong. It *does* pay to do crazy things."

"Just don't call me again at home."

A pause, then: "Let me describe my situation, Bear, so you'll understand, okay? I'm on my bed, and nobody else is home. I'm wearing my sheer blue panties—you know the ones?"

The image seized him and his mouth went dry; his anger began to crumble. "Yes," he said.

"Well, I'm wearing those panties, a white lace garter belt, and white stockings. That's all I have on. Can you picture it?"

Ted closed his eyes, his breathing thick. "I see it," he said.

"Okay, I'm lying on my back and my thighs are spread. "I'm holding something in my hand. Can you guess what it is?"

His blood was jumping. "No, I can't."

"It's a carrot, Bear. Don't think I'm hungry, it's not that at all. You see, what I've done is, I've carved out this carrot to look like your wonderful cock."

His heart was thumping; his groin was hot; his breath roared back at his brain from the holes in the phone.

"Now the carrot—impertinent fellow—has pulled my blue panties aside. He's rubbing and rubbing, and now—oh wicked boy!—he's poking his head inside, he's slipping in…. Oh, Bear, what a naughty vegetable!"

Ted's heart was crashing in his head. "Joy, Jesus…"

"Oh, Bear, you should see what he's doing! He thinks he's you, he wants to do what you're going to do very soon, he wants to be you. Hurry, Bear, hurry, I need you! Oh, Bear!"

• • • • •

Afterwards, with the rustle of leaves and the small uneven grinding of her dashboard clock the only sounds, when passion was a softly ebbing throb, he tried to get serious with her: about the tape, the note that Wally Blood had found, about her telephone call. She found the whole topic supremely amusing. The more he discussed it, the more it aroused her again.

"I can just see Blood now, his face all excited and red. He probably couldn't wait to get home and jack off."

"Joy, listen to me."

She tossed her head. "Oh Bear, calm down. I wouldn't call you at home if *June* was there." She looked at him with her big soft grayblue eyes and kissed his mouth.

"But we have to be *careful.*"

"I know we do, Bear." She pressed her lips together, hesitated, looked in his eyes and said, "Let's do it in your house."

His incredulous laugh. "Let's *what?*"

"Why not? June won't be back till Monday, I could spend the weekend there."

The idea thrilled and terrified him. Brad was staying at a friend's tomorrow night and it was possible.

"Impossible," he said. "Good God, if one of the neighbors saw us—"

"We'd arrive after dark, so how would they see us?"

"Some of those people have nothing better to do than spy on the rest of the neighborhood. They're good enough for the frigging CIA. They may even *work* for the CIA, for all I know."

"Oh Bear, we'll use your car, I'll hide, there's nothing to it." She begged him with those eyes, her pouting mouth, and how could he refuse? "Tomorrow's our anniversary," she said.

"One month?"

"One month since we had our first screw. What a marvelous month—the best month of my life." A silence, and then she said, "Tomorrow night let's celebrate. A new magazine, a bottle of good champagne, some dope—and your very own bedroom."

It was madness to even consider it. "No. Out of the question. I mean it."

She pouted. "I know you do, Bear." Reaching into her pocketbook, eyebrows raised, she said, "Good heavens, look who's hiding here! —That naughty carrot! Let me show you what he did in my house, in my very own bed." She spread her legs. "He did *this*, Bear. Can you *imagine?*"

As he watched her, his rectum felt warm and thick. His organ stirred—and hurt a bit.

"And then he did—*this!*"

He watched, tongue glued to his palate.

"You're smart to keep a filthy guy like him away from your bedroom, Bear, you really are…"

16 • REPLYING TO REALITY

Dear Sir:

At an "open house" on April 14th, I had the opportunity to examine our high school library's shelves, and was shocked to find a number of books which are clearly obscene, dangerous, vulgar, vicious, libertarian, and anti-Christian. One book in particular, *Our Bodies Belong To Us*, by something called the "Women's Health *Cooperative* of Greater Denver," is so disgusting that even now, nearly two weeks later, just thinking about its contents turns my stomach.

This work is a virtual handbook on fornication, homosexuality, abortion, masturbation, and contraception. It contains actual photographs of naked women with their *most intimate parts exposed*, and also photos of birth control devices such as condoms and vaginal foam. It is this sort of so-called "literature" that is striking at the moral foundations of our society and thereby destroying our youth and resulting in crime, unwanted pregnancies, venereal disease, and disrespect toward God and the Holiness of His Creations.

I am an aware, intelligent, and educated member of this community and have two children in your schools. I respectfully request that you remove this book from our library immediately. If you do not see fit to comply within two weeks' time, I shall have to consider further action (legal) to insure that such rot will not be imposed on our clean-minded youth with the aid of public funds. Below are some of the other books which I find objectionable…

The letter was signed, "Yours sincerely, Armand Dollinger," and underneath the name was a string of titles, among them *The Catcher in the Rye, Catch 22, The Naked and the Dead, Other Voices, Other Rooms,* and *Brave New World.*

Ted stared at the signature—at the bold, open dumbness of its A's and O's, the arrogant thickness of its I's. He handed the letter back to LeMaster. "Joy Dollinger's father?" he asked with blandly raised eyebrows. An assortment of visceral rockets was blasting inside him.

The principal nodded his serious, bloodhound face.

Ted remembered that open house vividly; remembered what he and Joy had done in the Plymouth directly afterwards. He did not remember Joy's father, though. As far as he knew, he had never laid eyes on the guy. "There's always somebody out there ready to make your job more interesting, isn't there, Marv?"

LeMaster's expression was slack and grave. "I'd like you to get a reply together, Ted."

Ted laughed, dismayed. "You'd like *me* to get a reply together? I thought the committee you talked about was going to handle these things."

"You're a member of that committee."

"But I'm not the *committee*."

"No time for a meeting," LeMaster said. "I discussed it with Howard and Allen, and they agreed—you're the one for the job. You draft the reply and we'll sign it. We'd like it by Tuesday. Okay?"

No, damn it, Ted thought, it *isn't* okay. "Marv, listen—"

"I appreciate it, Ted."

"But Marv, I—"

"Great," and LeMaster gave him the letter again.

Ted skimmed it, frowning hard. "Are you sure it isn't best to let this drop? Maybe if we just lie low he'll forget it."

"Not a chance," LeMaster said, "the guy's a bulldog, we're going to have to nip his bud." He nodded crisply, trying his best to look decisive, but came off looking absurd.

Ted frowned at the letter again. *Consider further action (legal) to insure...* He folded it and put it in his jacket, a black, barbed nugget of worry lodged deep in his mind. "I'll work on it," he said.

The letter wouldn't let him go, obsessed him all day long: through every minute of every class, through lunch, free period—and of course through his rendezvous with Joy, which he kept to a fondle and French kiss session, his lust short-circuited by his thoughts. (And, after all, there *was* tonight.)

In a way he could understand her father's position. The world the poor old fart had grown up in was falling apart, and he didn't know how to stop it. But damn it, the son of a bitch was making things *real*, destroying the fantasy. Reality kept intruding no matter what, with its slow and seemingly harmless tide, till the castles of dream were eroded and washed away, and now this oaf father was aiding its brutal cause. Did he have some second sense, some ESP that told him his daughter was sinning, defiling his values? Could be: there were more things in heaven and earth than even asshole Freud had dreamed about, and damn the luck!

At the end of seventh period, study hall, he read the letter again. He decided he wouldn't show it to her. Reality could jump in the goddamn lake.

· · · · ·

"Oh, what an adorable *dog*," Joy said as T.S. Eliot nudged her, licked her, nuzzled her, flopped to be scratched.

After Brad had taken off for his friend Jim Dinsmore's house, Ted hung around, drank scotch, watched late high blue fade out of the cooling sky. When the dark came down, he went for his forbidden prize and brought her home; drove into the garage with her slumped below window level, giggling madly, and here they were, where he'd swore she would never be.

"What's his name?" she asked as she rubbed T.S. Eliot's belly. "The kids must love him."

That motherly tone was completely wrong with her ass so cute and tight in her short white shorts, and seeing the dog writhe stupidly under her hand was also wrong.

"His name's T.S."

"T.S. Cute name for a cute, cute dog."

The fool plainly adored her; spread his legs in complete submission. She patted his head, then began to explore the house. "Nice place you got here, Bear. I like the drapes—much nicer than the Blue Note and Riviera." Here and there she went, transforming the familiar; everything she touched—formica table, kitchen cabinet, wine glass, stereo—retained her print, her heat.

They drank their anniversary champagne on the family room couch ("Mumm's, Bear. Don't get any cheap domestic crap.") and kissed and fondled in candlelight. They shared a joint till the flames threw golden splinters at his eyes, then headed upstairs—with T.S. Eliot trailing Joy devotedly.

Their wedding picture. Why hadn't he thought to hide it?

"Oh, my *God!*" Joy said, her hand on the glass, the brass frame. (More fingerprints! More evidence!) "You look so weird! That suit!" She tipped the picture slightly and said, "June's beautiful. Has she changed as much as you have, Bear?"

He was struck by a sudden, sick nostalgia; the room seemed furry, dim. He poured himself more champagne and drank, then kissed her, there by the dresser, closing his eyes.

What he saw behind his lids was—June. What he thought about was—the letter Joy's father had written. How did guys like that screw? he wondered. With folded hands, in supplication, hoping that if they just sort of held it there enough would seep out to further the family line? This Joy came from one of those stony unions? This girl with the tattooed ass?

She giggled. "Easy, Bear, you'll knock me down." Putting the photo back on the dresser, setting her champagne glass beside it, she fell with him onto the bed. His right hand traveled her thigh and cruised her shorts; he found her tenderness; she laughed.

And when he was free of his clothing she dipped his tube in her champagne glass and licked its length and said, "That tape on the dresser—one of ours?"

It was there where he'd put it the night before. "Yeah, *Big is Beautiful,*" he said. "The tape that nearly gave the junior history class the lesson of their lives."

She laughed again. "Well, what's it doing here?"

"I didn't want to leave it in school, so I brought it home."

"Jeez, Bear," she mocked, "you ought to be more *careful*. Somebody might break into your house and steal the thing, you know."

He laughed half-heartedly. No noises came from beyond the door; the dog was apparently sleeping.

She wet him again, looking up with round eyes, and said, "Just think of the great fund-raiser we could put on. They're always trying to think of ways to make money at that stupid school, well what if we showed our tapes? We could charge fifty bucks a head and people would pay it. They'd be *glad* to pay it. About three thousand students, right? They'd bring their relatives and friends, we'd rake in two hundred grand in a couple of hours."

"You're probably right," he said.

Licking, she said, "You better believe I'm right. All those magazine drives and bake sales and car washes, what do they net, a few thousand bucks? In just one night we'd raise enough money to buy new uniforms for the band and football team, new athletic equipment... We could probably build a new *gym* with the dough we'd bring in!"

"Sad but true."

She smiled at him, his shaft in her fist. "Sad? It's simply reality, Bear."

Reality, he didn't want to think about. He extricated himself and went to the closet—to the box in the back, on the floor—and took out the new magazine he had bought.

Joy said, "Of course, we'd have to assure that our audience, wimps that they are, remained anonymous. We'd give our show on Halloween, and everyone could wear masks! Just imagine how people would act if they always wore masks. That's what cars are, you know? They're masks. That's why we like to do it in cars so much."

He laughed and opened the magazine. Two people were pumping away on a Jaguar's hood.

"Good God, you're psychic, Bear. Wow, that is *sexy*. That ornament, that chrome, there's just something *about* it."

In his marriage bed, a gift from the Colonel, they read the magazine. It subscribed to the myth of female ejaculation, and was weird in other ways, too. Joy thought the vibrator part was a blast ("We'll have to get one of those real soon"), and she even liked the anal section, which totally turned Ted off.

They smoked a joint and fooled with each other, burning, prolonging things. She said, "Let's look at our tape now, Bear."

His mind was lost in tinkling, glassy stars. "We can't," he said. "My VCR broke."

"No! Damn! I thought that's *really* why you brought *Big is Beautiful* home."

"I'm sorry."

"Me too. *Very* sorry."

She worked on him with her slender fingers (woman fingers, child fingers), his wedding picture staring down from the dresser (June's sunny smile), and said, "Rod Rheingold used to rent these porno tapes, and we'd play them when his parents were out somewhere. Boy, talk about getting *hot...*"

"Yeah, tell me about it," Ted said as a pang of jealousy hit him.

"We'd do what they did in the tapes, we'd follow their lead. We'd even try to come when they came in the tapes."

He smiled, doped out of his mind. "No kidding," he said.

"Sure. Suppose in the tape she took his cock, like this" (she demonstrated), "well, I'd take Rod's cock—Rod's rod—the same way. If she put it into her mouth—like this—I'd do that too." She smiled, his organ against her flushed cheek. "When they ate, we ate, when they screwed, we screwed. Too bad your machine's broken, Bear. No *Big is Beautiful*."

Soft druggy music played in his ears. "We don't need *Big is Beautiful*," he said, and kissed her, held her, licked her left breast.

She grinned. "We could check out some stuff on the Net."

"I don't have the Net."

"You don't? Why not?"

"I'm not sure I like it."

"My father *hates* it. He says it's the work of the devil—which it is! A huge porno store in everyone's home!"

Ted thought of Brad—and Kim! "We don't need any of that," he said.

"You're right," Joy said, and straddled his hips, her sex on his, her sex a part of him.

In the Colonel's wedding gift they did the unspeakable, did the despicable. No matter how frequent the changing of sheets from this day forth, this spot was forever defiled.

After trips to the bathroom, drinks of water, they lay in the light that flowed from the lamp on June's dresser and shared a fresh joint, and he was the fool who broke reality's dam—by asking where her parents thought she was.

"I told them I had a pajama party to go to," she said, "and they *believed* me. They still believe there *are* pajama parties! Jesus, they're *hopeless*. You should read the sappy letter my father wrote to Grimsley about these library books."

Reality swirled around Ted's ankles, rose up to his kness. "I not only read it," he said, "I've been chosen to draft a reply."

She grinned. "You're kidding. How *comical.*"

"My sentiments exactly."

Pressing her lips together she said, "You want some help?"

"With the letter?"

"Sure. Let me write it, I really know how to get my old man's goat."

"I'll bet you do."

She sniffed."Can you *believe* that crap? This is the kind of thing I've had to put up with all these years. The guy makes Calvin look like a *liberal. The Catcher in the Rye,* for God's sakes! What would he think of *Big is Beautiful?*"

Ted lay there, organ limp, his glands content, a fullness throbbing somewhere behind his bladder—an odd, half-pleasant feeling that he wasn't so sure he liked. Pot and champagne bubbles swam in his brain. "You really want to draft the reply?"

"I'd love to."

"Can you get it to me by Tuesday?"

"No sweat."

"You have that scholarship interview Thursday, don't you? And isn't the class trip Friday?"

"No problem, really, I'll have plenty of time before then."

He grinned. "Okay, you're on."

"Fantastic!"

"I can't guarantee I won't edit it."

She rolled her eyes. "Okay, Mr. English teacher."

"Speaking of editing, we've got to get after that yearbook, the deadline is three weeks away."

"Don't worry, Bear, we'll make it. But after it's done, what excuse will I have to see you?"

"There are always some odds and ends to wrap up. The finishing touches."

"Finishing touches," Joy said, "a good title for one of our tapes," and she kissed his thigh.

He listened to the noises in his head and smiled and said, "Your father, Jesus. He's the kind of guy who gives God a bad name. How in the world did you ever—? It's mystifying."

She laughed. "For every action there's an equal and opposite reaction, right? I realized my father was a hopeless case a long, long time ago. He just *thrives* on repression and guilt." She spread her thighs. "See this?" she said, her fingertip touching her button. "You see this gizmo here? You know what it's for? To make us feel good. It has *no other function.* It has nothing to do with reproduction, it's there for fun, and that's *all.* That's what God, thoughtful guy that He is, designed it for. Can anyone deny it?"

"I don't see how," Ted said, pleasure creeping back into his scrotum. That semi-nice fullness grew stronger and not so nice: it felt like a heated orange was stuck up his tail.

Joy played with herself and he couldn't resist; dived into her folds again.

"Hey, fellow, I just had an oil and lube. And a ring and valve job, too, what is this, a ripoff joint?"

He looked up past her navel, between her breasts. "You still have a few knocks left in your engine."

She laughed. "You bet your sweet tools I do."

When they did it this time, he thought of his neighbors, the 7-Elevens and all the rest, and how shocked they would be by this scene. He thought of Armand Dollinger: *I'm screwing your precious daughter, you senile old fool!* As his orgasm drained his gland's reserves he felt a posterior sting. He winced. Then he rolled with her, lay entwined in her, with her hot sweet breath in his ear.

She said, "I love it in your bed. It's so good, so good."

He said, "Delicious." And it was, because of the terrible weight of taboo in this space: June's wedding eyes, his own young happy and hopeful eyes boring into his present eyes from the photograph there on the dresser.

"I'm glad we did it here on our anniversary," she said.

"Me too," he said, feeling suddenly tired and sad.

He made up a platter of cold cuts and rolls and they ate them in bed and then fell asleep next to each other. In the darkness he woke from a dream to hear easy soft breathing. She isn't snoring tonight, he thought, how wonderful; and then he remembered who this was and thought of his wife and daughter, an ocean away.

• • • • •

Forlorn, the very word is like a bell...

It *was* a bell! The doorbell, strange device, with its single deep and mournful bong! appropriate for a king's arrival or the start of an execution. A dagger of sun slit Ted's eyes; he pulled himself into a sitting postion; saw Joy in the ten o'clock bedroom, naked, asleep on her side with her legs curled up. The bellbuoy bell, bong! bong! Forlorn. Did all doorbells in Westdale sound like this? A rising panic, and quickly he covered his nakedness with his robe.

He closed the bedroom door behind him; hurried down the stairs. Good God, who is it, who can it be, and if Joy should wake up? The door was one of those foolish things with two little windows high at the top that only a giant could see through, and who—? He turned the knob, arms weak.

Brad. Brad and his pal Jim Dinsmore, standing on the sunny steps of home.

"Jeez, Dad, you just gettin' up? Forgot my key. I need my bathin' suit, we're goin' to the pool."

Sun-dazzled eyes and a million horrendous thoughts, and then: Brad rushing inside and mounting the stairs, Ted numb in the foyer, standing there stupidly, fingers still gripping the doorknob. T.S. Eliot, tongue long and loose, bounding into the cheerful sun. Brad banging around upstairs with Jim; their joking voices; thumping, bumping, down the steps, Brad's red athletic bag in his hand, his face with its teenage cool grin. "See you later, Dad." He was already halfway down the walk.

Ted called after him, "When will you be home?"

"I don't know. Around three or four."

"You got your key?"

"Yeah."

"Good. I might not be here when you get back."

"Yeah. See you."

"Have a good time. See you, Jim."

He closed the door behind him, leaned against it, sighed and thanked whatever gods may be. Hearing movement upstairs, he started across the foyer—when the doorbell sounded again.

Now what? Forgot his jockstrap, towel, his rubber duck? He opened the door—

And it wasn't Brad, but a couple of men, one old, one young. The old one was pasty, with wispy white hair and stooped shoulders; the young one was ruddy and thick, with a bushy, straw-colored moustache. The old guy carried a briefcase; was opening it. Ted knew what was coming but couldn't think quickly enough, couldn't act.

And the pamphlet was there in the old man's hand, he smiled an endearing false-tooth smile and the spiel began: "Good morning, sir, isn't it lovely today?" Ted allowed that indeed it was. "Our message for this morning is the message of spiritual happiness. If you'll take a look in this little book here, you'll find a story called, 'Is Happiness Possible?'" That plastic smile; brown stains between the teeth. "We believe that it is..." and on it went, the white-haired fellow underscoring lines with a palsied finger, gasping, obviously emphysemic, somehow not dropping his briefcase as he struggled to find a passage from Matthew that would give his words final authority.

Naked under his robe, Ted listened, furious with himself for not slamming the door. Mrs. Monsanto came out for her paper, saw his plight, and hurried inside to pretend that she wasn't home. As the frail gent rambled on, Ted thought of the letter (anonymous) he'd found in his mailbox a few months back. Obscenely religious and agrammatical, it warned: "Continue this chain and you will prosper. But if you oppose God's will and break it..." And then it detailed the horrors befalling those sinners who'd dared toss the tripe in the trash ("got cancer...went blind..."), and ended with a quote about God's love. He thought of his diabetic dying grandmother so many years ago, and that tract she had sent for: *With God All Things Are Possible.* That quote was from the Book of Matthew, wasn't it?

The young guy stood like a mafia enforcer, arms folded across his chest, as the old one persisted, handing Ted a leaflet with a wretched piece of doggerel called, "If Christ Dropped by Today" (Could you hold your head up proud?/ Or with shame would it be bowed?), and Ted felt his blood pressure rise. "Now here's a story I found most interesting," Mr. Emphysema wheezed, going back to his pamphlet again: "'Do All Religions Say the Same Thing?' You often hear that all religions say the same thing in different ways, but that isn't correct." (That smile!) "This pamphlet tells you about the *true* religion, the religion of Our Lord Jesus Christ, who—"

"I'm a Jew," Ted said.

This news didn't faze the old dude in the slightest. Ted saw him sift through his Alzheimer's to: Situation #8, The Jew. "Well in that case we have a *very* special message. It's right here in—"

"Thank you, but the baby's crying," Ted said brusquely, and he closed the door.

In the cool of the foyer he heard, "Waa, waa," followed by Joy's bright laugh. She was there on the stairs, on the carpeting June had bought with her Happy Trails Travel pay. Naked, she glowed in a shaft of sun. "Get up here, Daddy," she said with a grin. "Baby's hungry."

With a tang at the tip and root of his tongue he went to her; opened his robe like a flasher and kissed her hard; ran his hand down her golden shanks.

In the bedroom they did the libido-meter. She told him what was hooked to what and how it all worked and it drove him wild. When they crossed the finish line she said, "Not bad, Jewboy."

He laughed, out of breath. "I thought I'd never get rid of them," he said. "You give them an inch..."

"They're as bad as my father," she said with her crooked smile. "My father calls Jews Christ-killers."

"Nice."

"The Holocaust was a fake, he says."

"And people tattooed numbers on their arms as part of the charade?"

"He's absurd—but he's got religion, baby." She sniffed. "That's one thing I'm not going to lay on my kids, that Jesus crap. How'd you handle it with Brad and Kim?"

Brad and Kim—and June intruding from the dresser. "I let them make up their own minds," he said.

"And what happened?"

"Brad thinks it's a fairy tale. Kim isn't sure."

"Brad's cute," Joy said. "I saw him through the window."

That jarred him a bit and he said, "I thought you were dead to the world when they came in."

"They woke me up with their banging around."

"Oh."

That smile, that gap in her teeth. "How old is he?"

"Thirteen." He paused a second; said, "Your father's letter said that he had *two* kids in the Somerside schools. So who's the other one?"

"My brother Todd."

"You never mentioned him before."

"He's not worth mentioning."

"Why not?"

"He's Daddy's little boy, you know? The old man's got his brain washed clean as a whistle. It wouldn't surprise me if *he* came ringing your doorbell one of these days with a handful of stupid tracts. Sad case. I've done my best to make him see the light, but it's just no use." Her frown was quizzical. "Were you ever religious?"

"Sure. I went to church until I was fifteen, that's where I learned to drink."

She grinned. "You're kidding."

"Young people's meetings in the basement at night. They called adolescents 'young people' back then—still do, for all I know. Anyway, some kid, he's a minister now, used to bring a tiny bottle of booze and we'd sip it when no one was looking. Those meetings always ended on a cheerful note."

"That's a riot." Still smiling and looking right at him she said, "And when did you first get laid?"

He hadn't expected that. Could he tell her the truth? —That the first one he'd ever really done it with was...June? He said, "I can't remember. I was about eighteen, the girl was someone I met through a friend."

This smile was different; cut right through him. "Hey Bear, come on, nobody forgets their first lay. They might forget their name, rank, and serial number, but never *that*."

"I remember the incident, I just don't remember the girl."

"I see," she said, and smiled again, and he knew damn well she knew.

17 • MASTER MUSCLE

Gloomy in the airport's waiting room, Ted sipped from his plastic container of coffee, ran his hand through his graying hair.

Airports *always* made him gloomy—that mechanical sky, that gut-twisting tension of constant departure, those baggage checks with their x-ray machines, ticket people in red sportscoats—but this time the feeling was crushing.

Exhausted and nervous, he stared through a wall of tinted glass at a silently rising plane. Its purpose and power oppressed him still further; made him feel puny and weak. Into the heavy gray yonder it rose, spewing trails of black. Unhappy trails. Far off, sharp lightning flashed. Out of that darkening sky would come June and Kim. To him: the husband, father, traitor, mortal enemy.

He looked at the digital clock on the wall. The plane was twenty-two minutes late. What if the storm, so feeble from here, was serious up there? What if they crashed and were killed? He couldn't bear to think of it. He loved them and wanted them safe. That was the truth of it, right? He loved them? He drank his tepid coffee and watched the sky.

He thought of that leisurely breakfast with Joy on Saturday there in his kitchen, with T.S. Eliot lying beside his feet. In spite of his protests, they'd eaten nude. He hated the combination of food and nakedness; one cancelled the other, making enjoyment of either impossible for him. Casino shows and topless bars were not his cup of tea, but Joy had pleaded her case with passion, and he'd given in.

As they'd eaten their melon and scrambled eggs and English muffins with butter and strawberry jam, as they'd smoked their marijuana and gone back to bed, he'd sensed her melancholy. She chattered and laughed and was active as ever, but he knew it was all a charade. When they finished, she said: "I love it here. I wish I could stay here forever."

He felt suddenly sorry for her. She had so much to offer and yet, and yet... Behind her shield of cockiness there was something vital missing—and she knew it.

She went through a minor shaking spell before leaving the house, but recovered quickly, giggling again as she slumped out of sight in the car. As he made his Harmony Lane getaway he waved to Mrs. RCA, and Joy impishly stuck up her hand and waved too. Ted wanted to kill her, but no harm done, for Mrs. RCA was distracted the instant before the deed by Chuckie, her youngest, who'd tumbled face first off his trike.

"There it is," someone said, and Ted got to his feet, and yes, there it was, far away on his right, touching down. He watched it taxi to a stop, watched the door come open, saw strangers descend the steps.

People came through the passageway clutching their flight bags, looking around, looking tired, and suddenly—June and Kim. He hugged them hard with sweet powerful love and damn near cried. God, what was *wrong* with him?

Kim launched into a high speed travelog as June answered: "Not so good. Exhausted, of course, but I picked up some bug, turned me inside out on the plane." She rested on one of the naugahyde couches as he and Kim went to retrieve the luggage, and Kim, much older than she'd been a week ago, went on and on: the people's cheeks were so red over there, the toilet paper was hard and brown, for breakfast they gave you salami... Ted thought of his first trip to Europe with June so long ago, before the kids were born, how much they had loved it. June still loved it, but Europe was dead for him now and he wondered why.

• • • • •

When they walked through the door, June said: "What's that *smell?*"

"Lysol. I cleaned the bathrooms," Ted said.

The truth was this: Saturday evening, Brad had come home and said, "This place smells funny." "It does?" Ted had said with alarm, remembering Wally Blood's comment about the A-V room. "Yeah, it smells like flowers and smoke." So Sunday morning while Brad still slept, Ted stripped the beds and washed the sheets and pillowcases, searched the house obsessively for signs of Joy and doused the place with disinfectant spray.

Kim made a face. "It smells like—"

"The john at school," Ted said.

"Yeah, how'd you know?"

"That's what Brad said it smelled like."

"He was right for once."

"Let's open some windows before I vomit," June said, and went to the medicine cabinet and got out the Kaopectate.

Pretty soon it was just like they'd never been gone. All was normal again, right down to the last detail—Brad and Kim's first dinnertime battle. Ted ruled in Brad's favor and Kim said, "Jeez, that really sucks!" "Don't use that expression," Ted said. "Why not?" Kim said. "Just don't!" "Well why, is it *dirty* or something?" Ted didn't reply.

It rained like mad that night. Beside him on the freshly laundered sheets June said: "That roof leak. Ted, you've got to fix it, I just can't sleep." "Sorry, I didn't have any time this week. Next weekend, maybe." Five minutes later she was snoring.

Ted listened to the drip, the snores; he watched the lightning on the wall and thought exhausted stupid thoughts of Europe years ago; of Joy; of Kim, growing up; of Brad, growing up; of what would become of them. Brad had just learned at school that he was a prime contender for the Veterans' Legion Award. When Ted was his age he had won that same prize. It had seemed to him to presage a sparkling future ("I greet you at the beginning of a great career"—Ralph Waldo Emerson to Whitman), and, indeed, he'd won a scholarship to college, made dean's list all but one semester... And what had it meant, in the end? A happy life? Enlightenment? It hadn't even meant *security*.

The room was so filled with regrets and snores and drips that he threw off the sheet and went to the study and smoked some marijuana; then lay on the couch in the lingering Lysol smell in front of silent *House of Frankenstein,* until the voices in his head said, Yes, it was all right now, he could go to sleep.

• • • • •

In the morning June still felt rotten, with diarrhea and cramps. Ted made her some tea and toast and told her to rest, then went to school.

They had promised to finish the yearbook, bear down hard and get it off their backs, but yesterday they'd succumbed to a final showing of *Big is Beautiful* before erasing the tape. Today they worked like blazes, whipped through orchestra, athletic association, library aides and clubs. Toward the end of the period she said, "Oh, here," and handed him a typed page. It said:

Dear Mr. Dollinger:

Thank you for your letter of the 25th. We appreciate your concerns. As public servants, we are charged by the community with the responsibility of educating its youth, and we take that task quite seriously. The books you list in your letter have all been published by reputable firms, and, in our opinion, reflect aspects of our current society that the youth of today should be cognizant of.

As for *Our Bodies Belong to Us,* which you find especially disturbing: As we see it, this volume is not a polemic for or against particular ways of behaving, but simply a description of various behaviors which, whether we like it or not, do exist. We do not regard this presentation as an attempt to corrupt America's youth. On the contrary, we feel that this material will aid our young people to make informed choices in the areas of social commitments and personal hygiene, and we consider it a highly worthwhile part of our library collection.

Sincerely,
The Whitman High School Media Review Committee

Raising his eyebrows, Ted said, "It's excellent. I don't even think I'll change it."

"Jeez, I hope not," Joy said. "Did you like that 'young people' touch? I got that from you."

"It's perfect. Thanks."

"I had a blast."

She smiled and gave him a quick light kiss.

He felt oddly embarrassed. "I better get back to my class."

Her smile was wistful, her voice was soft. "Tonight then, Bear. Same time, same place."

"Under the 'J'," Ted said. She stared at him with wide, adoring eyes. He turned, her letter in his hand, and left the room.

• • • • •

In the weary blue Blue Note Motel they played libido-meter. "Push button and release," Joy said, and Ted, erect and red, said, "Rub hands briskly under nozzle." "You mean *on* nozzle, don't you?" Joy said, and she did it with expert strokes. As she used her mouth he felt distant, detached; he couldn't stop thinking of June. She'd been sick all day, hadn't touched her toast or any food. "Can I pick up anything for you after my class?" he had asked with concern as she lay on the mattress he'd recently slept on with Joy. His class. What a cheap bourgeois adulterer he was, what a perfect suburbanite! Excoriating himself, he rode Joy's tail, his hand on her sunny tattoo. He posted and galloped and drove to the stars—and it stung like a son of a bitch.

He jerked, cried out, and she said, "What's wrong?" "Foot cramp," he said, and kneaded the phony knot with both hands as the pain in his rectum died. "Better, Bear?" He nodded yes. She tried to start up all over again but he told her, "Not now, let's just smoke."

His denial disturbed her. She smoked in silence. She frowned, smoked, frowned, then said, "Bear, I'd like you to do me a favor."

He still felt the remnants of pain, that fullness again; he still had his mind on June. "What kind of a favor?" he said.

"Burk wants us to do this paper. It's not real long or involved, but I just never got around to it. I'm going away on Thursday and Friday, my weekend looks pretty full too, so I'd like you to help me out."

"Write it for you, you mean."

She touched his lip with her finger and looked in his eyes. "Could you, Bear?"

He hesitated, marijuana snowflakes falling, and said, "You should have done the paper instead of that letter."

"I know. It just totally slipped my mind."

His organs felt raw and drained. A part of his mind was thinking without him, saying all sorts of weird things. "What's the paper supposed to be on?"

"The theme of 'rain' in poetry. We're to find ten poems that mention rain, then show if the rain's used literally, symbolically, literally and symbolically…that kind of crap."

Ted rolled his eyes. "I always knew Burk was all wet."

"Oh funny, funny."

"How long does it have to be?"

"Ten pages—a page for each poem."

"Jesus! When is it due?"

"On Monday." She looked at him expectantly; the tiny peachfuzz hairs above her lip were deliciously blond. He weakened and said, "You got yourself a deal. But please—don't mention this to anybody. I mean *anybody*."

She smiled her quizzical smile. "Hey, Bear, you think I'm suicidal?" She laughed and picked up the magazine they'd been reading, *Tool Box,* the one with the dildo. "Just *look* at this," she said. "I mean all the *way.* We really have to get one, Bear." She arched her eyebrows, said, "Once more into the breach?"

"I can't," he said. "I told June I'd come home right after class. She really feels lousy."

Those soft blue eyes. "You still care for her, don't you, Bear?"

"It's…very complicated."

A silence. She just kept looking at him, then said, "I can't wait to meet her."

He sniffed a laugh. "No way."

Head cocked to the side, she smiled and said, "But I'm going to. You're a chaperone at the senior prom and surely you'll bring your wife, so I'll meet her there."

This startled him. "You're going to the *prom?*"

"Of course. Have to keep up appearances, play the game. It's the perfect cover."

"Yeah, perfect," he said. He frowned; looked vacantly across the room.

She laughed. "Hey Bear, don't worry, it's gonna be fun."

He looked at her, still frowning. "Well who are you going with?"

She tugged his member playfully, making him wince. "Why Rod Rheingold, of course."

"But he goes with Eileen Phillips."

"That's what's going to make it such fun, old Bear…"

* * * * *

Before he took his morning shower, the full length mirror gave him a nasty surprise.

The entire left side of his penis was purple. It looked like he'd gotten it caught in a door. He turned its limp tenderness over and gently probed.

It didn't really hurt, but that *color*, my God, it looked *dead*. He thought of that magazine, *Tool Box*. Maybe a little help from his friends was an idea whose time had come.

He picked up the "marital aid" after school. A "medium," seven inches or so, with a soft, flesh-colored sheath and the brand name "Master Muscle." The warty ectomorph who took his cash was completely impassive as he asked, "You want a bag?" Ted wondered: What would it take to produce some show of emotion in this guy? What a great executioner he'd make!

At a K-Mart, Ted purchased the size "D" batteries needed to bring Master Muscle to life, along with four cans of oil and a filter for the station wagon (he had to get around to that this weekend), and a gallon of windshield washer. In the parking lot he slipped Master Muscle into the K-Mart bag.

June's car, the Toyota, was in the garage. Even though she'd felt awful this morning, she'd planned to work, but either she'd changed her mind or had come home early. What was it with Europe? All these years of modern chemistry, and their water was still screwed up. But they didn't have any mosquitoes, you could sleep without screens. He had always marveled at that.

He got out of the Plymouth, clutching the K-Mart bag; felt the bulge of the vinyl dong through the crinkly plastic—and behind the door to the kitchen, the telephone rang. With a sudden irrational fear that the call was from Joy, he ran into the house.

Juggling his bag, he grabbed the wall phone, and heard from upstairs, "Is that you, Ted?"

He covered the mouthpiece with his palm and yelled, "Yeah! I've got it, June!" Then, into the white receiver, expecting the worst: "Hello?"

It wasn't Joy, it was Linda from LifeTime Books. Had he enjoyed the gardening series? He explained that his wife had ordered them, he hadn't read them, he hated gardening. Linda understood. Had the books arrived on time and in good condition? He assured her they had. Would he like to inspect the first volume of *Battles of World War Two?* He didn't think he—or his wife—would be interested in that, but Linda expressed the opinion that once he saw Volume I he'd be so impressed—

The K-Mart bag slipped from his grasp and fell—with a terrible crash of oil cans, and Linda dangled, strangled as Ted watched the flesh-colored horror go rolling across the floor. He scooted after it, pouncing as June made her entrance.

"Jesus, Ted, that noise, what—?" Startled eyes on the plastic dork. "What's *that?*"

Bland Ted recovered it and said, "It's a vibrator, June." Placing it calmly on the counter, his heart in a gallop, he picked up the cans of oil, the filter, the gallon of pale blue washer fluid, and set them beside it. Linda, thank God, was making a flat loud buzzing noise. He hung her up.

June stared at the ersatz erection. "A *vibrator?* What did you buy *that* for?"

"I thought it might help your stomach. You know, straighten out the kinks."

"You're kidding," she said. "You know what that thing *looks* like?"

"What's that?" he said.

June blushed a little. "Well, *you* know."

He feigned confusion. "They're supposed to be good. George Frangelli used one on his shoulder—that shoulder he pulled? Said it really helped."

She touched it gingerly. "Master *Muscle?*"

"Yeah. It's designed to relieve sore muscles."

June sniffed. "I don't have any muscle pull, I have something *internal*."

"Maybe not," Ted said. "Look, why don't we give it a try."

"Please. Don't be ridiculous."

"Did you work today?"

"No."

"Okay then, you still don't feel right, I went to the trouble of buying this thing, we ought to at least try it out. I mean what can you lose?"

In the bedroom she lay on her back in her panties and bra as the vibrator danced in his hands. "Christ, it tickles," she said.

He thought of *Tool Box*, Joy, their antics in this bed. "Does it feel any better?"

"It just makes me feel silly. —And looks obscene."

"I suppose it's the most efficient design," he said. Buzz! Buzz! Buzz! across her belly, the stretch marks, the looseness so different from Joy.

"Where'd you get it?"

"At Passwater Medical, Apple Heights."

"They ought to be ashamed of themselves for selling such junk. Turn it off, I feel like I'm part of some pagan fertility rite."

He clicked the button, thinking: *Over the top, Bear, all the way!* With a look of concern he asked, "No better?"

"Of course not, the problem's *inside*."

"Goddamn Europe," Ted said.

She sat up, slouching forward, her arms on her knees. "I'm going to see Dr. Dickle on Friday."

"Dr. Dickle?" he said. "The urologist? Why not Hodgkins or Buck?" (The internist and gynecologist.)

"I have blood in my urine."

Ted frowned at the plastic phallus, worried, guilty. "Jesus," he said, "some European parasite."

She looked at him. There were tears in her eyes. "Oh Ted, I feel so bad."

With genuine sadness at her plight (the sadness he'd feel for any poor creature in pain), he put his arm around her—around his old pal. Not his lover, his pal. "I'm sorry," he said. "Is there anything I can do?"

She looked at Master Muscle there in his hand and said, "Yes, get rid of that god-damn thing. And I'd like some tea."

18 • AN END OF MAY

On Friday Dr. Dickle told her she needed a hysterectomy: rampant uterine polyps were causing the bleeding and pain. The operation was scheduled for Monday, and the weekend was a blur of hurry, worry, waiting: packing her suitcase, driving to the hospital on Sunday afternoon and checking in, hanging around in that empty frightening hospital boredom, trying to read old *Newsweeks* and *Times* when conversation died.

Off and on, Ted thought about Joy. She'd gone for her scholarship interview Thursday, and Friday she'd been in Washington: class trip. As he scrambled some eggs for the kids Sunday night, he pictured her back in her father's house, that home he had never seen—young, healthy, secure from the weakness and worry of middle age. —And yet worried and insecure. To be haunted by time at seventeen seemed crazy—and terribly sad. When he had been seventeen he'd been damn near immortal.

He sat around listlessly watching TV and reassuring Kim that Mom (how that word never seemed to fit June) would be fine. But *would* she be? Without all those delicate clockworks? Would hormones be needed to keep her from sprouting a beard?

It was after eight when Brad came down from his room and said, "Dad, I'm stuck on my history paper, do you think you could help me with it?"

An alarm went off in Ted's head. Good God, that paper for Joy! It was due tomorrow! In the hassle of June's impending surgery, he'd completely forgotten about it! He said, "I'd like to, Brad, but I can't, I have work of my own to do."

"I just thought you were watching TV."

"No, I have some important stuff to finish."

"Oh."

"When's your paper due?"

"Tomorrow."

"Tomorrow? Why did you let it go so long?"

"I forgot about it."

"Well God, learn to write yourself notes, keep a list or something, you can't put things off till the very last minute and ask me to bail you out."

Brad's face was dejected and harried. "You can't help me out at *all?*"

"Not tonight. It's a bad time to ask, Brad, with all that I have to do and Mom in the hospital."

"Yeah."

"I could give you a hand in a couple of days, but I guess that'd be too late."

"If I don't get it in by tomorrow I get a zero."

Ted sighed. "Well give it your best shot, that's all you can do at this point. And just don't let things *go* like that."

"Yeah." Brad gloomily left the family room and went upstairs.

Ted went to the study, thinking: rain, rain, poems that deal with rain. *The rain, it streams on stone and hillock. It weeps in my heart as it rains on the town. Not sense to come in when it rains.* That's only three and I have to have ten. Damn Burk and his stupid assignments! Come on, for Christ's sake, think! *The doors clap to, the pane is blind with showers. Pass me the can, lad; there's an end of May.*

He looked out the open window and into the darkness, smelled the perfume of lilac and iris and thought: And it *is* May. *May will be fine next year as like as not: Oh ay, but then we shall be twenty-four.* Twenty-four! Next year I'll be forty-three! Forty goddamn three years old! He thought of June in the hospital, lying there waiting to have her exhausted organs carved away. She'd been twenty-four fourteen years ago, had been glowing with youth, and now... Life just shouldn't go so fast, it wasn't *right.* An end of May. Our mortal lot. It is in truth iniquity on high...

Five days had passed since he'd been with Joy; the bruise on his penis was gone; and he wanted to hold her, taste her, enter her, absorb her, ride with her out of the reach of time's iron hand.

He looked at the notes he had made. Rain, rain, go away, little Teddy wants to play. Damn Burk the Jerk! Think, think!

He found the rest of the poems he needed and got down to business. Brad went to the kitchen twice, used the bathroom twice, hit the sack around two. He was giving the history paper his best, and Ted hoped he had managed to finish. T.S. Eliot entered the study, flopped down on the rug and conked out. Envying him, Ted kept plugging away. It was ten after four when the last draft was finally typed.

He turned out the lights; sat in front of the window and took a few hits on a joint as he looked at the dark suburban carpet of lawn blending into the border of shrubs near Waughbach Cemetery.Thoughts of Joy and thoughts of June. Next year I'll be forty-three. The comforting little snapping sounds began in the back of his head. Far off, he saw lightning flash. *The rain is full of ghosts tonight...*

Low crackles of thunder and brighter lightning. Peaceful with dope and exhaustion, he watched the advance of the storm. A gust in the cemetery's trees, in the bushes below the window, and—soft rain.

He breathed with cottony lungs, feeling ancient; stubbed the joint out, closed the window, stepped across the gurgling dog and went to the bedroom, thinking: *Shantih, shantih, shantih,* peace and rain.

• • • • •

The operation went without a hitch: no signs of malignancy, everything fine. Ted brought her some roses and held her hand, and bleary with anesthesia, she openly cried. When her roommate—a chain-smoking toothless woman with frazzled white hair and pink slippers—went out to the nurses' station, June said, "I'm old. Oh, Ted, I'm already *old.*"

He held her hand in both his hands and said, "June, no, that's not true. Helen Trask had a hysterectomy, so did Valerie Miller. Do they seem old?"

"Yes, yes." Tears streamed down her cheeks.

"June..."

"Ted, I'm drying up."

• • • • •

In the Riviera Motel, he wallowed in wet. What was that phrase from Wallace Stevens? Concupiscent curds? Exactly! "Pump, Bear, pump, make it slap, give me noise!"

She lay on her back on the edge of the bed, knees bent. With his feet on the floor, he powered into her, stripping his fluid and heat. She winced and laughed. "Oh more, Bear, don't be finished, please..."

Amazed by her capacity, he shifted to fingers and mouth. He paused a second to catch his breath—and introduced Master Muscle.

"Bear! You got one!"

He started in gently. Joy watched with delighted, wide eyes. "Lick button C," she commanded, and he obeyed, his tongue meeting plastic dildo skin. "Caress flaps L and M." He readily complied. "Now finger hole A and activate pump G!"

She turned around and got up on her knees. He worked the surrogate with mounting speed, his eyes on her cheery tattoo. "All the way with tube D, all the way!" and he thrust the dildo up to its hilt and she shivered, hair flying, and shouted: "Yes, over the top, Bear, over the top!" He lapped her flanks as T.S. Eliot had lapped that springer spaniel. A beast, a fiend, a Boschian demon, he drowned himself—but couldn't stop thinking of June.

They lay in liquid laziness and smoked more dope. He asked, "How'd the scholarship interview go?"

"Oh, I snowed them, of course."

"Great. Aubrey's a real good school."

She smiled. "Yeah? *Is* there such a thing? The college kids *I* know say half of the teachers are senile and the rest are stoned."

"An exaggeration, I'm sure."

"I wonder."

He listlessly stared at the blood-red drapes.

"It must be horrible," she said.

He looked at her. "What must be horrible?"

"You know, to get old and have all your guts cut out. It happened to my mother. Do all women need that operation?"

"Not all of them, no," Ted said, feeling sick to his heart.

"I hope I don't. But I'll tell you one thing: before I'm old I'm going to have plenty of kids. I'm going to have *roomfuls* of kids."

"You are?"

"You better believe it."

"Ever hear of the population bomb?"

Laughing, she tossed her head. "I've heard of the population bomb, the atomic bomb, the hydrogen bomb, the neutron bomb... and I'll do what I damn well want to, Bear."

"So you think it's okay to bring kids into that kind of world?"

"Shit yes, because I'll raise them *free*. I won't lay all that guilt and Jesus garbage on them that my parents laid on me." Compressing her lips, she said, "My father can't answer this one, my shrink couldn't either, but maybe you know: Why did God allow the Sodomites to act the way they did?"

"Beats me."

"So you're no help either. God *created* the Sodomites, so they must have served some purpose in His overall scheme of things. Did He just want to make an example of them?"

"Could be." He looked at the curtain and drifted along on the dope—and thought of June, in pain, on drugs, and hoped she was peacefully sleeping.

"So us fuckers and suckers serve a valuable function."

"*We* fuckers and suckers," Ted said.

She squinted. "Hey, teach, you want me to mangle your dangling participle?"

"You bet I do." He kissed her left nipple and nuzzled it with his nose.

She laughed and said, "You tickle, Bear," and ran her fingers through his hair.

He could feel himself growing again, though he had no desire. "So what did your father think of your letter?"

Her eyes went wide as she said, "He turned blue. We haven't heard the last from the old fart yet." She kept fooling around with his hair.

"What will it take to satisfy him?"

"Nothing much—just total surrender. He's an ex-marine, you know."

"I know." He looked at her beautiful body, so close, so warm, and wondered: What would June's scar be like? He said, "God could have spared humanity so much pain by never inventing the penis-vagina system."

"You don't like the P-V system?"

"What problems it's given us all."

"And what *pleasures*," Joy said. "I mean what would *you* like to do—reproduce like fish? And spend your life in a search for a pile of eggs you can jack off on?"

"Sounds perverted."

"You said it, Bear." She fondled him, fooled with him, wet him down, and soon he stood fully alert. Looking up as she worked, she said, "By the way, thanks for doing the paper for Burk the Jerk, it should make him ecstatic."

"The kids call him Burk the Jerk too?"

"Doesn't *everybody?*"

"Probably even his wife," Ted said.

"You mean that little fruit has a *wife?*" Joy said, wedging his glans between cheek and gum. "Will wonders never cease." He sat there impassively, stoned and sad. She looked at him; said, "Hey, Bear, quit thinking about her. Visiting hours are over, what more can you do? Just because she's in pain, does it mean that you can't have fun?"

Sad, sad, he smiled. "That may sound logical to you, but it's not that easy."

She shook her head. "Old-fashioned Bear." She kissed his shaft and said, "Come on, let's play again before we leave."

When he didn't respond, she frowned, touching his tip, and said, "It's hard to believe that kids come out of here. —That we're all made of cum juice—Spoonfeather, Daddy—everybody on earth."

He pictured his own kids, Brad and Kim, as he watched her work; saw June, cut, aging, in pain. In spite of these thoughts, the psychology clicked, the biology won. In a dream, he observed as she mounted his hardness and rocked with her hands on her thighs. "Ride a cock horse, Bear, ride a cock horse," and his feeling rose and peaked and subsided, mechanical man that he was, and she brightly laughed.

He lay beside her, holding her. —And thought of June and those goddamn poems, those goddamn gloomy poems about the rain.

19 • CHAIN LETTER

Thursday he took off from work and brought June home.

They treated her like royalty. Brad's thoughtfulness was especially impressive: he made soft-boiled eggs and toast for her supper, picked a vaseful of flowers, brought aspirin and the *Courier-News*. Asshole Freud would probably talk about unresolved Oedipal complexes, but surely any normal observer (like Ted) would feel that Brad was simply showing love for his ailing mother. Ted was proud of the kid: there were touches of manhood in how he behaved. There was actually hope for him yet.

June was already feeling much better; the querulous edge had returned to her voice and she wasn't moaning about being old anymore. Propped in bed with the *Courier-News* as Ted put his pajamas on, she said, "Some guy's really steamed up over a book in the Whitman library. Have you read his letter?"

As he'd gotten undressed, Ted had thought of his session with Joy on the previous day. They'd recorded a show called *Championship Porking*, ten different positions in less than ten minutes of tape. In the chaos of June's operation he hadn't been sleeping enough, and there in the stifling A-V room his heart had been beating so fast he thought he would die. They were starting to play back the tape (as he worried about that nagging rectal pain) when Elfrieda Molt, the music teacher, walked in. Just walked right in! The goddamn door hadn't locked! They were fully clothed, no parts were exposed, the TV screen was facing away from Ms. Molt, and Joy quickly jumped up, stopped the tape and rewound it. Ted had damn near passed out.

He took the *Courier-News* from June. "I didn't see the paper this morning."

"You're going to love this letter."

He read:

To the editor:

I recently brought to the attention of the Somerside school administration the fact that the Whitman High School library is riddled with books that are suggestive, salacious, libertarian and anti-Christian. The degree to which the reply I received from the "Media Review Committee" is misinformed alarms and astonishes me. I would rather choose to believe that the administration, faculty, and school librarian are in the pay of the forces that promulgate such trash than believe they could be as ignorant as their letter implies.

Having received no satisfaction from the superintendent and his subordinates, I now wish to alert the public to what is happening in our schools; to let them know what garbage is being purchased and distributed to impressionable children with our hard-earned tax dollars.

While many books in the library collection are offensive and immoral, one title alone will serve to make my point. This is the volume OUR BODIES BELONG TO US, put out by an organization called The Women's Health *Cooperative* of Greater Denver. I ask any reader of your paper to obtain a copy of this paperback sewer and form his own opinion—especially of pages 42, 52, 90, 97, 131 and 235—pages with photos that leave absolutely *nothing to the imagination*. I ask the reader to decide if the topics this book discusses are proper for minors, some of whom are fourteen years old when they enter senior high. I guarantee that the majority of readers—those with a proper sense of moral values—will be as shocked and outraged as my family was when we found such filth in our school.

For the information of those who drafted the reply to my letter: Can you really be so naive as to think that OUR BODIES BELONG TO US—published by a *cooperative*— is not propaganda? That it is not a deliberate attempt to convince our children to shed those moral values that keep our country healthy? History has proven time and again that the greatest nations are those which repress their sexuality. The enemies of America are well aware of this, and will use any means in their power to destroy our mechanisms of control.

The "Comprehensive Plan of the Communist Party for the Destruction of the United States" lists the following goals:

Number 24: Eliminate all laws pertaining to obscenity by calling them "censorship."

Number 25: Break down morality by promoting pornography in books, magazines, and electronic media.

Need I say more?

A copy of this letter has been sent to Howard Grimsley, Somerside's Superintendent of Schools. If the situation is once again not addressed in a satisfactory manner by him and his committee, I will seriously consider taking legal action to subvert this pernicious influence on our youth.

Yours sincerely,
Armand Dollinger

"Incredible," Ted said. "The 'Comprehensive Plan of the Communist Party for the Destruction of the United States'?" The man should be institutionalized. He handed the paper back to June.

She said, "That's your committee he's talking about, right?"

"That's my *letter* he's talking about."

"Oh, great. I hope you don't have one of his kids as a student."

"As a matter of fact, I do."

"Is he like the old man?"

"It's a girl. No, she isn't like him at all." He thought of how ripped Joy would be when she saw this letter.

"Looks like your group's got its hands full. What *is* this *Our Bodies Belong to Us,* anyway?"

"I don't know, I've never seen it. I probably won't get a chance to now—it'll be the most popular book in the school."

"You never saw the book, and you defended it?"

Ted laughed.

"I'd suggest you read it."

"I guess I better."

"Speaking of wrecked moral fiber," June said, "Sally Williams called up to wish me well, and told me that Jerry Mandrill's been fooling around."

"You're kidding," Ted said, getting into the bed. Mandrill was a soft-looking, middle-aged dentist.

"He's been at it for months, and Sheila just realized. How the hell could she be so dense? Cheating for months and she just found out."

He pulled the sheet over his knees. "People are pretty clever at hiding those things, I guess."

June arched her brows. "Come on, any wife with half a brain would suspect what was going on."

"I guess you're right," Ted said, not daring to meet her eyes. "What I want to know is how did he ever find time with that job of his?"

"The affair was with his hygienist. He just left open spots on his schedule."

Ted pictured it: the dentist and his colleague at work on that odd sort of spaceship chair while unsuspecting patients read *People* or *US* in the waiting room. The scene had a certain charm. It would make a good movie or magazine. *Private Practice? Deep Cavity?*

June set her cup on the bedside table, laid the *Courier-News* on the floor. "Well, I'm ready for sleep."

"Me too," Ted said. He kissed her cheek and said, "I'm glad that you're doing so well."

She smiled at him. "Thanks, sweetheart."

He turned off his light and lay down, wide awake, staring into the dark. Sweetheart! She hadn't called him that in *years!*

"Oh, Ted?"

A paranoid flash that she knew about Joy, knew everything. "Yes?" Holding his breath.

"Have you seen my silver pendant around?"

Relief. "No, I haven't, June."

"I thought I left it on the dresser before I went to the hospital. I guess I put it away, but I don't know where."

"I'm sure it'll turn up soon."

"I hope so. I'd hate to lose it, it's one of my favorite things."

"We'll find it, don't worry about it."

"Okay. Goodnight, Ted."

"Sleep well, June."

He frowned at the dark. That pendant, yes. Hadn't it been right there on the dresser when Joy—? When she picked up the wedding picture? He thought so, but wasn't sure. He had given that pendant to June on their tenth anniversary. It was sterling, inscribed. He too hoped it hadn't been lost.

He thought about Joy and her father's letter, of Jerry Mandrill's affair. The "Comprehensive Plan of the Communist Party..." Any wife with half a brain...

June was already snoring. Poor June. He thought of Elfrieda Molt walking into the A-V room and broke into a thin, cold sweat.

• • • • •

If you love two different women
it'll drive you half insane...

He sat up and clicked off the country and western twang. With dismay he watched the clock radio's numbers flash. Power outage in the night—and he'd overslept twenty-five minutes.

Brad and Kim were already downstairs where automatic coffee tardily brewed. He showered quickly, shaved, got dressed; was hurrying past Brad's room when he saw his stapler sitting there on the desk. He didn't mind if the kid borrowed things, but couldn't he put them back? He went into the room and picked up the stapler, turned, and a dot of color—red at the edge of Brad's mattress—caught his eye.

Which one of the skin magazines was under there? *Playboy? Penthouse?* It was none of his business, but... God, only yesterday Brad was an infant, taking his first halting steps, and now he was into *this*.

Ted put his hands on the bedspread, thinking: No, I shouldn't pry. But one little peek... Delaying no longer, he lifted the mattress.

Cold panic. He thought he would faint. Good God, not *Playboy*, not *Penthouse*, but...*Spurts Illustrated!* The kid had discovered the hiding place! He stared at the

115

magzine's cover; the woman, the rod, the flow, and his throat closed up. Feeling cold all over, he lowered the mattress again.

Now what to do? He couldn't accuse the kid, admonish him, he couldn't say *anything* to him. A horrid red rush of shame flushed his body from navel to head.

He hurried back into his bedroom, where June was still sleeping. Creeping quietly past her, he opened the closet door (a tiny squeak! He winced), and leaned inside; plunged his hands in the box, felt a magazine's slick thick cover. Two, three, four magazines. He pulled them out.

On top, *Tool Box* (the one with the dildo); next, *Class Action* (the teacher-pupil relationship); third, *Y'All Come* (Appalachian hijinks); and last—*Spurts Illustrated!*

Huge relief: the copy Brad had was his *own*. But how the hell did a kid so young get his hands on a thing like *that?* Some older guy was buying the stuff and selling it at the school?

"Ted?"

He shoved the pornography back in the box, scuttled out of the closet backwards, crab-like, stood, and closed the door. "Hi, June, how you feeling?"

Looking puzzled, she said, "Pretty good. What in the world were you doing down there?"

"Oh. I can't find my running shoes."

"They're right under the bed, where you always keep them."

Lifting the edge of the bedspread, he laughed. "I must be blind."

"You aren't going to jog now, are you? It's late."

"No, I just didn't see them, that's all. Can I get you some coffee?"

"Sure."

"How about breakfast, you want me to make you something?"

"You don't have time."

"I'll rush."

"It's okay, I'm not hungry yet."

He hurried downstairs, and, thank God, the kids were gone. He got the pot, returned with it, and poured her a steaming cup. Kissed her cheek. "Well, I better get on my way. Have a good day now."

"You too."

As he left the bedroom he thought, *Have a good day now.* Jesus, why did he say that, what was he doing—turning into a teller, a clerk?

The garage and the car, down the driveway and into the street. Bright sunshine and Mrs. Bonanza out front in her robe. Embarrassed, she hurried inside. Ted thought: little *Brad* with a copy of *Spurts Illustrated.* Should he say something, do something, now that the option existed again? Do what? Steal the thing and destroy it? He turned onto Washburn Avenue, frowning. Well cheer up, he thought, it's bad, but it could be worse; it could be a copy of *Juicy Fruits* instead.

That cover photo—the platinum blonde with her mouth jammed full—seared his brain as he drove. If *he* had seen something like that when *he* was Brad's age, he'd have lost his mind, would have babbled and drooled through life in a padded cell. Brad! Little Brad! So soon!

• • • • •

In the staff room LeMaster nabbed him. Howard, he said, was displeased with Ted's letter to Armand Dollinger. "He feels we should've had the input of the full committee, Ted."

A fire flared up in Ted's brain. "Marv, what are you saying? You asked me to draft a reply, and that's what I did. You mean you sent it out before the others reviewed it?"

LeMaster's face was ponderous, gloomy. "See Dora," he said. "Draft an answer to this latest letter with her help, and we'll all get together on it."

"Does Grimsley think I sent that reply on my own?"

LeMaster stared in his basset-hound, stop-time way. "We should've had the full committee's input."

"That's not what I asked you, Marv."

The principal clapped his hand on Ted's shoulder. "Ted, gotta run, we'll discuss it later. In the meantime, see Dora."

Ted wanted to boot his fat ass.

• • • • •

In psychology class, Joy glowered and scowled. Afterwards, in the hallway, she said, "Let's talk for a minute."

They went to the A-V room. When the door was closed she sputtered, "Ignorant! Misinformed! The greatest nations are those that repress their sexuality!" Her eyes misted over. "Do you see what I have to put up with? *Do* you? Just wait till he sees what I write *this* time."

Ted said, "The committee will answer this time."

She glared. "What? You mean I can't get him back?"

"I'll welcome your ideas," he said.

"Thanks a lot. You sound just like LeMaster."

She was right, he did. "I'm sure you have plenty to do without working on that," he said.

"Yeah." She frowned at the floor in silence a second, then said with a petulant look, "I can't work on the yearbook tomorrow. Have a test to make up."

"Terrific. With all that we have to do."

"We'd probably only fool around anyway."

"No, we can't afford to, we don't have time."

She smiled. "Worried, Bear? Don't be, we'll wrap it up next week. I promise, we'll bust our asses."

"We'll have to."

She laughed, tears gone, and kissed his cheek. "I'll see you tomorrow night? At the usual place?"

"Sure."

"How's June?"

He wished to God she would stop these family references. "Much better."

"Good. Has she missed her pendant yet?"

"What?"

"You know, that silver pendant."

"Joy!"

She laughed again. "Hey, Bear, I only borrowed it."

"But you shouldn't *do* things like that."

She made a face. "Oh, what am I going to get, a lecture now? A spanking? Hey, that's something we haven't tried."

"Joy, I want it back. Tomorrow."

"Fine, fine, tomorrow night when I see you."

He shook his head. "I didn't expect that kind of behavior from you." The tone of his voice was precisely the tone he would use with Brad and Kim. He instantly regretted it.

Her gap-toothed grin. "Do you *want* to know what to expect from me? Wouldn't that be just too, too boring?" She kissed his cheek. "Gotta go now, I'll see you tomorrow."

The door wheezed shut. Alone, he felt slightly stunned. Why in the world had she done such a thing? What had ever possessed her? He looked at the table, the mess that would have to be squared away by next week, and thought: She's a kid. To her it's just a joke.

His eyes fell on a photo of Marty Zeller, taped to a sheet of copy—the yearbook's dedication. It said:

> *To the memory of Mr. Martin Zeller, whose caring was evident in all he did. To one who always thought of the little things, always lent a helping hand, always made each one of us feel special. Mr. Zeller, we'll really miss you.*

Ted stared at the photo, at Marty's defeated eyes, and thought of June's silver pendant, the inscription on its back:

> *To June, on our tenth anniversary.*
> *May there be a thousand more.*
> *With all my love forever, Ted.*

The bell rang, starting the period. He sighed, feeling heavy and sad. Four periods still to go. It was going to be a long day.

• • • • •

It turned out to be an even longer day than he'd feared.

When classes ended, he was cornered by Dora Rosen. LeMaster had asked her to see him; could he meet with her now for a minute or two? Depressed, Ted followed her to her office, a cubicle off the library. The nameplate on top of the cluttered desk said, MS. DORA ROSEN, LIBRARIAN. She closed the door, opened the window, and lit up a cigarette. Since smoking was totally banned in the school, Ted was shocked. They sat, and she brought out both of Dollinger's letters—the one to Grimsley and the one to the *Courier-News*—and Ted's (really Joy's) reply. She smoked and frowned and questioned him.

Did he have a copy of the library's book selection policy? He admitted that he did not. She smiled wryly, smoking, and gave him some xeroxed sheets. She didn't see how he had managed to draft a reply without knowing the policy, she said. Not that he'd done a bad job—as a matter of fact, she liked his letter—it was just kind of strange that he'd acted before consulting the school librarian.

He explained. Dora listened intently, nodding, and said, "I see. LeMaster. Mmmm. How interesting." They talked for half an hour, with Dora continually smoking, her lower lip protruding as she exhaled, a constant frown on her pixieish, round face. They would get together soon and draft a new letter. She assured him she understood why he'd acted without her. Even so, when he left he felt slightly chastised, and was more pissed off than ever at Marvin LeMaster.

When he got home he made June some tea, poured a scotch for himself, and read

Ms. Rosen's book selection policy, which he found intelligent and reasonable, though perhaps a touch too liberal for the public schools. Tired and a little high from the drink, he was starting to fix the meal, when Brad came home, walked into the kitchen, and, with a sick expression, gave him a note.

Ted read it in disbelief. Brad tried to explain. "No, I *don't* understand," Ted said as he slapped the note down on the kitchen table. "I don't!"

Brad's face was pathetic. He said, "Well, you wouldn't help me, you didn't have time—"

"So you copied Tammy Winslow's paper. Just copied it word for word."

Brad chewed on his lip. "Well, I changed a *few* things."

Grinding his teeth together, Ted said, "Oh, you did. How *big* of you. Good God, Brad, how dumb can you get, do you think Mrs. Harmer's a fool?"

Brad shrugged. "I just didn't know what to do."

"So you cheated."

"Yeah."

Ted thought of the paper he'd written for Joy and couldn't meet Brad's wet eyes as he said, "There's no excuse for cheating. I don't care *what* the circumstances are, there's simply no excuse."

Brad nodded. "I know. I'm sorry."

"Sorry? I *guess* you're sorry. You were first in line for the Veterans' Legion Award, and now your name's been taken off the list. Was it worth that to cheat?"

Brad chewed at his lip again and said, "I don't care about the Veterans' Legion Award."

"You don't."

"I feel bad about what I did, but not about the award. I don't even know what the Veterans' Legion *is*. They run a baseball league, that's all I know."

"That's all you know," Ted said. "Well, for your information, the Veterans' Legion's a hell of a lot more than running a baseball league, the Veterans' Legion is..." He stopped. "A *lot* of things!"

Brad looked up furtively. "You won it when you were in eighth grade, didn't you?"

"That's right, and I was damn proud of it, too!"

Brad frowned. "Yeah, but what did it mean? That you'd be a success or something?"

Ted could have slugged him. He said, "You'll rewrite the paper, do the extra assignment, and you're grounded for a week. You understand?"

Brad nodded, fresh tears welling up.

"Okay. And I don't ever want to hear that you've cheated again. I don't expect that kind of behavior from you."

The words went echoing through his brain. He had said the very same thing to Joy when he'd found out she'd taken June's pendant. He thought of that paper on "rain" again. If God was real and humanly vengeful, surely He would send the lightning now.

Brad sighed. Mouth quivering, he said, "You have to sign the note."

Ted snatched up a pen from the table and scrawled his name. Brad folded the paper and put it away. A tear rolled down one of his cheeks as he said, "Please...don't tell Mom."

Ted felt like a total cad. "Okay, I won't," he said.

Brad turned and went upstairs.

Ted sat at the table, completely wiped out. The Veterans' Legion Award. Today he'd win the Greatest Hypocrite Award hands down. He was thinking of pouring another drink when he heard June calling and went to the foyer. "Yes?"

Kim was watching TV in the family room. The CD was only $12.95 plus shipping and handling. "Kim, turn that down, I can't hear!"

June's voice again. "What was all the commotion?"

"Brad knocked something over, that's all."

"Could I have some more tea?"

"Sure."

He made it, sick with himself, and started dinner, a ground beef casserole. While he carried the tea upstairs, the garlic burned. Cursing, he chopped up another clove and glimpsed, through the window, a sudden white blur: T.S. Eliot taking off. After what? The Chryslers' cat? The Bonanzas' dog? The Bonanzas? He thought of Brad cheating again, of the paper he'd written for Joy, of Brad's mattress, that magazine—and the the telephone rang. It was Susan from LifeTime Books. He slammed her down. Kim was upstairs with Brad, doing battle. In the empty family room, the TV raged. June yelled at the kids and then called for some milk for her tea. T.S. Eliot barked to come in. The garlic was hopping around in the pot and Ted saved it in the nick of time.

When the dinner was finally over, he went upstairs to his study to grade compositions.

They were terrible, all of them, riddled with errors in spelling and grammar, confused in their logic. And these weren't freshmen but juniors; bright kids, the cream of the crop. What would it take to get them to write a clear sentence? A lot more than *he* had been giving them lately, that was for sure. For over a month now his classes had merely been drifting. It wasn't fair to them, he realized that, but one lapse in performance in sixteen years was certainly better than average. Half of his own high school teachers had been in a coma, and some of his colleagues, good lord...

He read the book selection policy again. As if he didn't have enough to do without loonies like Armand Dollinger. Religious loonies. He thought of that weird chain letter again (got cancer...went blind) and he had an idea.

He went for another glass of scotch, then turned his computer on. Stared at the screen a minute, then set to work. He wrote:

The Lord God Jesus Christ has Died for our Sins. "He that believeth in Me shall have Life Everlasting."

The letter you hold in your hands has gone around the world 19 times. Now I am sending it to you. Do not break the chain. Make 20 copies of this letter and send them to your friends and relatives within four days if you would have good luck. This is no Joke, it really works. Marlene Drubb, of Ice Cube, North Dakota, sent the letter out as directed and lost the unsightly embarrassing hair on her nipples. Joan Groan, of Heat, Ark., however, thought the letter was a joke, nine days later she choked to death on a chunk of snot the size of a billiard ball. Sister Rose Marie Blanch, of Our Lady of Perpetual Motion Convent, Dust, Oklahoma, answered the letter. She won a lifetime supply of Delfin Vaginal Foam. The Lord Thy God is a Jealous God. Alice Goon, of Moonscape, Utah, did not send the letter, 5 days later her buttocks were covered by a maculopapular pustular rash that necessitated 24 skin grafts. Fred Frump, who broke the chain, turned into a flaming queen. Jesus died so we could have Life Eternal. Jasper Wimp, of Dong, Minn., sent the letter. Three days later his penis grew two inches. Leonard Blup of Rust, Oregon, did not Believe and failed to send it out. Ten days later his cock fell off. This is no joke. Do not break the chain. God is the Light and the Life.

Ted read what he'd written. Not *quite* the tone of the original, but close enough. A few more comma splices? A few more superfluous capitals? The hell with it.

He folded the letter in thirds and stapled it shut (the stapler; Brad's room; *Spurts Illustrated;* Brad), addressed it to Armand Dollinger and affixed a stamp. Okay, you old fucker—or non-fucker, as the case may be—let's see what you make of this. He hoped the bastard would throw it away where Joy would find it, she'd love it.

• • • • •

That night (guilt over his childish deed?) he had a distressing dream.

He went to the bathroom to shave and the place was a shambles, with thousands of bottles and spray cans all over the floor. June was there in the mess; it was all her doing. He asked her where he could find his shaving cream. "In the medicine cabinet of course," she replied, but the problem was, there were dozens of medicine cabinets. He searched and searched as his beard grew rapidly, frighteningly, thick and dark. He tore off the cabinet doors and flung them about as Brad and Kim stood terrified. "What's the matter with you?" June shouted. Eyes blind with tears, Ted sobbed, "I'm having my mid-life crisis!" June said in a threatening voice, "Your *what?* I won't *let* you!" A murderous anger flooded him then. "You won't *let* me!" he screamed. "What the hell do you *mean* you won't let me? After all that I've done for you!"

He woke up to June's snoring. Furious with her, he gave her a poke in the ribs.

"Hey!"

"Oh!" He shuddered, himself again, not dream-Ted now. "Oh, sorry, June, you were snoring."

"Well God, take it easy, I just had an operation."

"I'm really sorry," Ted said. And he really was.

20 • THE CASTLE OF FEAR

She was wearing a navy blue skirt and a buff-colored V-necked blouse. The pendant hung in the depths of the braless plunge, its inscription against her cleft. It reminded Ted of those years with a different June, good years, and he wanted to tear it away, shove it down out of sight somewhere.

She started the Honda's engine, backed up, and drove through the parking lot. The tape was blasting,

Hot, it's so hot
And I'll show you what I got...

And it *was* hot, unusually sticky for spring. She squealed out onto the street. The windows were open, the sunroof was open, her hair was a golden banner in the sunset breeze. A marijuana cigarette lay on the dash, and she nodded at it. "Light that for me, will you, Bear?"

He did, and handed it to her. She smoked with an arrogant thrust of her chin, then gave it back, and he took a reluctant drag. *In the dark I'll turn your head around,* sang the tape. She was taking a street he didn't know. Still disturbed by the pendant he said, "So where are we going?"

She smiled, looking over the wheel. "You'll find out soon, it's a surprise."

"I don't usually like surprises."

She took the joint and smoked again. "Hey, where's your spontaneity?" Lifting her eyebrows, she held out the cigarette.

He'd been to The Spouting Whale and had drunk three beers and figured he'd better go light on the dope. "No thanks," he said.

She frowned. "Is something wrong with you?"

"That pendant bothers me," he said. "I'd like you to take it off."

"I will, Bear—in due time." She smoked again.

"I don't understand why you took it."

She shrugged. "I felt the need for something personal, something connected to you."

"I still—"

"Let's not make a big deal out of things, okay?"

She turned a corner—Exxon station and a bank—and sucked the joint.

"How come you always smoke that stuff?" he said.

She made a sour-looking face. "What is this, pick on Joy Dollinger night? Can't you take the suspense? Okay, I'll tell you where we're going, then—we're going to a carnival."

"A carnival?"

"First one of the year. Sid's Spectacular Shows, outside Pittsville."

"A *carnival.* Good God, you'd probably like Disney World."

She held out the joint with a grin and he shook his head no. One last huge drag and she snuffed it out; said, "I *love* Disney World. I went there when I was a kid, I have this aunt who lives near Orlando. But Sid's has a special ambiance that Disney definitely lacks—the tackiest rides in the world, and not only that, a skinny show. You ever seen one?"

He shook his head no again.

Looking incredulous: "Never?"

"Never."

She laughed. "Well do you ever have a treat in store for you, old Teddy Bear!"

She wheeled around another corner—Texaco and 7-Eleven (his neighbor's place? He didn't know)—and directly ahead were the lights: the sparkling ring of ferris wheel, the plunge of roller coaster, whirl of that horrible space ship thing; then tents and posters and booths and the backdrop sky, a dolorous orange-pink.

He hadn't been to a carnival in at least ten years. The closest he'd come was some fleabag circus in Barrenwold, a benefit for retarded kids that Joe Bishop had dragged him to, a pathetic affair with one "wild" beast—a mangy leopard just slightly bigger (and considerably tamer) than the Chryslers' cat—and a half dozen fraudulent clowns. "You sure about this?" he said.

"Positively."

She drove into the parking area, found a space, cut the engine and lights. The whomp-and-toodle carnival music was suddenly right beside them. Behind the slat and wire fence a merry-go-round pumped its baggage of snotnosed toddlers. In the line Joy said, "My treat," and bought handfuls of tickets, dark purple coils.

They pushed their way through the mob to a stand where she bought cotton candy, two huge spools. Ted loathed the stuff, had always loathed it, even as a kid. Joy's tongue flicked eagerly through the pink as she said, "Come on, eat up."

Ted munched the horror listlessly. Around him milled shaggy tattooed toughs, pregnant teens without teeth, giggling hags with pale ulcerous shins and sagging white socks. Nearly everybody, regardless of age, sex, or body type, wore a T-shirt. The "Do it" and "Shit" themes seemed most prevalent: "Mercenaries Do It For Profit." "Do It With Technique." "I'm So Happy I Could Shit" and its converse, "I'm So Pissed I Could Shit." "If You Ain't A Cowboy You Ain't Shit." What was the point of teaching grammar? Teaching anything? The point of life? On a woman with breasts as huge as basketballs: "National Sex Week—Give Till It Hurts." On a lean, scarred, mean-looking dude about fifty or so, a vicious silkscreened rooster and: "Super Cock."

Her mouth filled with sugary wool, lights pulsing across her face, Joy shouted above the din, "I forgot to tell you about your paper on rain."

"What about it?"

"Burk gave it a 'B'."

Ted stared. "He *what?*"

She munched with a little shrug. "Said it wasn't detailed enough."

Fury rose to Ted's throat. "Not *detailed* enough! Why that ignorant asshole, I ought to— Oh Jesus, *now* look!"

His fist had brought the pink mess to his leg and now clots of it clung to his pants. They reminded him of an insulation job he'd once done.

Joy laughed. She lapped her concoction avidly, already down to the stick.

"Want the rest of this shit?" Ted said with a scowl, and she shook her head no. "Where's a trash can?" he said.

"Just drop it, Bear."

He did, and it instantly found the foot of a vacuous two year old, hand caught in the palm of fat mamma. "Oh Jesus Christ, Hector!" mamma shrieked, "aincha got any brains in ya goddamn head?" Hector started to bawl.

"I'll still get an 'A' in English in spite of the paper," Joy said, "but it *was* kind of disappointing."

"*Disappointing*," Ted said. "I could *strangle* him! Burk the Jerk! How *dare* he give me a 'B'!"

She discarded her stick with a flip of her wrist. "Hey Bear, don't take it so hard."

They were standing beside the Star Invader, a mean-looking thing with missile-shaped, rotating cars. "First stop," Joy said.

"You're kidding," Ted said. "You expect me to ride on *that?*"

"Come on, Bear, loosen up."

"Joy, I really don't want—"

With a laugh, she grabbed his hand and pulled. "Come *on!*"

She gave the laconic tattooed kid some tickets; they entered the ride, sat across from each other; the kid clamped a metal bar over their laps with sadistic authority, locking them in. Ted tried to look only at Joy and not at the ground as with each new rider their ship jerked another notch higher.

Midway to the zenith, the huge wheel sprang into action: Up flew the car with gut-wrenching speed to its peak, then dived straight at the earth. Ted was sure the machine had malfunctioned and he would be flattened, but after a dizzying spin at the perigee, into the carnival-colored sky he rose once more, his heart whacking wildly, doppler-like shrieks from the other cars warping his ears. His wind-whipped panicky mind said: *No! I'm too old! This could kill me, I'm too damn old!*

Toward land again, and he closed his eyes. Joy laughed. The car began to rotate clockwise and his stomach churned. Another flip, then a spin in reverse, guts sloshing. All at once he was falling backward and Joy was above him, her face alight with a happy and mocking grin. He skimmed the earth then whipped skyward again, the objects on the ground receding, his stomach against his throat.

When the torment finally stopped he was shaking, his heart was racing, his stomach was queasy and full. The tattooed kid released him and he staggered away with weak knees. He braced himself against a post and Joy said laughing, "Too much for you, Bear?"

He tried to smile. "I'm afraid the merry-go-round is more my speed."

"I *loved* it," she said. "But you don't have to go on more rides if you don't enjoy them."

"Thanks."

He stayed in the crowd as she rode the Killer Coaster and Whirl-Around. The latter was a spider-like monstrosity that shot you outward with horrible force then dropped you, spun you, tossed you up. Just watching it made Ted sick. Each whirl flung June's pendant away from Joy's neck, to shine like a fishing lure in the sleazy light. Ted felt like a father showing his kid a good time, and wished they had never come to this goddamn place.

A sequence of flashing orange bulbs ringed the stand where Joy ate. She held out her chili dog. "Bite?"

"I just want to get out of here."

"Hey, the night's still young, we haven't seen what we came for yet."

"I don't know if I want to see that."

Wiping her mouth with her napkin and drinking some Coke, she said, "Of course you do. You'll love it, Bear."

The tent was a filthy blue and white striped affair with the red silhouette of a naked woman on it. The scrawny old guy at the entrance took tickets with washed-out eyes.

Inside, it was hot and dim; everybody was quiet and glum. It smelled like manure and sweat, and Ted's stomach felt queasy again. In they came, in they came, like lambs to the slaughter, packing the place. Every move meant a touch, meant a rub, and good God it was hot: hot breath, hot sweat, and the radiant heat of lust. Ted was much too close to these farmers and hoods, these pseudo-cowboys with chains on their necks, and he wanted air. Amazing how very few people spoke. More amazing still, the advanced age of some of the patrons. A couple of dudes across the way were eighty if they were a day. Joy was the only female in sight, as far as Ted could see.

In the background, filtered through canvas and heat, came the screams of the Whirl-Around riders outside, a kid crying, the clatter and hoot.

A dull spotlight splashed on, roamed, then jerked into place on the stage. Scratchy raunchy taped music began, and the woman appeared.

She was thirty or so, on the doughy side, with a brown-red hair and freckle combination that had never appealed to Ted. She wore a bikini outfit (black) and went into a listless leaden trot out of step with the blaring tune. Within less than a minute her top had come off, exposing her floppy loose breasts. A few cheers from the crowd, and Joy put her hand on Ted's crotch and began to rub.

The dancer turned her back on the audience, spreading her legs. With a quizzical, teasing look she peered over her shoulder while wiggling her ample rump. "Yeah! Yeah!" came the shouts, and she pulled the bikini string. The sad scrap of cloth fell away and Ted looked at her cleft, puckered anus, gross rust-colored hair.

Joy was working her fingers along his horn and in spite of himself he grew hard. As he watched the woman shuffle in dust, the spotlight white on her shiny caesarean scar, he was struck by a powerful feeling of *deja vu*: he had been in this tent with this woman before, years ago, in another life. What had triggered this weird idea? Thoughts of the burlesque show he had gone to in college? No, not that...

He needed to stand on his toes to get a good view, so stand on his toes he did, in spite of the fact that his stomach felt awful and all that he wanted to do was escape from this sexual sauna, flee this crowd. Sweating profusely, he looked at Joy; not a drop on her face. Working away on his organ, her lips pressed together, she said, "You catching this, Bear?" And the redhead, legs wide, was inserting a candle with steady firm pressure. It disappeared. The crowd grunted and snickered and laughed.

The woman stood grinning, retaining the candle, and then, by exerting the right combination of muscle, expelled the shaft onto the floor. Much commotion among the boys. Ted kept thinking in feverish heat that he knew this woman, had seen her before. But where?

She provoked a low rumble and gasp by producing a dildo. With a lustful gyra- tion she lowered her opening over it, taking it in. Dead quiet: a reverent hush. Outside, in another dimension, the screams of the Whirl-Around riders rose and died. In and in went the tube. The somehow familiar face was intense as the freckled hand steadily pushed. Ted felt his blood choke the bones of his skull, then the dildo was gone and the lights went out—and the woman's lower regions were glowing a dull blood-red.

"Cute trick, huh Bear?" Joy said with a squeeze on his joint. Salty sweat in his mouth and he thought he might faint. Then the spotlight came on again and the dildo- flashlight, shimmering now, was withdrawn. The assemblage cackled and clapped.

The redhead shined the light on a bald-headed man up front. "Now here's where it starts to get good," Joy said.

The bald guy stepped forward; the redhead said something absorbed by the tent, flashed a smile (two upper left front teeth gone), and then plucked at her crotch. She dropped the hairs curling and live on the bald guy's pate, and the gang went wild.

There was jockeying then, a shifting around, a semblance of order forming. "Now the best part," Joy said. "Chow line."

"Chow line?" Ted said, not liking the way he felt, needing air, needing sun on water, sky, a mountain, solitude. He wished to God she'd leave his pants alone.

"Look," she said; and a huge gross greasy hulk in a T-shirt, arms covered with fur, had grabbed the dancer—both hands on her cellulite rump—and had buried his face in her V. She laughed and went on with some patter Ted couldn't make out. All he heard was her voice, a high childlike nasal whine. She dispatched the gorilla and took on the next admirer, a runt about seventy-five with the pasty gray skin of an intensive care parolee. This fellow went at his task with exquisite calm and delicacy, as if any exertion would certainly do him in. Much laughter ensued.

"Finger me," Joy said.

"Joy..."

"Put your hand up my dress and do it."

He didn't move, so she grabbed his hand and shoved it up under her skirt. He felt her mound, slipped his fingers inside her panties. "Good, oh good, go on, go on," she said, and he did, staring straight ahead. The redheaded focus of lust seemed more and more familiar (who? where? when?), and all he could think of was church, the Eucharist, each worshipper taking his turn.

A tattooed and muscled young stud grabbed the harlot hard, shoved his angular face in her groin. She winced; then her face relaxed with a septic smile—

And Ted knew who she was. Good God, she was—

Sissy!

Sissy what? Some Polish name. How long ago? Oh long ago, when he was a new recruit at Whitman High. She'd been one of those dreadful cipherous pupils hell-bent on destroying each lesson, on mocking all learning, apparently having been put on this earth to snicker, pass notes, fool around. She had fooled around once too often; got pregnant; dropped out to the faculty's great relief.

And that's who it was! That horrible Sissy Whateverski, that's who it *was!*

His hand was stiff, immobile in Joy's soft pants. He felt suddenly cold. "Don't stop, Bear, please don't stop!" she said, but he sharply withdrew. She laughed disgustedly. "You think she's better than I am, Bear? Want to give her a try?"

"Joy, I have to get out of here."

He was struck by a wild fear that the crowd was comprised of his old pupils too, former classmates of Sissy's, come to pay their respects.

"What the hell is the matter with you?" Joy said. "You can't stop *now,* I'm on the *edge!*"

He was sure he would die on the spot. Fingers slick with her liquid, he pushed through the crowd. She pursued, saying, "Bear, come on, don't go, we might get to see..."

In the air, in the darkness of carnival music and spin, he stood in the shadows behind a baseball pitching booth as she said, "For Christ's sake, what is *wrong* with you? You've been no fun all night."

He breathed deeply, a long weary sigh, and said, "That dancer—I had her at Whitman, years ago."

Surprise; delight; a laugh. "You're kidding!"

"I wish I were. Her name was Sissy something, something Polish. My God what a horrible kid she was!"

"You're sure that's who it is?"

"It has to be. It looks just like her."

The ersatz buttery popcorn smell turned his stomach. He thought of June with her ovaries gone; of Kim, eleven years old. He watched the families roam among booths, rides, ripoffs, the toddlers clutching their parents' hands for dear life. He looked at the tent where, mired in heat and aroma, the chow line took its sustenance from Sissy Terroriski, Caesarean War vet (that flat white abdominal scar!). He started to walk away to he didn't know where.

Beside him, Joy said, "Jeez, Bear, you should've jumped in. 'Hey Sissy, remember me? Mr. Wharton from freshman English?' She'd probably give you an extra minute or two."

126

"She *did* tell me to kiss her ass once."

Laughing, Joy said, "No, turn around, Sissy, I don't want your *front*." Her grin; her parted teeth. "Well, wasn't it just the *tackiest?* The most of the gross? The *old* dudes are the ones who knock me out. One foot in the grave, and they're still sniffing at it like dogs. A good lesson to learn at my age."

"Why?"

"It just is."

"*All* men aren't like that."

"Oh yeah? If you find one who isn't, you let me know."

They had walked through a valley of relative shadow (the rear of concession stands; a stench of seared meat and assorted glop) and were now in a sequin-bright lane of amusements again—and the racket, the flash, the jostle of hostile hedonists. Ted's stomach still felt unsettled, his nerves were frayed, he just wanted *out* of this place.

He opened his mouth to convey his desire to Joy when he suddenly froze in his tracks. He grabbed her hand and turned abruptly, jerking her around.

With a look of surprise and annoyance she said, "*Now* what? *Now* what are you doing?"

"It's Kim!" he said.

"Oh no! Oh shit!"

"She's right behind us! Jesus Christ!"

Joy squeezed his hand tightly. "Come on!"

He ran with her through the crowd. "The gate's over there," he said.

She ignored him, pulling him, turning a corner and mounting some steps—and they stood at The Castle of Fear.

"Joy, what—?"

She gave the guy tickets. "It's perfect," she said. "There's an empty car right up front, in a minute or two we'll be gone."

"But Joy, I don't want—"

"What." She glared. "Don't want what, do you want to get caught?"

Resigned to his fate, he followed her into the car. They sat in the tiny seat, jammed into each other. He bent his head, put his hand up to cover his face, thinking: What if they come this way? —If they take this *ride?* He glanced to the side, still hiding himself with his hand. No sign of Kim or those she was with, obnoxious Joanie Dangerman and her still more obnoxious mother. With a neck-jarring jerk, the car moved forward, then stopped again. Come on, come on, let's get this show on the road!

He peeked to the left again; no Kim. Come on, come on! Ahead of him, the castle wall—gray phony stone, with painted bats and the comical-horrid gaping mouth of Dracula, King of Darkness. He ached to be swallowed alive by those sheltering jaws, to be out of this harsh, condemning light. The crowd filed by like the throng at a movie star's funeral. What dangers lurked in its core? Kids from Whitman? His neighbors? Maybe even LeMaster or Grimsley, who knew, who knew? The car cranked closer to the mouth. Ted closed his eyes, a cold slick sweat on his face. His stomach felt horrible now.

"Hey Bear, it's going to be all right." She was smiling. Actually smiling!

The car made a grinding, rasping groan, and clickety-slap they were violently yanked into black. A mechanical shriek, a maniacal ear-splitting laugh somewhere off to the left, and Joy yelled, "Quickly! We have to work fast! These rides don't last very long!"

Disoriented by racket and dark, Ted shouted, "What?" The hot stuffy wind on his face made him almost gag. Then he realized his pants were being unzipped; and his member was out and her face was down in his lap.

"Joy!"

Lightning flash of bright blue; gargoyle heads dangling over their car and then blackness again. "Joy! Don't!" He was wet and warm, felt her working away, was terrified. Aroused in spite of all that was decent by horrible Sissy's performance, his feeling rose.

More light, harsh crimson this time, with satan's leering face and piercing laugh. A flashbulb shot of Joy's hair, her mouth, and he thought: *This girl is nuts!*

"Joy, Joy…" June's pendant bouncing up and down on his root. He felt almost like crying, yet still his sensation was strong. In the wild hot wind she hollered, "Hurry, Bear, hurry!"

"Joy, please!"

"I *want* you to! You *have* to, before the ride ends!" And then she was jerking him with her hand, jerking frantically, desperately, hard.

A rush of mechanical bats, blue whoosh overhead. She yanked. Another crash of light. A witch on a broomstick flying away, old Frankenstein's monster gawking, and Joy kept working, her hand pulling faster, her voice in his ear saying, "Now, Bear, now!" and he thought: This ride will be *over* soon, we'll be *outside!* Then his fear and dismay came boiling up, splattering out—

And he felt no pleasure at all, just pain, excruciating icepick pain, and he cried out into the dark as the werewolf howled. An instant of noon-bright light and the girl in the car in front of them, her head craned in shocked astonishment, saw all.

Something cobwebby tickled his face. A scatter of yellow bulbs and he saw the crowd, the ferris wheel, the distant Whirl-Around. He'd been thoroughly tucked away and zipped by Joy, who sat primly, hands crossed in her lap. The pain in his rectum was almost gone, but his heart was fluttering, swooping in terror as the car slowed, creaked to a stop.

The girl in front put her hand to her mouth and whispered to her companion. Ted frantically scanned the bobbing mass of faces and saw—no Kim, nobody he knew. "Joy, we have to get out of here—now!"

He checked his crotch; his pants were clean. Joy grinned. That goddamn pendant!

"Joy! Wipe your mouth!"

She did—with her tongue. "Sorry, Bear, I must be slipping."

On the gravelly ground he felt weak and unsteady.

"Some ride, hey, Bear? A real libido-meter job, right over the top!"

He nodded, exhausted, his rectum tight. "Right over the top," he said. "Come on, let's *go.*"

· · · · ·

The sunroof still open, weak stars overhead, she drove. In a matter-of-fact and confident voice she said, "So when are you going to leave her, Bear?"

He stared through the windshield, sick and melancholy. "I don't know," he said.

"I hope it's soon." Quick glance and a smile. "I'd be terribly lonely at Aubrey without you."

He sighed, collapsing inside. "These things take time."

"You old guys always say that. Just walk *away*."

"It's not that simple."

"I don't mean now, while she's sick, but once she gets better, why wait? You might as well get it over with."

"Might as well," he said.

When they got to the shopping center lot she kissed his cheek. "I had a terrific time, Bear, did you?"

He looked at her, sad and confused. "Sure," he said.

"I'm glad," She reached behind her neck; unclasped the pendant; took it off. "Don't want to forget about this," and she handed it over. In his palm it felt magical, precious.

When her taillights were gone and he was alone in the Plymouth, he looked at the pendant. The pink lonely glow of the towering lamp highlighted its design: a rose, June's favorite flower. What masochistic need made him turn the thing over, he didn't know.

To June, on our tenth anniversary.
May there be a thousand more.
With all my love forever, Ted.

His rectum burning, his mind still dancing with horrible Sissy, Joy's question— When are you going to leave her, Bear?—still ringing in his ears, he started the car.

When he pulled out into the street, there were tears in his eyes.

21 • SPOONFEATHER DEATH

After the next time they did it he went to the motel bathroom (Surprise Motel: appropriate name, as fate would have it) and urinated blood.

He managed to con an emergency appointment out of Dr. Dickle's receptionist. Dickle was the guy that he and June had seen for bladder infections years ago, the guy who'd discovered June's polyps. Ted tried for appointments with three unknown urologists first, but all were booked solid for periods ranging from four to six months. Only his status as a long established patient of Dr. Dickle's (three visits eight years before) and a heap of persuasion ("Blood. Pain. Discharge.") allowed him to crash the line that would never terminate—even when the doctor himself had terminated—but would simply submit to a different set of instruments, a different pair of hands. Ted supposed if it hadn't been for his veteran standing and debating skills, he'd have been abandoned, fated to bleed to death through his damaged tube.

Actually, the Surprise Motel surprise was the only time he saw blood. But Christ, that spicy apple up his tail, the effort it took to urinate! For a week he did nothing with Joy—except work like a fiend on the yearbook (still not done!). When she tried to start up, he pleaded intestinal flu.

Awaiting the lab reports, he kept busy, busy; grading assignments (he'd given a ton of them lately), doing jobs around the house (almost got to the leak in the roof, but thought better of it), even going to one of Brad's baseball games (two hits and a diving catch). His activity didn't distract him sufficiently though, and he thought of the frightening possibilities over and over again: Some horrid disease? A virulent teenage strain immune to antibiotics and fatal to those over twenty? (Joy had lain with that scum Rod Rheingold—and others? so it just might be.) A ruined prostate, which had to be reamed away with potentially dire results? Not AIDS, it couldn't be AIDS, these weren't the symptoms, but maybe (oh God) he did have the dreaded Big C, apt punishment for trying to beat time's game, death's game.

And if he *did?* The torture and diminution, that's what he dreaded, not death. Dragging on and on in illness and pain like old Walt Whitman—horrible. But the end of consciousness, was *that* so bad? What was the point of it all anyway? More crepes and steak, more wine, more ejection of sperm? Was he living for June and the kids? If he died, would they even *miss* him? He certainly wasn't living to see the world, like June. The "world" was the same stale advertising hoax no matter where you went. (The castles, the beaches, the platters of food.) Was his mission on earth to impart precious knowledge to acne-pocked ingrates who thought the sole purpose of school was to help them land better jobs? Some mission. When he thought about it, it really didn't make sense to continue, and yet...

He remembered that tabloid headline, "New Proof! There *Is* Life After Death!" God forbid! If he had to go, what he wanted was sweet oblivion, the nothingness he'd known before birth. How tragic that life was so stuck on itself in spite of its grievous faults. The Buddhists were probably right: the very desire to stay alive was the most grievous fault of all.

The concept of immortality had never made sense to Ted; it was more than his mind could grasp. What could heaven consist of? Eternal youth? With its endless frustration and hopeless passion? Eternal middle age? With its boredom and repetition? Maybe you'd constantly swing back and forth from infancy to senescence: one year goo-goo, one year ga-ga. Oh God, if there is a God, please, just let the lights go out.

But not yet. Not right this minute.

No? Why not? Did he really believe there was some dark undiscovered mystery that could give his existence *meaning?* And that he could *find* it? Or did he just want more Joy?

They do not sweat and whine about their condition,/ They do not lie awake in the dark and weep for their sins,/ They do not make me sick discussing their duty to God...

Whitman was in hell, of course, for such blasphemy. And yet there existed the Whitman Bridge, the Whitman Mall, the Whitman Plaza (luxury "homes"), Walt Whitman High School, and he wondered: would fame like this come to Henry Miller one day? Would there someday be a Henry Miller High? (It sounded like a triple X show at the Pikesboro Drive-In.) A Henry Miller Shopping Center, perhaps? (That strip of motel and porno palaces on General Haze Boulevard?) No, it would never be.

Why was that lab taking so damn *long?* Was it doing additional studies to confirm...? He kept busy. And his meetings with Dora Rosen, which only a week before would have been unbearable, were a welcome distraction now.

This Dora was a deceptively tough cookie. Soft-spoken and thoughtful, she was nevertheless quite determined and stubborn. At their first two meetings they analyzed her book selection policy in great detail. They had to be perfectly clear on the policy, she said, before they could draft another reply to Dollinger.

Ted questioned the word "recreational" under the "challenged materials" paragraph. "Any work without educational, artistic, literary or *recreational* merit." In his opinion, such a broad definition of "objectionable" would allow nearly anything. Staring him right in the eye, Dora asked, "Well what do you think I'm going to do, stock the library with hard-core porn?" They hashed the issue over for forty-five minutes. Dora put up a valiant tussle, but Ted finally won.

They went over the letter that Ted (really Joy) had written. Dora thought it was fine. (Wouldn't Joy be pleased?) "As a matter of fact, it's a lot like the letter *I* sent to Dollinger." The letter *she* had sent?

At the open house, Dollinger had complained to her about various books—and had asked for the names of the children who'd checked them out. She'd refused his request, of course, and had put her refusal in writing, sending a photocopy to Howard Grimsley.

Grimsley didn't like her letter (it had sparked the first missive from Dollinger), and the next thing she knew, he had asked Ted (through Marvin LeMaster) to fire the next shot. He had criticized Ted's attempt too, and now he was asking both of them to draft the third reply. He trusted them jointly, but not on their own? The whole was greater than the sum of its parts?

Third meeting; reply still not drafted—not even *begun.* When the hell was LeMaster going to form his committee? Were these letter-writing assignments the tryouts? If so, Ted had luckily flunked the first round. Thinking about the lab again, he said, "Dora, just what *is* this *Our Bodies Belong to Us?* I've never seen it."

She was smoking again. In her office she always did, in spite of the rules, and now she exhaled in her typical manner, projecting her lower lip, then went to the shelves and came back with a large format paperback book in the overdone catalog style.

Ted took it, glancing at the cover photo of women linked arm in arm. It reminded him of a thirties Communist propaganda poster. He turned to the first page mentioned in Dollinger's letter, page 42.

—And was taken aback to see a young woman in stirrups, legs spread. To his great chagrin he blushed as he said, "It *is* pretty explicit."

Dora smiled a puckish, wry smile. "Whose side are you on, anyhow?"

He laughed and turned to the next page Dollinger listed, page 52.

A baby's head extending from the "birth canal," as they called the vagina at this and no other moment. "The facts of life," he said with a little shrug.

"So you approve?"

"Sure."

"And what do you think of the first photograph—the gynecology exam?"

He didn't commit himself. With a smile he said, "One thing about Armand, he lets you know right away where the good parts are."

Page 90: Two women in rugged attire and defiant smiles, arms over each other's shoulders. Under the photo, a treatise on woman-to-woman love; how Donna and Gladys had found each other, their first shy physical contacts, their decision to live together. The reaction of the community, etc., etc.

"Well?" Dora said.

"Reality."

Smoking, Dora said, "Some of the kids in this school don't know this kind of love relationship *exists.* Some of them, believe it or not, have never even *looked* at themselves—at their intimate parts. They've been taught that it's bad, that it's *dirty* to look at themselves." She scowled in her anxious, questioning way. "Isn't that awful? To grow up thinking that some of your body—some part of what you were *born* with—is bad? This book explores these kinds of concerns in the words of women who've dealt with them, who've come to terms with them. I think it can be a tremendous help to kids whose minds are filled with myths and half-truths and unwarranted fears." Unblinking, she stared at him.

He picked up his pen and prepared to write. If they didn't get down to this letter soon, they never would. He said, "Could you repeat that, please?"

Her ironic smile. "Quite an outburst, huh?"

They worked on the letter for over an hour. LeMaster and Grimsley would probably tear it to shreds, but Ted thought it was good: low-keyed and reasonable, but firm.

Dora had given the issue a lot of thought. With her nervous and somehow coercive frown she said, "If you let them ban one book, you open the gates, and soon it becomes ridiculous. *Huckleberry Finn*'s been banned in a couple of places, you know."

"I heard about that."

"In Illinois, they claimed it was racist."

"While it's just the opposite."

She smoked. "In California, the objection was different; some people felt it depicted a homosexual relationship."

"Absurd."

"Of course. But what if it *were* a homosexual relationship? Should that be reason enough to ban it?"

Her sharp eyes made him uneasy, and all at once it occurred to him that *Ms.* Rosen, thirtyish, unmarried, just might be… Oh boy, wouldn't *that* be a pretty mess? To have *Our Bodies Belong to Us* defended by a lesbian? Dollinger would have a field day. Ted tried to be cagey: "Do *you* think that should be reason enough to ban it?"

Dora didn't hesitate. "Of course not!" She took a huge drag of her cigarette, squinting, and snuffed it out in the ashtray. It seemed impossible for her lungs to have held all the smoke she exhaled. She said, "An Ohio school board almost pulled *Tarzan* off the shelves."

"*Tarzan?*"

"He and Jane never tied the knot."

"Oh, brother."

"Know what kills me about all this?" Dora said as they left, as she clicked out the lights, locked the door. "*Our Bodies Belong to Us* has been borrowed exactly six times since we've had it here. If it's smut, it sure isn't turning on kids at Whitman High."

As Ted wondered about her again, he thought of the porno shops and *Talented Tongues* and *Thigh to Thigh*. "Just between you and me," he said, "do you have anything that *would* turn them on?"

Lifting her eyebrows, she smiled and said, "They might try *Slaughterhouse-Five, Beloved, Of Mice and Men*."

"*Of Mice and Men?*" he said. "Bestiality leaves me cold."

She looked at him oddly. Offended? Confused? Had he gone too far? Then she laughed sharply, brightly, and Ted laughed too.

•••••

He didn't have any fatal disease, he wasn't doomed, it was simply that "The human fabric becomes less elastic with age, less capable of withstanding stress." In other words, he thought as he listened to Dr. Dickle's drone, time wipes you *out*.

Ted hated physicians. They could never pronounce words right, never laughed at your jokes, and had odious habits like reading the Sunday *New York Times* no matter where they lived. Dr. Dickle, typical of the breed, had the odious habit of pressing his palms together and touching his index fingers to his nose. He was sitting in this pseudo-thoughtful fashion as he said: "You've been giving your sexual equipment too much of a workout, you've got to slow down. Daily intercourse for a man your age is too strenuous over more than a brief time period. You'll have to refrain completely till the symptoms subside, then resume on a gradual basis—say once a week for the next two weeks, twice a week for the two weeks following that, etc."

Etc., Ted thought as the doctor frowned, his fingertips still in his nose, as if he were puzzled by something; as if there were some connection he ought to be making; as if in his overscheduled mind he saw someone he knew, some woman whose ovaries he'd just removed and who somehow had something to do with the sex life of this man he was talking to. Pretty sure that the link would never be forged, Ted felt reasonably safe. Dan Jefferson, a former colleague, had gone to the same fertility specialist as his wife. The doctor had treated them separately, Dan for a prostate infection and Gloria, his wife, for blocked fallopian tubes. After months of treatment he'd called them into his office—separately again—to tell Dan he was cured and would soon be a father; to tell Gloria she would never have children. Physicians, oh yes, they were peaches, all right.

Sure enough, Dickle's frown dissolved. He leaned forward again, hands away from his nose, and told Ted to call him again in two weeks if the abstinence didn't suffice. If it didn't, they'd have to consider (unspecified) treatment, okay?

"Okay," Ted said.

Dickle smiled then, as if he'd remembered a joke or had worked some miracle, and bade Ted good day.

•••••

Refrain completely. It wasn't *Dickle* who had to put Joy off. The day the yearbook was finally ready to ship to the printer, she said, "We did it, Bear! Let's celebrate!"

He made a face. "This flu…"

"Flu schmoo. God, Bear, it's been over a week, don't you love me anymore?" — One hand on his cheek and the other between his legs.

It *had* been over a week, and desire spread into his throat. He grew.

"You *do* still love me!" Her teasing smile.

"Joy, listen, we…need to come to an understanding."

"Let's not," she said. "Let's screw instead."

"Tomorrow night."

"No, *now*. I didn't get it all last week and I want it *now*." She was rubbing her hands along her thighs and hiking her flimsy skirt. Ted's heart began skipping all over the place and his mouth felt rubbery, weak.

She lifted her skirt to her hips—to reveal bikini underpants he'd never seen before, a diaphanous wedge of film rimmed with pale blue lace. "Bear, Bear," she whispered, rubbing against him, her skirt still high, and he groaned.

133

The hell with Dr. Dickle. The hell with his "aging fabric." Seven days without screwing makes one weak (to paraphrase a sign he'd seen on a pizza place), and he set to work as if he were back when his system was fresh and strong. They were well along the primrose path when the knocking began at the door—which was locked, he'd made sure of that.

"Hello? Is anyone in there? Hello?" —Ethel Spoonfeather's piping voice.

"Jesus Christ, not again!" Ted said.

"Don't answer it," Joy said—astride him on the table, bouncing, breathing fast.

"We *have* to answer!"

Gritting her teeth, she pumped like mad. "No, no, we can't! If we don't, she'll go away!"

She was doing it *too* hard now and he winced as he said, "She has a key! She'll catch us! Joy—"

She shook her head, lips pressed together. "No!" she said, and clutched his shoulders, her nails digging into his flesh. "Don't stop! Don't stop!"

He was raw, he was numb. "Joy…"

She stared at him hard with those grayblue eyes and said, "Spoonfeather is Death! Death always knocking, coming for us, we have to defeat it, we must!"

"A key!" he said. "I hear a key!" and he slid off the table, taking her with him, slipped out, jammed his member away. As her feet hit the floor, she said with a hoarse flat gasp, "It beat us, it beat us!"

The door came open. Joy stood at the table, assuming an air of complete composure as Ted, his voice disintegrated, said, "Hello, did you want me?"

Ethel Spoonfeather's face had a puckered look, as if she smelled something rank. "I want Joy," she said.

Joy leafed through a pile of papers and said, "Well, here I am. Or you want me to come to your office?"

"As soon as you can," said Miss Spoonfeather, smiling.

"I'll be right there."

Ethel Spoonfeather left and Ted closed the door. A sickening watery chill swept through him; his forehead was pocked with sweat.

Joy smiled. "What's wrong? Flu attack?"

He didn't like the tune his heart was playing on his ribs. He said: "That's it, we can't use this room anymore."

She shrugged. "Of course we can."

"We can't, we'll get caught. We're bound to get caught."

"You mean no more tapes?"

"No more tapes." His heart was crazy, quick and light, completely beyond his control.

"Bear, what's happened to you?" A frown; those cool blue eyes. "We almost beat Death, we almost did, we had it on the run, and you let it win."

Ted's heart abruptly slowed; he felt the sudden scary shift. "Nobody beats Death," he said. "You've read Shakespeare and Donne and the rest and you ought to know that."

He expected a protest. None came, and she didn't try to start up again. Instead she simply looked at him, expressionless, her blue eyes beautiful and calm. She said, "I have to see Spoonfeather now" and left the room.

22 • PROMISES

The following night, in the Monaco Motel (a velvet portrait of Princess Grace in the office), they finished what they had started the day before. Age gave Ted one dubious edge over youth: he could hold back damn near forever. Yesterday's passion had faded as soon as Joy left for Miss Spoonfeather's office, and hadn't resurfaced till now. Let a twenty-year-old try that!

His organs felt okay, thank God, but he couldn't get into things. The marijuana made him too mellow, too bland. When he worked from behind he observed a small pimple above her tattoo and he wished he could wish it away. His mind roamed as it did when he made it with June, and release brought a hot gush of sadness and high dull pain—a pain reminiscent of that caused by Dickle's sheathed finger.

They smoked more dope in silence in the fatal yellow light. She said, "Well, we didn't kill Death, but it was still good." Her grayblue eyes were soft and wide. "It's always good with you, Bear, always *will* be good."

She kissed him lightly on the lips; his prostate throbbed in its sickening way. She said, "My father didn't like that new letter."

He snorted softly. "Surprise."

It had gone out almost the way he and Dora had drafted it. Grimsley had toned it down with some pious "community standards" stuff, had added some crap about "careful study by the full committee," but had otherwise left it intact.

"So what's his next move?"

"He made some noise about suing the school, but I talked him out of that. Daddy's little girl still gets her way, you know." Ted looked at her flat, firm belly, her delta's pale down. "He wrote to the paper again."

"And what did he say?"

"I didn't read it."

"Oh."

She kissed his cheek, then touched his glans. Her finger felt sandpaper-rough on his damaged skin. "Ms. Rosen's nice."

"Very nice."

"I wonder how come she's not married."

"I don't know."

He had asked George Frangelli if he thought she was gay. George pointed out that she'd gone with Gary Haslam, a science teacher who'd transferred out of the district. "It doesn't *prove* anything," he said. "But I *think* she's straight."

"My father says she's to blame for the 'dirty' books," Joy said. "Jews are ultral-iberal radicals, he says."

"All Jews?"

"A Jew's a Jew."

Marijuana hummed songs in his brain as she said, "I can't wait to meet June."

He closed his eyes, saw stars revolve. "I don't know if she's going to the prom," he said.

"If not, you'll go alone?"

"Of course."

"Then I'd have to arrange to meet her some other time."

What the hell was this woman *thinking?* "So who are you going with?" he said. "Rod Rheingold?"

She screwed up her face. "Rod's still hot for Eileen Phillips. Turkey Tits must know some clever tricks. So—Frank Pippa's the lucky guy."

Ted grinned. "Frank *Pippa?*" Pippa was the quarterback on the football team, a dense, good-looking, dark-skinned, dark-haired boob.

"I'm sure the air will flash with stimulating repartee," Joy said. "Believe it or not, four-fifths of the senior females would give their hymens—if they had any left—to go with that yokel, who's had a tiff with Melanie Ward and is therefore available."

Ted couldn't get rid of his smile. "Frank Pippa!"

Giving his mangled tube a squeeze she said, "That's right. And you make one smart remark when you see me there and I'll spill the beans. I'll tell the whole world everything, you bad old Bear."

He laughed, not without anxiety. "What did Spoonfeather want to see you about?"

"Well, what do you think?"

"You haven't said anything, so I was afraid to ask."

"Of course I got the scholarship, what else?"

He sat higher against the headboard and said, "That's great! Aubrey's a real good school, there aren't a whole lot of kids who get scholarships there." He had that fatherly flash again, and felt like hugging her, kissing her cheek, but it seemed absurd with his penis still there in her hand.

She shrugged. "Big deal. It's a scholarship given by some insurance foundation my father knows about. As if he needed help with my tuition. It's not much money, just sort of an honor."

"You bet it's an honor."

"Yeah. But you see, I don't know if I'm going."

A white space spreading across Ted's mind. "You might not go? But why?"

Her eyes on his. "Because of you, of course."

"Because...of me?"

"Well, sure. You haven't told me when you're leaving June, and I can't go away till I know you're free to go with me."

He jerked himself upright; his organ flopped out of her grasp. He said, "Joy, don't be nuts! Take the scholarship, go to Aubrey, it's a once in a lifetime thing!"

Her mouth was vulnerable, soft. "But Bear, I want to be with *you*."

In marijuana undergrowth, his mind searched frantically for words. All it could find was, "Joy, I'm forty-two years old. I'm married. Who knows what will happen with us?"

With an injured, worried look she said, "But you won't *stay* married, will you? I mean *can* you, after all this?"

"I don't know."

"But you love me, don't you?"

"Joy..." He frowned; he wet his lips. "You've brought me tremendous excitement. You've made me feel so *alive*..."

Those eyes, right on him, riveted. "But what about *love?*"

He sighed. "Look. Listen to me and go to Aubrey. You'll probably meet some guy—"

"Are you trying to dump me, Bear?"

Those eyes! "Of course I'm not, I'm thinking of your future. A scholarship to Aubrey College, you have to take it, you really do. What will your parents think if you turn it down?"

"Who gives a damn what they think?"

"You do. Admit it, you do."

How absurd it was to be saying all this in the buff on a motel bed! How unerotic nudity could be! How *dreadful* it could be!

"I *don't* give a damn what they think!" she insisted. He sensed the beginning of tears; was she going to start that shaking again? "But if you *really* want me to go, and if you *promise* to leave June as soon as you can and join me there—I'll go."

A hundred thoughts in the space of about two seconds. He swallowed and said, "I promise. I'll leave her as soon as I can and join you at Aubrey."

"And marry me?"

Yes, that was always the bottom line, the script never changed. Father her zillion kids and all the rest. He'd gone this far, so why not go all the way? "Of course."

"I'll always love you, Bear. I'll love you forever."

"Just promise you'll take the scholarship."

"I will. I do." She smiled then and flung herself backwards, spreading her long lithe legs. Ted thought of that woman in stirrups in *Our Bodies Belong to Us.*

"Use your tongue on me Bear, nice and slow. I love how you do it, that flip of your chin."

Anxiety, guilt, and crinkly dope sounds in his ears. With Dickle-like indifference, he regarded her crotch.

"Come on, Bear, do it."

He lowered himself and lowered himself, remembering horrible Sissy again, and obeyed.

23 • HAT IN THE RING

June had fully recovered. She was brusque and efficient again, back at work again, and was already planning her next excursion abroad. She hadn't called him "sweetheart" since she'd gotten back on her feet, but her operation had wrought a distressing change: a resurgence of sexual desire! A *pronounced* resurgence. How? Why? What was it, an effort to prove she was still a woman? God only knew, but her first full week at Happy Trails they did it four times! One third of their former yearly output! No extended gymnastics were called for, thank God, and he managed to fake it twice, but all the same it was mighty tough on the goddamn aging fabric.

With Joy he relied on The Wharton Method and good old Master Muscle. Without this combo, he'd have been doomed. Joy wasn't pleased: "I don't want Master Muscle all the time, I want *you,* Bear!"

He complied, and my God did it hurt! At home he sat in four inches of steaming water per Dr. Dickle's directions, but all he got for his effort was a scalded scrotum.

He read in a magazine that pumpkin seeds were good for the prostate gland, so he kept a supply in his jacket and munched them between his classes. Each morning he gulped six capsules of Vitamin E, supposedly good for the whole soft tubular system. He didn't have any more bleeding of parts, but good lord was he sore and abused! He needed a break!

• • • • •

"I just thought it would bore you to tears," he said.

June was smearing her toast with butter. "Oh, no," she said, "it ought to be fun. Besides, how would it look if you went by yourself?"

"Who cares how it looks?"

She spread strawberry jam, took a bite and said, "World opinion no longer concerns you?"

A reference to an old cartoon they'd liked—of a recluse curled up in a box. Remembering it, he laughed—and felt the laugh in his prostate gland. He said, "Teachers are *always* concerned about world opinion. If a—well, a vacuum cleaner salesman—gets stopped for drunk driving, what happens? Does he lose his job? Not on your life. If a *teacher* drives drunk, it's another story."

Saturday sunshine was bright on the shrubs and lawn. June bit into her toast again. "Life is cruel," she said. "You ought to join the carefree world of us travel agents." A dot of jam adhered to her upper lip.

"You have jam on your lip."

She wiped her mouth but missed the dot, so Ted erased it.

"Thanks. Did I tell you that Sally and Jerry Mandrill have split up?"

"Uh-uh."

She shook her head, looking exasperated. "I still can't see how she didn't know what was happening."

"Some people are just oblivious."

Voice muffled with toast, June said, "You see the editorial page? Mr. Dollinger's letter?" She handed him the folded *Courier-News.* "Right here."

> To the editor:
>
> Having been unable to obtain a satisfactory response to my concerns regarding what I consider to be objectionable reading matter in our high school library, I find that I have no choice but to deal with the problem in a more direct fashion. I am thus announcing my candidacy for the Somerside School District Board of Education, the elections for which will be held this coming November.
>
> I call on all parents who want a decent education for their children to support my candidacy. I pledge that with your help I will restore morality to our schools and eradicate the forces which have dragged the honored names of our community and our high school into the mire.
>
> Yours sincerely,
> Armand Dollinger

"Oh Jesus," Ted said.

"Looks like the guy means business," June said.

"He means business all right. 'Eradicate the forces'?"

June shrugged. "Is his daughter like him?"

"His daughter?" Ted felt himself flush. "I don't know her that well." He poked at the thin line of eggwhite lace on the edge of his breakfast plate. June had never been able to fry an egg without making that lace. With a frown he said, "So you are going to go to the prom."

"Sure. I'd like to see what a prom *looks* like these days. When was the last one you chaperoned? About twelve years ago?"

"About that."

The coffee had worked on Ted's bladder. He went to the downstairs bathroom to urinate; when he did, it felt puffy and strained, with a heavy, congested warmth. He had to refrain, restore himself! What was the point of seeing doctors if you didn't heed their advice?

He thought about Dollinger's letter. Deciding to run for school board! The guy was obsessed! The letter that Dora had helped him write had been so *mild*—especially with Grimsley's changes. How had he ever allowed himself to get involved in this mess? He should've said no to Burk and LeMaster right from the very start.

In the shower he thought of the prom again, then thought of his own senior prom, how many...God, twenty-five years ago! His class would have a reunion soon, no doubt. Ted Wharton? Dropped out of sight, no one knows where he is. And thank God for that, for he sure didn't need that scene: the slack, bald men and potbellied women who only moments ago in his mind had been lean and firm and bushy-haired. Lord, twenty five *years,* he thought as he gingerly soaped his limp tube. A quarter of a *century.*

Before putting his clothes on, he checked himself out in the full-length mirror: examined the sag at his hips, the soft roll at his waist, that silvery stretchy quality on his thighs. Something's wrong, he thought. A seventeen year old girl who could like *this* body? Something's *wrong.*

24 • STARDUST RAIN

The lousy feeling between his legs simmered on for almost a week. He put June off (committee meetings, headaches), put Joy off (return of intestinal flu), didn't meet her at night, didn't go to the A-V room. But he couldn't avoid her eyes in psychology class, and twice she approached him afterwards with indecent proposals. He said he just couldn't, his stomach was really bad. Well soon? she asked with an anxious, haunted look. As soon as he could, absolutely. He promised. Before he could keep that promise—prom time!

—With rain, that bane of tuxedoes and gowns. Ted seemed to recall it had rained at his own senior prom. (Did it rain at *all* proms?)

He and June arrived early, as required, manning their chaperone station, a table beside the door. They shared it with Hilda Peck, a typing teacher, and her husband, Max, a squat, robust, cigar smoke-saturated guy who instantly bored Ted stiff. The kids straggled buoyantly in, looking grown-up and stilted and dislocated in their formal clothes. When Joy arrived with Frank Pippa, halfwit quarterback, she looked so gorgeous Ted's mouth went dry.

Her gown was satin—white, tight, elegant—totally different from what the other girls wore. Max Peck, with a leer, remarked that she sure was one hell of a dish for a high school kid, and Hilda slapped the back of his hairy hand. June said, *"That's* the daughter of the guy who writes those letters? Maybe he's got more to worry about than he thinks."

Ted watched Joy dance with dense, compact Frank Pippa (What was that line from Markham? *Whose breath blew out the light within this brain?*); he watched her body liquify the satin, eyed the silky shadows of her thighs. He listened to Max Peck's fishing stories, set in vast Canadian wilderness where he wished Max would go this minute and never return; he danced twice with June to please her and the crowd, smiling and nodding to bright, dull, bad and good.

The rain streamed down past half-closed casement windows in the blowy night. Ted thought of the paper he'd written for Joy. Insufferable Rod flowed by with Eileen, who smiled, said hi. No Rick and Allison, and Ted felt sorry for them. (Allison did plan to march her swollen belly through graduation, though.) "Six and a half pound rainbow," Max Peck said, and Ted, worn out, feigned amazement still one more time.

The band took a break, the floor cleared, and the room filled with talk. Much milling around and punchbowl business, and Max dispatched the wilderness. Time to talk about gardening now. He'd planted ten rows of gold 'n silver corn this year, and by God, you should see 'em—

By God, Joy was right at their table—without Frank Pippa—demure, subdued, and wearing a charming smile. "Hello, Mrs. Peck. Hello, Mr. Wharton." Ted's skin felt hot. Then the introduction of June, and he felt *creepy.* June smiling, extending her hand, and Joy—the perfect lady, perfect Aubrey-student-to-be—clasping it with aplomb and saying how pleased she was. The band had regrouped and it started up. Joy said, "May I have this dance, Mr. Wharton?"

Ted's heart skipped a beat. "Why certainly, Joy." He smiled, stood, took her naked illicit arm, and walked out onto the floor.

One hand held her hand, one hand held the small of her back, and he looked at June and rolled his eyes in an oh-well-what-can-you-do sort of way—and Joy rubbed her satin against him.

"Joy! Not so close!"

She pressed her lips together and looked at his eyes. "I've missed you, Bear. It's been over a week since we've done it."

June was watching them dance. He acted normal, smiled and said, "That flu…"

"It couldn't have been *that* bad, you didn't miss any school."

"Every day I went home and collapsed."

"Really." Sad, sad eyes.

"Yes, really."

They danced; she clung; he felt stifled, acutely aware of the crowd. "Not so *close,*" he hissed.

She pressed into him harder and said in his ear, "I miss your body, Bear."

He wished they could do it right now, on the floor, in her wonderful satin dress. "I miss yours, too, but for Christ's sake, we have to be careful!"

"Okay, okay."

She backed away and they danced half an arm's length apart. She said, "June's pretty, Bear. She looks much older than your wedding picture, but she's pretty."

"Yes, she is."

"It's sad for her. It's going to be so hard."

"Joy, please, not here."

"Okay, I'll shut up, I'll be good. We'll just dance like this, like good little bourgeois puritans, and talk about nothing. Wouldn't Daddy be proud?"

Was this song going to last forever? "So he's running for school board now."

She grinned. "Oh, yes, and he's never lost an election. A born politician."

"Terrific."

She sniffed. "Oh Bear, forget about him. By election time we'll be married and living at Aubrey."

Strained, agonized, he danced. Without a hiatus the band slipped into another number: Stardust, the all-time favorite—and everything came back.

It had *poured* on that prom night so long ago, he remembered it clearly now: the last night he'd spent with Elaine. They had gone with each other for nearly six months, were madly in love, and then something had changed. He didn't know how or why it had changed, but it had, so fast, irrevocably, terribly, in the space of less than two weeks. It wasn't anything she'd said or done, she was somehow just different, not someone to love anymore. She knew how he felt, but couldn't believe it; and they danced on that sad dim floor with the rain coming down in torrents, two adolescents drowning, drowning. *Stardust. Sometimes I wonder why I spend the lonely night...* She cried and cried in the car on the way back home and he kissed her goodbye forever in the lush May rain before she ran inside the house and he never saw her again.

Now Joy had that same mournful look as Elaine. That suffocating clinginess surrounded her, spun a web that was dragging him down. If the lights would go out and the people would disappear he would screw her right here and now—but he knew he would never love her. Never. And what to do?

"How's it going with Frank?" he said, forcing a smile.

"How do *you* think it's going?" she said. "The creep already made a pass at me on the way *over* here. I told him I'm having my period."

The slippery rub of her hip against his. He would dump her this week, he swore he would, but before he did... Maybe they could meet tomorrow night, she could wear this gown... He said, "*Are* you having your period?"

She looked at him, said nothing, smiled, said: "No, Bear, I'm three days overdue."

An electric shock came out of her hands, flowed into his arms. He kept dancing. "Is that unusual for you?"

She continued to smile. "It's only the second time it's happened since I was twelve."

His thighs felt feeble; sweat blushed on his brow. He looked at her smile, that gap in her teeth, and thought: unattractive. Not seductive, but unattractive. He remembered the way that Elaine's face had changed from an object of adoration to...just nothing. Just nothing at all, so fast. It had scared him to death.

The saxophone player was doing that head-down-end-of-song blow job all saxophone players do—*the memories of love's refrain*—and the music stopped. They were standing there facing each other, not touching now, and people were going back to their tables. He said, "Joy, what if it's...it's the real thing?"

She kept smiling. That gap! "I'll have an abortion," she said. "It's as simple as that, I thought we discussed it before."

Sweat traveled along a crease in his neck. "And how will you keep your father from finding out?"

"I'll go to another pajama party—an extended one." She shrugged offhandedly. "Or maybe I'll change my mind and keep the kid."

He felt naked, surrounded by too much space; could see June watching. "We have to start walking," he said.

"Why do we?"

"To keep up appearances, play the game. You're good at the game, remember?"

She walked toward where Pippa the airhead sat with his football pals. The band jumped into something fast, and the floor came alive with a rush.

"You're not going to keep any kid!" Ted said above the sudden raucous din.

"I'll damn well do what I please!" Joy said. She smiled broadly and defiantly, then turned and walked away. Ted swallowed, heart thick in his throat, and went back to June.

There was a thing at some giant milkshake hangout afterwards, but Joy didn't show. Ted sat there gloomily, eating nothing, as June and the Pecks had sundaes and kids came over and cracked their dumb teenage jokes. Little by little the place thinned out, and Max Peck, chomping his cigar, put Hilda's sweater over her solid typist-teacher's back and they all went out in the rainwashed air of late May and said good-night.

On the way home, June said she'd enjoyed it; it was cute to see all those kids attempting to act grown up. She yawned, looking old. Ted drove in a silence filled with sick, dull thoughts.

In bed June nuzzled his cheek and said: "I'm glad I'm not their age. I couldn't go through all that again—those *emotions,* that *uncertainty.* It's all in the future for Brad and Kim, but when you're young you can take it."

"Yeah," Ted said. He remembered Joy's heat against his body, saw her shape in the satin dress. Just stop taking the pill, that's all she had needed to do, and how would he ever know? The standard sucker trap, and he'd fallen right in. No, he told himself, not Joy, she had plans for *Cosmo* and *Vogue,* she wouldn't destroy herself like that.

"Goodnight, Ted."

"Goodnight, June."

He lay there watching the ceiling, thinking of Joy and actually growing hard in spite of himself. He felt so helpless and foolish he wanted to scream. The leak in the ceiling was dripping, but June was asleep. When she started to snore he went downstairs and drank two shots of Red & Black and sat in the dark silent kitchen thinking: No, she can't be serious. Keep the *kid?*

25 • BLUE NOTES

He was up after five hours' sleep and out on the sun-splintered Saturday street and he ran four miles, thinking, thinking, ribs aching, sharp blade in his side. He ate no breakfast, wasn't hungry. To keep himself busy he measured the broken downspout (almost fell off the ladder), then drove to the hardware store for a new one and everything else he needed to fix the roof. He didn't dare mount the ladder again when he got back home, he was certain he'd kill himself (thinking: going around in circles), and he went to the mall with June like a docile lamb.

They had the Phillipses to dinner. Through talk of investments and Phillies he tried to convince himself that things were okay, she wasn't pregnant. And if she was, she would have an abortion, he'd somehow persuade her to do it.

He fell asleep late to a dark dream of Mabel, his mother-in-law, in a nursing home. She was lying alone in a ward of identical beds, he approached with the kids, a spray of bright roses in his hand, she turned around—and was June instead. This was her final day on earth, but she gave him a smile and took the flowers and kissed both kids, man Brad and woman Kim. He awoke with a start and said, "Is she all right?" and June stopped snoring abruptly and said, "What? Who?"

"Your mother," he said, regretting it, the dream stuff flying away.

"As far as I know," June said. "She didn't mention anything wrong in her card. Is that why you woke me up? To ask me that?"

"Yes."

"Since when do you care about my mother? You must have been dreaming."

"You're right," he said, "I was," and apologized. —Then thought of Joy again, and didn't get back to sleep for a long, long time.

On Sunday, more rain, but he jogged anyway. Self-flagellation? The penance that would save his life? He'd been stiff-upper-lip with Rick Castle all right, but now that *his* turn had come… In the afternoon, like a model Dad, he took the kids to a movie. Bought take-out Chinese food so that June wouldn't have to cook. Could anything terrible happen to such a nice guy?

He struggled to avoid her eyes as he lectured on Monday morning. As the class was leaving he said, "Joy, I'd like to see you a minute." He had her wait by his desk until everyone else had gone and then said softly, "Well?"

"Well what?" she said. Her face was impassive, her eyes cool gray—yet with something hurt and imploring in them.

"Well *what?* Well what do you *think?*"

"Is that all you care about?"

Next period's "students" were gathering in the hall. "Of course it's not *all* I care about, but Jesus Christ!"

She shook her head. "I'm six days overdue now, Bear."

His heart took a sickening plunge.

She asked: "Can you meet me tonight?"

"What time?"

"The usual, Bear, under the 'J'."

• • • • •

They were back in the Blue Note Motel again. Through a rip in the musty, dark blue drape, he could see the flashing red Vacancy sign and imagined the rooms around him, the various acts of perversion they housed. Toilets flushed, cars screeched and roared away, trucks whined on General Haze Boulevard, highway of hell.

For half an hour they sat on the bed fully clothed. They shared a joint, she smoked another by herself and lit a third; got halfway through it, snuffed it out. — Then looked at him with sad and sorry eyes and said, "What's happening to us, Bear?"

He didn't reply. The room—gray shaggy rug, harsh ticking air-conditioner, headboard of plastic walnut attached to the wall—revolved to the cellular reefer tune in his brain. Her lips and chin were speckled with threads of gold.

"It's June," she said. "You have to leave her, Bear."

Her hand was soothing his cheek and he wanted to tear it away—yet he liked it, he liked it. In spite of the air-conditioning the room was stuffy, suffocating, dead. "I will," he said.

"But I mean *soon.*"

He stroked her hair—as if she were an animal, a pet. "I will."

He felt her tremble, saw tears in her eyes. "I've only been close to one other person in my *life,*" she said. "Just *one,* and I need you so *much.*"

He took a sad, deep breath. "Joy, look…you're only seventeen." Which was, after all, the impossible truth.

Her quivering lips. "Who *cares?* What difference does *that* make? Is *that* the problem? Her eyes were smeary now, and pleading. "All I know is I *love* you, you just *can't* leave me alone. It can't happen twice, not so *soon.*"

He looked away: at the hole in the drape and the Vacancy sign. He stood up and went to the window; pushed the fabric around so the slit was hidden; returned. Sat down on the bed again. "Rod?" he said. "Was *he* the other person?"

She sucked mucous into her throat with a sneer. "*That* creep? Are you kidding?"

"Well who—?"

"It isn't important, you don't want to know."

She was probably right. Some pustular crud even worse than Rod who made teaching torture, no doubt. Let it ride.

Her tongue pressed into the gap in her teeth. "You're the only person I really feel *with,*" she said. "Without you I'm all alone, and I can't *stand* being alone. My father… Christ! His ice is inside me, I can't burn it out!" Moisture rushed to her eyes, spilled over. She said, "My brother's *dead.* He was only two years older than I am now when he died, do you understand?" She stared at him with frightening intensity. "Death's in the rug, it's in the walls, it's coming through the door! I'm *scared!*"

She was starting that horrible shaking. He held her. She said, "We're living in the earth's last days! The dark is coming down! The rain is poison, we've killed the air! It's too late to reverse it, we're going to die no matter *what* we do, it's just too *late!*"

A heavy tremor shook her then. He said, "Joy, no, it's okay. You're all right, we're all right, no one's going to die."

Her face was twisted painfully and her eyes were closed. "No, no, nobody beats death, you said it yourself." Staring at him again, her eyes suddenly wide, she said, "The sun's a cancer! The whole *world's* going to die!" Then she wrenched herself out of his arms and ran to the bathroom.

Retching: violent and loud.

He found her on her knees in the bare bright light. She clung to the toilet, her face in the bowl, the bowl full of yellowish gruel. She heaved again; more liquid erupted and plopped; strands hung from her lips.

He held her shoulder, felt her chills, heard the click of her shivering teeth. She spasmed again with a horrible rasping sound.

Sad eyes on the toilet, sad hand in her back, he thought: Now isn't *this* a pretty piece of porn? There was no doubt a section he'd overlooked on those decadent bookstore racks she had sent him to that catered to just this thing: *Vomiting Vixens. Barfing Bimbos. Upchucking Chicks.* He held her as she jerked and groaned again. The dazzle of light on porcelain tank and fiberglass tub; the shower curtain, torn at the top, a haze of fungus at its base; the thin cold twitch of her flesh.

Then all at once with a pitiful cry she said: "Tell me you love me! Promise you'll never leave me!"

He stared at her, shaking his head. "Joy…"

"Promise! Promise me now." White fire was in her eyes.

He wet his hot numb lips. "I…promise," he said.

She retched again, but nothing came up. Leaning back with a gasping breath she said, "Oh Christ." She ripped a wad of toilet paper off the roll and wiped her mouth; hung, head over soiled bowl, eyes closed, and time stood still, eternity trapped in the fixtured glare. It was just the two of them, alone in all the universe.

Slowly she got to her feet and tripped the lever. The contents of her guts disappeared with a gurgle and swirl. She washed her face and rinsed her mouth, the toilet sighed, he helped her to the bed.

His thoughts were scattered sparks. "Do you want anything? Can I get you some Coke?" He was thinking of Kim and that virus she'd had before Christmas; thirteen hours of throwing up and then Coke, good old Coke, had at last done the trick.

"Okay," she said. "Yeah, Coke."

Into the dark satanic night he went with the plastic bowl, the growl and headlight rush of the road assaulting his ears and eyes. Pinkorange crooknecked lamps, gas stations and liquor stores. A car pulling up to the Blue Note office, two muscular T-shirted toughs jumping out with a shout.

In the breezeway he punched the ice machine and filled the bowl. Stuck the coins in the soda machine, heard the hollow deep crunch and collected the can of Coke. Faced nightmare night: Joy's Honda in the lot, its red distorted, bloodied by the lamps; the swish and rip of traffic in his eyes; exhaust smell, diesel roar; a slamming door, a woman's loud coarse laugh. He went back to the room, a cable of tension tight and sharp in his chest.

Joy was leaning against the headboard. The color was coming back into her face, but her eyes didn't look quite right.

"Feeling better?"

She nodded. "Yeah."

He iced the plastic cup and snapped the Coke: quick fizz, brown liquid hiss, tan foam. She took two tentative sips and said, "It's good. Thanks, Bear."

He watched her drink. Her hand was shaking as she raised the cup.

"You want me to pour some more?"

"No, that's enough." Her funny eyes. She set the cup on the brown formica nightstand, smiling wanly and said, "Come here."

He sat beside her.

"Put your arms around me. Hold me."

He did: felt her tremor; diminished, sporadic. He said, "Joy, maybe that doctor could help you. That therapist you said you saw last year."

A scornful sniff. "*That* guy? Forget it." She stared with adoring, blurry eyes. "No, all I need is you." She was silent a minute, just staring, then said: "Say you love me."

"I love you."

"Tell me again that you'll never leave me."

"I'll…never leave you."

"Oh Bear, my wonderful Bear."

She leaned her head against his chest and it burned him, melted him down. He held her for long hot mournful minutes and didn't know what to do. Oh this was a blue, blue note, all right. He breathed her sad soft hair.

Her shaking stopped. She kissed his ear and smiled and said, "I'm better now. When will I ever learn not to smoke so much when I'm having my period?"

He stared at her. "Your...period?"

"I checked while you were getting the Coke. I figured that's why I got sick."

The cable inside his chest unraveled and snapped.

"I guess you're glad," she said.

"Glad?" he said, his heart on wings. "Yeah, I guess I am."

She said she was totally gross and needed a shower, and disappeared into the bathroom again. He watched TV, the Phillies without any sound, his mind a happy blank.

The door clicked open with a rush of steam and she came at him naked, her skin aglow. She sat beside him on the bed and said, "Make love to me."

"What? Joy, you're...*sick.*"

"Oh no, I feel wonderful now."

"But..."

"But, but, but. Come *on.*"

"Joy, to tell you the truth, I'm kind of worn out."

The Phillies had made a terrific play and the fans across the river, under the lights, were silently going wild.

She held him and smelled unbelievably sweet. He thought of her puking, her head in the bowl, the vomitus slick on her lips. "Bear, *please,*" she said, and a tremor went through her again.

This *clinging,* this *begging.* He remembered Elaine, from so long ago, and what did she look like now? After all these years? "It's time to go home," he said.

She held him tighter. "Not yet, not yet."

He sighed. "Half an hour ago you were sick as a dog, and now—"

"I bounce back fast. I always have."

He stared across the room at the dark blue drapes.

Frowning, she let him go and said, "Oh Bear, what's wrong? I got my period, we ought to *celebrate.*"

He looked at her. "You were close to another person," he said. "Who was it?"

A sharp, hoarse laugh. "So *that's* why you're bent out of shape. I *thought* that was it. Will you do it with me if I tell you?"

"Joy..."

She smiled. "Yes or no?"

"Okay, okay."

The inning was over; a commercial was on. She said: "It was Marty, of course."

"Marty..."

"Zeller."

Her face had a druggy, languid look. She continued to smile.

"Marty Zeller," he said with a soft hissing sound in his ears.

"Well certainly, couldn't you guess? Why did you think I was so shook up when he died?"

Thinking a million death-before-drowning thoughts, he looked away. When he faced her again, tears were staining her cheeks. "He left me," she said. "He abandoned me. Don't ever do that, Bear."

And then she was holding him tight again, so tight it hurt. Eyes closed, she said between taut lips, *"Now.* Do it with me *now!"*

She rubbed his crotch. He looked at her rich young skin, her rose-hued areolas and the gooseflesh on her arms. She kissed him hard, and her taste was sour. Features limp, she said, "Use your mouth on me, Bear."

"Joy, Jesus—"

"You said you love me."

"I know, but—"

"Then use your mouth."

The light from the TV set was medicinal, raw, as he got underway, and he thought of Marty. Had he too feasted at these portals? *Beauty is momentary in the mind—but in the flesh it is immortal...* She writhed and sucked breath hoarsely, tossed her head. Oh God, oh God.

Isn't it funny
How a Bear likes honey?
Buzz! Buzz! Buzz!
I wonder why he does?

With decerebrate surgical skill he worked, employing his patented Wharton Method, and sure enough, in spite of himself, his member began to respond. And soon he was up on his knees behind her, facing the colorful sunny tattoo on her moon. "Yes, Bear, yes," she moaned as he entered, "Oh yes," and he said to himself: *So this this is the way it's going to end? Not with a whimper but a bang?*

• • • • •

It was after ten by the time he called June. And explained, with naked unconscious Joy on the bed beside him, that the car had conked out, he was at a garage, he'd be home quite late. Did he want her to pick him up? No, that was okay, he'd wait, it was only a water pump, no big deal. Okay, so long, good night. Good night, sweet ladies, good night.

He lay back on the bed and waited: half an hour, forty-five minutes, an hour. When she started to snore (snore! Seventeen years old!) he shook her. She lolled her head, said, "Huh?" and went back to sleep. She snored for ten more minutes, driving him nuts. He tried to wake her up again but she was floppy, comatose, and he waited; watched the silent TV throw its shifts of hard light on the wall; heard somebody laughing and banging around upstairs; heard toilets flush, doors slam, cars start with angry squeals.

She rolled over, groaning, at ten after one, as he finished a ragged thought about Dr. Zahara's class. (The semester was probably over, he'd have to check.) She stared at him thickly, looked at her nakedness, wanted to sleep again. He propped her awake, got her into her clothes, helped her out to the car. She dozed as he drove to the shopping center where his car stood lonely under the huge green 'J' in the massive lot. He managed to wake her again, and they sat for twenty minutes in the asphalt desert in muggy late May warmth. She cried, said she didn't know why, and finally said yes, she was all right now, she could drive.

He followed her back to her house to make sure she was safe. When he walked through his door at three twenty-five, T.S. Eliot barked and sprang, knocking him backward, waking both Kim and June.

26 • CLOUD ON THE HORIZON

Joy wasn't in school the next morning. Ted, zonked, a zombie, wondered what lie she had told her parents. The Honda breakdown story? Had she even remembered it? Worried and preoccupied, he fumbled his way through the day, a fraction of his harried brain performing the teaching function.

It bothered him more than he cared to admit that she'd had an affair with Marty. Marty had always seemed so defeated, so old, and why would a pretty young girl like Joy be attracted to someone like that? He was almost as bad as that corpulent, bald, cigar-smoking mate of the camp director. Anyone who could fall for a burnt-out, dried-up geezer like Marty Zeller could fall for...well, for *anyone.*

Time dribbled away. Good God was his aging fabric beat! Since Joy had passed out in the act he'd been spared a complete performance at least, and now, at last, he was finished with her. Amen. June's passion had entered remission again, and so, with luck, his glands and ducts would now receive their doctor-ordered rest. But *all* his fabric needed rest, not merely certain parts of it, and sweet sweet dreams of a ten hour sleep consumed him as his last class left, he locked his door and headed down the hall. He had to cook tonight, but after that—

"Ted? Do you have a minute?"

Dora Rosen. If there was anyone he didn't want to see right now...

But see her he did, in her office, the newspaper on her desk folded back to the editorial page and Armand Dollinger's letter.

"Grimsley wants me to pull *Our Bodies Belong to Us* off the shelves," she said.

"Oh, no."

"You bet. He says if we keep on fighting the guy it will help his chances of getting a seat on the board."

"So what are you going to do?"

Dora picked up her cigarettes. "Well what do you think? The book's going to stay where it is." She lit up, intent on the lighter's flame, and said, "When I came to this school a year and a half ago, I drew up a book selection policy. The school board approved it. Until it's officially changed, I go by that policy—which does not allow a superintendent to arbitrarily remove a book from the shelves." She exhaled a tight stream of smoke. "Grimsley approved the purchase order for *Our Bodies*—which Miss Page selected, by the way, not me—and now because some two-bit fascist attacks it, he's running scared. We talk about our precious freedoms in this country, and then when it's time to defend them, we roll over dead."

Ted pictured himself in the Blue Note with Joy, flopping down next to her, panting. He saw Marty Zeller collapse. Gagging a little on the smoke, which stung his exhausted eyes, he said, "Grimsley probably doesn't even read the purchase orders. I bet all he checks is the cost."

Raised eyebrows. "Well, that's not my fault."

So tired, exhausted, and what would he make for dinner? Tuna casserole *again?* Souffle *again?* What did Dora *want* from him, anyway?

She smoked and said, "Grimsley asked LeMaster to get his committee together—

fast—ostensibly to review my book selection policy. According to SUN, there's a lot more to it than that."

SUN was an acronym for Secretaries' Underground Network. If you wanted the inside dope on the Somerside schools, you had to hook into SUN: their methods were thorough, their knowledge was awesome. The powers of Eleanor Crux, LeMaster's secretary, bordered on the occult. LeMaster's door had a translucent pane of glass that would vibrate whenever he spoke. To the ears of the casual listener, like Ted, these vibrations were just so much noise, but Eleanor Crux's ears, after years of exposure, had somehow evolved to decode those buzzes, imbue them with meaning again. The woman knew *everything.*

"So what's SUN's scoop?" Ted asked.

"They say that Grimsley wants to take away my power to deal with complaints about books and give it to the committee."

"Oh, brother."

"That's right, and we meet on Friday."

"Friday!"

"Okay," Dora said, "so The Spouting Whale or whatever it is will have to wait for a while. We're dealing with something *critical* here."

Ted felt like a scolded child.

"In the meantime, I'm going to draft another letter to Dollinger—and I'd like you to help me with it."

Now? Did she mean *now?* "I'd like to, Dora," he said, "but I have an appointment."

"I don't mean today. Tomorrow."

"Oh." He frowned and said, "Don't you think you should wait till after the committee meets?"

She smiled sardonically, smoking again. "The committee has nothing to do with this letter. The committee is going to work on the book selection policy and the method of handling complaints, but *not* on any replies to Armand Dollinger. That's Grimsley's edict."

"Really."

"Really. We obviously failed again."

"But he *approved* our letter. It went out from his office, didn't it?"

With a shrug, Dora smoked. "What I told him is this: You can stop me from using my school librarian title, but you can't stop me from sending a letter. As a U.S. citizen I have that right, and I won't allow it to be abridged."

"Good for you."

"So you'll help me with it? You'll sign it too?"

"You mean as a private citizen, not a school employee?"

"Exactly."

A thin cold prickle of sweat. "Well…"

"You're concerned about freedom, aren't you?"

"Of course."

"Well, then?"

Oh sleep, if he could only sleep! When school let out, he had a whole week free before his summer job began. Could he possibly spend it in bed?

She was staring. "Okay," he said, "I'll do it. But I think we should show the letter to the committee."

"Why?"

"Oh, courtesy."

She sniffed. "Let's see what kind of courtesy they show *us.*"

· · · · ·

At home, wrung out, Ted took a brisk shower to wake himself up; changed into a pair of shorts and a polo shirt; made tuna casserole for about the twentieth time in the last six weeks.

Everyone ate it sluggishly as T.S. Eliot skulked below the table with anxious eyes, praying, as always, for bountiful leftovers. (This time, his prayers would be answered.) It was June's opinion during this meal that the trim on the back of the house (which Ted had started scraping weeks ago) looked like it had some scabrous disease. Ted promised he'd work on it this weekend, provided the weather was good. And the leak in the roof? That too, he would work on that too. And when would his course on wackadoo kids be finished? He'd taken his final exam last night, he said. At this, the kids, who found it amusing that their teacher-father still went to school, both laughed. The Media Review Committee, how were things going with that? Hot and heavy, Ted said, it would tie him up for the next two days. He talked about the letter Dora wanted to write.

And June didn't like *that* idea in the slightest. It was fine for a single woman like Dora to challenge the administration, but he was a family man. On a really important matter, okay, but over this? He explained the principle of the thing. June said she'd have to see this book that was so controversial, *Our Bodies Belong to Us.* Brad suddenly turned beet red. The telephone rang, and he instantly jumped up to get it.

"Who? No. Uh-uh. So long," and back he came to the table.

Everything hung suspended as June said, "Who was that?"

"That lady asking for 'Bear' again," Brad said, sitting down.

"For 'Bear'?" June said.

A sharp little bolt of lightning zapped Ted's chest. To hear her say "Bear" like that... His life was a hair's breadth away from collapsing.

"She called before, one time," Brad said, "when you and Kim were in Europe. I guess some clown named Bear has a number almost like ours."

Sick, Ted excused himself, he had papers to grade. He went to the study and sat at his desk, mind blazing. Good God, what was *wrong* with her? He stared out the window, coiled and tense, anticipating the dreadful ring of the phone. An hour went by. No call. He went to the kitchen and drank two shots. As he started up the stairs, the bell exploded.

He pounced on the family room phone so fast he scared Kim half to death. — And the call was for her.

He went to bed at eleven thirty, wide awake in spite of his heavy fatigue. What to do, what to do? The *nerve* of her calling him here, she had to be nuts! A week and a half until graduation—and then?

Without any help from the Colonel this time, he'd gotten the job he'd had two summers ago: checking servicemen's cars for damage before they were shipped overseas. It would get him away from the neighborhood, keep him occupied, wear him out, give him fine excuses for not being able to meet her. But Christ, three months till she left for Aubrey! How could he possibly stave off disaster for three whole months?

Layers of dark fatigue ringed his burning eyes and he pictured her retching again, felt her quivering form in his arms, smelled her vomit's sharp tang. June snored. He sighed. And then he was jogging with Brad, Brad opened his mouth to speak, and a telephone ring came out.

He jumped awake. His blood was audible, hard in his neck. In the darkness he grabbed the receiver.

"Hello?"

"Hi, Bear."

An ice pick, smack in his heart. June's snoring stopped. Quick sweat as he said: "Hi, George."

"Come on, Bear, don't play games."

Throbbing deep in his brain. "I'm in bed now, George, we can talk tomorrow in school." He thought: the kids. Asleep? There was always a hollow, tunnel-like sound when someone was on the extension. That sound was absent now, thank God.

With a frantic edge to her voice, Joy said, "Bear, you're going to leave her anyway, so what's the *difference?*"

June silent. Joy silent. He was trapped on an antimatter planet where his life would play backward, evaporate. His heartbeat hammered in his head. If he hadn't kept in shape by jogging, he'd surely already be dead. "We'll talk about it tomorrow. Sixth period."

"Promise, Bear? Promise? Please?"

"No problem, George."

His roaring breath in the silence, and then: "Say you love me."

Jesus! "Fine."

"No, I want you to say it! Say you love me! Now!"

June stirred, rolled over, her wrist on her forehead.

"Not now, no, I'll see you tomorrow."

He hung up—and waited, waited.

June said, "Who was that?"

His pulse hurt his throat. "It was George Frangelli."

"What in the world did *he* want?"

"Oh, nothing important."

Black silence. June turned on her side again. He waited, waited, waited—for over an hour. The phone didn't ring. Fragments sang in his brain. All he wanted was sleep, but some part of him wouldn't allow it.

He went downstairs, had another drink, skimmed a magazine June subscribed to. It informed him that eighty percent of American men married twenty-five years or more had had an affair.

He watched TV without any sound, a Doris Day-Rock Hudson film. He waited for the phone to ring and wondered what to do, what to do about Joy.

The next thing he knew, it was early dawn, he was still on the couch in the family room, and T.S. Eliot was barking frantically, running from window to window because of—the Bonanzas' dog: loose, roaming, without any collar. In heat?

27 • WOUNDED

The A-V room was a prison, an oven, a gas chamber, hot and dead. The videotape equipment—silent witness—sat merciless, black, in the corner.

"But I *have* to see you," she said with a huge thick sob. "I have to *have* you!"

He kept his voice low and calm as he said, "There are eight more days until graduation. All I'm saying is, we can't do anything for those eight days. Once you're no longer a student here, it's a whole different story. Okay? Do you understand?"

She smeared her tears with her fingers. "I understand."

"Okay. And foolish things like calling me at home can foul things up completely."

She pressed her lips together, her eyes red and wet. "But you *are* going to leave her."

"Of course."

"As soon as possible."

"Absolutely."

She fumbled around in her brown leather bag for a handkerchief; wiped her tears. Put the handkerchief back. Came close to him, submissive, beaten. "You understand that I can't live without you."

"Joy..."

"I can't." She shrugged. "I didn't want it to be this way, it just happened, and now... Oh *Christ*..."

She fell against him, kissed him wetly, hot and sticky, clinging. He wanted to push her away. But then she was reaching between his legs and he closed his eyes and allowed it: let her open his fly. He watched her work, watched his organ grow, watched it disappear into her mouth.

He caught his breath. "Joy, no—"

Looking up with imploring eyes, she said, "Oh yes, oh yes," and swallowed him again.

The reasoning part of his mind was a shadow as pleasure spread into his groin. "Don't worry," she said, "I'll just use my mouth, just my mouth."

He pictured the door at his back, the hall, the sophomores working away at their desks; his colleagues, normal and conscientious, performing their dreary tasks. He looked at her eagerly working and thought: Sex is truly amazing. Such power—and over so fast! All the lives that were lost in this cause, for this blaze of sensation. He stayed quiet, compliant, and let her go on.

The feeling was suddenly fast and full; his whole body lit up. She was pulling him now with her hand. "I want you, I want you!" she said, so loud he was sure they could hear her out there in the hall. Then in almost a whisper she said, "Lie down."

He stretched out on the empty formica table. She operated on him frantically—with mouth, hand, mouth—then only hand, teeth clenched, and said: "Come out! Come out!" She yanked, mouth tight, eyes wide, and said, "It's life that comes out of here! *Life* comes out!"

And dies, Ted thought. And dies and dries and disappears. His feeling had shifted, was growing remote. Come on, let's get this *over* with, he thought. But now she was working *too* fast, and the look on her face, that desperation—*terrifying.*

She rocked like a Jew at prayer, transformed. He was trapped, immobilized, numb. Sweat slimed him as she bounced and jerked, her features agonized. "It's *life!*" she said in a loud hoarse voice, and he burst with thick pleasure and stinging pain, and her fingertips were red.

With a horrified face, she let him go. He sagged, his glans oozing blood.

"I hurt you!" she gasped. "Oh my God!"

With shock and alarm in his voice he said, "It's all right, it's okay."

"But I cut you! I made you bleed!" She stared at her soiled fingers like Lady Macbeth.

He sat up quickly, reached in his pocket, gave her his handkerchief. Looking dazed, she wiped her hands. "Oh God—"

"Forget it, it's nothing," he whispered between clenched teeth. He tucked his battered flesh away and hurriedly zipped his fly.

"But I *hurt* you," she wailed. There were tears in her eyes. "Oh, no," and she tried to hold him.

He caught her arms. "Did you hear me? I said I'm all right! Now that's it until graduation, you understand?"

She shook her head. "Yes."

"Good." He let her go sharply.

She wept; bit her lip. "I'm so sorry, so sorry, please, say you forgive me."

He did.

"Say you love me."

He did.

"Kiss me."

Yes, he even did that, quickly, next to her ear.

"I'll keep your handkerchief. I'll wash it for you."

"No, let me have it."

She did.

Before going to Dora's office to work on the letter, he checked himself out in the mensroom. The skin on the rim of his glans had been rubbed away. *Only a flesh wound, podner,* he thought, *you'll survive.* When he was eighteen he'd once masturbated three times in the space of an hour. My *God* had he declined! It was tragic, tragic, how quickly the body went sour. The aging fabric. *Aged* fabric.

The only redeeming part of the episode was, it had thrown a good scare into Joy, and maybe, just maybe, she really would leave him alone until school was out.

• • • • •

The Media Review Committee was rounded out by—of all people—Gordon Hoover (history teacher, part-time minister), and Wanda Pottsweather (parent, tie-breaker). Mrs. Pottsweather, forty-nine and going on sixty-five, had sent eight children through dear old Whitman High. Her youngest, Wendy, fully as timid and taciturn as her brothers and sisters had been, was among Ted's woefully neglected sophomores.

Howard Grimsley—tall, trim, balding, bearded—was not a committee member, but he was present at this initial meeting to offer "suggestions" and "guidance." He was the third superintendent Ted had worked for, and Ted liked him even less than the other two creeps.

Stroking his pointed silvery beard, Grimsley first "suggested" that they take up Dora Rosen's book selection policy—which of course they all did at once. All went well till the part about "challenged materials." The written complaint form was a fine idea, Grimsley said (Dora passed around copies; all murmured approval), but to have the librarian give the initial response to a complaint was—well, to place too much *responsibility* on one person's shoulders. It wasn't the most *professional* way to go about things, he said, and suggested the policy be revised to state that the Review Committee would give the initial response, not the librarian.

Dora protested. Ted, vaseline on his injured dong, protested too. He said, "You mean each time somebody complains about a book, we'll have to have a meeting?

Why not keep it the way it is? If Dora's response doesn't satisfy the person, *then* we can deal with the issue. A lot of people will probably accept what she says and it won't have to go any further."

Grimsley countered that the number of complaints was small, not enough to impose a burden on the committee; repeated his point about the responsibility placed on Dora (What if she *agreed* with the complaint? Should she have the sole power to *ban* a book? Did she really want that?); suggested to Marvin LeMaster that the matter be put to a vote.

Gordon Hoover moved that "Media Review Committee" be substituted for "librarian" in the third sentence of section four. Wanda Pottsweather, whose glasses gave her an underwater, fishy appearance, seconded the motion, muttering, "Too much responsibility." Any discussion?

Dora scowled; said again that the change seemed to guarantee wasted time. It meant that when someone complained, the whole committee would have to read some book that she herself had already read, then meet to hash it over and take a vote. She was sure she could satisfy most objectors herself. At which point Grimsley, eyebrows arched, said, "The same way you satisfied Armand Dollinger?"

The motion was voted upon. Those in favor? LeMaster's and Hoover's hands went solemnly up. Mrs. Pottsweather, dense and opaque behind her lenses, also raised a timid hand, and the motion passed.

Grimsley then handed around fresh copies of *Our Bodies Belong to Us* and "suggested" that everyone read it right away. Next week they would meet to decide if it should or should not remain on the Whitman library shelves. If nobody had any further business, LeMaster said, would someone make a motion that the meeting be adjourned?

Dora, steaming, said she had further business; smoothed out the paper in front of her; read:

> "To the editor:
>
> In a recent letter to your paper, Mr. Armand Dollinger said he'd received no 'satisfactory' response to his objections concerning certain books in the Whitman High School library. He did, however, receive a response—a carefully thought out response—which was drafted by members of the Whitman Media Review Committee." (She paused after this and glared at Howard Grimsley.)
>
> "Perhaps a few excerpts from this letter will help your readers determine whether or not the response was 'satisfactory.'" (Here she quoted extensively from the Grimsley-sanctioned letter that she and Ted had composed.)
>
> "The undersigned feel that suppression of information is one of the top priorities of totalitarian regimes. Freedom of information, on the other hand, is a hallmark of democracies. As concerned citizens, we oppose Mr. Dollinger's attempts to restrict the information available to our children.
>
> Sincerely,
> Dora Rosen
> Theodore Wharton"

As Dora read, Grimsley plucked at his beard. When she finished, he said in a quiet voice, "I suggest you don't send that out."

Dora glared. "It's my right as a U.S. citizen to send it out."

Grimsley nodded. "True, but I still suggest you don't."

A silence. LeMaster cleared his throat. Was there further business? Nobody spoke. Mrs. Pottsweather stared with her fishy frown. Hoover moved that the meeting be adjourned. Mrs. Pottsweather— clearly an expert at seconding motions—did her thing, and the vote was unanimous.

In her office, Dora said, "What a whitewash job. I wonder what the vote will be on *Our Bodies?*"

"Hey, it's all very democratic," Ted said. "Parliamentary procedure, majority rules."

"Democratic, you bet! Wanda Pottsweather! Gordon Hoover!" She lit up a cigarette.

"I'm going to The Spouting Whale," Ted said. "Want to join me?"

"I don't think the 'boys' would approve."

"I don't think they'd mind."

"I do." She blew smoke. "Let me tell you the rest of the open house story. When I wouldn't let Dollinger have the names of the kids who had borrowed *Our Bodies,* he asked to take it out himself. I told him that school regulations restricted borrowing to students, and you should have heard the tirade. 'I'm a taxpayer! I have two children in this school!' I gave him a complaint form, and two days later his daughter, Joy—you know her, don't you?"

"I have her in honors psych," Ted said just as cool as could be.

"In she comes with a sour face and a sealed envelope. She probably didn't know what was in it, but it was the filled-out form. The guy's listed twenty-two books! I tried to call him, but couldn't get through. I wrote that letter I told you about and asked him to stop by and talk—and he never replied. Instead, he writes to Grimsley— who dumps all over me for not responding properly to a parent's complaint. What am I supposed to do, make *house* calls to these lunatics?" She shook her head, exhaling a quick blast of smoke. "I'm not going to give him an inch," she said. "Not an *inch.*"

"Good, Dora."

She smoked again. "I pity poor Joy," she said. "Imagine what it must be like to have a father like that."

"It must be pretty bad," Ted said.

"You bet!"

28 • ONSTAGE

The end-of-school frenzy was in high gear now. Dreams of freedom spurred the faculty through hot distracted days, providing the surge of martinet strength essential to maintaining order. (The final grades had been turned in; the kids knew it; this was all a charade.)

Ted's year-end happiness was dulled by thoughts of labor on South Philly's docks, but how great it would be to be far from Whitman, far from Joy. Attending more to teaching now than he had in many weeks, he was shocked to find that his sophomores had learned quite a bit. What in the world could account for this? The busywork he'd assigned? The not-quite-arrested process of neural growth? Was he superfluous even here?

It was during this crazy week and a half that June (at last!) found her pendant—deep in the bottom of her middle drawer, buried in nightgowns and underwear. She concluded she must have put it there in pre-hysterectomy hysteria, precisely what Ted had hoped she'd conclude. ("You found it? Where? No kidding?" A stellar performance; he should've made the stage his career.)

He saw little of Joy. Most of the seniors were tied up now with graduation rehearsals and other such stuff, and honors psych was a shadow of its former self. She showed up twice, slouching down and staring out the window, sometimes fixing her moony eyes on him, which gave him chills. He took no chances: asked no questions, called on no one, immersed himself in mock work at the period's end. He had a few practically sleepless nights, but she never telephoned.

In the midst of this chaos and heat, LeMaster called the next meeting. (Dora and Ted had sent their letter and the *Courier-News* had run it, but so far Armand Dollinger hadn't replied.) Before Mrs. Pottsweather came, Ted said, "So has anybody thought of new ways to corrupt our youth since the last time we met?" Dora laughed; Gordon Hoover sat stiff as a statue; big Marvin LeMaster, with sagging face and rheumy eyes, said, "This is serious business, Ted." Wanda Pottsweather made her appearance then, looking slightly unsteady, and close behind her came non-committee member Grimsley, to offer more "guidance," no doubt.

As soon as LeMaster started the meeting, Ted asked if he'd taken the new review procedure before the school board. Not yet, said Marv. How could they use it if it hadn't yet been approved? Ted wanted to know. LeMaster hesitated, eyebrows raised, eyes wide. All waited.

It was Grimsley who broke the silence. The idea of forming the Media Review Committee had come from the board in the first place, he said—as had the suggestion that the committee, and not the librarian, should respond to complaints about books. It was obvious that the board would approve its own recommendations the next time it met, but there wasn't time for that before taking up *Our Bodies Belong to Us*.

Stroking his beard, Grimsley said that he hoped they all knew that he didn't like banning books. Prudence, however, proscribed what a public school library could contain. Keeping *Our Bodies* on the shelves could result in a serious problem (Dollinger's election to the school board and—happy thought!—Grimsley's replacement?), and thus it behooved (how superintendents loved that word) the committee to consider the book most carefully. At this point he nodded to Marvin LeMaster, who said, thick eyebrows raised, "Has everyone read the book?" All murmured yes.

It took nearly an hour of wrangling (total silence from Wanda P.) before Gordon Hoover moved to remove *Our Bodies Belong to Us* from the library shelves. (He was not in favor of banning books either, but community standards, etc....) "Maybe we should have a referendum on every book I want to order," Dora said, and Grimsley glared. Wanda Pottsweather (expertly) seconded Hoover's motion. Discussion? Dora fumed. "Pretty soon it'll be *Tom Sawyer*," she said, "and I'm not *kidding*." All in favor? Hoover and LeMaster's hands went up.

A pause, then LeMaster said, "Mrs. Pottsweather, we're voting to remove *Our Bodies* from the library shelves."

Mrs. Pottsweather, blinking her codfish eyes, said, "I'm aware of that."

Ted and Dora glanced at each other. LeMaster, frowning, crossed his gigantic legs. "All those opposed?"

Ted and Dora, of course—and, miracle of miracles, Wanda P.!

LeMaster's face went slack and sad. "Mrs. Pottsweather, you're *opposed?*" he said. "You seconded the *motion.*"

"Right," Wanda Pottsweather said, her mouth chewing at something, "I love to second things. But as far as the book goes, I read it cover to cover, and think it's great. I gave birth to eight kids, but lots in there was new to me, and I want it to stay."

Stunned silence. LeMaster looked at Grimsley, widened his eyes and said, "The motion has been defeated." Dora looked like she wanted to jump up and shout hooray.

In her office she said, "Wanda Pottsweather! Who woulda thunk it?"

Ted laughed. "I loved the look on LeMaster's face."

"And what about Grimsley? What about him?"

"Good old Wanda the Wonder. There's hope for suburbia yet."

"You bet!" Dora said with bright eyes.

• • • • •

Six days after this meeting—the day before the graduation exercises—Marvin LeMaster crippled his ankle jogging; was plastered into a cast and plied with pain-killing pills. Ted couldn't believe it. Huge Marvin *jogging.* Didn't the idiot realize his ankles could never withstand such strain? He *deserved* to get hurt.

Why was he jogging, anyway? To get in shape for *what?* Could it be he was...? Highly unlikely, but if Marty *Zeller* could fool around... He pictured those huffing tons in T-shirt and shorts, and laughed.

But not for long. It was LeMaster's duty to hand out diplomas on graduation night. Phil ("You Can Do It") Shuck, vice-principal, distributed awards and scholarships—in theory, that is. In practice, he always managed to palm the job off on somebody else. Last year his excuse had been sterling: chicken pox. This year it was rather shaky, but it served: he was off to Mississippi for an extra-early resumption of work on his doctorate, that ever-elusive Ed.D. he'd been chasing as long as he'd been at Whitman. Big Marv had agreed to assume Shuck's duties—to give out both diplomas *and* awards (as he'd done the year before)—but now he was out of the action and all was chaos.

To the graduation committee's profound relief, Grimsley said he'd present the diplomas—but insisted that the Whitman staff handle scholarships and awards. A logical choice for the job was Ethel Spoonfeather, guidance counselor, but Miss Spoonfeather, sad to say, had a pathological dread of public speaking; the very thought of the platform set her aquiver. Rumor had it that certain members of the English department could use their native tongue gramatically, and Burk was asked if he could think of anyone on his staff who... Of course he could: Mr. Wharton had served as yearbook advisor, had chaperoned the prom, knew most of the class quite well, and would surely be glad to help. Ted, still not over the "B" he had gotten from Burk on the rain poems paper, felt like murdering him.

• • • • •

The yearbook copy for graduation night had been written a month in advance. It was Joy's work, and said:

With lumps in our throats, we took our places on the Whitman High School stage for the very last time. With misty eyes we received our diplomas, fond memories filling our minds. Soon we were marching down the aisle and our high school days—

incredibly—were over. Another chapter of our lives had closed. How short it seemed to us now!

September will not find us together again in Whitman's familiar halls, but we fervently hope we will never be forgotten there. We know that we shall never forget our Whitman High, and never lose our gratitude for all we have learned within its walls. ("You think that's sappy enough to satisfy them, Bear?")

As things worked out, there wasn't any stage and aisle involved: the event took place on the playing field behind the school, on a portable platform set up on the edge of the track. It was a perfect evening: mild and fragrant, a copper sun going down in a purpling sky, a pale breeze rustling the sycamores on the edge of the park to the east.

Ted, bringing up the rear of pomp and circumstance, watched kids ascend the platform and take their seats. In her pure white mortarboard and gown, Joy glowed angelically. Ted tore his eyes away from her, faced front, sat down in the first row of chairs: felt her eyes boring into his back.

Grimsley opened the show with some drivel. The valedictorian (Mary "Virgin for Life" Willis) and salutatorian (Freddie "Motormouth" Wilkinson) spewed the obligatory guck (America...future...hopes...). The seniors stood and belted out a song. The orchestra's last sad notes died out in the darkening air as Grimsley took the podium again, told how certain members of the class had earned through their dedicated efforts, etc., etc., and Ted was standing up and walking, taking Grimsley's place.

In the hush—sheet music fluttering on stands below him—he picked up the first of the envelopes in the pile; half turned to the graduates and firmly read: "A four year scholarship to Pine Grove College, Pine City, Pennsylvania, to...Leslie Ambler." Little ("Lemon Cunt") Leslie smiled, came forth to the hearty applause of the crowd; took the envelope out of Ted's hand with a "Thank you," as if he himself were responsible for the award; then smiled again and returned to her seat. Ted read another envelope, another kid came up, smiled at him, took her loot. The next one got him a little: "The Whitman School Service Award to..." (dramatic pause) "...Rick Castle."

And Rick, who should have been going to Brown but was going to work to support his new family instead, came up and shook Ted's hand. "Good luck, Rick." A bitter smile: "Thanks, Mr. Wharton."

A four year scholarship to Dale Withers, a pudgy denasal drip who'd written an infuriating letter to the paper on the folly of disarmament; four years to Delaware Union College for Susan ("Pocketbook Pussy") Merry; and when Joy's name appeared—on the next *two* envelopes—Ted's heart went slushy, backed up on itself.

"The Martin Zeller Award for Academic Excellence to...Joy R. Dollinger!"

She rose, came forward, stood in front of him, more beautiful than he had ever seen her, the white of the gown setting off the deep tan of her skin. His arms felt weak as he said, "Congratulations, Joy," and gave her the envelope, shaking her hot electric hand. "Wait, don't go yet." Her bluegray eyes. He looked at the audience, smiling, dying inside: "To Joy R. Dollinger, the scholarship of the North American Insurance Institute to Aubrey College, Danesville, Pennsylvania."

He gave her the ticket out of his life as the audience clapped. She smiled and shook his hand again, the sadness three dimensional in her eyes. Her gappy teeth; a quick flash of *The Joy of Sucking.* "Thanks, Bear."

His heart did another backflip as she walked away. Stippled sweat flushed his forehead and neck.

On he went till the envelopes finally ran out. He asked all the winners to stand again, there was loud applause, he sat down on the metal chair; looked away to the long black line of pines at the field's far end—at Venus, a perfect jewel in the high June blue. Then Grimsley gave out the diplomas and Joy came forward again. Ted wished with all his heart she would go to some party, stay out all night and get drunk, meet some guy, and just be a high school kid.

When the music stopped and the marchers scattered and mortarboards bobbed among bald and bleached and gray bent heads, and little kids in dresses and sport-coats were running all over the place, Ted heard her voice: "Mr. Wharton!"

He turned to see her, ten paces away. She said, "Could you come here a minute?"

He took a deep breath as he suddenly understood.

The guy was slightly taller than Ted, with bluegray eyes behind trifocal gold-rimmed glasses; sculpted cheeks and thin blond hair. Age indeterminate. Fifty? The cheeks were infused with a rosy glow, an almost cherubic flush. He was well on his way to becoming an angel? His wife was also tall, but darker, with coppery hair and green eyes. Her face had a puppet-like First Lady look, the look of a woman who'd sell cosmetics or vitamins door to door.

"Mr. Wharton, I'd like you to meet my parents."

Solemn handshakes. Ted nodded. "Mr. Dollinger, Mrs. Dollinger..." Why was she *doing* this? Her father had a no-nonsense insurance man's grip; he stared with his hard blue eyes. "Joy's told me a lot about you," he said, his diction as crisp as frost.

"She did a tremendous job on the yearbook," Ted said. With pure mischief he added, "And she was a pleasure to teach."

Mrs. Dollinger smiled tightly. "She told us that you were her favorite teacher."

"I'm flattered."

Placing his hand on his daughter's shoulder (did he rouge those cheeks of his, or what?) Armand Dollinger said, "She's quite a young lady, isn't she, Mr. Wharton?"

"She is indeed," Ted said as he thought of *The Joy of Sucking* again, her puking bout in the Blue Note Motel. "And I'm sure she'll do well at Aubrey."

"I'm sure she will too."

The letter that he and Dora had written—would Armand sully this happy occasion with that? No. With cool finality he said, "A pleasure to have met you," and his eyes were laser beams.

"Oh, yeah," Joy said, "that stapler I borrowed last week, I never returned it, it's in our car. Can I give it to you?"

"Sure," Ted said.

"We're parked on the hill. You're going that way, right?"

Resigned to this minor fate, Ted answered, "Right."

To her parents Joy said, "I'll be right back, I have some other people I want you to meet," and then she was walking with Ted through the happy-sad crowd.

When they reached the car—a pale blue Lincoln—he said: "So what was the point of that little scene?"

The tip of her tongue touched the gap in her teeth. "Just wanted to give you a look at your in-laws-to-be."

He stared. She laughed. "Actually, it was his idea, not mine. Wants to see what the enemy's made of, I guess."

"Terrific." The Lincoln's rich, high sheen. "So where's this stapler?"

"What stapler?" People trudged up the hill to cars and parties, restaurants, night clubs, homes. She fixed him in her gaze and said, "So when will I see you again?"

"I don't know," he said.

A desperate look, that firm press of her lips. "Bear, it has to be soon. I miss you so much, I *need* you."

"Hi, Mr. Wharton!"

Sue Merry, waving. "Hi, Sue. Congratulations again on the scholarship."

"Thanks."

A quick cold rush in his chest as he turned back to Joy. He said, "Not this summer. We can't see each other this summer."

"What?" Pain in her voice.

"We can't, it could ruin everything. Getting out of a marriage isn't easy, and we can't take chances. If we do, it could all fall apart."

"But I *need* you, Bear."

Little pinpricks of sweat. "I need you, too, but we have to act...maturely. Whatever you do, don't try to get in touch with me in any way—phone, letter, in person, *anything*. When it's safe, I'll get in touch with *you*. Do you understand?"

"But Bear..." Her face was strained, flushed, anguished, and passersby looked at them oddly. With moist and pleading eyes she said, "I *love* you. And I want to kiss you—*now*."

He wished he could vanish, evaporate.

"Congratulations again on your scholarship, Joy," he said with a stiff wide smile. "You're going to love Aubrey, it's great."

Tears were staining her face; she was lovely, pathetic, horrid. "Of *course* you'll miss Whitman," he said with a shrug. Around him kids in gowns walked past, the cast of the X-rated yearbook. "But things will work out just fine, you'll see." He stared at her. "Okay?"

She bit her lip; the tears streamed down. In a tremulous voice she said, "Okay."

To his left he saw her parents and a blond-haired boy—her brother, he assumed—start walking up the hill. He smiled and shook her hand. "Been a pleasure having you in my class," he said.

She pressed her lips together, fighting tears; said softly, "Love you, Bear." Then turned and started down the hill to join her family, just like any other graduate. Linda Straub said, "Bye, Mr. Wharton, have a nice summer," with a cheery smile. Ted smiled back, waved, and moved with the upward flow.

Behind the Plymouth's wheel he felt tired and old. Kids laughed and shouted, posed for pictures, took off caps and gowns. A cluster of girls he'd had in English—last year? the year before?—broke into a happy song. He listened, catching only a few of the words. Joy was nowhere in sight. He drove home.

29 • FAREWELL TO A TROUBLESOME FRIEND

What a scorcher of a summer!

He would get to the wharf in South Philly at eight (the heat in the eighties, humidity close to ninety, the mud-brown Delaware River shrouded in orangepink stink), and as soon as he left the station wagon his sweat glands would shift into high. Up, up the sun would crawl, throwing dizzying glitter on hundreds of hoods, roofs, trunks. He would swelter and drip through the morning, distracted and sluggish. At noontime, the wharf ablaze, he would listlessly gnaw on the flaccid sandwich he'd packed, then sit in the shade of the brown-brick warehouse walls with the morning paper till one o'clock, when he had to get moving again.

The job wasn't hard, it was just so incredibly *mindless*. What he did was go out to the brutal lot with some serviceman about to be sent overseas and check his car for damages. (Decades since the end of World War Two—and all these troops still shipping out to who knew where!) He'd circle the proper numbers on the form attached to his clipboard, go back to the office, have the serviceman sign the form, and turn it in. Not a whole lot of challenge, and plenty of time to think. And a lot of his thoughts, perversely enough, were of Joy.

Her father's letter appeared in the paper on Ted's second day at the job. Certain persons at Whitman High, it said, were attempting to smear him by linking his efforts to those of the Fascists. These persons, he was happy to note, did not have the school administration's support. He urged the community to help restore decency to the schools by voting him into office in November. As Ted read the letter he pictured that cool, imperious face. And he thought the *Colonel* was bad as a father-in-law! Just imagine *this* guy!

He was scared to death those first few weeks that Joy would attempt to see him, but she kept her word. She was waiting for him to do his part. She trusted him. What a rat he had been to lie like that about love and divorce—but he'd had no choice. Someday, he hoped, she'd be able to understand that.

As he sat in the nine-tenths vacant warehouse waiting for servicemen to arrive, as he read the paper in the fetid and steaming shade, he remembered those scenes in the tawdry motels, in the cars, in the A-V room. As time went by it seemed more and more like a dream. He had actually done those things! In school! With classes in session around him, with teachers and students just inches away in the hallway beyond the door. To have risked ruination for the sake of an animal need—he could hardly believe that now.

His fervent hope was that during the summer she'd meet someone new, someone close to her age, and start a real relationship—if that was possible for her. She was charming, brilliant, beautiful, expert in bed—and vitally deficient in some hard-to-pinpoint way. He could easily picture her having a string of affairs and marriages, a battalion of men, and—because of that fatal flaw—never really connecting; always being, in essence, alone.

As tropical July wore on and Joy maintained her silence, his optimism increased.

Maybe she *had* found someone new. Oh Jesus, let it be so! A summer fling to fill her up till school began would do just fine, for once at Aubrey some lecherous classmate would certainly win her hand (etc.).

When he thought of their times together it stirred him up all over again, but uh-uh, no more of that, he was off it for life. His fragile mind, his fragile flesh—he simply wasn't *equipped* to have affairs.

He felt good again. Unenthusiastic, bored, but good. All signs of his troubles belowdecks had disappeared. A couple of weeks of abstinence had fully renewed him, and little by little his drive, that vile devil, had revived. He'd propositioned June a few times; she'd consented twice and his hopes had been high, but that fire she'd shown right after her hysterectomy (A.H.) had definitely died.

She was back to staying too late at the office and wearing herself to a frazzle; hoping in vain for chateaubriand with sauce maitre d'hotel and sighing at his casseroles; letting dirt and disorder obsess her (the Electrakween whined every morning and night). In short, she was settled into the old B.H. (Before Hysterectomy) routine—though she claimed that she hated routine.

As in the B.H. days, her only adventurous area was travel. Her next jaunt to Europe would be in October, to Denmark. Her last vacation had been wrecked by tumors, she hadn't seen Denmark in over two years, and wouldn't he come along? She'd planned it for the Columbus Day weekend; all he'd have to do to be able to go was take a few personal days. He reminded her that personal days were for critical things like funerals. Always some excuse, she said. And what about the shore at the end of August, had he made up his mind about that? Okay, okay, they'd go to the shore, but Europe was out of the question. "You mean you'll *never* go to Europe again?" (Oh God did he hate that tone!) No, he didn't mean that, but how could he go in October when he had to teach? Next summer, then, she said—a tour of Greece. He thought of heat, white blinding space, dry rugged stones, though his knowledge of Greece was strictly from travel posters. Why not Denmark next summer? he wanted to know, where it would be cool. Well why would she want to go back to Denmark next summer after going this fall? That's not what he *meant,* he said. They started to shout. They threw up their hands. Angrily he went out back and scraped the goddamn trim.

His existence was back to square one. (He was even full of intestinal gas again!) How could he live this slow suburban death after all he had tasted with Joy? Well, he'd have to, that's all. (Some putty required here and this molding was rotten, needed to be replaced.) He'd have to be happy with what he had; another affair would destroy him. It would, he knew it would, and yet—would that knowledge deter him? Seventeen years of faithfulness and he'd dived right off the deep end. It had happened once, so why not again—and again and again? The idea revolted, intrigued him. (No doubt about it, he'd have to caulk this entire goddamn seam.)

· · · · ·

It shook him up when the Phillipses split toward the end of July. No hanky-panky going on, it was simply that after twenty years they'd decided they were "incompatible." Incompatible! In Ted's mind they'd been fused together like Siamese *twins* they'd been so well matched, and now... No more dinners with *them* on Saturday nights, and that was a blessed relief, but their breakup was highly disturbing. There had to be *some* stability in the world, and if not the Phillipses—who? He thought of their Rod-sodden daughter, Eileen, of how she was taking it all. Well, maybe it wouldn't last. Maybe they just needed time apart, a change of scene. He hoped so—for Eileen's sake. Maybe they'd get together again, decide that Saturday dinners had caused their rift, and forswear them. That would be perfect!

He still had a lot of Joy's dope. Late at night, if the day was especially hard (a mealtime tiff with June, the news about the Phillipses, a nonstop stint on the docks), he'd roll a loose and clumsy joint (recalling Joy's dexterity) and sit in his study and smoke. Sometimes in the dope's false clarity he'd think he had sorted things out, and would sleep the dreamless sleep of the redeemed. In the morning the sky would be jumbled and hot, the horizon fried. As he battled and cursed the traffic his thoughts would be leaden, confused. Where had those smooth and smoky late-night insights gone? All he saw was his neighborhood—forever—and June, his teaching—forever—until he was old. The same things over and over. Well what did he want, a life full of thrills? Then why not try auto racing? Or skydiving. Hah!

For exercise, he worked on the house. It kept June off his back, and anyway, it was much too hot to jog. After the scraping and painting was finished, he finally tackled the roof. As always, there was much more to it than he had anticipated. How pathetically optimistic he'd been to buy one can of roof cement!

Every Saturday after breakfast he'd haul out the ladder and make the climb. Off with the old and on with the new: new sheathing (in some spots), new flashing, roofing paper, shingles... Talk about hot, he damn near broiled, but didn't rush to finish, took his time: for he found an odd peace up there above and away from everybody, felt like a minor god. The dull remote dramas of the neighborhood dwarves—the Chryslers, the 7-Elevens, Monsantos, Bonanzas—were somehow comforting. Their trips to the shopping malls and the shore, the release and retrieval of cats and dogs, the coming and goings of UPS and the mail—all seemed perfectly ordered and inconsequential. He remembered those Christmas gardens he'd had as a kid, those miniature trains.

From his perch he could see a good chunk of Waughbach Cemetery, and observed two funerals, one sparsely attended, one packed. When everyone left, he was there to see the green awning removed from the hole and the dirt shoveled in, and he thought of Keats's "easeful Death," of Freud's death wish, of Whitman's craving for the end. But Whitman was sick for so long, in pain for so long. Had he felt that way about death in his open road days?

Ted's view of the road in front of his house—flat Harmony Lane—was extremely open (pale Jersey landscape, puny trees). He could see to Washburn Avenue in one direction and all the way to MacArthur Drive in the other. On two occasions, spaced only three hours apart, red Hondas a block and a half away had sent him down the ladder so fast he'd damn near broken his neck. False alarms both times, thank God.

• • • • •

He was up on the roof when the tragedy struck.

The first Sunday in August: the Bonanzas' dog, in heat for sure this time, got loose again, and T.S. Eliot, also loose (Kim's fault) and horny as ever, went charging after his pleasure across the street. A rough roar of teenage engine as Ted gooped a shingle with roof cement, then high staccato yelps—and Ted turned, amazed to see T.S. Eliot rapidly whirling around in the street, as if frantically chasing his tail. The car ran the stop sign at Washburn Avenue, was gone, and Kim screamed, "No! Oh, oh!" and ran into the street, and Ted rushed down the ladder, his fingers sticky and black.

It was spinal cord damage; the dog had to be destroyed. Ted couldn't stand how the glassy-eyed animal stared at him—as if begging him to reverse the hurt and make things right again. As the vet did the deed, Kim vomited. She had never known a time without old T.S.; they had grown up together. He was the first creature close to her heart to die.

That evening, at Kim's insistence, they held a memorial service in the dining room. Standing in front of the clear blue vase of blackeyed Susans that Kim had arranged, Ted made a few kind remarks—and actually meant them. Oddly enough, he was going to miss that fool beast; for whatever irrational reason, he'd grown attached to it. The dog had been, after all, a part of the family, and a part of the family was gone. Kim cried through the whole ten minute affair, and even big grown-up Brad had tears in his eyes. Grandmothers and dogs: in the world of kids they were sacred, could do no wrong.

30 • SUMMER JOB

He had just about convinced himself that Joy had found a new flame, when she made her appearance.

It was a torpid, hazy day in the middle of August, the day before Kim turned twelve. (Good grief, she was getting breasts!) June played hooky from work to go over to Philadelphia to buy some presents (for herself as well as for Kim, of course), drove Ted to the wharf in the morning, then went on her way. She would pick him up around noon, they'd eat lunch together, she'd shop some more and come back when his day was done.

He was checking an unbelievable Chevy—one so covered with scratches and dents that he felt like drawing a single gigantic circle around his inspection form—when suddenly he saw, miragelike, not more than a hundred yards away—the little red car gleaming bright in the orange sun.

His heart wobbled, fell in on itself. He looked at his watch as the pimply serviceman followed him back to the office. Twenty of twelve. His sweat thickened. He had the serviceman sign the form and sit on the plastic couch. Through the window he saw Joy get out of her car and start walking his way.

A major delight of these summer jobs was the company one kept. Eddie Kracovitch, a burly, chain-smoking, hairy-armed guy with a limp and a constant leer, said, "Catch *this* piece," as he crushed out his butt in the lid from a mayonnaise jar. Dick Masterson, dark and wiry, missing his teeth and possessed of boundless energy (caffeine-and sex-inspired, no doubt) said, "What a chunk! I'll handle *this* customer!"

"No, I will," Ted said. "She's my daughter."

A silence fell. Kracovitch mumbled, "Pretty girl," and lit another Camel.

Pretty? She was dazzling: in a flimsy sleeveless yellow dress, sunglasses and sandals, her sunblond hair tied back, her skin pure bronze. "I wonder what she wants," Ted said to the "guys" as he went out the door, and his heart was going a zillion miles a minute.

They came up to each other, stopped. She said, "Hi, Bear."

The heat and the shattering glitter of chrome. How the hell had she found him? "Joy, what are you doing here?" Up close she looked different, more mature.

"You told me that when it was safe, you'd call. You never did."

Thick droplets of sweat on his forehead. Good God, June would be here soon! He said, "I didn't call because it *wasn't* safe. The time was never right."

"Come on."

"I mean it. It still isn't safe—especially *here.*"

She pursed her lips. "I have to talk to you."

He looked around; the car lot gleam, the hissing sounds of factories, the clack of a slow freight winding along the river. "Okay."

They walked to her car and got in. He told her where to drive: down the cobblestone street below the wharf and under the vacant pier.

She turned the engine off and set the brake. Trash plastered the muddied cobblestones and clung to the rotten pilings; slats of fuzzy sunlight slashed the planks above their heads. She looked at him with her sunglassed eyes and said: "I love you. I haven't been out with anyone else all summer, I love you, I need you."

Her lips: so soft, so sweet, so sad. He said, "But I told you, we have to be *careful. Extremely* careful. Christ, June is supposed to meet me here for lunch, do you realize what could happen?"

She pressed those soft sad lips together and said, "Let's have it out with her right now and get it over with, I can't wait anymore."

He swallowed, his throat thick, painful. "Joy, that would be suicide."

"Why? Didn't you tell her yet?"

"Of course I did."

"She knows about the divorce?"

Oh God forgive him. "Of course."

"Then what's the problem?"

"The—terms of the settlement. I've told her I want a divorce, but I haven't talked about *you.* If she knew there was another *woman* involved..."

"Woman, yes," Joy said, "remember that, I *am* a woman now, not one of your little high school students. I'm stronger than I was—and richer, too, Daddy's loosened the purse strings now that I'm going to college. So I don't really give a damn about the settlement, it's not important."

He closed his eyes on a dizzy brownness. Opened them and shook his head. He was clammy, sticky, the Honda was gathering heat. "It may not be important to you, but it is to me," he said, "and I don't want to blow it. All you have to do is hang in, be patient."

A tightness around her mouth as she said, "I'm *tired* of being patient. I've been patient and patient and patient for two months now, how long will I have to wait?" She licked her lips quickly and said, "I want you to do it."

"*Here?*" he said.

"Right here. Right now—to prove you still love me."

A heavy and painful breath. "Joy, June will be here any minute."

"Not *here.* You didn't tell her to come down *here,* did you?"

He didn't answer; looked at the brown and fetid river, saw the long slow freight on the opposite shore.

She said, "I'm not wearing anything under this dress," and slid her hands along her thighs, slowly lifting the silky fabric. Shifting position, she bent her knee and drew her leg up, showing everything.

He thought, Oh Jesus Christ, and said, "But I'm sweaty, I'm dirty."

165

In a ragged, breathy voice she said, "That's how I like you—dirty," and that was it.

His back was cramped; he banged his leg against the gearshift as she squirmed and wriggled up and down, intent on her task, eyes closed. He thought of June. Drum rolls, the guillotine! She worked harder, harder; the windshield steamed, the car was filled with her heavy scent, she shivered and winced, said, "Good! Oh, good!" His tension and fear and frustration exploded. She held him, panting, her rich flesh smothering, slick on his shuddering skin.

A seagull mocked; another one mucked around at the foot of the pier. Thick brass-plated sun threw bars on the Honda's hood. "I'm eighteen now," she said. "Did you notice the difference?"

His face was slimy, sour; his stomach burned.

"Oh Bear, I've missed you so much."

The soft, slick lick of the water on the ooze. He said, "Joy, you have to believe me, I'm doing the best I can. When things are settled..."

She still had her sunglasses on: reflections. "When, Bear? When?"

He wet his lips. "Well when do you leave for school?"

"September eighth. Can it be before then?"

"I don't know. I'll do my best. But please...don't come here again, it's just too dangerous. I'll let you know when it's safe, I promise I will."

His ankle hurt. Reflections; lips; her pulse enveloping him. "I'll wait, Bear, I'll wait."

When she'd gone he walked back to the office. The grade was steep and his heart pounded hard with that odd occasional slushy sound he'd heard on graduation night. It didn't sound good, it didn't feel good, he would have to get back to his jogging. He thought of Marty Zeller as the sun beat down. Sweat gushed, and he felt sick.

When he reached the top of the hill June was there in her car. "Where *were* you? I've been waiting ten minutes, it's bright as hell."

He fought for breath. "I'm sorry... We're running late... Let me get cleaned up."

"Well hurry, I'm starving."

He went inside, washed his hands and face, put his tie and jacket on. Came out and opened the door on the passenger side, sat down. Still breathing hard, he stared at the warehouse, the cars.

"What's this nonsense about your daughter?"

He laughed as his heart did another reverse. "The wife of one of the soldiers came by to pick up some clothing she'd left in their car. I told the guys she was my daughter. It was a joke."

She started the engine. "Oh."

His organ throbbed as she pulled out into the street. He said, "Did you find what you wanted this morning?"

"I got Kim's stuff, but I didn't get mine."

He leaned back, closing his eyes. June and her things, her goddamn things. The car rattled over the cobblestones. He opened his eyes and looked in the sideview mirror—and was startled to see a red Honda behind them, half a block back. Was it really *her?* It trailed them north to Lombard Street, and when they turned off, it went straight.

They ate at a fine French place in Society Hill that June had read about in *Downtown* magazine. Ted agreed that the food was superb (at those prices it better be!), but he hardly touched it. "Was everything satisfactory, Monsieur?" the waiter asked with a fine Philadelphia twang and a look of concern at Ted's plate. "Just great," Ted said with a pallid smile. "Everything was just great."

• • • • •

That Saturday he resumed his jogging; was panting along at a snail's pace on Washburn Avenue, dripping with sweat, a slight stitch in his side, when his ankle gave way.

The pain was astounding. He buckled and fell knees-first on the gravel shoulder, scraping his hands, crying out, his mind brilliant with disbelief.

He stayed there awhile, then, grimacing, struggled up. The ankle would not bear weight. On his healthy leg he hopped on the gravel, each jolt dealing arrows of pain. He waved at the shooting cars, but on they flashed, zip, zip, throwing cinders and dust.

He remembered how cramped he had been in the Honda with Joy, how funny his foot had felt. That must have set him up for this. His just penance. He fluttered and hopped like a wounded bird as the cars zinged by, and thought of the way he had laughed when LeMaster had hurt *his* foot. Just penance, all right. He fell, skinning his arm on the gravel. "Shit!" he yelled. There was no one to hear. He thought of T.S. Eliot spinning around in the street, his plaintive yelps. Christ, how was he going to make it home? "Goddamn it, somebody stop!"

They all thought he was drunk, of course—or trying a con of some kind. They'd pull over to help and he'd whip out a gun and rob them or rape them. Oh yeah, it's a great country, folks.

He struggled up once again. *Goddamn!* Hop-hop. A pause. Hop-hop. At this rate he'd get home by Monday for sure. He started to laugh, it was all so absurd. Half a mile away from his house and he was a total stranger, nothing; could die on this road for all anyone cared. He kept hopping. Just penance. His damaged ankle grazed the ground and he yelped.

It was Mr. Chrysler who finally pulled over and asked if he wanted a ride. Ted thanked him profusely; sank into the "oatmeal gray" Imperial with plush maroon upholstery and throbbed in air-conditioned agony on the brief ride home. Mr. Chrysler (what was his real name? Balzetti? Baretti?) told him about a friend who'd thrown his back out jogging and had to have major surgery. That was two years ago, and he still wasn't right. "Best leave that exercise stuff to the young," was his advice. Ted thanked him again and hopped into the house.

He had torn several ligaments (just as Big Marvin had! but not as badly), and that was the end of his job for the rest of the summer. Laid up with his slippered foot on a hassock, the accrued fatigue of the last several months crashed down: he was *exhausted.* During that week between school work and wharf work, June had kept him busy with house work. He'd never had a chance to feel his tiredness, but now... He dozed, he read, he watched TV. Watched clouds and daydreamed, tried not to think about Joy. Jumped alert at each ring of the phone. It was never for Bear.

By the time they left for the shore he could walk pretty well, but the foot still hurt. As he limpingly packed the car, June claimed he was playing it up, malingering. Malingering! What for? To get out of swimming? Did she think he wanted *sympathy?* She had never shown any patience with his infirmities; an occasional twenty-four hour flu was okay, but stretch it to forty-eight hours and she was resentful—and now this foot thing was already in its third week.

In the car he swore his senses were deceiving him. "That smell, what is it?" he said.

"My new perfume."

"I don't like it."

"You're just still mad at me."

"I'm not. (He was.) "I just don't like it."

June took a poll. Kim loved it, Brad thought it was "fair," and what could Ted do, tell the truth? —That June had picked *Joy's* scent? "I wish you wouldn't wear it anymore," he said.

She shrugged. "I like it and I will."

Sullenly he drove, his ankle throbbing. At the first rest stop the cat (yes, the cat!) took off and they had to wait for half an hour till it finally came yowling back. Ted didn't like cats, but Kim had been so upset by the dog's demise that he'd given in and let her take it—free, from Joanie Dangerman. He'd wanted to call it W.H. Auden—even though it was a girl—but Kim had won out with "Missy."

What a great way to start a vacation! But once they got settled in, it wasn't bad. They had beautiful weather, saw movies, ate out every night; he dragged himself into the water to keep June happy, played miniature golf with the kids. June relaxed, he relaxed (no phone to worry about!), and lo and behold, they even got it on a few times when the kids were out bowling or feeding the video games. On their eighteenth anniversary, they ate at a fancy expensive place and June ordered Mumm's champagne. (Mumm's! *Joy's* champagne!)

Back home he felt rested; his foot seemed good. He finally finished repairing the roof, and, wonder of wonders, during the first downpour—no leaks!

31 • THE RETURN OF BLUE NOTES

Anxiety built as September eighth—Joy's day of departure for Aubrey—drew near, but Ted kept himself busy, and soon he was back at orientation-workshop days for the seventeeth year in a row. (He knew the routine by heart.)

Then classes started, the eighth went by like any other day—without any word from Joy—and everything was just as Ted wanted it: boring.

Brad was at Whitman now, a freshman. He'd turned fourteen on September first, had his braces removed the next day, and now during most of his hours at home he wore an atrocious facial appliance known as a positioner, which gave him a sinister, simian look and rendered him practically mute. His attempts at communication consisted of gutteral grunts and inscrutable signs, he skulked around the house like a wounded ape, but his teeth, when visible (mostly in school), looked great. When he ran into Ted in the Whitman halls or walked past his room, he'd flash him his brand new expensive smile, proud that his dad was a teacher.

When he made the freshman soccer team, *Ted* was proud. He went to the weekday games with Kim and the weekend games with Kim and June. The Saturday Brad scored his first goal (in early October), the four of them celebrated at McDonald's (like any other American family), then went home and watched TV. (How *normal* life was now.)

But Joy was never far from Ted's thoughts, especially since her father's school board bid was starting to gather steam. After a silent summer, the paper was noisy with ads. "Dollinger for Decency"—the slogan was everywhere. As part of his master strategy, he'd filed a formal complaint against seven books in the high school library, spreading the word with more letters to the *Courier-News.*

He was getting attention. Responses, pro and con (dishearteningly, mostly pro) appeared for days after his letters ran. A couple of these were from kids. One came from Ellen Clooney, a girl in Ted's junior English class, saying that she was a hundred percent behind the Dollinger for Decency campaign. Teenagers weren't adults, she said, in spite of what people might think. They were scared to death (of what, she left to the reader's imagination: Sex? Their bodies? Life?), and Mr. Dollinger would defend their right to take time to grow up. Vote for him on November fourth! Ellen Clooney was a clunky dink who played solo flute at assembly programs. Always over-prepared in Ted's English class, her answers were just like her music: completely correct and completely lacking in soul.

Brad read the letters and asked what the big deal was. This guy thought *A Separate Peace* was *dirty?* Ted wondered what new goodies Brad had collected since spring, and thought of his own magazines in the back of the closet—with dormant Master Muscle lying on top. He'd have to get rid of that crap before somebody found it. —Before *Brad* found it and was shocked (and he would be, of course). Was life nutty, or what?

· · · · ·

At the meetings of the Media Review Committee, Salinger, Hemingway, Vonnegut, Hesse and Steinbeck passed with no trouble. LeMaster saved Dollinger's top priority—*Our Bodies Belong to Us*—for last.

"What?" Dora said. "You mean we have to vote on a book each time a person complains about it? —Even if we've already voted before and agreed to retain it?" No, LeMaster said, but in this particular case, another vote was warranted. At the time of the vote in the spring, the school board hadn't yet passed the new review procedure (which, in a summer session, it had). At this point he looked to Grimsley, who, as before, was present to offer counsel, and Grimsley nodded.

Ted was livid. In the spring, when Grimsley thought the vote would go his way, he'd said that board approval of the new procedure was a mere formality; once he had lost, though, he'd changed his tune. A typical superintendent mind at work.

But Dora jolted everyone then by standing her ground—and moving that the committee abide by its previous vote on *Our Bodies.* Wanda Pottsweather, true to form, said, "I second the motion."

When LeMaster called for the ayes and nays, the ayes carried it three to two. Gordon Hoover kept his nay hand up an inordinate length of time. When it fell, Dora asked if LeMaster, as chairman of the committee, was going to write to Dollinger and inform him of their decision. LeMaster looked blank for a minute, then glanced at Grimsley, who nodded again. "Of course," Big Marvin said.

Then Grimsley stroked his beard and cleared his throat and said how much he disapproved of the action that Dora had taken. It meant, he said, that Dollinger would surely appeal to the board. The board had approved the committee procedure with the clear expectation that complaints would be resolved at committee level and not take up board time.

Dora, squinting, eyebrows knitted, asked him to clarify. Did he mean the committee should ban all books that people objected to so that no appeals would ever reach the board? Had they done that? Grimsley asked. They'd passed Hesse and

Vonnegut and the others, hadn't they? Then just what *did* he mean? Dora wanted to know. He meant, he said, that a tremendous amount of trouble could have been forestalled if *Our Bodies Belong to Us* had been removed from the library shelves in the spring—or even now.

Even if they'd done that, Dora said, Dollinger would appeal their decision to retain the Hesse and Vonnegut and other books. Grimsley disagreed, saying that Dollinger would probably never have challenged the other books if *Our Bodies* had been removed. Dora quickly disputed that. Dollinger had challenged the other books along with *Our Bodies* in April—and Grimsley knew it, he'd seen the complaint form.

Ignoring her, looking straight ahead, Grimsley said that having to hear appeals like these could cripple the board. It had far more important things to do than spend its time making petty decisions over some foolish book.

Foolish book? Dora said. She didn't think *Our Bodies* was foolish at all, and perhaps such "petty" decisions might prove to be some of the most important a school board would ever make.

Now Grimsley was really ripped. Turning from Dora as if she had ceased to exist, he reminded LeMaster to offer Dollinger a chance to meet with the committee. LeMaster assured him he would. There was a silence in which Gordon Hoover coughed and Dora picked at her lip. Then, looking at Ted with a blank soggy stare, LeMaster said, "Any further business?"

There wasn't, and the meeting (the third of the series—on a Friday, yet) was adjourned.

•••••

Dollinger, of course, never took up LeMaster's invitation to meet with the group. His new letter to the paper said that this "self-appointed Media Review Committee" obviously had no respect for the wishes of the community, and he urged his supporters to write to Superintendent Grimsley and voice their displeasure in no uncertain terms. With their help he would score a resounding victory next month. Dollinger for Decency!

The weekend after this letter appeared, June and the kids took off for Denmark, and Ted was alone in the house—except for Missy, a nice enough kitty, but not much of a conversationalist.

At first he enjoyed the quiet, but after a couple of days he looked forward to getting his family back. Brad had matured amazingly since starting high school, and was actually human now. Kim was also progressing, and things with June...weren't bad. Ted was making an effort. He didn't complain about seeing the Sleepers and Grays on Saturday nights, he stifled his protests and went to the movies and restaurants she liked, and it seemed to help. Or maybe her hormones were calming down. Whatever, things were better. While June still worked too hard and cleaned too much, she was more content. He'd prefer it if she were *exciting* as well as content, but Jesus, you couldn't have *everything*.

Wednesday morning of the week that his family was overseas, he was looking through his staffroom mailbox and—paralysis!

There among all the crap—the blandishments of this and that educational publisher, the Dailygram, a flyer announcing a conference on teaching the classics to illiterates—was a pale blue envelope with an unmistakable scent—the scent June had taken to using—and a postmark from Danesville, PA.

He took it into the john to open it, locked himself in a stall. Sat down.

The letter said she still loved him madly, was confused and upset that he hadn't been in touch, and wondered how the divorce was coming along. Please write as soon as possible, or, better, call—and she gave a telephone number where she could be reached. She adored him, couldn't possibly live without him. She was sorry he'd hurt his foot and hoped it was better. What she loved about his cock was how the head was ever so slightly larger than the shaft. How she wished she was sucking it right this minute!

He slumped on the pot. Oh God, *now* what to do? Hoped his foot was better. How in the world did she know about his *foot?* He read the blue missive again. The obscene part, disgustingly, firmed him right up. "God, oh God," he whispered; tore the letter to shreds and dropped it between his legs. *Wham!* the thundering rush of water whisked it away. If only he could erase his connection to her with a blast like that!

The letter obsessed him. In senior English, Peter Oakes, an outdoorsy-dyslexic kid, asked a question that Ted never heard; he only knew he'd been spoken to when the giggles came filtering down through the wall of his worry. Soon after, he made a boo-boo of the type all teachers dread: said "peter butter" for "peanut butter," causing himself (and Peter Oakes) to blush bright red. Not as bad, perhaps, as Gordon Hoover's "Napoleon Bonafarte" or Paul Whiteside's "tit for tit," and certainly not in a class with George Frangelli's beauty about news leaks ("Some reporters will take a leak and make a whole story out of it"), but it *was* pretty bad (and *very* Freudian).

At the start of sixth period—junior English this year—he went to the A-V room for the overhead projector. It was the first time he'd been there since spring. What a weird sensation! He felt as if all they had done back then was preserved in these cream-colored walls, might come oozing out any minute. The birch formica table, monitor, VCR— He broke into a sweat when he thought of how reckless he'd been. He reached under the table to feel in that crack where they'd hidden their notes: nothing there. He opened the drawers and looked inside, reaching all the way into the back: a couple of old Dailygrams, and that was all.

There was nothing left of their presence here, no clues to their sins, yet the room made him queasy. What a perfect spot for an interrogation! Surely he would confess if they gave him the third degree here. Surely the walls would shout Guilty! Guilty! as he mouthed his despicable lies. He wheeled the projector into the hallway, the door clicking shut behind him. His well-trained heart surprised him with its rapid beat.

• • • • •

June and the kids had a fine time in Denmark. If only he'd come along! Next time he would, he promised. Had he missed them? June wanted to know. Yes, he had, he replied. (It was true.)

Brad and Kim had grown again, about an inch apiece. They brimmed with amusing stories; told: how they caught the wrong train and almost went to Germany; how a waitress brought them chocolate cake for breakfast when they thought they'd ordered eggs; how teenagers there wore sweatshirts with the names of non-existent U.S. colleges—University of New Hamster, etc. Ted chuckled and nodded and thought of Joy's letter. Denmark was great, he agreed as he watched the slides, and the bomb kept ticking.

He decided he wouldn't respond. Surely she'd get the picture if he was silent; surely she'd realize the truth of the situation; surely, with all her beauty, with all her libido, it couldn't be very much longer before some stud hooked onto her and washed away her Wharton days with his lust.

• • • • •

The second letter arrived on Halloween. There in his box at school was the same blue envelope, the same familiar, terrifying smell.

She missed him frantically. She was thinking of dropping out of college and coming back home. She had gone to Aubrey sure that he'd join her soon, and without him she felt like an exile. "I'm a prisoner in this goddamn room at this goddamn school with my goddamn infantile roommate—who plays the goddamn cello! —And it isn't funny, Bear." At night in the dark her heart ached so much she was sure it was going to break. When she got the shakes there was no one to help her. No one!

When he left the john this time *he* had the shakes, and he taught all day in a daze. At home he went into the study and opened the window on crisp fall fragrance and zonked himself out on her dope. Trick or treat. Jesus Christ, what to *do?*

• • • • •

Armand Dollinger won a seat on the school board by just a hair—two dozen votes—but he *won*. His letter thanking all who had helped his campaign was so sanctimonious, so smug, that Ted felt like torching the *Courier-News*. LeMaster, face heavy with gloom, said Whitman High had better prepare for a seige, and Dora was in a tizzy.

Three days after Dollinger's victory, Ted came home to find a pale blue scented envelope on the dining room table. Kim had brought in the mail after school; June, praise the Lord, was still at work. Ted took the envelope up to the study. Heart pounding, he ripped it apart.

Since she hadn't heard anything from him, she thought maybe the mail that she'd sent to the school hadn't reached him. From now on she'd send it to his home. She repeated the points in her earlier letters; she was crazy about him, hated Aubrey, was desperate to know how things were going with the divorce. If she didn't receive a reply this time, she said, she'd be forced to question his sincerity, and would have to consider what action to take to bring him back to her. Following the usual pornographic part she said, "I guess you're really ripped that Daddy won the election. You ought to be, you're number two on his hit list, you know. (Ms. Rosen is number one.) Please, *please,* Bear, do what you have to do and we'll run away and get married and fuck our insides out and have zillions of kids. The libido-meter's getting rusty, if we don't start using it soon it'll fall apart."

Ted stared at the pale blue page, thinking: *Daddy?* Since when was she on such cozy terms with her father? Consider what action to take to bring him back! What the hell was she *talking* about? She sounded just like the old man!

He took the letter into the bathroom, tore it to pieces and flushed it. The toilet gurgled, sent half of it back again. A blue scrap of paper with "fuck our ins" floated, whirled in the water. He flushed again. More evidence disappeared, but not all; the trap seemed to be clogged. He attacked with the plumber's friend. Outside the door Kim said, "You in there, Dad?" Sweat dotted his brow as he said, "The toilet's plugged up, use the one downstairs." He rammed the plunger down, sucked hard: saw Joy, her face, that mouth, those teeth. He flushed again. Only one scrap was rejected this time; it said, "hit list, y." He scooped it out of the bowl, rolled it into a ball, then shoved it into the sink drain and turned on the tap.

He stared at the porcelain gleam, breathing hard. What the hell was he going to do, this girl was *serious*. More sweat on his forehead; he wiped it away. Okay, okay, keep cool, it was simply a matter of finding the right way to handle this mess, and he'd do it. *Must* do it. He heard Kim flush downstairs; looked into the toilet again to make sure all the blue had stayed down; flushed again for good measure. In the whirlpool's aftermath, one tiny azure speck. My God was she tenacious!

32 • A TALK WITH DADDY

"George, could I see you alone for a minute?"

The "gang" had been in The Spouting Whale for two hours now and was pretty well gone, the racket was loud, it was black outside. "Sure, Ted. There's an empty booth in the corner."

Ted had already had four beers. As he got off the stool he felt wobbly; the room looked dim. He sat across from George in the booth. George grinned and said, "What's up?"

Ted broke into a sweat, wet his lips, tried to start, found he couldn't. He took a deep breath and exhaled.

George frowned. "Hey Ted, are you okay?"

"Sure, George." His dark heart fluttered, fell. He ordered another beer and sat in silence, watching the Miller High Life sign go around. The waitress came. He tipped her generously. —Then sipped the bitter brew and steeled himself—and told George everything.

George stared through his heavy hornrimmed glasses, devouring every word. When the story ended, he said in a voice filled with genuine pity, "Fever forty-two."

"What?"

"Fever forty-two," George said. "Your thirties are great, right? You're feeling good, the kids are fun, you're starting to think you might actually figure life out, and all at once, you can't believe it, you're forty. And it starts to hit you: twenty more years and you'll be sixty. Sixty! Ready to die! Then, around forty-two, it really hits, and God, you go wackadoo, off the deep end."

"You *know*," Ted said. "But how? I mean— Did you—?"

"I didn't, but I came close."

"And now you're what? Forty-five?"

"Forty-six."

"So you made it."

"I hope so." George shook his head sadly. "My God, in the *A-V* room?"

Ted's mind was giddy; his skin felt numb. "George, Jesus Christ, I was crazy or something. It's no excuse, I know that it's no excuse, but the thing is, what do I do? Three letters! She's sending them to my *house*." His throat closed up; he looked at the table and held his head, heard the dizzying rattle of laughter and talk at the bar. Too hot in here, too hot!

George looked at him closely, his round cheeks flushed. "What you do," he said, "is you get out to Danesville as fast as you can and meet with her. Go see her, Ted. It's the only way you're going to calm things down."

"But that might just start it all *over* again. Are you sure?"

"I'm positive. Go see her this weekend. *Tomorrow.* Promise her that you'll come to see her every so often, then *do* it. It'll show her you care."

"But what do I *say* to her?"

"Tell her things have changed. You're getting on better with June and you can't leave the kids."

"She'll go nuts. She *is* nuts. She was under psychiatric treatment for over a year, she's liable to—Christ, do *away* with herself, for all I know."

George shrugged. "So you don't make her take the whole dose all at once, but you *have* to go see her. *Believe* me, Ted."

It was nine twenty-five when he walked through the door. June was angry, alarmed. He said he didn't feel so hot and went to bed. —And lay awake half the night semi-sick, thinking over what George had said.

When he woke up at six fourteen he had made up his mind: George was wrong. He just didn't know the situation well enough, he didn't know Joy. To see her again would only stir everything up.

To be perfectly honest, he didn't *trust* himself to see her again. If she threw herself at him he might not resist—in spite of how he felt about her now.

He went to the study and wrote her a letter explaining his situation. He and June had discussed their problems and realized they still loved each other. He knew she would be distressed to hear this, but he was a married man, she'd known that all along, and a married man's allegiance was to his family. She was young and bright and beautiful, etc., and she should forget him and find a nice guy her own age who wanted to spend the rest of his life with her. Time would heal, etc., etc. He walked to the corner mailbox, pulled the door down, dropped the letter in and right away wanted it back. Dark visions assailed him. He pictured her reading the words he had written and hanging herself in that dorm, being found by her cellist roommate... If that happened he'd never forgive himself.

· · · · ·

A week went by, two weeks, and not a word. She had taken his letter to heart and had come to her senses? Dare he harbor such hopes? The bomb in his brain would not stop ticking.

Thanksgiving dinner was scrumptious. June cooked the turkey perfectly, Ted made his special stuffing (superb), and Kim made marvelous candied sweet potatoes. Brad, the ever-amazing, baked a pumpkin pie that didn't look bad at all. June was ready to slice it when the telephone rang.

Expecting a call from Lee Carswell, a friend who wanted information on a St. Croix cruise, June said, "I'll get it," set the knife on the dining room table and went to the kitchen. And Ted, staring into the pie, already knew.

"Hello? Who? Just a minute," and June was holding the receiver up, her hand on the mouthpiece. "Joy Dollinger," she said.

Ted's knees were rubbery as he rose. He went to the kitchen and took the phone, forced cheerfulness into his voice as he said, "Hello?" —And a delicate, intricate structure inside him collapsed and crashed into dust.

A moment of nothing, the hum of the line, then: "Oh Bear, it's so good to *hear* you."

"Of *course* I remember you," Ted said, his voice sounding hollow and flat in his head. "So how's college?"

"Oh Bear, don't start with that happy horseshit. I'm home for Thanksgiving, when can I see you? I'm totally *desperate*."

Thin sweat. "That's terrific," he said. "So Whitman was adequate preparation for Aubrey?"

"I have to go back on Sunday, Bear. Let's make it tomorrow, okay?"

"No, I don't think so," Ted said, just as pleasant as he could be. And all at once the Little Man was there! He'd been gone for months and now he was back, and was moaning and holding his head.

"I *do* think so," Joy said. "I think you'll *have* to, Bear."

Ted's heart took a sudden plunge. "I don't believe—"

"I've told Mommy and Daddy everything."

All breath was gone. His mind was a vacuum, empty blackness; time spiraled away from his eyes. He heard his failing voice say, "Is that right?"

"That's right. My father wants to see you tomorrow morning at ten o'clock, here at the house. The address is 14 Hollingswood Drive. You know where the neighborhood is, you followed me home one time, remember? You'd better be here, Bear."

He was numb from his neck to his waist, his arms tingled, his mouth was all mushy and soft. "Terrific," he said. "I'm glad that it's going so well." June pointed the knife at the pie as she looked at him, raising her eyebrows. He shook his head no. "Great, good to hear from you. And lots of luck."

"You better show up, Bear."

"Goodbye."

He hung up—and thought he would die on the spot. He went to the sink, ran a glassful of water and drank, feeling bloated and ill. "You sure you don't want some?" June said said from the dining room. "It's delicious."

"I'm sure it is."

"You'll hurt Brad's feelings."

"I'll have some later, I'm really stuffed." He leaned on the counter, trying to steady himself. Armand Dollinger, Jesus Christ!

He felt clammy and cold. Wiping his forehead, he went to the dining room, started to clear the table. Keep busy or faint, keep busy or go insane.

June said with a smile, "What did she want? Another dance?"

June never forgot a thing, had it all stored away somewhere. "Just wanted to say hello," he said.

"I think she has a crush on you."

Brad said, "Oh Mom, come on." Kim giggled, "A crush on *Dad?*"

The dishes clattered as he stacked them beside the sink. Keep busy. He said, "She's doing real well. It looks like she'll make the dean's list."

"Terrific," June said.

As she put the milk in the refrigerator, Kim said, "Dad, you still taking us skating tomorrow?"

Ted, scraping garbage, winced theatrically. "Oh darn it, Kim, I can't. I have to take the station wagon to Herb's."

"What's wrong with it now?" June asked.

"Exhaust pipe. Rusted through." He rinsed the plate. "Can you possibly take them?"

"No, tomorrow's not a holiday for me."

"Oh, right. Well what about Saturday, Kim? The car should be fixed by then."

Kim pouted, but said okay.

"Terrific." He went to the dining room to get more stuff. Keep busy, keep busy, keep busy, keep lying, oh God…

•••••

The "village" of Hemlock Run was an upper middle class violation of the Jersey pine barrens, six years old. From Ocean Pike—the two lane strip of road that ran to the seashore, sixty miles east—all you could see were trees and the hand-carved goldleaf-inlaid sign at the entrance of Hollingswood Drive. The Drive looped into oak and pine, and from it sprouted other loops ("ways" in the lingo of the image makers), each of these forming a "mews." Each mews was screened from every other mews by trees and shrubs; each house was screened from every other house. In short, it was a really classy place.

Thinking about America's love of aristocracy, Ted left the Plymouth three houses away from his destination and walked past the clusters of yews and rhododendrons, the lawns still green even now, on the edge of winter. Parking his car at the end of the "way" made him feel not quite so vulnerable, though he wasn't sure why. Maybe arriving on foot would unsettle the old fart a bit.

The Lincoln Continental stood in the driveway. Its bumper asked, "Your child's textbooks—have you read them?" and asserted, "It's so great to be a CHRISTIAN!" In the open garage sat Joy's Honda.

A thin cold whisper of wind brushed the trees as he went down the brownbrick walk to the Dollingers' door, a solid construction of robin's egg blue set deep in the tan vinyl wall. A swollen hurt engulfed his heart. As he rang the bell, he saw that his hand was shaking.

Armand Dollinger's face was pinched and pale—except for those two bright quarter-size balls of red on his upper cheeks. Religious fanatics quite frequently had that blush. Why? Overindulgence in Communion wine? It was mystifying.

Ted entered the padded hush and followed Armand into the living room, where Helen (he'd found her name in the phone book) stood in a trim, blue dress looking tired and totally sexless. Did daughters really become like their mothers as time went by? Was this sad-looking woman a sign of the future Joy? Armand, nodding to the couch, said, "Please sit down."

Ted sank into the deep gray plush. Armand and Helen sat opposite him in matching gray plush chairs.

There was a suffocating, mausoleum quality about the place: the heavy furniture, the thick beige rug, the brocade draperies tied back with bows… One corner held a floor-to-ceiling knickknack cabinet lighted inside like a waterless, fishless aquarium. The room seemed expressly designed for somber occasions like these; it was impossible to picture a person relaxing in it.

Armand was wearing a gray flannel suit that looked several sizes too big. In each of his jacket's lapels was a pin: one was a tiny American flag; the other one was obscure. He stared at Ted for a couple of minutes, and then, in a calm and quiet voice, began.

Ted was a degenerate, he said, a traitor to his profession. Coercing Joy into foul acts of sin was a crime that could not be forgiven. "That my very own child should fall victim to the curse. That the forces of evil should desecrate her innocence, in spite of all I have done to protect her." The eyes behind the goldrimmed glasses looked moist.

Ted gritted his teeth in the stifling stillness. Force of evil—he'd never been called *that* before. What your innocent daughter likes about my cock, he wanted to say, is that the head is just slightly larger than the shaft. What he said was, "I didn't coerce her."

Helen Dollinger snapped to life. "Don't you *dare* say that! We refuse to tolerate your lies!"

Ted steamed. Did they actually think that he was the first one to get it on with their daughter? He hadn't even been the first *teacher.* He cursed himself for having destroyed the letters she'd sent. Where *was* she, anyway? The house wrapped its smothering silence around him.

Armand Dollinger cleared his throat. Looking down at a spot on the floor, he launched into a long tirade against the decadence of modern life, which included a really freaky attack on computers, which he called "machines of the anti-Christ." As he spoke, the flush in his cheeks intensified. He looked unreal, embalmed, like those plastic TV preachers ("What a glorious day it is, my friends!") whose speech and manner were so bizarre you'd call the funny farm in a flash if anyone acted that way in your home. He expounded with blind unwavering certainty. How wonderful it must be, Ted thought, to know without question what's *right.*

On and on he went: to explain how liberal organizations behind the spread of pornography (like the Mafia? Ted thought) were controlled by "secular humanists" and "anti-Christians"; how the Whitman High School library was run by an "anti-Christian person." With pious false concern he said, "Mr. Wharton, tell me—what is *your* relationship with God?"

The "anti-Christian" crap had really ticked Ted off. How refreshing if the guy would just say "Jews." (Why were there never any bumperstickers saying, "It's so great to be a JEW!"?) The reply he wanted to give to Dollinger's question was: My relationship with God? It's not too comfortable. Know why? Because God doesn't have a representative form of government, He's a dictator. That's what he *wanted* to say, but he bit his tongue. His role for the day was repentant sinner; if he played it well, he just might be able to pull himself out of this goddamn mess. Calmly, trying his best to sound sincere, he said, "Mr. Dollinger, I don't think your major reason for calling me here was to have a religious discussion."

Helen Dollinger, looking as if she had a broomstick up her ass, frowned, shifting in her chair. Her husband said, "Very well, then, let's get to the point. Joy has talked of"—his eyelids drooped—"of marrying you. You have twisted her mind to such a degree that she'd really consider that. —Consider marrying *you,* a heathen, degenerate anti-Christian opposed to all the values that she has held dear her whole life. This is the extent to which you have brainwashed her."

Ted exhaled a deep breath, thinking, *Where the hell is she? Where is she hiding?* How he would love to expose that tattoo on her ass right here in this morgue of a living room! What would the old man say to that?

Lips pursed, eyes pinched, Armand said, "I don't know what blasphemous garbage you've put in my child's head, but I certainly hope you don't intend to marry her."

A touch of sweat. Was she listening? In a soft voice, almost a whisper, Ted said, "No, I don't. I never did."

"I am very relieved to hear that," Armand said. Still squinting, his eyes impenetrable discs, he gravely shook his head and said, "Mr. Wharton, I am forty-one years old. I've met many, many people in my life, I've seen a lot of the ways of the world, and believe me, a relationship like that would never work."

Ted looked at him: at his pallid face, his receding forehead and wrinkled eyes, as the thought sank in: He's younger than I am! The "old fart" is younger than *I* am! A horrible flush of embarrassment struck and he turned bright red. Wetting his lips and swallowing hard, he said, "I agree with you. It wouldn't work."

Armand Dollinger crossed his legs and nodded; said, "I would like you to promise me that you'll never—under any circumstances whatsoever—see my daughter again."

That's *it?* Ted thought. Can that be *it?* Barely able to stifle his glee, he said with a glum expression, "I promise."

"I would like you to swear on the Bible," Armand said.

He pushed himself out of his chair and went to a large mahogany desk near the wall; returned with the black pebbled volume; stood before Ted and said, "Please rise."

Ted did, feeling totally foolish. He placed his hand on the Book, remembering inaugurations and thinking about those loyalty oaths, how absurd they were; how any subversive with half a brain would sign one in a flash. After calling him a heathen, how could Armand put any faith in this? He had to believe that the Bible itself could extract the truth from all, believer and pagan alike. It was all so comical and painful that he nearly laughed. But he kept a straight face and repeated his promise. When he finished, he said, "I suppose that concludes our business."

"Not quite," Armand said. "Please be seated again."

Ted sank against the bristly plush, thinking: *Now* what?

Sitting across from him again, Armand stared with a curious frown—as if Ted were some strange mutation he'd been asked to study—then said, "About this book in the high school library, *Our Bodies Belong to Us.*"

"What about it?" Ted said.

Armand's brow remained furrowed. "I want you to help me remove it."

Ted almost laughed in his face. With a sniff he said, "Really."

"Yes, 'really,'" Armand said. "I want you to write to the *Courier-News* and retract your position. I want you to condemn *Our Bodies Belong to Us* as a piece of vulgar trash."

Ted's heart was racing now and his jaw was tight. He ran his tongue along his upper teeth and said, "I've agreed not to see your daughter anymore. I'll honor that agreement. But as far as retracting my views on censorship, no, I can't do that."

Armand, nodding slightly, said: "I think you can—and here's why. You can, because if you don't, you will soon be charged with sexual assault."

The stuff of nightmares. He'd talked to George about it. "She'd have to be under sixteen," George had said. "You're sure?" "I'm positive. It's only statutory rape if she's under sixteen."

"Joy's over sixteen," Ted said. He could feel his pulse in his throat.

Armand shifted position; rubbed his forehead with thumb and two fingers; adjusted his glasses; said: "But you see, Mr. Wharton, that only applies if no force was involved."

"No force *was* involved."

Helen Dollinger snorted disgust.

"In a court of law," Armand said, "it would be my daughter's word against yours. Whose word do you think a jury would sooner believe?"

Ted didn't reply.

"If you are found guilty of sexual assault," Armand said, "do you know what it means? It means five to ten years in prison."

Nausea struck as Ted heard a sharp scraping sound. He turned to see a tall, blond good-looking boy leave the house. The kid was a Whitman freshman. Ted had seen him around, but hadn't realized that he was Joy's brother, he'd grown so much since graduation night. The door clicked shut. Good God, had he heard? If so, all Whitman would know the whole story by Monday. Sweat started to roll down Ted's cheeks.

"Court proceedings can be so messy," Armand said with a tight, pained look. "Expensive, time-consuming... Even if one is found innocent, his community standing is often impaired. A man with a reputation to protect, with a wife and children to support, must exercise prudence. Even to be *charged* with a few counts of sexual misconduct—"

"Okay," Ted said, feeling suddenly shaky and cold. "Okay...I'll write the letter."

"Thank you," Armand said, and leaned back in his chair.

Helen Dollinger suddenly burst into tears, then stood up and left the room.

Armand's pale eyes were squinty with loss and hurt. "You have brought a terrible sadness into our home," he said. "I can never forgive you for violating my child. But if you write the letter against *Our Bodies Belong to Us,* I will never say anything further about your sin—to anyone. I give you my word as a God-fearing Christian man."

Silence rang in Ted's ears, and an urgent, painful pressure welled up in his bladder. Sweat rimmed his lips as he took a deep breath and said again, "I'll write the letter."

Dollinger nodded, got up from his chair. "I'll expect it in the *Courier-News* by Friday."

Ted rose. "I can't guarantee they'll print it," he said, "but I'll mail you a copy to let you know that I've sent it."

"That only lets me know you've written it."

"Well, true, but—"

"If you send it to them, they'll print it."

That was that, and they went to the door.

The sun was gone and the sky was a pearly white. Ted hurried down the walk, the drive, the "way," sure Joy was watching him. Behind the station wagon's wheel, he stared at the threatening sky. A sharp pain jabbed his chest below his throat. He thought of Dora Rosen, closed his eyes and said in a soft voice, "Jesus Christ." The pain stabbed his breastbone; his bladder burned. He drove to The Spouting Whale and pissed and pissed and pissed, his whole body shaking like mad, then drank three beers.

• • • • •

By the time he got home he was in a horrendous mood. Kim asked if he'd take them skating this afternoon instead of tomorrow. "I said tomorrow and I *meant* tomorrow!" he snapped. Kim stared and June said, "You don't have to be so sharp with her, there's no reason for that!" "Don't start telling me how I should *be!*" he said, "that's for *me* to decide!" He stomped to the study and started to work on the letter, head sluggish and sad with beer.

It was agony, pure agony. *What* did Dollinger want him to call *Our Bodies?* Garbage? Filth? Vulgar trash, that was it. But he couldn't say that, he just couldn't. He typed a draft, crossed out, erased, read it over and tore it up. By the time he had something suitable, the sky was dark.

He stuck the copy in the envelope addressed to Dollinger and sealed it, hating himself. In cold November blackness, cursing, he walked to the mailbox, pulled down the door, and…gone, irretrievable, done. He stared at the mailbox, his damp breath white in the streetlamp's pink glow, feeling sick with himself. Well okay, what else could he do? Disgrace his family? Lose his job, put them out on the street? Dora would be furious and George would think he'd lost his mind, but he had no choice. *I give you my word as a God-fearing Christian man.* A god-fearing Christian blackmailer, that's what he was!

As he walked back home he remembered something Joy had told him long ago, something about her father's insurance firm. —Some story about an endorsement by a phony professional group—The Association of Retired Pharmacists, was that its name? He could have kicked himself. Why hadn't he thought of that at Dollinger's house? It might have given him some leverage.

When he came inside and hung up his jacket, June asked if he wanted to eat. There was leftover turkey and stuffing and sweet potatoes. No, he said, and he went to the study again and worked on another letter—to the State Consumer Protection Bureau. This one was easy, a pleasure to write.

He had recently received some promotional material from the Colonial Safeguard Insurance Company, he said. Their insurance plans, this material claimed, were endorsed by something called The Association of Retired Pharmacists. The name hadn't rung a bell with him, so he'd looked it up—and failed to find it in the listings of professional associations. A pharmacist friend of his said there wasn't any such group. So what was this company trying to pull? Maybe some other organizations they listed in their brochure were non-existent too. Such fraudulent advertising made him seriously question the integrity of this Colonial Safeguard outfit. What was the Bureau doing to protect the public against such criminal practices? He demanded an investigation. Etc.

He really piled it on, and it made him feel slightly better. In the cold he dropped the new letter on top of the others, thought of Dora, felt sick again. When he went back in he still didn't eat, but drank two double shots of scotch and went to bed. He lay there, a firm, sharp pain pressing into his chest—the pain he had felt in the car after leaving Joy's house.

He was drifting toward boozy sleep when he jerked awake to the image of Joy's tattoo—a hot sun searing his eyes—and lay there in darkness and pain, June next to him now and snoring. At last he gave up and went down for more scotch, and stared in misery at his bright suburban carpet and appliances, the cat rubbing into his leg for her pleasure till finally he booted her one. Then, following his long-established custom, he watched some crap on TV with no sound until consciousness seeped away.

• • • • •

In the morning, that stake in his chest was worse. Had he pulled a muscle? Cracked a bone? Was it simply trapped gas? —Trapped misery, fear, trapped disgust with himself, was that it? He drank coffee and restlessly looked at the *Courier-News*; at the heavy sky. When he couldn't bear to sit still anymore, he put his sweatsuit on.

"Are…we going skating today?" Kim asked, looking slightly afraid.

"After my exercise," Ted said, trying hard to sound kind, and he went out the door.

A good clean bite to the air, the smell of snow, and he started to jog right off. He had to break that tension, dissolve that pain. But what if it was something serious? What if it wasn't just fear and disgust, but real pathology? Jogging just might be the worst thing to do—the thing that would throw him over the edge to die a Zellerian death. He thought of Marty and Joy as he shuffled past Mr. 7-Eleven's house, his breath making moist gray clouds. Another lover bites the dust, Joy joyrides on.

In front of the Snap-On Tools' place he started to pick up steam. Mr. Snap-On, contributing to the suburban ecology by raking leaves into plastic bags, nodded slightly as Ted inadvertently caught his eye. Around the bend and onto Washburn Avenue, the scene of the twisted ankle fiasco.

The fog of his breath was thicker, his legs started limbering up. He thought of the letter he'd written, of Dora Rosen, the Dollinger boy going out through the door—carrying the secrets of Ted's shame? He thought of June and Brad and Kim waiting back at the house as Daddy indulged in his foolishness. The knot in his chest was as hard as ever but the jogging felt good, so he turned on a bit more speed.

He paused at the traffic light—and heard the thunder of his heart. Looked carefully both ways, then jogged across the street and along the road's shoulder. An occasional car rushed at him, whooshing past, stirring spirals of dust and leaves. His breath coming hard, he wished he could run down this road to a whole new world where all would be fresh and new again. What a coward he'd been, giving in to Dollinger's demands like that. But he'd had no *choice,* it was write the letter or else. Now he'd have to face Dora, and what could he say? The goddamn pain in his chest just wouldn't melt.

Another car in the distance, coming closer. Size, shape, color—and the shock of recognition. The hood bearing down, the squeal of the brakes—and the Honda was on the shoulder in front of him; stopped, dust puffing around its tires. And Joy was there as beautiful as ever, slamming the door behind her.

His ribs were heaving, he gagged on his breastbone pain. He had run and run and run and had not escaped. Would he ever escape? She said, "I have to talk to you."

It was the first he had seen her since summer. She'd changed again: her features were firmer—she looked like a woman now. Her voice had a certain softness that he'd forgotten, overtones the phone had not conveyed; and suddenly all they had ever done came back in vivid color. He was terrified: of her, of himself, of the fact that she was so close to his home, his real life, to June and Brad and Kim. They could come out of Harmony Lane at any minute and he would be stone cold dead.

"He wouldn't let me see you yesterday," she said. "He said he'd handle everything, I couldn't be involved." She pressed her lips together in that way she had, then suddenly she rushed up, threw her arms around him, held him tight. A car whined by. He stood there frozen, smelling her scent, that perfume June used now.

"I love you, I love you!" she said, her voice lost in his chest, in his sweatshirt's gray. "I have to have you back, I must!" She was shaking against his pain. My God, somebody would see them! He said, "Let's get in the car."

She turned away, got back behind the wheel. He opened the door on the passenger's side, slid in. It was warm in there. Her tongue was pressed against her teeth. "I love you, Bear."

He looked at her sad, imploring face and said, "You love me and you told your father everything. Is that how you show your love?"

She shook her head. "I was just so *desperate.* That letter you sent, you were just going to throw me away like that, without even coming to *see* me. It wasn't right."

Why didn't I listen to George? Ted thought. Why didn't I *listen?* He said, "Well you've made things impossible now. I promised your father I'd never see you again. I can't break that promise, he'll take me to court and I'll lose my job. I'll go to *jail.*"

Tears stained her cheeks. "My father is so damn *dense,*" she said. "I wanted him to say you had to marry me, *that's* why I told him about us. How could he *do* this to me? I *live* for you, Bear." She wet her lips, leaned close to him; in the warmth he smelled her hair. "My life is totally empty without you, I *have* to have you. Say you'll marry me and I'll change Daddy's mind. I can do it, I know I can."

It was one of those moments when past and future were nothing but thin, pale scraps; where all that existed was Now, this instant, swollen and hard and huge. "Joy, the best thing to do for the present is what your father asks. Go along with him, let him cool off. Give him a few more months and *then* approach him, he just isn't ready now."

Her red, wet eyes. "And what do I do in the meantime? Live at that idiot school with that idiot cello-playing roommate? Keep screwing myself with a carrot carved into the shape of your cock?"

A lightning bolt of lust went through him. He swallowed hard.

"We have to be patient," he said. "It will all work out in the end, I'm sure, but we can't rush things."

She rolled her eyes, exasperated. "You *always* say that. Take your time, don't rush. Well I won't be young *forever.* I'm not going to live *forever,* and neither are you. We have to act now, now is all that *exists.*" She pressed her lips together again and said, "Yesterday I almost died when I saw you on the walk. When I heard your voice again I went out of my mind. As you and Daddy talked, I listened and pictured us doing the things we did, and I used my finger, Bear." Slowly she licked her lipsticked lips and said, "It can be the same as ever, you know. It can be, look." And suddenly she raised her skirt and under it she was naked.

He stared at her delta; familiar heaven.

"Why fight it, Bear? You're not going to live forever, so why resist?"

His mouth was dust. He said, "I made a promise. I wrote to the paper. I'm doing what I have to do, please, try to understand."

"I understand how good it feels," she said, "and so do you." She slithered down and parted her thighs, revealing slick inner vermilion. "Bear?"

His sweatsuit's flimsy softness kept no secrets. "No," he said. He shook his head, tripped the door handle, turned, got out. His erection pointing, he stood with his back to the road.

"Goddamn it!" Joy said. "Goddamn it, what's *wrong* with you?"

He kept facing away from her. "I promised!" he said. "I wrote a letter! It's done! I can't do any more! I'd like to but I can't!"

A silence. A car rushed past, then another car, and "God*damn* it!" Joy said, her tearful voice drowned in the Honda's small cage; and her engine started, her tires tossed gravel, ripped onto the asphalt road. He heard the sound diminish; turned and saw the red spot disappear.

Shaking all over, weak all through, his erection thoroughly wilted now, he closed his eyes. Behind them the universe swam. He opened them; breathed streams of dampness into the dead gray sky. The pain in his chest was worse than ever. Slowly he started to walk back to Harmony Lane.

He crossed at the light, feeling shattered and small. When he turned into Harmony Lane he forced himself to start jogging again. Play the game, keep up appearances. His legs were leaden, his heart congested, his breathing hoarse in the frosty air. He stood on the mat outside his back door, heard the roar of his blood, felt his pain. Bit his lip, put his hand on the latch, went inside.

Kim was at the kitchen table with chocolate chip cookies and milk. In a tentative voice she asked him, "Dad, can we go skating now?"

He nodded, gasping, closing his eyes. "Yes, we can go skating now, Kim."

33 • TRAITOR

As Dora held the clipping in her fist, the muscles at her mouth were tight and her cheeks were an angry red. She said, "How could you *do* this, Ted? I don't understand, I just don't."

He sat on the other side of her cluttered desk, unable to meet her eyes. In a hesitant voice he said, "You know I was never completely convinced about *Our Bodies,* Dora, and—I just had a change of heart."

"A change of heart." She slapped the clipping down on her desk, ripped into her purse for a cigarette. "Seems more like a brain transplant to me." Struck a match and inhaled and looked down at the clipping again. "'Question the wisdom of exposing children to this type of explicit detail...' 'Unwholesome ideas about sex...'" She fixed him firmly with her eyes. "Do you really believe this crap?"

He looked away again. "It's...very complicated."

She sucked on the cigarette quickly and sharply exhaled. "We agreed on our position, Ted. Don't you think you should have informed me about your 'change of heart' before making it public?"

He looked up sheepishly. "And what would you have done then? Censored my letter?"

Her eyes burned into him. "Of course not! You're free to write whatever you damn well please, but at least I'd have been prepared. To put it in the paper like this without giving me any warning—it's like stabbing me in the back!"

She was right, she was right, and he felt like the rottenest person on earth. "I'm sorry you feel that way," he said. "I was simply expressing my changed opinion, that's all."

She smoked, mouth tight; kept looking at him; smoked; then said in a quiet voice: "You're the only one I could count on, the only one who seemed to understand what this whole thing's about. It's not a matter of a *book,* it's a matter of a constitutional *right.* And all of a sudden it seems you're against that right." She frowned at the clipping, her face more hurt than furious now. "'I call for the removal of *Our Bodies Belong to Us* from the library shelves.'" The cigarette's thin line of smoke trailed up, away. "Do you know what kind of a spot you've put me in? I can't believe it, Ted."

The pain started up in his chest again. He hadn't felt it yesterday—Sunday—and now it was back. He said, "Dora, listen...I'm not even sure myself why I changed my mind. I looked through the book again in a bookstore and...I just felt different about it."

As Dora raised her cigarette, her hand was quivering. When he looked at her eyes, they were moist. "I think you just chickened out," she said. "I think you're just like LeMaster and Grimsley and ninety percent of the others around this school, you'll take whatever position will save your skin." She took a last drag of her cigarette, crushed it out in the ashtray, and stared.

She was right on the mark, yet he felt compelled to defend himself. He said, "Dora, you can't allow *everything* in a high school library. There has to be a limit, you have to draw the line *somewhere*."

She glared at him. "I think we discussed this point before," she said. Then snorting a quick, short laugh, she said, "Do you know what the world is like today? Do you *know?*" Her face was so filled with emotion it scared him; he thought she might burst into tears. She looked at the papers on top of her desk. "Let me tell you a little story. Remember a girl named Allison Walker who graduated last June?"

"She was in my psychology class."

Dora stared. "That was me when I was in high school. You get the picture?"

He nodded; said nothing.

She fumbled around in her purse and came up with another cigarette; lit it, shook out the match.

"I was sixteen years old. The boy I loved was seventeen. We thought you could only get pregnant during your period. So did a lot of other kids, incredibly enough. We found out otherwise." She smoked, lips trembling now, and said, "Three times. We did it three times, and I was pregnant. That's when I learned what it is to be scared—and I mean *terrified.* The scene with my parents, the stuff at school, it was horrible, pure torture. Abortion? Unheard of. Immoral, illegal, dangerous. I dropped out of school to have the baby—*terrified.* My lover, of course, was long gone by the time it was born."

She smoked; held it in, closed her eyes, breathed out. Looked at Ted, her chin trembling, and said: "Born dead. Born dead after thirty-six hours of labor that wrecked me inside so I'd never have babies again."

Outside, in the hallway, a bell went off; stopped, echoing in Ted's ears. The hurt in his chest was a sword. He watched the smoke from the cigarette rise and rise.

In a soft, resigned voice, Dora said, "Years later, when I finished college, I met a guy. We fell in love. He asked me to marry him and I told him everything—I told him I couldn't have kids. He loved children and wanted a family."

She stopped. She winced as if in sudden pain, then it happened—what Ted had been dreading: tears spilled from her eyes and went coursing along her cheeks. "He decided to think it over," she said. "So he thought it over... And every time..." She swallowed; began again. "Every time I see an Allison Walker it's me all over again. I just get so damn *furious,* because it doesn't have to *be* that way. It doesn't have to *happen* that way anymore. Even if it turns out well, it turns out *horribly.* Rick Castle and Allison Walker, what chance do they have with a kid at their age?" Her voice was thin and choking now and her eyes were flooded. "It... Oh, it just makes me sick."

The sword twisted into Ted's heart. His face was a mask; heavy, tired and stiff. No air in this office, just heat and smoke. For a second he thought he might faint.

Dora felt in her pocketbook, brought out a handkerchief, wiped at her tears as she said, "These people who say that sex education should be confined to the home are the people who never *talk* about it at home."

Ted suddenly realized that *he* had never talked about it at home.

"The kids need information, Ted. They need the facts. It isn't fair to deny them the facts and expect them to make the right choices. We say we believe in democracy, but what do we do? We tell them to do what we say and the hell with the logic behind it. We hide things from them, hoping they won't find out. Well it just can't work that way anymore. The sooner we realize that, the better off we'll be. Dollinger and those who think like him are living in the nineteenth century. And you—" She stopped, shook her head and looked down at the desk. "I've said enough. Now you know why I feel as I do."

Ted felt like the world's greatest heel. He didn't know whether he bought her argument—kids who knew the facts got pregnant too—but he felt incredibly sorry for her. He stared at the cluster of dead cigarettes in the ashtray, sick with himself.

She looked at him. "I won't give up, Ted. I won't, I won't quit."

"Don't," he said. "Don't you dare quit, Dora, stick up for what you feel is right."

"I will—because at least I *know* what I feel."

Ted shifted position; the pain in his heart didn't budge. He said, "There's a lot I'd like to tell you, Dora, but I can't. I simply can't."

She stared. "You still have time to change your mind before the next meeting. Think about it."

"I will," he said.

Ashamed, he left her office. Think about it. Think about ruin, prison, disgrace.

At the end of the hallway he ran into Madeline Bisbee, the teacher he'd seen at the porno drive-in the night he had gone with Joy. She told him how glad she was that he'd changed his mind about that awful book, and how much she agreed with his letter. He thanked her for her support, sad, sick, and drove to The Spouting Whale.

• • • • •

He didn't head for home until his fingertips were numb from booze. It was almost six, pitch black, and cold—the coldest it had been all fall. An icy wind cut through his coat. Preoccupied, anesthetized, he felt it dimly, distantly.

June was even later than he was, thank God. Under the unforgiving fluorescence he started spaghetti sauce, burned the garlic, threw it out and began again. Everything happened in time delay, too bright, and the voice in his head wouldn't stop, but he had the sauce at a simmer and the pasta cooked by the time June came through the door.

They sat down right away and June asked him about his letter; she'd seen it in the *Courier-News* at work. Why hadn't he told her about it? And why had he suddenly changed his mind about *Our Bodies?*

He'd simply forgotten to tell her, he said. And he'd changed his mind because he'd finally had a chance to read *Our Bodies* thoroughly. His temples pounding wickedly, his chest still hurting, he suggested she visit a bookstore and see for herself what the fuss was about. *Our Bodies* was downright indecent in his opinion—not the kind of thing that high school freshmen and sophomores should be exposed to, you *had* to draw the line *somewhere.* His mouth felt like cotton; he felt like a total creep.

Brad ate his spaghetti slowly; his face didn't look quite right. Ted said, "Is something wrong?"

Brad shook his head. "It's nothing," he said looking down at his bowl. His odd expression heightened, and he flushed.

"It must be *something.*"

"No. No...nothing," Brad said in a breaking voice.

Ted got up from the table and said, "Come with me."

They went up to the study. Closing the door, Ted said, "What is it, Brad?"

Brad shook his head with downcast eyes. "It's too...*embarrassing,*" he said.

"No, tell me, that's what a father's for."

Brad swallowed. He took a deep breath and let it out and said, "I think you're right."

Ted frowned. "Right about what?"

"You know—the letter you wrote."

"Oh?" (Jesus!) "Why?"

Brad chewed on his lip, averting his eyes again. "I never saw the book you wrote about, but there was this other book..." Pain, agitation on his face.

"Yes?"

"Not a book exactly, a magazine... This kid I know let me borrow it. He snuck it off his brother."

"'Sneaked it away from his brother,'" Ted said.

"Yeah." Looking up, looking even more worried, Brad said, "You think I'll get you for English next year?"

"I don't know yet," Ted said. (God forbid!) "So what about this magazine?"

Brad breathed deeply, a long, hurt sigh. "It was awful," he said. "It had pictures—real photographs—of people doing these really disgusting things. I mean it was just so *gross.* I never knew..." He looked away again. "I wish I'd never read it, that's all. I wish I'd never *seen* those pictures, I can't get them out of my mind. Why do people...? Why do they *do* those things?" There were tears in his eyes as he looked at Ted's face again.

Ted remembered his own encounter with the facts of life: fifth grade, the school-yard, Shirley Blattner brazenly miming the act. Shocked, Ted had said, "I'll *never* do that!" "Wanna bet?" Shirley Blattner had said. Brad—modern child that he was—had known how babies were made since the age of six, but it was a long way from that to *Spurts Illustrated*'s blond. Ted said, "Brad, you...well, you just have to be older to understand certain things."

Brad's chin was trembling as he fought his tears. "Does *everybody* do that stuff? I mean it wasn't *normal,* it was sickening."

Ted wet his lips. (Oh boy, oh boy.) "No, everybody doesn't do that stuff," he said. "And nobody *has* to do it, it's a matter of choice. I know it's terribly confusing at this point, but please, try not to worry. You saw some things you weren't ready for and it was scary, but the scary feelings will go away, it just takes time."

"But I saw it months ago and it keeps coming back."

"I know. But it's not as bad now as it was back then, right?"

"Right," Brad said.

"And as time goes by it will keep getting better."

"I guess so."

"It will. Believe me it will."

Brad sighed again. He blinked to clear his eyes. "You're sure?"

"I'm sure."

"You aren't mad or anything?"

"Why should I be?"

"I don't know, I..."

Ted wanted to hold him, to hug him—as he had not so terribly long ago, when Brad was a little boy.

Brad shrugged. "Thanks, Dad. The talking helped. I wanted to tell you about it before, but, well...*you* know..."

"I know."

"I'm glad you're trying to stop these things, Dad."

Ted felt his headache again, felt the pain in his chest. He said, "Uh-huh."

"Now I guess your spaghetti's cold."

"It doesn't matter, I've had enough. Tell Mom I'm going to do some work up here, okay?"

"Okay. And thanks again."

"You're welcome, Brad. I'm glad I could help."

Brad left. Ted went into the bathroom and took three aspirins, sat at his desk and turned out the light and held his throbbing head. On the movie screen of his mind flashed scenes from *Mastering the Art*. He pictured Brad beside him, watching too. He turned on the light again to chase the images, and thought of Dora Rosen; went downstairs and poured a double scotch.

34 • HIGH NOON

With ponderous solemnity, Big Marvin LeMaster informed his committee that during the past two weeks the school had received a total of sixty-eight letters concerning *Our Bodies Belong to Us*. All but twelve of these letters had asked that the book be banned. In light of this, it behooved the committee to vote on *Our Bodies* again. If it didn't, the matter would go to the board, which would surely support the ban.

Dora Rosen objected. Did Mr. LeMaster really think he had gotten a true idea of what the community wanted? It was *Dollinger's* people who'd written in—at his request. Give her a couple of weeks and she'd flood the school with letters demanding the book be retained.

LeMaster disagreed. He recognized the names of many of the correspondents, all of whom were "independent thinkers" in his opinion. Only six of the letters had mentioned Armand Dollinger, while twenty-three had referred to Mr. Wharton's rather surprising letter to the *Courier-News*. If the committee failed to act in the face of this evidence, what would the school board think? He looked at Grimsley, who simply sat stroking his beard.

Gordon Hoover supported LeMaster, making the further point that removing *Our Bodies* was no big deal, as the book would still be available in the Somerside Public Library. Dora blew her cork. Ninety percent of the kids at Whitman never *went* to the public library, she said—it was hard enough to get them into the library at school. But Gordon Hoover made the motion to reconsider removing the book, Mrs. Pottsweather quickly seconded, and the ayes had it, four to one, Ted feeling like total scum as he raised his hand.

Mrs. Pottsweather said she had changed her mind about *Our Bodies* because of Ted's letter. Her daughter Wendy had told her so much about Mr. Wharton, about what a marvelous teacher he was, that she knew he had to be right about the book.

Some people were easily impressed, Ted thought. As one of last spring's neglected sophomores, Wendy had scarcely caught sight of him all term. When the next vote was taken, the one to remove *Our Bodies* from Whitman High, he cravenly avoided Dora's eyes. All she said in the hall before walking away was, "I'm disappointed in you, Ted."

A few days later, her letter deploring the ban appeared in the *Courier-News*. Ted admired her courage and loathed himself even more. When they met in the staffroom or hall he would mutter hello, his lids lowered, and quickly move on.

Ever since Joy had ambushed him jogging, he dreaded the mail. He caught his breath when he looked in his staffroom box, flipped fearfully through the daily pile as soon as he got home from school—but never found a pale blue scented envelope with a Danesville, PA postmark. As December deepened, he began to believe that she'd finally seen the light. If he got through the holidays without any calls, he figured he was in the clear.

• • • • •

The day before school let out for Christmas vacation had always been dreamlike to Ted. The kids were cheerful, hyperactive, unable to keep their minds on their work, and all that a teacher could do was hang in and go through the motions till time ran out.

He was deep in fourth period English, thinking about what to get June for Christmas, when Allen Burk rapped on his door.

In the hallway Burk said, "Mr. Grimsley wants you. I'm taking your class."

Ted frowned and said, "Grimsley? Wants *me?* What for?"

"You'll have to ask *him* that."

"Where is he?"

"In the principal's office."

Ted informed his kids of the change (scattered chuckles and groans) and started down the hall. It's about the Media Review Committee, he told himself. But *what* about it? Maybe LeMaster had quit as chairman and now, because of his letter opposing *Our Bodies,* Grimsley was tapping *him.* He felt a slight twinge of that chest pain again. He hadn't felt any of that in weeks. And facing Mrs. Crux in the outer office, his heart flipped upside down.

Mrs. Crux stopped her typing; looked over her glasses. She went to the door behind her, opened it slightly, received a message, forced a smile and said, "They're ready for you now."

Ted's mind said, They? They *who?* With a horrible sinking feeling he walked to LeMaster's door. The knob was cold in his hand. He pulled.

As soon as he entered the room it was instantly clear that life as he'd always known it had come to an end.

LeMaster was seated behind his desk, tilted back in his swivel chair, his fat legs crossed, his expression more hangdog than ever. On his right side sat Grimsley, face grave. Vice-principal Phil Shuck, looking fretful and scratching his fringe of reddish-brown hair, was sitting on LeMaster's left. —And next to him sat Joy, wiping tears from her eyes with a pale blue handkerchief.

Grimsley nodded to the one remaining seat—the chair that faced the other chairs—and said, "Mr. Wharton, please sit down."

Ted did, knees rubbery, weak. He clutched the arms of the chair with ice-cold hands. Cloudy with fear and rage he shouted at himself: *Stay calm! Play dumb, it's your only chance!*

Grimsley placidly listed the accusations: Mr. Wharton had forcibly seduced Joy Dollinger in the audio-visual room. Too frightened to resist his advances, she had let him engage her in numerous acts of sexual perversion both in and out of school, even making her pay for motels. As Grimsley spoke, a deadpan executioner's expression masking his delight, Joy sat demurely, straightbacked, weeping quietly and dabbing at her face.

When Grimsley finished, swollen screaming silence filled the room. Heart blasting, Ted put on a baffled smile. "Joy, why are you saying these things? Did I treat you unfairly in class, or what?"

She didn't meet his eyes, didn't answer. Instead she reached into her purse and came out with some papers. "These are the motel receipts," she said, and gave them to the nearest inquisitor, Phil Shuck.

Ted thought: The motel receipts! Jesus Christ, she'd kept the motel receipts— from the very beginning, like a secret agent!

Bald rumpled Shuck looked through the papers, his eyebrows raised, and passed them to LeMaster. LeMaster examined them closely, holding them up to the light as if they were counterfeit bills. "Mmm," he intoned. "Well, Joy, I see your name on some of these, but who are these other people? 'Howie Bangs,' who's that?"

"He used an alias," Joy said. "A different one each time."

Grimsley had clearly caught the pun; his ears were a brilliant crimson. Thumbing through the sheaf of receipts, he said, "These don't prove anything."

"But the writing is all the same," Joy said in a quivering voice. "And it matches Mr. Wharton's writing, see?" She passed another paper. Ted recognized it as an English quiz from last year, with a comment of his scrawled across it in red.

Scanning it quickly, Grimsley said, "It isn't proof." He handed it back to LeMaster, who returned it to Joy.

A clear cool stream rushed into Ted's chest. Round one to Mr. Wharton. Shaking his head with an injured frown, he looked at Shuck and then at Grimsley. Poor child, she's lost her mind.

Ignoring him, Grimsley said, "I think we'd better see the other evidence you spoke about." He clasped his hands and touched his knuckles to his nose.

Joy pressed her lips together in that firm, determined way Ted knew so well; put the motel receipts in her purse again. She hesitated, took a breath, then brought out shiny colored squares of paper wrapped in a rubber band. Removed the rubber band, gave the squares to Shuck.

Shuck stared at the paper on top of the pile, his cheeks and shiny pate suffused with a rich vermillion. He looked like he'd gazed on a Gorgon and turned to stone.

Ted's mind was so full it was blank. The Polaroids! Thoughts spinning and flashing, he pictured the Little Man losing his grip, falling over the edge of the cliff to the rocks below. He flushed with a slick cold sweat.

Shuck examined the photographs, taking his time. His blush had faded now. The squeak of LeMaster's swivel chair and the delicate scrape of one photo against another as Shuck moved on. The sweat on Ted's forehead collected above his brow. To take out his handkerchief and mop himself would not look good at all, so he sat like a statue, soaking, and tried to seem calm.

Shuck passed the photos to LeMaster, screwed his mouth up, frowned, and looked down at his shoes. Ted thought he detected a smile.

LeMaster, wide-eyed and boyish-looking, plowed his way through the pile. He too went red. He gave the photographs to Grimsley; swallowed heavily and looked at Ted with huge cow eyes as if he were terribly, terribly sorry for him. Skin drenched, Ted looked away.

Grimsley stared at the Polaroids. He rubbed his chin, leaned forward, gave the photo on top to Ted. "Is this you?"

When Ted looked at the picture he swore he was going to die.

It was one of their libido-meter super-specials, with Joy on a motel dresser. He was wearing cowboy boots with spurs and a holster with toy six-guns—and nothing else. She too was naked except for a ten gallon hat and a lasso around her neck. Her left hand was hoisting the lasso, which lifted her breasts. They had called this scenario "High Noon," since they'd both been stoned out of their minds.

"What about this one?" Grimsley said, and passed another photo.

Good God, it was "Delicate Operation." She was dressed as a nurse, and he had a phony cast on his foot. (Portent of his ankle injury? Had he *meant* to hurt himself?) Her nurse's skirt was slung high on her back; he was tumid and aiming to enter.

Next came "Illegal Procedure," in which she was clad in nothing but football shoulder pads while he wore a referee's shirt (stolen out of Hank Springer's office!), and "Girl Scout Cookie," with Joy in non-essential parts of her faded uniform.

Ted's eyes were swimming. Every one of his organs was poisoned and maimed, and his skin was a horrible slime. He felt something break in his throat when he tried to speak.

Grimsley said, "May I have them back now, please?" As Ted complied, his arm weighed tons. Over and over he saw Marty Zeller collapse on the golf course, dead.

"You have two choices," Grimsley said. "You can either resign, effective now— or you can be fired, also effective now."

The first thing he did when he left the office was go to the mensroom and vomit. He sank to his knees in front of the john and retched so hard that he actually feared for his life. How much could the aging fabric take?

It was over and just beginning. He was out of a job, he was finished at Whitman High after seventeen years. It was too much to grasp. His marriage, his first years at Whitman, the trips to Europe, the kids, T.S. Eliot hit by the car, Joy, Marty Zeller—a hundred images sped through the wreck of his mind like tracer fire.

He got up weakly, shivering, shaking, rinsed his mouth and washed his face. Saw his sad red eyes in the mensroom mirror, a stranger's eyes. Then Wally Blood came in and he quickly left.

In the hall he saw Allen Burk.

"Allen—wait. Can I see you a second?"

Kids swirled around them as Burk said, "I don't have time."

"Just for a second. It's really important. I have to see you alone."

Burk sighed. "All right, let's use the A-V room."

The A-V room! The door hissed shut behind them, clicked.

Ted stood in the silence, dizzy, a high ringing sound in his ears. "Allen, listen, I'm in a fix. I need your help."

Burk sneered. "I *know* about your fix," he said. "I can't do anything."

Ted wet his lips. "But Allen, you're the department head. You know I've been a good teacher. I've been a good teacher for seventeen years."

Burk pointed to the corner of the room, his features tight. "Do you see that machine over there?" he said, his face coloring.

Ted simply nodded.

"Do you know what happened to me the week before last when I used that machine? I was running a tape I'd recorded when what do you think I saw? I saw a member of *my* English staff and one of his former female students engaging in the most *disgusting* sexual aberrations that one can imagine."

Ted's throat closed up. He stared at Burk's piercing eyes.

"I *almost* showed that tape to my class before running it through. Do you *realize* what that would have meant for me? For Whitman High? For the entire Somerside system?"

Ted shook his head, gasping for breath. "Allen—"

"Of *course* I erased it instantly," Burk said, "and never breathed a word of it to anyone. But if you have *any* idea that I'll defend you now, you are sadly, sadly mistaken."

Ted braced himself against the birch formica table; swallowed hard and quickly left the room.

He hurried out of the building and into the parking lot. The area next to the lot held a scatter of kids who had finished lunch and were killing time till the bell. Tomorrow these kids would know. Everybody would know, the whole world would know. He started to shake again. A girl whose name escaped him said hello. He hurried past her toward his car—and suddenly Joy was there.

He opened his mouth to speak and she fell to her knees: threw her arms around his legs and held him tight. "Take me with you!" she cried. "Take me with you, wherever you're going! I can't live without you, please, take me with you!"

He wanted to kick her, to crack her jaw with his knee. "Let me go!" he said, and the lunchtime pupils stared.

"Take me with you!"

In a low and threatening voice he said, "You bitch! You didn't even warn me!"

She was sobbing now, her face on his leg. "You ruined me! You made a slave of me!"

"Let me go!"

"You lied! You said you loved me, and you didn't!"

"Let me *go!*"

She continued to cling. At the edge of his vision, he saw the crowd. He twisted, and still she clung. "I want those Polaroids," he said. "Hand them over."

"Bear—"

"I want the Polaroids!"

She looked at him, eyes pleading. "I let Grimsley keep them," she said.

"You what? You *what?*"

"Take me with you. We can make it together, we—"

Violently he wrenched away, breaking her grip. She fell forward. Kids stared. He fled.

Joy knelt on the asphalt, her fists clenched in rage, her frantic face streaming with tears. "You promised to marry me!" she screamed.

All watched as Ted ran to the Plymouth and unlocked the door, got in, turned the engine on; backed up with a squeal, almost smashing a purple sex bomb, an old Chevy, and drove away.

He was trapped in a bubble, aquariumized. The car seemed to float on its own down the sunny December street. He drove in his numbness for half an hour to a town where he'd never stopped before, to a bar he had never seen before. He pushed the Christmas-wreathed door aside and went to the beery and sullen formica guts of the place and got himself smashing drunk. He didn't know what to do after that so he drove to a mall and paid his way into a movie; fell asleep, waking up hours later, still drunk, not remembering where he was and how he was changed. Then the memory crushed him as giants with meaningless voices dissolved on the screen, coalesced in a blast of brass. He slumped against the sticky seat, his head throbbing, thoughts dead. There weren't any answers, just imperatives: he had to get home, see June, explain. *Explain?* He had no *job*.

Finally he roused himself, made his way to the mensroom; splashed his face, ran his comb through his hair. His eyes were baggy, his next day's whiskers were coming in, it was ten thirty-five. In the huge mall parking lot a shimmery mica-like snow sifted down. White Christmas. I'm dreaming. Need a present for June.

He drove home slowly, cautiously, sick, and what came to him was: the tattoo on her ass hadn't showed! She'd selected the Polaroid shots where it hadn't showed, the conniving bitch! Traversing an underpass, he thought: if he smashed himself into those concrete posts it would all be over, what he drove toward would never take place. He shuddered at the image and drove on.

Only one light, in the kitchen. He parked and closed the car door softly, opened the door to the house very gently, hung his coat in the closet and went to the kitchen—and June.

She was there at the table, so old, so old. Her eyes were froglike, swollen, bruised, and her hair was all stringy, askew. Her smeared mouth opened and said, "You lousy bastard."

He closed his eyes; pirouettes of light; he opened them, saying, "June. June—"

He stopped. Why continue? To tell more lies? He was sick of lying, sick of deceit, he just wanted oblivion. "Are the kids asleep?"

"They're in bed," she said through narrowed lips, "but that doesn't mean they're asleep. They're in bed because they don't want to see *Daddy,* but I doubt very much if they're sleeping."

His stomach curdled. "Let's not make a scene in front of them," he said. "Let's go out in the car."

She glared at him with redrimmed eyes. "Why *not* make a scene in front of them? Do you think that could hurt them more than you've *already* hurt them?"

"June—"

Her face flashed fire. "Brad was outside at lunchtime," she said. "He saw it, he was there!"

Ted closed his eyes. The room tilted and dipped.

They left the house. He drove three blocks and parked across from a frozen field that would bloom with construction come spring. As she screamed and he sat there sick and sad, a part of his ruptured mind escaped, thinking, Odd that so many momentous events take place in cars: conjugations and conceptions, shady deals, births, deaths… So many deaths, fifty thousand a year. "And how do I get the news? From Alice Phillips, who calls to console me. Console me for what? For what happened with Ted, what happened at school, what Eileen had told her. 'Oh no, oh June, you haven't heard? Oh God, I'm so *sorry.*' Yeah, I'll *bet* she was sorry. Then Brad coming home in tears and crying three hours, Ted. Three hours! He saw it all, the whole thing! Do you know that slut's brother is on Brad's basketball team?" Another quick shock wave hammered Ted's heart. He'd seen a few games but the kid hadn't played and Ted hadn't noticed him on the bench. "Did you think for even a minute of what you were doing to us? To *all* of us?"

For a minute, yes—but not for much longer than that. Thoughts of family and future, respectability, responsibility, morality—of anything but his freedom and pleasure had been so weak, so gray.

192

"To think that you deliberately arranged to dance with her in front of me. That you deliberately mocked me like that."

"June, no, that isn't true!"

"Pretending to care about me when I was sick, when I was in the hospital, and all the time—" Tears choked her words.

"I *did* care about you. I *do* care about you."

She looked at him, eyes flooded, skin flushed. "Oh, sure! Oh, right, you really care! You could have *infected* me, did you think of that? You could have caught some disease from that whore and given it to *me,* did you think of that? How many other sluts have you done it with?" She wept heavily, hands on her face.

He had done it with nobody else, he swore. And he swore he had never meant it to happen, it had simply...*happened*—as much because he had wanted to know someone new as for any other reason.

"Oh sure, you have to *fuck* somebody to know them! Sure, you wanted to get to *know* a seventeen year old girl!"

It sounded like nonsense, and yet it was true—or at least he thought it was. He was so confused, so exhausted, he wasn't sure. He'd committed an indiscretion, he said, he had been a fool—but now it was over and he was so terribly sorry...

"And how are we supposed to live?" June said. "On your apologies? On what *I* make? How long do you think *that's* going to feed us?" He didn't know. Well she'd give him some time to think about it while she took the kids to her parents' for Christmas. He begged her not to do that. "We can still have Christmas together, don't let it wreck Christmas." "You have to be joking," she said, her mouth curled in contempt. "Do you actually think that they want to spend Christmas with *you?*"

He felt like the biggest shit in the world, a huge festering turd. "I never loved her, never!" he said. "It was physical, purely physical." "Oh that explains *everything!*" June screamed, and that was when the cop came up and shined the light inside and asked to see Ted's license and said all the shitty things that cops say in those situations, making them freeze with the window down before sending them home—as if sitting there in a car that they owned was some sort of threat to the neighborhood. Ted drove silently back to the house in sick anger, the painful knot hard in his chest. Not once in all his times with Joy had a cop interrupted, not once on those long spring nights.

June started to cry again. He wanted to hold her, to make things right, but didn't know how to begin.

In the house they said nothing. She went up to bed and he lay on the couch in the family room, his chest pressure hard and huge. This time it was real for sure, this time he would die, like Marty: another notch in Joy's belt. He swallowed a shot of scotch and gagged, afraid he would vomit again. He watched TV with the sound off and tried not to think. The Polaroids! My God, he had let her keep the Polaroids, where was his brain?

He slept for five hours; awoke to a sharp ray of low winter sun in his eyes. He shaved in the downstairs bathroom; drank instant coffee, nauseated; glanced at the paper's meaningless headlines, was jumpy and taut in the silent house and went out. Drove away to a mall; window shopped at the grille-fronted stores. When things opened up he bought June's present, a ring with a pearl (she was nuts about pearls), a lot like the ring he had bought years ago when their love was new, the one she had lost at the shore.

He hung around watching mechanical fountains spray water on penny-lined pools, hoping that June had changed her mind about taking the kids away. Surely they could work something out, at least for the holidays.

But when he got home, no June, no kids, no cat. He put the gift-wrapped ring on the mantel and poured a scotch.

He was pretty well gone by the time the telephone rang. It was George. Good old George. Was there anything he could do? Ted said no, not really, ashamed, ashamed. Did he want him to stop around? After Christmas he'd like that a lot, Ted said in his numbness, so glad he was numb. Oh *God* this was embarrassing! It wasn't the end of the world, George said. Ted said he would try to remember that. When he hung up he wondered: would he ever see George again?

That night, when he was thoroughly bombed, the carolers came. He heard them next door at the 7-Elevens': Oh Little Town of Bethlehem, Oh Come All Ye Faithful, Silent Night—so mournful, soft and sweet—then heard them shuffle past his house, *past* his house and across the street. Surely they hadn't deliberately skipped him, had they?

In the morning, mouth bitter and thick, he stepped outside for the paper and found that his doorstep was black. The oil paint covered the door and the welcome mat, and paint like black blood hung in strands from the Christmas wreath. Good will toward men. He discarded the mat and the wreath and wiped up what he could, but only a whole new paint job would set things right.

The first telephone caller—attacking at twelve twenty-six—proclaimed him a "snotsucking motherfucker." The second one said he ought to have his cock torn off and fed to alligators. The third caller struck the next day, Christmas Eve, at six o'clock, when Ted was bombed, and explained that Ted was a shiteating scumbag who'd burn in eternal fire. Ted wished him a Merry Christmas and switched off the phones.

35 • CLEANING UP

A Christmas without any presents, the first in his life. No pre-dawn excitement (only now were the kids beginning to grow out of that), yet he woke in early darkness all the same. Remembering everything, he moaned, took a leak, ate three aspirins, crawled back into turbid sleep. Felt warm in those muddy dreams and woke again to pleasant sun and a temperature in the fifties, the streets black and runny with melted snow, a day like early spring.

He turned the phones on, thinking of June and the kids ninety miles away at the Colonel's, their presents meaningless because of him, disgust with him filling their minds. All those years he'd been Daddy, respected and loved, and now in a flash all that love and respect was gone. He stared at the phone in the kitchen. If only they'd call. He wished with all his heart they would have a good Christmas, a wonderful Christmas, knowing it wasn't possible, and he started to drink at noon.

He spent the day in a bar, a restaurant, another bar. At the restaurant he sentimentally ordered "traditional turkey." It came with canned ersatz gravy and he ate two bites.

At home, chest throbbing, he watched TV, the evening still oddly warm. He still had a bit of Joy's dope, and rolling his typically sloppy joint, he smoked. It eased his chest. He watched the lousy TV show and despaired that he had no friends. He had buddies, pals, and no friends—except possibly George. Had that been what he'd wanted in Joy—a friend? It seemed absurd, but he actually didn't know.

He drank, wishing that June would call. Hopelessly drunk and devoid of hope, he hit the sack at ten.

In the morning he called Howard Grimsley at home; made arrangements to go to the school and clean out his room. He was shaking so badly afterwards that he drank some scotch. When he finished it, he got a fire going in the fireplace, then went to his closet and took out his secret cache and burned it all—as if doing so would make partial amends for his crimes. He put Master Muscle in last, on top of the magazines. It wilted quickly, then sputtered and gurgled black sulfurous smoke and was gone.

• • • • •

As he neared the school he thought of LeMaster, Grimsley, Burk: how they'd relished bringing him down. His chest began hurting again. This wasn't right, he should go to a doctor—*soon*.

The weather was even warmer than yesterday—in the sixties. It was almost as if all New Jersey was out of joint, not just him. Far off, on the athletic field, he saw kids tossing a baseball around. He hoped they didn't realize who he was.

The janitor—Stanley or Mr. Stanley—let him in, and he carried his empty cartons through the halls. His footsteps echoed hollowly. He had always hated school when the kids were gone; there was nothing creepier.

He went into his room, the room he had taught in for six straight years. He had practically grown up at Whitman; had started there at twenty-five, a year after his marriage, and now...he still couldn't believe it. A patch of his handwriting—"lives of quiet"—was still on the board. He erased it and set to work.

He had emptied all but the bottom drawer of his desk when he heard a sound, looked up, and saw Dora Rosen.

She was wearing a thoughtful, fretful frown, as if something important had just slipped her mind.

He could feel himself blush. "Dora. What are you doing here?"

She didn't answer for a second, then said, "Catching up on my cataloging. Got a minute? Want some coffee?"

They went to her office. She poured two coffees from her giant thermos, and they talked. He explained everything as best he could, apologetic, ashamed. Mostly she just said, "Mmm," like a parody of a therapist, but nevertheless it helped. Just getting it out of his own obsessive head made him feel a bit better.

"I felt like a rat when I didn't support your stand on *Our Bodies*," he said, "but I was desperate. If I didn't come out against it, I'd end up in court, and *then* what would people say? *This* is the kind of person who wants that book on the library shelves? This child-molester, this *degenerate*? Maybe now I've confused them. This guy supports censorship, then he does *this*?"

Dora smoked and said, "I think they'll figure out pretty fast that Dollinger blackmailed you."

"I guess. But that won't hurt you as much as if I'd supported you, will it?"

She shrugged, and he said, "I hope you'll keep fighting, Dora."

"Don't worry," she said, "I will."

She asked how his family was holding up. When he told her, she said she was sorry. He threw out a thought that had come to him earlier: "How can they simply dismiss me like that? There's such a thing as due process, Dora, and I sure didn't receive it." Trying to convince himself that he had a case, he excoriated Grimsley and LeMaster. Dora said she didn't think denial of due process was a path worth following. After all, they hadn't fired him, he had resigned. Had been *forced* to resign, he reminded her. "You're not giving up *your* fight, and I won't give up *mine*," he said. "Do," Dora said.

• • • • •

When he got back home, the Toyota was in the driveway.

Kim was at the kitchen table eating cookies, drinking milk. She looked at him with nervous eyes. He wanted to hug and squeeze her, but checked himself and said cooly, "Hi. Did you have a good time at Grandmom's?"

Before she could answer, June came in looking exhausted. "Hello, Ted."

"June… I'm so glad you're back."

She sighed. "The kids and I had a talk. We agreed to try to make the best of a bad situation."

With gratitude so great he could have kissed her feet, he said, "We'll work it out. I'm sure we will."

She looked at him. The space between them seemed to crystallize. "My father's found you a job," she said.

Kim got up from the table, went into the family room. Ted said, "He did? What kind of a job?"

"There's an agency in Sellerstown called Helping Hands. It's for families in crisis. They need an assistant director. You'll do publicity, write brochures and press releases, interview people to determine their income levels, that kind of thing."

Ted held out his helpless hands, palms up, thinking: Families in crisis! "But June," he said, "I don't know anything about that kind of work."

She sniffed. "You can *talk,* can't you? And you teach *kids* to write, so I assume *you* can write."

"But a social service agency… I've never had anything to do with a social service agency. I'm not even sure I *like* them."

"This is hardly the time to be choosy, Ted."

"But we'd have to move. I don't *want* to move."

She rolled her eyes. "Oh Ted, for Christ's sake, be realistic. I guess you didn't see the paint that's splattered all over our door."

"Every neighborhood has its assholes. Those feelings will fade."

"Right. In how many years? Think of Brad and Kim. Do you realize how embarrassed—?"

"I know, I know."

"Do you also know you'll never get another job around here?"

"Not in teaching, I guess."

"Not in anything, Ted."

She was probably right. But he would be *damned* if he'd take the Colonel's job. He would not be indebted to him for anything—ever! He told June he'd think about Helping Hands, but he had a few other leads—which of course was a baldfaced lie. Then he went to the mantel and gave her the present he'd bought. She opened the package, examined the ring and said, "Very nice, thank you," and that was the end of that.

He exchanged some mumbly words with Brad, who talked with his head low and turned to the side, as if looking into his father's eyes might prove contaminating. He got Kim to show him her presents and told himself things would work out. Other families had gone through these crises and come out okay, so why not his? Why should he have to give up his home on account of one stupid mistake? Time would heal. In time, the slingers of paint and the phone blasphemers would find new things to fill their sick minds, June would forgive him, and all that would stick with the kids would be a sore nick of memory, a faded scar. From this day forth he would be the best father in history, and the whole damn stupid affair would amount to nothing.

He hoped. Employment, that was the kicker. Okay, if worse came to worst, he'd move. But a job through the Colonel—on the Colonel's turf? No way.

•••••

In the morning, June nagged him about Helping Hands. "I have to check out my other leads first," he said, and gave George Frangelli a call.

They met in a restaurant-lounge in Apple Heights, a place where no one would know him; drank beer in a dark anonymous booth. George listened intently, then said, "Take the Sellersville job."

"But damn it, I was denied due *process,* George. What's the union *for* if it isn't for things like this?"

George stared with his owlish eyes. "Ted, please—*forget* due process. Even if you have a case—which is highly unlikely—think of all the *publicity.* Think of the turmoil your family would have to go through."

Ted drank some beer, swallowing hard. "You don't know of any openings, do you?"

"In teaching?"

"That's all I know how to do."

"Yeah, you and me both. But Jesus, teaching jobs are as scarce as hen's teeth now, I haven't heard of a thing. I'll ask around. Maybe somebody else knows of something."

Ted frowned at his glass. "I guess it doesn't *have* to be teaching. I *ought* to be able to learn how to do something else."

George looked at him, his expression grave. "Ted, take the Sellersville job. In a year or two you can try for something different, but take the job."

•••••

On the way back home, Ted thought: I *ought* to be able to learn how to do something else, Jesus Christ, I'm still young! The beer had depressed him; the lowering, cooling sky was depressing him too. Helping Hands! I'll be damned if I'll work for a place with a name like that!

As he drove, his beery determination grew. The Colonel could go to hell, Helping Hands could go to hell, he would find a job on his own. Yes, maybe he'd have to move, but he'd call his own shots and not owe anyone anything—especially not the Colonel.

He'd apply to every junior college in the country. College—that's where he should have been teaching all along. A brief fling with a student? In a college setting, no big deal.

The house was empty. In the silent study, head fuzzy, he worked on his resume. He tapped the desktop with his pen and stared at the cemetery. The sky—a scalloped gray—pressed into his brain. Jesus, what could he say? Except English and psychology teacher, Walt Whitman High School, Somerside, New Jersey. Part-time automobile dent inspector? Not very impressive—and neither were part-time supermarket clerk and part-time bartender, other jobs he had held in past lean (always lean) summers. Seventeen years at the same damn job! It looked awful! People didn't expect that these days. They thought if you didn't jump around there was something wrong with you: you lacked initiative, were nuts, incompetent.

He got out his college record, that endless stream of courses, master's plus plus. Now *that* would be impressive—to a high school administrator. But to a college administrator? If only he'd gotten his doctorate!

He put down his pen and reached in his drawer and pulled out his stash of dope; sucked the smoke till the room went soft. He stared at the hopeless resume, then went to the family room, lay down on the couch...

Someone was pounding a stake through his heart! He jumped awake, gasping for breath.

It was Missy—miserable cat—who had leaped from the end table onto his chest. She yowled as he cuffed her, his heart thumping hard, the Dracula-dream still lingering in his bones.

They came tumbling into the house, Brad giving Kim grief about something. Ted sat up quickly, tucking his shirt in and combing his hair with his fingers. Yes, George had a couple of real good leads, he said, he was getting right on them. June, dropping her keys in her pocketbook, stared without comment.

The kids muttered hi and started upstairs. "You can watch TV if you want," he said, "I'm leaving." They filtered past him. He went to the study. English and psychology teacher, Walt Whitman High School, seventeen years. All gone in an instant. He thought of Joy. He sighed. The smell of something cooking—pork chops?—hit his nose. He gagged.

He forced himself to eat (how loud the forks were on the plates!) and told June the meal was superb.

36 • THE POSITIVE MENTAL ATTITUDE PATH TO SUCCESS

In the morning he finished his resume (changed "dent inspector" to "auto assessor," "supermarket clerk" to "retail sales"), and wrote a cover letter.

He had two hundred copies made of the resume, purchased a reference book on colleges, checked off two hundred names. Two days later he mailed his packets, enclosing return envelopes. If he didn't get any bites from this batch (God forbid), he would send out two hundred more.

Three recent obscene phone calls had convinced him that June was right, they would have to move—especially since Kim, poor kid, had answered the last of these calls. The creep had asked to talk to her toad-fucking father, making her burst into tears. Ted had picked up the bedroom extension as the filth was spewed and had blasted the guy with some epithets of his own. Kim had heard all this too, of course, and had cried even harder.

The shit really hit the fan after that. What was he doing, June demanded—deliberately torturing them? What happened to all those leads George Frangelli had talked about, and what about Helping Hands? That job wouldn't wait forever, what was he *doing?*

He locked himself in the study and smoked more dope. Maybe jogging would make him feel better, he thought; then decided that no, it would only remind him of all his transgressions (smoking Joy's weed was reminder enough), and anyway it was cold again. He stared at the snow-covered graveyard and smoked till his ears went numb.

On New Year's Eve they went to sleep early, lying as far apart as they could, as was their custom now. Would they ever be able to touch again? Yes, all it would take was the right combination of words and glances, of gestures and vocal tones—that elusive magic—and they'd fall in each other's arms as if nothing had happened. But how to begin? The chasm—those few hot inches—seemed unbridgeable. When he accidentally brushed her arm in the night she recoiled like a wounded snake.

He couldn't sleep, and heard the New York New Year's crowd flare up as the ball came down (Brad was watching downstairs). Poor Brad—two more days and the Christmas vacation was over and then it was back to Whitman to face the abuse. He hoped Brad would paste the first wiseguy who made a remark and end it there, but the first kid who made a remark would probably be a gorilla with muscles on top of muscles. Happy New Year, dear Brad.

• • • • •

But Brad seemed no more sullen than usual his first days back at Whitman. If stuff had been said, he'd been able to handle it, Ted guessed—or maybe no stuff had been said. He remembered a boy some years ago whose father had run away with another man, and as far as he'd known, nobody had teased the kid, who was very popular. But then that Lenny…Lenny who?—that dingaling whose father died of cancer of the cock—good Christ had they raked him over the coals for that.

Brad was fairly popular, so maybe they'd treat him okay. Ted prayed that the bullshit wouldn't descend on Kim. For either of his kids to have to pay in the slightest—at *all*—for his crimes was a crime in itself—and the way of the world. How people loved to see their fellow humans squirm! LeMaster, Grimsley, Burk, his "neighbors"—what glee they must feel. Yes, damn it, June was right: they couldn't remain in Westdale. Maybe come back in five or ten years, when half the current residents had moved away, but to stay here now would be madness.

The first replies to his resume came that Friday, four of them, from nearby schools in Jersey, Pennsylvania, Delaware—and all of them said no thanks. They would keep his name in their files, and if… The following week eleven more schools said they too would file his vita and keep him in mind.

June panicked about Helping Hands. What the hell was he *waiting* for? Was he suicidal?

"I'm just not *qualified,*" he said.

"You have thirty psychology credits, what more do you need?"

"But my master's degree is in English."

"Your background is perfect. *Ideal.* Take the job, you can learn as you go along."

"Give me two more weeks, I'm sure I'll land something by then."

• • • • •

They were horrible weeks. Brad quit the basketball team and holed up in his room. The rejections kept pouring in. Alone in the house with his dread of the mail, with June at work and the kids at school, Ted drank. Around and around and around it all went in his head. He'd let her keep the Polaroids! How? Why? June's question rang in his baffled brain: *Are you suicidal?* Could it possibly be? Had Freud been right about the death wish after all? Hemingway's shotgun, Kerouac on the lam from death and running straight at it with open arms... No, no, he wasn't a crazy writer, he wasn't like them, he'd been running to freedom! (But hadn't they also been running to freedom? He frowned, confused.) All he knew was a person's life should not be totally planned, controlled, accounted for; sometimes you had to just smash all the rules and *go!* And how they hated you for that! How people made you pay for that! They loved the independent spirit, and, too cowardly to embrace it themselves, would punish those who did.

With every rejection, his rage increased: his rage at Dollinger, Grimsley, Joy, the Colonel, the mailman, the whole damn world. He wanted to raid every porn shop in Jersey and drag all the hypocrites into the light, Maddy Bisbee and all the rest. They were playing the same kind of game he'd played, but just hadn't been caught. They were punishing him for his carelessness, not his deeds; his mistakes were a threat to them all. Well he hoped they all burned in hell.

Dinners were truly pathetic now. He was usually sloshed, and his cooking—marginal at best in his pre-Joy days—was now nothing less than atrocious. June and Brad didn't even show up most nights, and he'd eat in silence with sadfaced Kim, who would leave half her food on her plate. When June and Brad did show, the knot in Ted's stomach was huge. The one time he found himself alone with Brad at dinner's end he said as gently as he could, "I think it's time we had a little talk." Brad scowled and muttered through his plastic mouthpiece, "Murph! Wabba! Goo!" Frowning, Ted said softly, "What?" and, pushing the stringy positioner out of his mouth with his tongue, Brad screamed, "I said I don't *want* to talk to you!" and ran upstairs. Ted, numb with drink, felt as low as he'd ever felt in his sorry life. He thought of his days with baby Brad, with toddler Brad, those days on the schoolyard swings and slides, and damn near cried.

After dinner he always had more booze, then went to the study and smoked. Joy's dope was disappearing fast. It let his mind slip, settle onto ledges, slide away. In spite of everything, the sex urge hadn't died, and twice he masturbated—necessary chore—to fantasies remembered from *Spurts Illustrated* and *Y'All Come.*

• • • • •

The end of January, mail arrived from the State Consumer Protection Bureau—a reply to his Colonial Safeguard Insurance complaint. It was a printed form that said:

So that we can assist you further (Further? They thought they had already helped him somehow?), please answer the following questions:

Where did you buy the product?
How much did you pay for the product?
In your opinion, what is wrong with the product? Please be specific.
Thank you.

Two days later—February now—a Dollinger letter appeared in the *Courier-News,* thanking his supporters for their help in his war against smut. "As chairman of the Somerside Board of Education I will do my utmost to expunge this evil..." Chairman! They'd elected him *chairman!* Stunned and furious, Ted wrote the Consumer Protection Bureau again, explaining in excess specificity the nature of his complaint. He knew it would do no good, but thought it would make him feel better. (He was wrong.)

He hung around, cut off from the world, the house his jail. He thought of how he had tried to dissuade June from taking the job at Happy Trails (a mother should be home with her children; he didn't know how to cook; since when was a job *liberation?*). Jesus, if she'd listened to him, they'd be dead ducks!

He felt totally ineffectual, emasculated. The mail: "We are sorry to say that at present... If in the future..." He drank, smoked dope; had the creepy feeling that Joy had dropped out of school and was spying on him, and he kept all the curtains closed. That goddamn grass *did* make you paranoid. Well, soon he'd run out. (Then what?)

• • • • •

In February's second frigid week—on the day of Ted's eighty-sixth rejection—the Colonel called to say that the Helping Hands job had been filled.

June went berserk. She'd had it with his moping around, what the hell did he think she was going to do, support him the rest of his life? He was dreaming if he thought he was going to get a junior college job, he'd be lucky to get a *high* school job. She dissolved into bitter tears.

He kept searching the ads in the *Courier-News,* the *Inquirer,* the *New York Times.* The jobs at social service agencies—case worker, counselor, that sort of thing—required credentials he didn't possess. In the course of three weeks he found a grand total of two English teaching positions—one at a school for the deaf in upstate New York (sign language required), the other for a debate coach-teacher in Newark. He called about the latter job the day the ad appeared. It was already filled.

As he read the ads, he suddenly realized that time had passed him by. While he'd been serenely expounding on Poe, Thoreau and Frost in his classroom capsule, the world had turned upside down. "Data capture shift manager." What the devil was *that?* Did people actually go to college to study such things these days? "Fluid dynamicist"—another mystery. "Flavorist" sounded a bit more understandable, but where were the jobs for *him?* Not "flavorist" but "wine-taster"—that sort of thing. (How did one ever *get* a job like that, anyway?) "Export traffic specialist." Huh? "Does your fluency in English and German match your expertise in export traffic?" His fluency in *German* did. Seventeen years ago schools had been begging for teachers and now he couldn't *give* his skills away.

He signed up with a placement agency. They were not optimistic. English teacher at the top of the scale? The man at the desk gave a shrug of thick shoulders, a shake of bald head. Feeling ill, Ted entered the ground floor bar (the placement agency's *real* business?), and ordered a double scotch.

Jesus, he was totally expendable! All the courses he'd taken, the kids he had taught, all he'd learned and had done meant nothing! He drank. There had to be *something* he could do—besides ringing up groceries or mixing drinks or checking cars for dents. He thought of his work as yearbook advisor. Editor or journalist? The magazine or newspaper field, something like that?

There *was* another possibility, one he didn't like to contemplate; but during the rush hour drive across the dark Walt Whitman Bridge (the murky river fused with the graybrown sky), he decided to give it a shot. All he *really* wanted to do was teach, he knew that now; he already missed it like mad. He'd never missed it those busy summers, had actually dreaded Labor Day, but now with all this time on his hands oh *God* did it appeal! He'd get back to it soon, he swore he would, but right now he needed a job, any job—some temporary thing to tide him over till—

• • • • •

"Hello, is this Joe Bishop?"

"This is Joe Bishop, who's this?"

"Joe, this is Ted Wharton."

A pause on the other end of the line, a *long* pause, then: "Ted! What's up, your Electrakween giving you trouble?"

"No, Joe, it's not that, it's…well, I'm looking for work."

"For work?"

"I was thinking about that offer you made when you sold us our vacuum. You know—the salesman job?"

A long, *long* pause. "Well, that was a while ago."

The hum of the line. "You mean there aren't any openings?"

Joe's voice took on a confidential tone. "Ted, look, let's face it. After your troubles at Whitman… Selling door-to-door around here after that…no way."

Ted licked his lips. "Well Jesus, Joe, I'm not a *rapist.* I mean what do you think will happen?"

"It's not what I think will *happen,* Ted, it's your *image.* A male is always a negative image in this line of work. He can often overcome it with effort, but in your case…it's just not possible."

"Joe, listen, I'll take another neighborhood. —Someplace where they've never heard of Whitman High."

Another pause. "Sorry, Ted, but we can't take the chance. Electrakween *has* to protect its image."

Ted gritted his teeth. "Hey Joe, let's not be hypocritical. Did you show me a magazine in the mensroom at school?"

"I fail to see—"

"Did you say—referring to the centerfold—'What a chunk of tail'?"

"Ted, that's irrelevant."

"I don't think so."

"Well it is. You've got a negative reputation, a negative image, and—"

"Stop it with all this goddamn *image* shit!"

A silence. Ted's breath was hot in the phone. Joe said, "Ted, I know that you're having it rough and I'd like to help, but I can't. Not in this way I can't. In another way though, perhaps I can. There's a book that I think you should read. It's called *The Positive Mental Attitude Path to Success* by Napoleon Murphey."

Heat rose in Ted's head. He said, "Joe, I'll tell you what. You can take your positive mental attitude and shove it up your ass, then set your Electrakween on four ball suck and suck it out again. I don't need any goddamn *attitude,* I need a *job!*"

The silence, hum, the click.

Ted banged the receiver into its cradle, shaking with rage. Damn! Not even a *vacuum* cleaner salesman! Not even *that!*

He went to the study and smoked the last of Joy's dope: the very last, every shred, too fast; sat stupified and forgot about dinner. But Brad and June never appeared, and Kim cooked a soft-boiled egg for herself and ate it while watching TV; and Ted fell asleep in the overstuffed chair in the study and stayed there till dawn.

37 • EACH LONELY NIGHT

On the day he received his ninety-fourth rejection—from Peyote Junior College in California—June announced she was leaving: Her father had found her a job as a travel agent in Sellerstown.

She and the kids packed the station wagon without Ted's help. He felt that his help would imply he *wanted* them to leave, and since he *didn't* want them to leave, he simply watched, which made June furious. She said she would send a van for furniture and the rest of her stuff when she'd found a place to live.

When they'd gone, Ted felt empty and guilty. Why guilty? Would guilt have assailed Henry Miller or Kerouac? Joy's words came back: *Fuck guilt.* He'd love to, but couldn't. What the hell was the *matter* with him?

The house was a tomb. Quieter than when he was home alone while June worked and the kids were in school? Objectively, how could that be? What else was missing? The cat? Had it filled that much space?

Resentment, rage and loneliness crashed down. He hated them for leaving him— and he wanted them back. All the hassles they'd had—yet he wanted them back. He would *get* them back too, he swore he would. He'd get a good job somewhere and they'd move to wherever that job might be, and things would be fine again. He looked out the window, saw Mr. Monsanto setting out bags of trash, and imagined the glee that his neighbors had felt when they saw June packing. He wondered where Joy was now and what she was doing.

He searched the bottom drawer of his desk, hoping to find some dope he'd missed, but no, so he poured himself a double shot of scotch and tossed it down.

The week after June's departure, the rejections dried up: he got nothing for six straight days. Apparently over a hundred schools had steamed off the stamp he'd enclosed and used it for other purposes.

The very thought of sending out more resumes exhausted him. He called the placement agency; no news. He searched the want ads. Nothing. Drank his scotch. If only he had learned to use the Net!

Before he had gotten involved with Joy, he'd felt distanced from life, screened off, as if a caul were covering his senses. That fog had been sunshine compared to his present state, in which all enthusiasm, all ambition, had died. He found nothing appealing: TV, food, sex, books… Spent hours staring blankly at Waughbach's stones and drinking his Red & Black.

In the course of that terrible week he received two calls: one was from Donna at LifeTime Books, inviting him to enroll in their needlepoint "program." The other was from a credit bureau, asking him to rat on the Monsantos.

The Consumer Protection Bureau sent another letter. It said that on the basis of the information that Ted had provided it would be very difficult to determine the facts of the situation to which he referred.

Two and a half weeks after June left, it snowed like mad. The loneliness of wind and whirling sky put Ted in a frightful mood. He started to drink soon after lunch and by suppertime he was gone. He ate cold cereal—a habit now—and went to bed; slept soddenly, then fitfully; and sometime in the early morning, the storm still raging around his room, he dreamed.

He was taking a shower. The shower enclosure was filled with steam and he couldn't see, but a certain fantastic blind perception told him that wires were coming out of the shower head. Those wires, he suddenly realized, were attached by means of small clamps to his penis and scrotum. The ultimate libido-meter?

Through the steam, far off, he could hear June's voice—or *was* it June's? He strained to hear. The voice—so distant, wet and small—was giving him a command. What was that gray breath saying? Press the button on the cord—the cord that he held in his hand. He felt the slippery plastic bulb, rubbed its nub with his thumb. The demands (was it one voice or two? Did he hear Joy now?) grew louder, shrill. The shower hissed tropical, gasping clouds; he couldn't breathe. His body, he was shocked to see, was oozing beads of blood. "Press it! Press it! Press it!" screamed the over-lapping echoes, and shattered with fear, he did. A fierce jolt of power tore through him, the world was fire, he sizzled and snapped—

And awoke in the dark in a drenching sweat to see lightning flash outside.

The snow had stopped. A thunder roll ripped his heart. He gasped for breath and turned on the bedside light. He lay there, panting like a dog, trying to chase the last fragments of dream from his mind.

Gradually the terror seeped away—to be replaced by a horrible longing for June and the kids. He lay there with the light on, feeling a lovesick, homesick sort of sick-ness, wanting to sleep and wanting to get some scotch. He did neither; kept watching the pink freak lightning flicker at soft wide intervals till morning came, then dozed. Woke up with a start, felt that mushy sad sickness again, got up, took a fretful shower (those wires, that jolt, my God!), watched a soundless talk show.

It was Saturday, and shortly after ten o'clock, fortified by three cups of black coffee, he gave June a call. Sun shone on a foot of new snow as the telephone rang. The Colonel's aide-de-camp answered and put June on.

The first thing she asked: "Did you find a job?"

"Not yet. I have some good prospects, though."

"Such as?"

"The agency has a bead on a couple of things. They're not definite yet, but we're getting close."

"I'm glad."

He felt his falsehood soaking through the wires. "So how are the kids?"

"The kids are fine."

The telephone burned his ear. He cleared his throat. "June, I'd like to come see you."

It seemed an eternity till she answered. When finally she did, she said, "Ted, I guess I can't stop you from seeing the kids, but *I* don't want to see you. Not yet at any rate."

And that's how they left it. It was hard to believe they were that far apart. All the mornings they'd lain in each others' arms, all the evenings they'd shared their dreams, their flesh... The intimate web of their caring, frail for years, was now hopelessly knotted and torn.

He told himself not to think of the good times—to think of the terrible times: all their arguments, misunderstandings, her snoring—and he noticed his hands were trembling.

One minor indiscretion and he was destroyed. It just wasn't fair! Did his act negate all the diapers he'd changed, all the meals he had made, all the ferrying to orthodontist, skating rink and gym? Did it cancel the fishing trips, the trips to see Eagles and Phillies and Sixers games while he sat there bored to tears? And what about the kids he taught to form the possessive of plural nouns—or to love the words of Dickinson and Millay? All the hours he'd spent after school with kids who were struggling, his work with those who might not have made it to college if not for his help—had that all been *erased*?

Of course. Look at Benedict Arnold: valorous general, head of West Point—and who ever remembered *that?*

The libido-meter horror dream came back. He felt a sick plunge in the pit of his stomach, his thoughts turned thicker, a ringing began in his ears. Stars grew in the core of his brain, expanded, pressed against his skull.

The Little Man was screaming, trapped in bone. Dope was the only thing that would calm him down—and it was gone. Ted rushed to the bathroom, the medicine cabinet, and shoved things around. June's Valium—had she taken it all?

She had. He sat on the toilet seat, quivering, weak. Good God, what was *happening?* He felt the way he'd felt when Marty died—but much, much worse. He thought of how Joy used to get, so shaky, so sick...

He stood up quickly, afraid he might faint; went back to the bedroom and put on his running shoes; fumbled the laces into knots, his fingers stiff sticks.

He didn't remember the foot-deep snow till he opened the door. Sighing, he closed out the glare and sat on the couch in the family room, the stars in his head spreading into his chest and squeezing out the air. He couldn't breathe, he couldn't think, he had to see somebody. He grabbed the phone and dialed George's number.

He let it ring twelve times: twelve mournful times, then put the receiver down and went to the kitchen and drank two shots of scotch. He took deep measured breaths and stared out the window and told himself to calm down.

All the people he'd met in his life, all those "pals" at work, and no one to tell his troubles to—besides George, and George wasn't home. One person in all the world, my God that was sad. Sad, but certainly not unusual: millions of people were caught in the same situation, trapped all alone in their minds with their fears and guilt.

The trembling and pressure and queasiness wouldn't let up. He had to connect with someone, have somebody listen. To what? To his babble, his screams, to anything, just *listen.*

He took the phone book down from the shelf and fanned through it. To his great relief he found that her number was listed. He dialed.

Three rings and, "Hello?"

"Hello, Dora?"

"Yes?"

"Ted Wharton."

A silence. "Hi, Ted."

"Dora, how are you doing?"

"Okay, how are you?"

"Okay."

He felt better already. Just that link with another person—anybody—made things better. He gripped the receiver hard. He had nothing to say. "I just wondered how things were going."

Her laugh was ironic, soft. "Oh, I've had better times—but I've had much worse times, too."

"Dollinger's putting the screws to you."

"You bet."

"Persistent sucker."

"Obsessed is more like it." A pause. He hoped she wouldn't say goodbye. "Have you found a job yet, Ted?"

"Not yet. It's a bad time of year. In the spring I think I'll have more luck." She didn't respond to that, and stupidly he said, "Do you think there's any chance they'd take me back?"

"At Whitman?"

"Yes."

"No way."

He felt like a fool, but he had to keep talking. "You don't think it'll ever blow over?"

"Never."

And now what to say? If he hung up, he'd shatter like glass. "So is Grimsley going along with Armand's purge?"

"Of course. Anything on my order he doesn't like, he crosses out."

"No matter what the committee thinks?"

"He says the committee's job's to review books already on the shelves, not books on order."

What a bastard, Ted thought. "Is there any way I can help you, Dora? Anything I can do?"

Her laughter was sharp this time. "The best thing you can do is stay out of things."

Well, that was that. It wasn't fair to waste any more of her time. His heart hit a snag as he said, "Listen, Dora, the next time you run into George Frangelli, ask him to call me, okay?"

"Sure."

"Thanks." He was starting to shake again, and instead of saying goodbye he impulsively asked, "Do you have any free time today? Can we get together for coffee?"

"I'm afraid not, Ted, I'm tied up."

His heart sank. "Oh. Well, good to talk to you. And please don't forget about George."

"I won't."

"Good luck, Dora."

"Thanks. Goodbye, Ted."

He had another double scotch, then shoveled the snow off the walk. He went at it savagely, heart pounding thick and fast in his ears as if ready to burst—and he didn't care if it did. He brushed off June's Toyota—his car now—then kept on shoveling, clearing the driveway, and thought about Dora, and June, and Joy, and Brad and Kim, Joy's father, Grimsley, LeMaster, the Colonel, the sun on the bright snow confusing his eyes. His heart just kept thumping away with a regular beat. Still in good shape from past jogging, he figured.

He quit as the plow made its sweep up the street. Inside, in the contrast dark of the house, he had another Red & Black and sat at the kitchen table. The telephone rang and he jumped for it, shaking all over. It was Betty from LifeTime Books.

38 • DORA ROSEN'S WESTERN PLAN

For five straight days he awoke before dawn with an urge to empty his bowels. His gut rumbled and gurgled, cramped him, stabbed him, and up he would get in the bitter dark and sit on the cold, cold john (the whole house was cold; he had lowered the heat disastrously to save money), and out it would come in loose shreds, smelling foul. A terrible sadness would cripple his chest and throat as he purged himself, and he couldn't shake it; its cloud would oppress him all day. And what would be next? Hot flashes?

What was he so afraid of? That things would never be right with June again? That he'd never live with his kids again? He'd never get a job? That last one was ridiculous. Of *course* he'd get a job, what was he, washed up? At the age of forty-two?

This thought sent him back to the toilet again. So this was the dread that motivated Burk, LeMaster and the rest. How had he been so blind to the facts of life? And yet he despised those facts, despised them even now as his insides groaned.

Well what if he *didn't* get a job? What would happen? Would he starve in the street? In *America?* If he did, he would starve right here, in front of the 7-Elevens, Monsantos and Chryslers, he swore he would.

When he drank, he grew more confused. Should he go to a shrink? No, damn it, no, he would rather live with this pain for the rest of his days than resort to that!

• • • • •

In the heart of that frigid and colicky week—the first week in March—some Jehovah's Witnesses came. He hid till they stuck an *Awake* in his door and left for the 7-Elevens'. Harbingers of spring? He hoped so, he was *freezing.* Nobody else stopped by and nobody called except Sears, who wanted him to know about their special on vacuum cleaners.

He got one more rejection, from a tiny school in Kelvinator, Minnesota. He collected June's mail and shipped it off in a large manila envelope. She didn't call. He got bills.

Bills, Jesus did he get bills! He had only a few hundred dollars left in the savings account, and forty-five dollars and seventeen cents in the checking. He'd made the February mortgage payment, but now March was due—and no money. Nobody to borrow from. He called the placement agency twice. No jobs, and he lowered the heat another five degrees.

His intestinal problems persisted. Night after night he spun through black oblivion and fire-hot frightful dreams. He couldn't sleep at all unless he drank. He didn't jog.

He lived on cereal and eggs. He was eating poached eggs on toast on a wickedly windy night that had him in total despair, when the doorbell rang.

He answered it warily—and there was George.

"George! Jesus, come in!"

That rosy smile. "Hi, Ted."

"Come *in.*"

George stepped inside. His smile died. Ted suddenly realized the house was a mess and he hadn't shaved for two days. "George, it's so good to see you."

They went to the family room. Ted cleared some newspapers off the couch and had George sit down. He got him a beer, a Lite, the kind he always had at The Spouting Whale.

"I was talking to Dora," George said, "and just thought I'd stop by." He looked very concerned—and cold. Turning up the thermostat, Ted said, "Little chilly in here, it'll warm up soon." He sat in the easy chair opposite George and sipped his Red & Black.

"Did June and the kids go out somewhere?" George asked.

Ted cleared his throat. He took another sip of scotch—and told the truth.

George said he was sorry that things were so bad. Then his eyebrows went up. "Hey, why don't you come for dinner tomorrow night? We'd love to have you."

Ted hesitated. "What's tomorrow? Wednesday?"

George squinted a little, as if to say: You don't know what day it is? "Yeah, Wednesday," he said.

"I can't," Ted said. "I'm busy."

"Well how about Thursday, then?"

"That might work out. I'll give you a call."

"Great. I hope you can make it."

"Me too."

He of course wouldn't go; to be with a happy family would only depress him further. "So what's new, George?"

"Well, Marvin LeMaster injured his ankle again."

Ted laughed for the first time in weeks, and at what?—at another man's pain. "Jogging in *this* kind of weather?" he said.

George swallowed some beer. "No, just stepped on it funny. I guess it never really healed from before, and with all his weight... He did it at school. It took five guys to carry him out to the ambulance. Quite a scene."

"Too bad I missed it."

George drank. He said, "You know about Joy, of course."

A pain in Ted's heart and a flash of bad dreams. "No, what about Joy?" he said.

"She eloped with Rod Rheingold, didn't you hear?"

Ted stared at George's flushed, round face; set his drink on the floor and said, "She *what?*"

"That's right, last week. Her old man is fit to be tied. Rod spirited her away from Aubrey, drove her to Elkton, and that was it."

Ted felt giddy. "Rod Rheingold," he said. "Rod *Rheingold.*" He laughed, feeling suddenly light. She was married and gone, he was free! He laughed again, sardonically this time. Some freedom. She'd sabotaged his job and family because he had "ruined her life," and now she'd run off with *that* creep!

"I thought you'd appreciate that one," George said. "The only other item is, they're not renewing Dora's contract."

Still tangled in angry thoughts of Joy, Ted didn't react right away. Then George's statement registered. "They're letting Dora go?"

George nodded. "Troublemaker, you know. Puts principles above expediency."

"They're letting Dora go because of this Dollinger crap? Because of this stuff with the books?"

"No one on the Media Review Committee backed her, not even Wanda Pottsweather. You knew that Warren Volstead took your place on the committee?"

"Warren Volstead! Can he read?"

"Since when is that a qualification for banning books?"

Ted shook his head. "Jesus, letting her go for stating her honest opinion. They can't *do* that."

George shrugged. "Of course they can. All they do is change her job description, you know how it works."

He did indeed: he'd seen it happen to a special ed teacher and a home economics teacher. No one got fired anymore, they had their job descriptions changed—beyond all recognition. They were hassled with extra duties until they cracked. "Is she going to fight it?"

"Doesn't look that way. She said that you wanted to see me, we talked a little, and that's when she gave me the scoop on her contract. She seemed matter-of-fact about it, resigned to her fate."

Ted was hit by a huge wave of guilt. He shot the bull with George for another hour, but all he could think of was Dora. *Damn* Grimsley, *damn* Marvin LeMaster— he hoped his goddamn ankle *never* healed!

At the door George said, "Try to make it for dinner Thursday. And listen—if you need anything, a loan or anything, just let me know."

Deeply touched, Ted said, "I appreciate the offer, George."

"I'd've stopped by before, but I wasn't sure if you wanted me to. You know how confusing these things can get."

"Stop by anytime. I mean it. And thanks for coming."

He closed the door and sat at the kitchen table, dizzy with scotch. As he thought about Dora Rosen, his anger surged. She was losing her *job* because of him—because of that letter he'd written against *Our Bodies* to save his own skin. He poured more scotch, then thought: *What the hell are you doing?*

His father had been an alcoholic, and now he was heading down *that* dark road? He poured the scotch back in the bottle and thought: Enough of this moping around! (*They do not sweat and whine about their condition...*) If worse came to worst he would work for his brother Frank, but enough of this crap! Restless, furious, he paced the kitchen floor. Dora! Damn it, it wasn't right!

Three hours later, in bed, he still wasn't calm. Dora. Dora and Joy. A clean bright energy burned in his brain. He wanted to kill it, to melt, to sleep, but refused to drink more scotch.

The runs came earlier than usual—shortly before three A.M. It was then that he realized he'd fallen asleep after all—and had dreamed of Joy. And that nearly forgotten pain in his chest (he hadn't felt it for several weeks) was slowly wedging its way back into his heart.

• • • • •

He woke up at seven to find that sleep had hardened his resolve, and at nine he called Grimsley's office and made an appointment. His bowels were so loose that he went to the john four times in less than an hour. Before he left, he downed a double Red & Black—the only thing he'd put in his stomach all day.

The superintendent's office was in a converted house in the center of Somerside. Not a mansion, exactly, but close. Ted sat in a metal chair and pretended to read *Time* magazine as Mrs. Carbone, the office manager, typed. The place was hot; a huge cast iron radiator clanked in the corner. During the forty-five minute wait, Ted's guts produced a symphony of sighs. Twice Mrs. Carbone stared up at him oddly over the tops of her glasses. When his moment arrived, the pressure in his bowels was such that he thought he would surely break wind if he so much as moved. But no; as he faced Howard Grimsley the pain decreased and settled behind his ribs.

The first thing that caught his eye was the copy of *Our Bodies Belong to Us* on the fireplace mantel behind Grimsley's desk. Grimsley asked him to sit; then, tilting his chair back, he said, "Mr. Wharton, perhaps we can save some time. There is absolutely no chance at all of your being reinstated."

Ted sat forward, his hands on his thighs. Something wheezed in his stomach. "I didn't come here about that," he said.

Grimsley stroked his steel-gray beard. "What *did* you come about?"

"Dora Rosen. I understand her contract's not being renewed."

Grimsley stared with his cool blue eyes. "I am not at liberty to discuss Ms. Rosen's contract."

"But it's true that you're letting her go."

Grimsley simply continued to stare.

"I *know* it's true," Ted said. "And I also know that you're making a big mistake." The superintendent stroked his beard; kept staring.

Sweat formed on Ted's forehead (good God it was hot in here!) as he said: "You're making a *huge* mistake. A *foolish* mistake." He paused. Had he hit anything?

"You're entitled to your opinion," Grimsley said.

"I'm happy to hear that," Ted said. Wiping sweat from his chin, he said, "At least I *have* opinions. Do you? Or does Armand Dollinger tell you what to think?"

Grimsley stiffened. He narrowed his eyes and said, "Mr. Wharton, you're wasting my time."

"I'm sure I am," Ted said. "—And I plan to waste even more of it."

The stone man didn't change expression.

"Okay," Ted said, "be Dollinger's puppet, don't open your mouth, but I'll tell you what I think—I think you're sacrificing Dora on the altar of your fear."

Grimsley rocked, his back rigid. He said, "Mr. Wharton, the fact of the matter is, Ms. Rosen has no respect for decency—and seems driven to force upon Whitman High her own warped conception of what constitutes proper reading for adolescents." His eyes were sharp and hard.

A gurgle down below; Ted hoped it wasn't audible. He said, "As I understand it, the Media Review Committee as a *whole* decides on whether or not a book will remain in the library. Dora doesn't decide alone, she's part of a *team.*"

Grimsley said, "Before Ms. Rosen came to Whitman High there was no *need* for a team. Only after she came was it necessary to form one. And since its inception it's had to meet a minimum of once a month—because of her."

Ted frowned. "Just what are you saying? —That *Dora's* responsible for all this flap about the books? It's *Dollinger* who's responsible. A lot of these challenged books were sitting in the library for *years* before Dora came, and nobody ever said boo."

Grimsley shrugged. "Times have changed. —And Ms. Rosen refuses to change along with them. She continues to openly—defiantly—flout the standards of this community."

A trickle of sweat ran down Ted's neck. He said, "The standards of this community? You mean Dollinger's standards, don't you? If you want to know about this *com-*

munity's standards, listen to the radio or watch TV, read the stuff on the shelves at your local drugstore, go to the Pikesboro Drive-In on weekends. That's where you'll find your *community's* standards."

"Or the standards of the entertainment industry," Grimsley said.

"Well *somebody* reads and watches that stuff, or it wouldn't make any money."

Again, Grimsley simply shrugged.

Infuriated, Ted said, "Dora hasn't done anything wrong. Protecting a constitutional right, is that *wrong?*"

Grimsley toyed with his beard again. "I'm not going to discuss this further," he said. "Do you have other business?"

Ted gritted his teeth. The sweat rolled down under his collar; his skin was flushed. He looked at Grimsley's impassive face; reached into his jacket and took out a paper, unfolded it, said, "I want you to listen to something." Aloud he read:

"'It is I, you women, I make my way,
I am stern, acrid, large, undissuadable, but
    I love you.
I do not hurt you any more than is necessary
    for you,
I pour the stuff to start sons and daughters
    fit for these States, I press with slow
    rude muscle,
I brace myself effectually, I listen to no
    entreaties,
I dare not withdraw till I deposit what has
    so long accumulated within me.'"

Grimsley's face had turned crimson. He opened his mouth to speak and Ted said, "Wait a second, I haven't finished:"

"'The babes I beget upon you are to beget
    babes in their turn,
I shall demand perfect men and women out of
    my love-spendings,
I shall expect them to interpenetrate with
    others, as I and you interpenetrate now.
I shall count on the fruits of the gushing
    showers of them, as I count on the fruits
    of the gushing showers I give—"

"Mr. Wharton," Grimsley interrupted, "that is more than enough. I refuse to sit here and listen to these vulgarities."

Ted stared. "Do you know who wrote those lines, Mr. Grimsley?"

"Certainly not. I would never read such trash."

Ted said: "Walt Whitman wrote those lines, Mr. Grimsley. The man this school is *named* for wrote those lines. 'The honored name of Walt Whitman High School'— what pious crap! You and Dollinger would ban the work of the man who *bore* that 'honored name.'"

Grimsley's face was a frozen mask. He said, "I had nothing to do with naming this school, Mr. Wharton."

Leaning forward, his teeth on edge, the Whitman poem tight in his hand, Ted said, "That letter I wrote to the paper about *Our Bodies* was *garbage*. I wrote it to save my neck—and Dora Rosen shouldn't have to pay for that—for my cowardice. She shouldn't have to pay for *your* cowardice either. Look, she's a *hell* of a librarian. She puts in far more time than she has to, the kids think she's great, she gets even turned-off pupils to read—"

"And gives them information on birth control," Grimsley said, his eyes piercing and cold.

A tremor passed over Ted's arms. "I don't believe that," he said.

"Believe what you want," Grimsley said, "but it's true."

Ted's hands—to his great dismay—were quivering. "So Dora doesn't have a chance," he said.

"No chance at all."

Ted shakily folded the poem; put it back in his jacket. He looked at his traitorous hands a second, and then looked up. He said: "The manner in which you fired me was illegal."

Leaning back in his chair and caressing his beard, Grimsley said, "Fired you? You resigned."

"Oh come off it!" Ted said. "You denied me due process, and damn it, I'm going to sue this district—and you—for all I can get!"

Grimsley's face wore a slightly bemused expression. "Mr. Wharton, I possess certain photographs—"

"That belong to me!" Ted said, a cold thrill coating his bones. "They're mine, and I want them back!"

With a sniff that was almost a snort, Grimsley said, "Joy Dollinger says they're hers and has entrusted them to me."

"Joy *Rheingold* is a goddamn liar and I want those photographs!"

Grimsley sat forward and leaned on his desk. He said, "I'll tell you what I'll do. If you'll agree to sign a statement saying you'll make no claims against this district or against me personally—no claims of any kind—I'll destroy the photographs in your presence."

The radiator hissed. The pressure in Ted's chest was hard; a rumble traveled through his bowels. He stared at Grimsley, thoughts of murder flaring in his brain. He said, "I'll sign the statement. —But you have to take Dora back."

Grimsley's smile was stiff and thin, a smug suppressed retraction of his mouth. "Ms. Rosen has nothing to do with any claims of yours against this district," he said. "That's a separate issue entirely. Sign the statement as I've proposed it, or I keep the photos."

Ted ground his teeth together, forehead hot, bones cold; then sighed, collapsed inside, and said, "When will you have it ready?"

"Tomorrow at ten."

He berated himself all the way back home. He was scum, a pariah, the kiss of death, and anything he said on behalf of Dora could only hurt her cause. Why had he even bothered with Grimsley; merely to vent his emotions? He'd sunk so low that he needed *catharsis?* No, no, he had done this for *Dora.* But why the Whitman poem, why *that* grandstand play? Oh Christ, he should've stayed out of it as she'd asked.

He nearly ran a light as he thought of the Polaroids; when he slammed on the brakes, the Toyota's old body groaned. Maybe his true subconscious reason for seeing Grimsley was those photos. What had the creep been *doing* with them all these weeks since Christmas?—using them to spice things up at home? Now they would be destroyed, so the trip had been worth it. But that wasn't why he'd gone, he swore—

A chorus of horns informed him that the light was green.

• • • • •

He met Grimsley at ten the next morning, signed the statement and watched the Polaroids burn—in that fireplace with *Our Bodies Belong to Us* on the mantelpiece. With impassive precision, Grimsley flicked each photograph face down into the flames. A draft caught one of them, flipping it over: for a second Ted saw Joy's mouth on his organ, his hand in her crotch—and blushed dark red. He thought of Rod Rheingold enjoying that expertise.

As he sat at the bar and nursed his scotch he thought about Joy: relived those lush intoxicated days when he'd drowned himself in scent and heat and wet. He thought about June and the kids and the way life had been a few years ago, before it had started to sour. Maybe things would have straightened out with time, it had only been time that had made them go wrong in the first place, right? Maybe they still *would* straighten out. He drank, watched the customers come and go, heard the regulars— sloshed at noon—air their petty complaints. Depressed, he ate lunch at McDonald's— which started him thinking of Brad and Kim again. Woozy and worn, he drove home. On the car in front of him, a bumpersticker: FLORISTS DO IT TILL THEY WILT.

The phone woke him out of his nap. It took him a minute to grasp who was calling. "Dora?"

"Ted. Do you have time to meet me for coffee?"

She'd heard. She had already heard somehow. Mrs. Carbone, the rotten fink! SUN strikes again! "I have time, Dora." What else did he have *but* time? "So when do you want to meet?" His head was a heavy bulb on the stalk of his neck.

"In an hour? At the Firefly in Haddonwood?"

• • • • •

She was already there at a corner table, smoking, her coffee half gone.

"Hi, Dora."

"Hi, Ted."

His stomach tight, he pulled out a chair and sat down. Why had he agreed to this? How much punishment did he need? "Dora, listen, I'm sorry, I lost my head. I should've stayed out of it, I know, but—I just got so damn *mad.* I mean it isn't right. You do a good job, a *damn* good job, and for them to shaft you like that…" She smoked; she stared. She knew about the Polaroids? A stipple of sweat hit his fore- head. "You told me not to interfere and I should've listened, but see—"

"I think it's great," she said.

The swing of the kitchen door and a flicker of bluish light. He said, "You do?"

She smoked; she smiled. "I wish I had been there to see his face when you read him the Whitman poem."

Sun shone in Ted's heart. "I'll just have coffee," he said to the sudden waitress. When she left, he said, "Pretty childish, wasn't it?"

"You bet it was—but delicious."

He laughed. "You mean Mrs. Carbone even told you about the poem?"

"She told Eleanor Crux, Eleanor told Madge Nader, and Madge told me." She squinted from smoke in the eyes as she drew on her cigarette.

"I thought you'd be ticked," he said.

Raising her eyebrows, Dora retained the smoke for a second, then slowly exhaled. "My case was closed before you ever went in there," she said. "There was no way that you could have hurt it. The last committee meeting we had, I blasted them—Grimsley, LeMaster, Hoover, Volstead—everybody except poor Wanda Pottsweather, who was so upset by my tone that she cried anyway."

Ted's coffee came, and he ordered a scotch. "Would you like a drink?"

"Sure."

"Whiskey sour? Pink lady?"

"Gin on the rocks."

He waited until the waitress left then said, "So you let them have it."

"You bet."

"But your job… You're not going to fight what they're doing?"

"No, Ted, I've resigned. I don't want to work at a place where I'm not appreciated."

"But the *kids* appreciate you, Dora. I think you should fight."

"And go through all that business about my breakdown again? Drag all *that* out again?"

Ted frowned. "I didn't know about that. You never mentioned that."

She smoked. "After David died?"

"David?"

"The guy I was in love with? —Who wasn't sure if he wanted to marry me, since I couldn't have kids? I told you that story, I know I did."

"But you didn't tell me he died."

"Well he did, and I had a bad time. And they'll rake me over *those* coals again, and if I beg and *promise* to behave, well *maybe* they'll take me back—but only so they can *really* shaft me later."

"Well what are you going to do?"

"My sister runs a boutique out in Albuquerque. I'm going to stay with her for a while and help at the store while I look for a permanent job."

"Albuquerque," Ted said. "God, the desert."

Dora snuffed out her cigarette. "You ever been out there?"

"I've never been west of St. Louis. To Europe, yes, but west of St. Louis, no."

"It's an interesting place."

"So I've heard. One of Whitman's English teachers moved there three years ago, Dan Jefferson. Good guy. I got a couple of cards from him saying he liked it."

"I liked it too. But I missed the seagulls after a while and finally came back."

Missed the *seagulls?* "How long were you there?"

"A year—last time."

"And when are you going out again?"

"Next week."

"That soon."

"The sooner the better."

Ted stared at the ashtray, the crumpled butt with Dora's lipstick on it. "That's probably what I ought to do," he said,"just move someplace."

"Are you serious? Why?"

He looked at her eyes, at the splinters of green in her irises. "Dora, I sent my vita to two hundred junior colleges and didn't get a nibble, not a one. I signed up with a placement agency, searched the want ads every day, and—nothing."

"You'd have a better chance out West."

"You think so? I was turned down by places in Arizona, California, Nevada—"

"If you went there, I bet you'd find something."

The waitress arrived with the drinks. Ted took a sip of the scotch and said, "Well, maybe I ought to try it."

"You think your family would go for a move like that?"

"What family?"

"Oh," Dora said. "Oh, that's too bad. Is there any hope?"

"Doesn't look that way." He drank in the awkward silence, then said, "Albuquerque. Who knows, it might work."

Dora sipped at her gin. Lighting another cigarette she said, "If you're serious, I could use some help with the driving."

"You're driving?"

"I'll need a car out there. I'd like a new one but can't afford it, so I'll drive the bomb." She smiled a little. "Also, I'm scared to fly."

"That's silly, you know."

She blew out smoke. "I guess, but I haven't taken a plane since David died."

"Why not?"

She looked at him as if he were totally dense. "Because that's how he died."

"Oh."

Another deep silence. She drank her gin and said, "He'd gone away for a while to think things over, decided he did want to marry me after all, was coming back...and the plane crashed on takeoff. Nobody survived."

"Oh. Terrible," Ted said. He looked at his drink, at the miniature ice.

"I lost my bearings after that."

"Who wouldn't?"

She sighed out a stream of smoke. "So if you're serious about the trip, please let me know. I'd like the company."

They had another drink and talked about New Mexico. Dora's sister, Sylvia, had lived there for nine years now, and Dora had gone out to see her three times. For a year she had had her own apartment in Albuquerque, a safe and convenient city of manageable size ringed by beautiful mountains. Winters were cool but seldom frigid, and the sun shone practically every day. There were Native American pueblos nearby, and Santa Fe, with a downtown made of adobe, was only an hour's drive. Ted used his VISA to buy two dinners, and listened to Dora talk. By the time they finished their food, he'd decided to go. "That's great," Dora said. "It really is, I hate to travel alone. A person alone on the road can just *disappear* these days."

When Ted got home, he still felt high enough to call Dan Jefferson. Directory assistance gave him the number (the Albuquerque operator grainy and exotic-sounding), and he listened to the brittle, far off ring.

Dan's voice held the hollow weight of two thousand miles. "Ted Wharton! I don't believe it! You're coming out here? With everybody, or just by yourself? What? Jesus, that's too bad. As a matter of fact, there *is* an opening—my job. I'm going to be the principal next year. Yep, giving up the front lines, Ted. It's junior high, do you think you can stand it? Love to see you. Terrific, just call when you get into town. The weather? It's been fantastic! Sixty-five today—and sunny, of course. It's *always* sunny! Look forward to seeing you!"

He sounded as if he meant it, but did he really? Ted imagined him groaning to his wife, "My God! Ted Wharton! He's coming to Albuquerque, he might even *stay* with us!"

"The hell with it, I'm going," Ted said to himself aloud in the desolate kitchen. He poured himself a double scotch and sat at the white formica table—the table that Kim had sat on as he'd laced up her first pair of skates—and thought of his family in Sellerstown, of Dora Rosen, of sand and adobe and sun. What should he take on the trip? he wondered. What, he wondered, were Rod and Joy doing now?

39 • STARTING OUT

The sky was still dark when Dora pulled up in her sagging green Pontiac with—surprise!—a silver and orange U-Haul trailer coupled to its tail. The emphysemic engine idled roughly as Ted locked his soiled front door and walked to the street. The morning air was damp and cold. Spring seemed as far away as it had a month ago.

He carried one piece of luggage—a leather travel bag (his twelfth anniversary gift from June, meant to encourage globe-trotting), and the sleeping bag he had bought for Brad's first summer at Camp Ambergris. (How long ago was that? Four years? Five years? A lifetime ago.)

Dora was wearing a furry, comical, Russian sort of a hat. Through the partially rolled-down window she said, "Good morning."

Ted looked at the U-Haul. "You didn't tell me about this thing," he said. "You ever tow one before?"

She shook her head. "Is it hard? I had no choice, I couldn't afford a mover."

"I don't know if it's hard, I've never towed one either."

"Oh. Well, I guess we'll find out."

"I guess. I'd've helped you pack if I'd known you were renting it."

"Thanks, but it wasn't too bad. Put your things in the back, the trunk's full."

The back wasn't exactly empty; clothes and bulging shopping bags took up all but a sliver of space. The ledge below the rear window was littered with books, one of which was *Our Bodies*. Ted crammed his stuff back there and sat in the passenger seat.

The engine's vibration ran up through his feet and he felt a deep stomach-pit thrill. He'd felt that excitement before long trips as a kid and had never outgrown it. Sometimes he liked it, sometimes he loathed it. On airplane rides with June he loathed it; almost felt sick with his fears about engines sucking in birds and the huge plane falling, careening, grinding the concrete, squashing its human cargo like rotten fruit. This morning, however, the feeling was pleasant.

Mr. 7-Eleven was leaving for work. Giving them a sidelong glance, he got in his Buick and started to warm it up. Dora looked in the mirror and pulled out slowly, the Pontiac farting. As Ted watched the neighborhood slide away, he thought: Good riddance, dear Westdale.

Dora was frowning. "How come your door's all black like that?"

Ted chuckled. "A little reprisal for my crimes."

"Aren't people grand? You should've heard the rumors at Whitman regarding my sexual preference. I wonder who started *them*."

Ted blushed, and hoped it didn't show. It was probably *he* who had started them—with the question he'd put to George. "Vicious, Dora."

She chewed on her lower lip as she drove. "So why don't you repaint the door?"

"That's just what my wife kept asking me. Too cold, the paint won't dry right."

"Oh."

The Pontiac's windows were covered with film, the residue of months of tobacco smoke. Why hadn't she cleaned them off for a trip like this?

"Ted, do me a favor and get me a cigarette, will you? They're right in my pocketbook, right on top."

He got them and shook one out. She took it, stuck it in her mouth and touched the lighter to it; set the pack on the dash. Thick smoke replaced the air.

"I have to stop for gas. Is a station open around here anywhere?"

There was, he said, a half mile down Route 9. Why hadn't she filled the tank last night? The smoke and blasting heater made him gag.

At the gas station Dora used the ladies room. When she got in the car again they discussed what route they'd take.

She wanted to go down I-95 through Washington and Richmond, swing through western North Carolina, then pick up Route 40 outside Greensboro and follow it to Albuquerque. Ted said a better way was to cross to Philadelphia, take the expressway to the Pennsylvania Turnpike, pick up 81 past Harrisburg and follow it down to Knoxville, then take Route 40 from there. It was fast and foolproof—you couldn't get lost. And he hated the drive to Washington, it was always so frantic.

Dora objected. His route was more northern, so there'd be more chance of snow. She wanted to hit the South as soon as possible. Also, she'd never been to western North Carolina and thought it might prove interesting.

"Dora, this isn't a *sightseeing* trip, we want to get to Albuquerque *fast*."

His appeal to practicality won out, but she frowned all the way to the Walt Whitman Bridge. It was daylight now, but the sky was a dingy gray. "If we run into snow, this route will be slower," she said.

Ted didn't respond. He stared at the poisoned Delaware, wondering what it had looked like in Whitman's day. "Could we turn down the heat a little, Dora?"

"Sure."

She did, but not much.

"You don't have a radio."

"No."

"I was hoping to get a weather forecast."

"Sorry."

They were quiet until the turnpike, when they shared a banana and started to swap Whitman High School stories: about blunders that they and others had made, about Grimsley's and LeMaster's foolishness. Dora's mood improved, but she still wore a worried look and drove slowly, very cautiously, though the traffic had thinned considerably. To Ted, she seemed too small to be driving such a big car.

She stopped at a Burger King to pee and buy coffee. When she came back out, snow was starting to fall. "I knew it," she said. "It's sunny as hell in Washington, I bet."

She drove even slower, hands tight on the wheel. By the time they got to Harrisburg, they had already spent an astounding three hours and thirty-five minutes on the road.

Ted took over the driving. The Pontiac handled heavily with the U-Haul on its tail, and the snow turned steady and thick. He had meant to clean the windows back at the service station, but the dialogue over which route to take had distracted him. He wiped the gray film with his hand. "That only makes it worse," Dora said. She took some tissues out of her purse and rubbed the glass. "Better?" "Not much," Ted said.

The snow made them silent and tense, and the going was painfully slow. With a stop for lunch, a stop for gas, and two more bathroom stops for Dora (did the woman have a bladder infection, or what?), it was nearly four o'clock when they left Pennsylvania and crossed into Maryland. The snow had stopped, but the sky was still heavily gray and the dark was coming on fast.

It was totally black by the time they arrived at a place called Endless Caves, Virginia and decided to call it quits. They had fallen short of their destination, Pulaski, by a hundred and eighty miles. At this rate, Ted figured, it would take them till April to get to Albuquerque.

This snail's pace really bugged him. On auto trips with his family he was a stern taskmaster (worse than the Colonel!), severely restricting the number and length of stops. He wanted to *get* there, not spend his time in a car. But it was impossible to hurry Dora: she dawdled over lunch, took twenty minutes to use the john, bought coffee each time they stopped. When he mentioned their extraordinary tardiness, she said, "Let's just relax, okay?"

He figured there would be some hassle over the sleeping arrangements, but no, she agreed they were both mature adults and could certainly share a room. They found a small motel (The Siesta! What memories *that* brought back!), and got a decent room with two beds for a low off-season rate. (Was there really a *season* in a godforsaken place like this?) He thought of an alias—Willy Ball—but signed his real name and paid with his VISA card.

They put their travel bags inside, and, too bushed to get in the car again, had supper at the diner beside the motel. The food was quite edible trucker-type stuff, and cheap. Ted had roast beef with mashed potatoes. Dora had Salisbury steak with "smothered" onions, also mashed potatoes, left half of it on her plate. Ted polished it off. They both had cherry pie for dessert, with coffee, and Dora smoked a cigarette before they went back to the room.

She used the bathroom first, as she had to pee, and came out in her robe, a long shiny thing with huge flowers. Ted urinated silently, then put on the pair of pajamas he'd bought for the trip.

"Brand new, huh?" Dora said from her bed when he came back into the room.

"How'd you guess?"

"The tag's still on them."

So it was, on the back of the collar. He removed it; got into the other bed, feeling dizzy, exhausted. His runs had woken him at three that morning, he'd never gone back to sleep, and now he was shot. No chest pains, though—or stomach pains or any of that kind of crap. Feeling odd with her in the room with him, he said, "Well, good-night, Dora. Let's try to get up real early and make some time."

She laughed a little. Mocking him? "Sure, Ted. Goodnight."

Despite his fatigue, he lay awake; heard her breathing lapse into a gentle rhythm, and thought of June. He thought of the kids again and it made him sad, so he switched his thoughts to his times with Joy, *those* motel rooms. Despite his exhaustion and melancholy, he got a bit hard. He wondered what Dora would think if she'd seen those Polaroids. Would she have dared to share this room with him? He listened to her breathe, and thought of her poisoned pregnancy, the lover who had died. And he thought *he* had problems. As the cold wind whistled around the window he thought about New Mexico, a whole new life in warmth and sun, and slept.

40 • BREAKDOWN

When he woke up and looked at his watch, it said 8:05. He'd hoped to get up at the crack of dawn, but...

Dora was still asleep, which was good, since his shaft, as usual in the morning, was perpendicular to his thighs. Mature adults or not, he wasn't about to get caught like this.

He sneaked across the rug to the bathroom, closed the door, sat down, and his tip hit the bowl—a foreign bowl used by hundreds of transient strangers. He backed off, cringing, urinated softly, flushed; washed up, shaved, brushed his teeth; came out to find Dora leaning against her headboard, smoking a cigarette.

"Morning, Ted."

"Morning, Dora. Sleep okay?"

She smoked. "I could've done better. Maybe you could arrange not to snore so much tonight."

"Snore? *Me?*"

"You bet. June never complained?"

He scowled. "No, never. I can't believe I did it."

"Well, you did."

He continued to scowl. She smoked. He said, "Jesus, Dora, you're going to kill yourself with those things."

"I don't especially care," she said, exhaling with a pout.

"You aren't serious."

"If I cared, I'd stop."

"I guess. But it doesn't make sense. You're scared to get on a plane because it might crash, but you'll kill yourself with cigarettes."

"It has to do with time, I guess. I mean lung cancer's twenty or thirty years off."

"That's not so long."

"Does it bother you? Do you want me to put it out?"

"No, no, go ahead." He was suffocating.

When she used the bathroom he put on his clothes, rushing so she wouldn't catch him in his underwear, but he needn't have been concerned: she took forever. He heard things clicking and clinking, he watched the news and weather on TV, was absorbed in a talk show (dealing with married women who had affairs), when she came out looking nice, with makeup on, and said, "You want to get breakfast next door?"

"I think we should hit the road," he said. "It's almost quarter of ten."

"Aren't you hungry?"

"I still have some fruit in the car."

"Fine with me, I won't be able to eat for a couple of hours yet—but I would like to get some coffee."

They paid their bill and got coffee to go. As he sipped and drove, she grinned.

"What's so funny?" he asked.

She laughed. "Well really, what's the point of this? You could have sat in the restaurant and *savored* the coffee. Was it worth it to get on the road a few minutes sooner? Now you don't even know what you're drinking."

"Of course I do."

"You don't."

"I *do.*"

"Hey, don't get testy now."

"I'm not getting testy."

"Mmm."

This day followed the same general pattern as the one before: lots of stops for pee and coffee; flurries; a protracted lunch. When Dora drove, she crept along at barely forty-five. Ted tried to resign himself to her leisurely style. What was his hurry? he asked himself. He didn't have an actual time set up to meet with Dan, so why the rush?

The day's destination was Knoxville. Ted figured that given his normal traveling speed the Endless Caves to Knoxville run would take about eight hours, but after nine hours (with Ted exceeding the speed limit during his stints at the wheel) it was dark and going on seven o'clock, and Knoxville was still a hundred miles away.

After their lunch stop, the time had flown. They had kept up a steady stream of talk—about their childhoods, the places they'd lived, the books and movies they liked and hated, Whitman High again—and Ted was amazed it had already gotten so late. Tired and stiff and munching on peanuts to quell his advancing hunger, he vowed to make Knoxville before they stopped for the night. But the dashboard lights—didn't they look dimmer than before? It had started to snow again and the wipers were sluggishly—feebly?—brushing away the flakes, and the headlights just didn't seem *bright* enough. "Hey Dora," he said, "does the dashboard seem dim to you?"

"Turn the headlight knob," she said.

He did—and found it was already all the way up. "And the wipers aren't moving fast enough."

"They do seem kind of slow."

A twinge of panic hit Ted's gut. "We're dying," he said, "we're losing power." He pressed on the gas; the car didn't accelerate.

"Oh damn," Dora said. "I was praying this piece of junk would get us there."

"Jesus," Ted said, "we're out in nowhere."

They both fell silent. Ted drove in agonizing slowness, straining to see in the snow, the headlamps' beam growing duller and duller. An exit sign swam up on the right with a faint: GAS LODGING FOOD. "I'm getting off here," Ted said.

"You think we should?"

"Of course. We have to find a garage before we're dead."

He braked, put his turn signal on. It blinked lethargically, twice, then stuck. At the foot of the ramp he stopped at the sign; turned right, and the Pontiac gasped.

"Where *are* we?" Dora said.

"Your guess is as good as mine. Somewhere east of Knoxville, that's all I know."

The road was black; no cars on either side. Snow beat against the glass. The dash was a sickly orange now. They inched along.

"The sign said gas," Ted snapped. "Well where the hell is it?"

The car started shaking; he pumped the pedal. The engine sputtered, the wipers stuttered, he pulled to the side of the road and the engine stopped.

Dead quiet. "Now what?" Dora said.

Ted looked out the window. Nothing but trees on both sides of the road. The snow came down. "They always say never to leave your car in these situations," he said. "— Unless you can get a ride, of course. Fat chance."

Dora stared at him, frowning; took out a cigarette, lit up. "Well why did you turn off the interstate? They have phones up there, they have patrols."

"I thought I could make the service station. Anyway, I didn't see any phones up there. You don't have a cell phone?"

Projecting her lip, she blew fretful smoke. "I lost it," she said, and then,"I have to go."

"Well go in the woods."

"Are you kidding? There might be bears out there."

Ted rolled his eyes. "Bears. What do you think this is, the wild west?"

"I've never been in Tennessee before."

"Me neither, but I'm sure there aren't any bears."

"Well rabid foxes or something."

He stared at her. "Dora, what do you want me to do? Go pee, for Christ's sake, I'll be right here, nothing's going to hurt you."

She hesitated, then opened the door, the cigarette still in her hand. A cold gust of air blew in. She got out, closed the door and went down the snow-covered bank. In the dark he saw the tip of her cigarette glow brighter, then disappear—clear evidence that a bear had consumed her.

He waited. No cars came by. The Pontiac was cooling rapidly. He bet she wouldn't take twenty minutes *this* time.

The door shot open. She popped inside and said, "My God, it's *freezing!* I thought the South was warm!"

"Come back in July."

"It's the coffee."

"What?"

"That makes me pee so much, I ought to cut down." She shivered. "You sure know how to show a girl a good time."

He was forming a tart reply when she sneezed—just once. He waited expectantly, but no more came. June always, but *always* sneezed twice.

She wiped her nose with a tissue and said, "When you got off 81, you should've turned left."

"I should've turned left," he said. "Well thanks for telling me. What do you mean, I should've turned left? There weren't any signs for anything either way."

She crossed her arms and clutched her shoulders, shivering. "Well there sure isn't much in *this* neck of the woods." She sneezed again—again just once. "Now I'm catching a goddamn cold." She looked at him. "Well what are we going to do, just sit here like this?" She said it without any anger, as if she just wanted to know.

"What else *can* we do?" Ted said. "If I knew what was wrong I'd try to fix it it, but I don't know shit about cars."

"Me neither."

"And it wouldn't be smart to try to walk anywhere. I think we should wait here till somebody comes along. If nobody comes, we'll have to sleep here and try to find help in the morning."

"We'll freeze to death."

"If worse comes to worst, we'll take off our clothes and get in my sleeping bag. It's the best way to keep from freezing."

She sniffed. "Oh, yeah, I *bet* it is! Is that how you snagged your little cookie? Stranded her on some godforsaken road somewhere and told her she'd die if she didn't crawl into your sack?"

"The mad rapist has all kinds of devious ploys," Ted said. "Seriously—it's the best way to keep your core temperature up."

"I'll bet that's not *all* it keeps up! I'd have to be damn near dead before I'd get into that bag with *you!*"

Ted sighed. "The other thing we can do is start a fire."

"Out there? In that wind and snow? I'm not going out *there.*"

"Well if nobody picks us up and it gets any colder—"

"Okay, okay, we'll cross that bridge when we come to it. What do we have to eat—besides peanuts?"

"Sardines."

"Oh, ugh. Well, let's eat them."

Ted reached in the back and opened his travel bag, groped around. "Here we go." He lifted the ring on the can and pulled—and the ring broke off.

He stared at it there in his hand. "Oh for Christ's sake," he said.

"You pulled too hard," Dora said.

"What? It isn't my fault, the can's defective, they made a defective can! Christ, they ought to be sued, a person could die because of their negligence. Now what?"

"I guess it's peanuts."

A handful apiece was all they could stomach. They waited. No cars came by. Ted said they should get some rest. He went to the woods to take a leak (good God was it damp!), came back and unrolled Brad's sleeping bag, unzipped it, and they wrapped it around themselves. They held it tightly, shivering, exhaling white air.

Their knees touched briefly and they both recoiled. Forced intimacy, how Ted loathed it. Those parties he'd gone to in junior high, those games—how horribly wet and cold those kisses had seemed. He didn't actually mind this closeness with Dora, but there was a terrible awkward tenseness about it, at least on his part.

She smoked another cigarette, clutching the sleeping bag to her neck, her funny Russian hat pulled over her ears. She looked like a first grader bundled against a blizzard—except for the cigarette, of course, which was smothering him. Trying to lighten things up, he said, "You shouldn't smoke in bed. Didn't anyone ever tell you that?"

"No," she said with a quizzical frown.

"We'll have these moments to remember."

"If we live." She smoked. "How would taking your clothes off make you *warmer?*"

"They say it does."

"Mmm."

When she finished her cigarette, they were quiet. Ted was actually dozing off when the spotlight hit the rearview mirror and the flashing revolving blue pulled up behind them.

The cop asked the usual nonsense about the driver's license and where they were from, then radioed a garage. Ted was standing outside in the snowfall, asking about a place to stay, when a call came over the squad car's radio. In midsentence the cop jumped in and roared off, his blinding blue strobe slashing into the lonely trees. And there they were in the cold and the dark again.

But twenty minutes later (three cheers for the men in blue) the wrecker actually came. The guy unhitched the U-Haul; then, with Ted and Dora in the cab beside him, towed the ailing car to his garage.

While Dora used the ladies room, Ted tried to start the car when given the signal. The mechanic—a lean, grease-blackened guy with slick gray hair and few teeth—said it looked like the voltage regulator. He could probably find the part and fix it tomorrow. Dora insisted he get the U-Haul, so he locked them outside in the snow and took off. When the trailer was safe in his parking lot, he ran them into town—a block of stores, all closed—and left them at a woodframe white-porched guest house run by a pair of old women. Dora gave him a handsome tip.

There was one guest room, quite tiny, with a double bed below a pull-chain light, a sink on a wooden stand in the corner, a huge dark chiffonier, and walls with faded stained paper. They said it was fine. The bathroom was in the hall, and Dora used it.

Ted had brought Brad's sleeping bag in with him, thinking he might be needing it, and offered to camp on the floor. Was he sure he'd be comfortable there? she asked. Yes, he replied, he was sure. They turned out the light and lay down without getting undressed.

In the dark, Ted's stomach growled. He said, "You must be starving, Dora."

"I'm okay."

"Maybe the ladies have something to eat."

"I just want to sleep."

So did he. He lay on the cold linoleum floor, his belt cutting into his hips. After about ten minutes of that, he slipped off his pants. Dora seemed to be already sleeping.

Through the floorboards he heard the old women conversing. For them this was home, the world's center; for him it was foreign and far away. He felt lonely, cut off from all he knew, and immensely sad. He thought of his family—June, the kids—in Sellerstown, PA.

He listened to the jumbled, lilting talk, unable to understand nine-tenths of it, but finding the sound of the conversation soothing, comforting, as he'd found the sounds of his parents' downstairs conversations soothing when he was a child. He listened, lulled, his heavy lids closing...

41 • BREAKDOWN (CONTINUED)

When he woke he was next to her in the bed. How had it happened? He remembered being cold in the night, getting up off the floor—and now here he was, curled up beside her, facing her back in the softspringed sag with the sleeping bag over them both.

His matinal firmness was at its peak, and the tip of it brushed her spine through his boxer shorts. Good lord! Wincing, he ever so gently retreated. She stirred. He tried to sneak out of the bed and the springs creaked rustily, gratingly, jiggled like Jello. He stood up quickly, grabbed his pants and frantically pulled them on.

She turned and stretched and opened her eyes. "Is it morning already?"

"It's almost nine," he said with his back turned toward her, his bulge directed at the chiffonier. His mouth had a foul brown taste and his breath, he knew, was obscene. "I'm going to use the bathroom, okay?"

"You mind if I pee first?"

"Go right ahead."

Still hard, he was standing at the window when she returned.

"So what do you see that's interesting?" she asked, coming up beside him.

He twisted his torso abruptly and moved toward the door. "That store over there. See the old Coke sign?"

"That's interesting?" she said.

In the hallway he softly moaned; hurried down to the john.

• • • • •

The sun was cheerful on the inch-thick fluff of fresh snow. From the nearby cafe they called the garage. The part had been found and the job would be finished by noon. They lingered over eggs and compulsory grits and had multiple fillups of coffee. When Dora finished her cigarette they walked back to the boarding house, where the ladies corralled them, plied them with questions, and told them about the town's old days, which sounded like the old days anywhere. At quarter of one the mechanic (the old ladies' nephew) picked them up.

The repair cost a hundred bucks. Ted put it on his VISA card. Dora had paid for the guest house (the ladies would not accept credit). Ted insisted she keep a strict account of expenses and he'd settle with her as soon as he landed a job. She said okay in her offhand way, and they left with her at the wheel.

A couple of hours past Knoxville, still beat from the night before, they decided to stop; checked into a decent motel, had a meal at a place that took VISA. It was early, ten of seven, and Dora suggested they go to the Main Street movie—her treat.

The film was about a guy who cheated on his wife, got caught, lost his family and friends. Not such a treat for Ted, who felt like Claudius at Hamlet's play.

When they went to an ice cream place, Ted felt like a teenager out on a date. He had a few spoonfuls of sundae and quit, feeling vaguely ill, like the last time he'd eaten a sundae, that time with Joy. In the dark of the motel room the movie assailed him, making him toss and turn.

"What's wrong," Dora said, "can't you sleep?"

"No."

"We shouldn't have seen that movie, I guess. Is that what's bothering you?"

"I guess."

A pause, then: "I might be able to help."

"How?"

"I'll show you."

She turned on the light. She was wearing bright red pajamas. Taking a chair from the dresser, she sat at the foot of his bed. When she lifted the blankets he said with a twinge of anxiety, "What are you going to do?"

She took his left heel in her hand. Her touch was warm. "Foot reflexology," she said. "It's a form of massage. There are points on your soles that connect to each one of your body's organs. It's a safe harmless way to relax."

"Are you serious?"

"Wait and see."

He had taken a shower, his feet smelled okay, so no worry on that score, at least. She kneaded him gently, diffusely at first, then just as he started to let himself go, she bore down.

"Ow!"

A look of intense concentration. "Hurts, huh?"

"A little."

More pressure. Jesus! A crunching noise. "What's that?"

"The crystals breaking up."

"The crystals? What crystals?"

"It's junk that your system collects. The massage breaks it up and flushes it out so your energy paths are clear again."

"You're kidding. That's *weird.*"

She kept working. The pain subsided, the crunching subsided, and now the massage felt good. He *was* relaxed—but stimulated too, a bit...aroused. She was pressing the point for *that* organ? He hoped she would move on soon. She did. His stomach growled. "It's making me hungry," he said.

"That's good, the energy's really flowing. I still have some cookies from the ice cream parlor, you want them?"

"Okay."

"When we're finished."

She switched to his right foot. His left foot felt tingly and loose. When his right foot was done he felt totally calm.

"Well?" she said.

"Incredible," he said. "Thanks. Thanks a lot." He tried to imagine June doing a deed like that, but couldn't; she just didn't have it in her. He remembered that time he'd massaged her with Master Muscle.

"I think you'll sleep fine now."

"Thanks again. Oh—your cookies."

He ate them, three Oreos, and his stomach felt great. She went to the bathroom again and got into bed; turned the light out; began to breathe deeply, and soon he was drifting off too, the movie pale and harmless at the far green edge of his mind.

"June, I really don't want to go."

She sniffed disdainfully, arms folded, and turned away.

They sat in the widebody's center section, Brad on his left, Kim on his right, and June beside Kim. The plane vibrated, taxied down the runway, picked up speed—and he saw on his left, through the window suddenly huge in front of his eyes, the swift thick pepperblack flock of starlings. The jet engine vacuumed them up and he felt the huge plane stutter, falter. People were screaming. He saw Kim's terrified face. Runway lights were rushing at them and he was the pilot, he'd done something wrong, too late, too late, and why did the band on his cap say "Electrakween?" He pulled the lever back, too late. A terrible jolt and Brad's seat belt cut him in half—

"He isn't dead!"

The shout sent him shooting straight up in the darkness, pulse racing, his skin slick with sweat. He didn't know where he was. On a plane? Home? Where? "He isn't dead!" he heard again and the voice was Dora's. He turned on his light.

She was leaning against the headboard, mouth open, the covers pulled up to her chest. She stared at him wildly, fearfully, as if she had never seen him before in her life. Then closing her eyes and tilting her head back, she let out a huge deep sigh.

She sat there motionless a minute, her eyes still closed, then looked at the covers; looked at him.

He frowned. "Are you okay?"

She nodded. "That goddamn dream again," she said. "I haven't had that dream in almost a year."

"You said, 'He isn't dead.'"

She nodded. "Sometimes it's David and sometimes the baby. Sometimes it's both of them mixed up together somehow."

The bedlamp was hurting his eyes. He said, "You won't believe this. I dreamed of a plane crash too. My son was killed."

"How terrible," she said. The covers were still in her fists.

"I heard you shout. In the dream I was trying to scream but no words came out. The words you said were the words I was trying to say." He shook his head. "For both of us to have a plane crash dream..."

"I was dreaming about the birth this time," she said.

"Oh."

Her covers hadn't stopped their quivering. She got out of bed and went into the bathroom. He heard the faint hiss of her urine, the flush. In the room again, she said, "I'm a wreck." She searched through her pocketbook.

"You want me to try to massage your feet?"

"There are limits to foot relexology. Look, I hope you don't mind, but I'm going to smoke some dope."

She came up with a pre-rolled joint and lit it; sucked it deeply; held it out. "Want some?"

He sat on the end of her bed and took the cigarette; smoked, gave it back.

"If Dollinger could only see us now," she said. "What decadents we are, they were right to banish us."

He sniffed a sad laugh and smoked again. When he started to feel it he said, "Did you ever go to anyone about those dreams?"

"You mean a therapist?"

"Yeah."

"Back when I had my breakdown."

"Did it help?"

"I guess so. I got better."

"What was it like?"

"The therapy?"

"The breakdown—or maybe you'd rather not talk about it."

"I don't mind," she said. She smoked the joint, which was tiny now, and said, "I couldn't walk. My legs wouldn't work. I had to crawl to the toilet, I couldn't go out of the house, there were all these noises in my head..."

"My God."

"I don't know if the therapy helped or not. I think Sylvia helped me the most, I stayed with her. I slept a lot. The bad part lasted three months. After that I just felt rotten and had attacks sometimes—blurred vision, weak legs. I guess dreams are the last things to go."

Ted sucked on the roach; held it out, fingers hot. She declined. Squashing it in the ashtray, he said, "You're still in love with him, aren't you?"

She smiled sadly. "I guess, in a way. In a way I guess I'll always love him. Is anything wrong with that?"

"Not unless it prevents you from loving somebody who's living."

"It won't." She looked at him, "Do you still love June?"

"I don't know," he said. "Sometimes I think I do, and sometimes I think all I love is the memories. Sometimes I think...that maybe I'm like those guys who are sick and tired of teaching but can't do anything else or don't want to do anything else. They don't want to lose their investment. Maybe that's all it is with June, I don't know."

"But you miss the kids."

"I miss the kids. But soon they'll be grown and gone anyway."

She stared at the bedspread, a quizzical frown on her face, and said, "I've often tried to imagine what it's like to have kids. I enjoy my sister's family, but I don't think I'd want my own kids now. When I was young, yes, but not now."

"Why not?"

"I don't have the nerve I had back then."

"You seem to have plenty of nerve to me."

She smiled. "Thanks."

He said, "I wouldn't want to start a family either at this point, but I liked having kids. They added a depth..." Remembering then in his lazy high that Dora could never give birth he felt suddenly awkward, and shut his mouth.

She looked at him, frowning again. In his druggy calm she was quite attractive, in spite of the fact that her makeup had all worn off and her hair was messed up. "What are people like Dollinger so afraid of?" she said.

"God only knows," he said. "A million things. Chaos, I guess, the way of the world. I guess they're afraid that what happened to Joy will...happen." Light and floaty, he thought about what he'd just said. Had it made any sense? "I wonder..."

"Wonder what?"

"I wonder if Joy got pregnant. —If that's why she ran off with Rheingold."

"My God," Dora said, "her old man would die. Would he stake her to an abortion?"

"The way he hates abortion? Never."

"Well who *doesn't* hate it?" Dora said. "It isn't a matter of *like*, it's a matter of *need*."

He frowned at her. "Dora?"

"Yes?"

"Did you really give birth control information to kids?"

A sardonic laugh. "Birth control information. A girl came in and asked for the address of Planned Parenthood. I showed her how to find it in the telephone book." She raised her eyebrows. "You ever try to look up Planned Parenthood?"

"No."

"Well try it sometime."

"So what happened?"

"She went there, they gave her some birth control pills and her mother found them. She panicked and said that I was the one who'd told her where to get them."

"Jesus."

"Precisely. Dollinger said I was part of the faculty's secular humanist plot to destroy our country's youth."

Ted laughed. "Plot! Jesus, can he really believe that crap? The Whitman staff part of a *plot?* They can just about plan a *faculty* meeting."

"Who *knows* what he believes. He's just sad—and dangerous."

"He sure is."

A mellow silence hung in the yellow light. Ted listened to the crackles in his ears. This dope was decent stuff, as good as Joy's. He wondered if they used the same supplier.

"Joy is so bright," Dora said. "Such a beautiful girl."

"She certainly is," Ted said, his mouth suddenly heavy, "and no one will ever love her. She knows it, too. That's what drives her. It's what she's fighting against."

"You don't think Rod loves her?"

"Rod? Rod loves his car and his hair."

She stared at him. It made him uncomfortable. To think about Joy again was disturbing, even behind the dope. "You feeling okay now, Dora?"

She nodded; her face was soft. "How about you?"

"I'm fine." A tingle of sweat as the dream came back and he saw Brad sliced in two.

"God," she said, "it's three o'clock, we better get some sleep."

"I guess we better." Strands of his life with June and the kids sent melancholy colors through his brain. "Well, Dora, goodnight."

"Just let me use the bathroom first before you turn out the light."

42 • CLOSE CALL

Despite the interrupted sleep, in the morning they both felt fine. They poured two paper cups of the motel's coffee and got on the road right away. The day was beautiful, their conversation flowed with fluid ease, and they made it to Nashville shortly before one o'clock.

By then they were starving, and left the highway in search of some decent food. Ted drove down a city business block, scowling and mentally cursing the traffic, when Dora said excitedly, "A Jewish deli! The genuine thing, it has that *look.* In Nashville of all places!"

It was steamy, noisy, aromatic, jammed. Ted wanted to order a corned beef sandwich, but Dora said, "Don't, you can get that *anywhere.* Look! Kreplach, knishes, blintzes!" and she ordered a meal for them both.

It began with borsht, a cold purple liquid with boiled potato in it. Dora spooned sour cream into hers, but Ted ate his plain. It wasn't too bad, but the next thing he tried was awful.

He took one bite, rolled the fragment around on his tongue, laid his fork on his plate. With a look of chagrin, he managed to swallow. "What *is* this stuff?" he said, "cat food?"

"You've never had gefilte fish?"

"I've never even seen them in stores. What do they look like?

She laughed. "It's a mixture of carp, whitefish and pike."

"Carp! Jesus, it *is* cat food! Carp are nothing but giant goldfish."

"You don't have to eat it."

"Believe me, I won't."

The blintzes were good. He kind of liked the knishes, too, though they had a pasty texture and a foreign mix of flavors. "'Knish' is Jewish slang for vagina," Dora said. "Some inside information that I thought I'd pass along."

Ted picked at the kishka she'd put on his plate. No way was he going to eat *this* stuff. "What *are* Jews anyway?" he said. "I've never quite understood it. I always wanted to ask Marty Zeller or Murray Sheinstein or some of the other guys, but I felt too embarrassed. At my age you ought to know that stuff."

"You ought to."

"Yeah. But I've never had any Jewish friends, so I don't. A religion, a culture—just what *is* 'Jewish'? Moses and the Ten Commandments, or what?"

"It's all those things."

"But you can be Jewish and not be religious, right? That's the thing that I don't understand. I mean you can't be *Catholic* and not be religious."

Dora reached for a cigarette. She lit up, frowned, blew smoke. "It's not that easy to explain," she said. "It's a set of shared attitudes, traditions, food preferences...all of that."

"But are you religious? You believe in God?"

"You mean a Big Guy in the Sky who directs the universe?"

"Yeah."

"No."

"But you're Jewish."

"I am. But not *real* Jewish."

Rolling his eyes, Ted said, "Now that's the kind of thing I mean. How can anyone understand a statement like that?"

She smiled. "Maybe you have to be Jewish to understand."

He sighed.

She said, "Let's put it this way. Even if I never ate another bite of Jewish food, even if I never set foot in a synagogue, I'm Jewish enough to be persecuted by Hitler."

"So what are you telling me? It's a race?"

"No."

Shaking his head, he said, "I give up."

"So do I," she laughed.

He frowned. "Speaking of Hitler—or Dollinger, for that matter—why do people *hate* the Jews so much?"

"Well, *you* didn't like the gefilte fish—and wouldn't even *try* the kishka."

"Seriously."

"Perhaps it's because they're so much smarter than Gentiles," she said.

"I'm beginning to understand."

They laughed, then fell silent. Behind the steam tables, dishes clattered, men shouted. Dora smoked with a serious look on her face. "No," she said, "I don't believe in God. I don't believe the universe has a plan. Was it part of God's plan for my baby to die? For David to die? For six million Jews to die in the ovens? Is it part of God's plan to give children cancer and third-degree burns? What kind of a plan is that?"

The waitress cleared off their plates. When she left Ted said, "You really ought to cut down on your smoking, Dora."

"You care about my health that much?"

"Well...yes, I do."

"It's good of you, but I'm not quite ready to give it up. In my next incarnation, maybe."

"So. You are religious after all."

She shook her head. "Are you?"

"I'd like to be, but I just can't be."

"Me too."

"And yet you're a Jew."

"That's what my mother told me."

On to Memphis, constantly talking, Dora driving, constantly smoking; stopping to pee and get gas and a snack of some devils food cake. It was dark when they reached the city, but feeling good they kept on going, Ted behind the wheel. By the time they'd had enough it was almost ten.

Dora had been briefing him on Jewish ceremonies—Hanukkah, Rosh Hashana, Yom Kippur—and was into Passover (coming up soon) and the seder—when Ted, going down the ramp, saw the sudden headlight: *Wrong, wrong way, in the wrong direction, coming fast*— Instinctively, he swerved and hit the brakes.

A grinding shriek as the tires hit gravel and the Pontiac started to slide. The headlight belonged to a car with its left light dead. Protruding teenage faces laughed and jeered as the car roared past, just inches away. The Pontiac slid in a slow calm dream then stopped, the U-Haul yanking its tail with a wicked crunch. The engine died. The quiet headlights glared on brush and rock.

It had all taken place in the space of ten seconds. Ted stared at the bushes, a cold sick prickle scattering through his chest. His head felt light, his heart was crashing, he suddenly felt sharp pain in his arm and he turned and saw Dora—saw her clutching his arm with both hands, her eyes tightly closed.

"Those bastards!" he said between clenched teeth.

She kept gripping his arm; exhaled, and her eyes came open. "Oh my God," she said. She stared at her hands and released him, looking confused; took her cigarettes off the dash. She shook the pack and three fell in her lap. She put two back, stuck the other one in her mouth. "Goddamn," she said. Her hands were trembling violently.

He pressed the lighter in. When it popped he held it up to her. She puffed smoke gratefully.

"That could have been it," he said.

"You bet," she said. "You bet." She blew out smoke and said, "I'm sorry for being so bad about it." A car went slowly past; its stoplights flicked at the yield sign, turned left. "Frailty, thy name is woman, right?"

"Are you kidding? I'm a basket case."

"That's good to hear—in a way. Too bad you don't smoke, it might settle you down."

"I'll be okay in a minute. Those crazy bastards, how can they act that way?"

"Brainwashed by secular humanists in school, no doubt."

Ted sniffed. "Wouldn't Dollinger be ecstatic if we were killed? The Avenger at work. The sinners' just demise."

"Good God it was close," Dora said. "Look at me, I'm still totally wrecked," and she held out a quivering hand.

"Me too," Ted said. "God, I dreamed of a crash last night and we almost had one. I wonder what Freud would say about that—that I put those maniacs there?"

She was silent. He stared out the windshield at bushes and gravel and rocks and thought: And what if it *had* been the end? Would it matter? Would anyone care? He felt a perverse adolescent poignancy as he thought of his children weeping over the news. But who gave a good damn if they wept? Or if *anyone* wept? Was that the point of life? —To make someone cry when you died? He glanced at Dora. Did anyone care if she lived or died? Did she care if anyone cared?

He waited until she finished smoking, then checked things out. The U-Haul was still attached and the Pontiac started right up. He drove off cautiously. That damn chest pain was back again and his arms on the wheel felt like lead.

They stopped at the first motel they saw, a small brown cement block affair with a stuttering neon Vacancy sign and lots of white gravel. The available rooms had only one bed. Ted signed the card, took their stuff inside, rolled his sleeping bag out on the floor.

"Forget that nonsense," Dora said. "If it makes you feel any safer, I'm having my period."

He got into bed beside her. It wasn't too saggy; they didn't roll into each other. "To tell you the truth, I feel like having someone next to me after *that*," she said. "No insult intended, but I'd ask a *dog* into bed if I had one and you weren't here."

"I'm insulted."

"I figured you would be." She took a joint out of her purse and lit up. They lay beside each other, sharing it.

"So when did you first start smoking dope?" she said.

"Joy turned me on to it."

"Bad girl."

He smoked the joint, thinking of Joy, wondering if she missed the Wharton Method. Maybe she'd taught it to Rod. He wondered how experienced Dora was and thought: Her period? Yet she can't have kids. The pain without the payoff, yuk.

They finished the joint, she used the john, he turned out the light and they faced away from each other on opposite sides of the bed.

• • • • •

A terrific sharp pain in the eye woke him up in the dark. "Ow! Jesus!"

"Ted! What's wrong?"

Only then did he know. "You hit me with your elbow—right in the eye!"

"Oh, no! I forgot you were there!"

He covered the throbbing pain with the palm of his hand.

"I'm sorry, Ted." She turned on the light. "Let me look."

He took his hand down and let her examine him, suddenly feeling deceptive—as if he'd arranged all this. The fuss felt nice.

"It looks okay. How's your vision?"

"Blurry."

"That ought to clear up soon. Still hurt?"

"A little."

"I think I can fix it. Just try to relax."

She pressed on his temples again and again. The pain dissolved and his vision cleared.

"I'm okay now," he said. "You're amazing, Dora."

"Acupressure massage. You see—"

"I know, there are spots on your head that correspond to these various energy centers."

"How'd you guess?"

"You're as wacky as Armand Dollinger."

She laughed. "You want me to show you how to increase the pain?"

He grinned. "Let's go to sleep."

"I want to use the bathroom first."

He awoke in the morning to find her snuggled against him. He lay there, his hardness constricting him, breathed the clean scent of her hair, then eased himself out of the bed and went to the bathroom. His eye was already dark.

"Looks pretty bad," Dora said when he came back again. "What will Sylvia think?"

"I'll tell her I hit myself on the bedpost."

"Bedpost? In a motel?"

"The hell with it then, let's keep them guessing."

"Sure, why do we feel compelled to *explain* everything?"

Ted looked at himself in the mirror beside the door. He frowned, he stared, he rubbed his chin.

"What's wrong?" Dora said. "You look like you've seen a ghost."

"I just realized what day this is," he said, still frowning at his image, his blackened eye.

"What day *is* this?"

"My birthday. I'm forty-three."

43 • THE CUB REPORTER'S FIRST DREAM

Sun, sun, an endless sky, a piercing, eye-filling light. How marvelous the warmth felt in his bones! But could he *live* with this? Pinion and yucca, sagebrush and sand—so different from the Northeast's lush bluegreens.

Sylvia Schuster was taller than Dora, with soft brown eyes and graying hair and a pleasant, open manner. Her husband, Al, the owner of a print shop, was rotund, balding, cheerful, and equally forthright.

Ted took to them right away, and vice-versa. They insisted he stay at their house, and he slept on the couch in Al's home office, while Dora moved into the guest room.

Richie was twelve and Mike was ten. Ted took them to bowling and video games and had a good time in spite of his constant thoughts of Brad and Kim.

Dan Jefferson's hair had silvered a bit, but he seemed more relaxed than when he'd taught in Jersey. Ted talked about his separation from June and his need for a change of scenery, mentioning nothing about the fiasco, of course—or that he wasn't at Whitman High—and Dan was quite encouraging.

"Ted, you're my man. It has to go to the board, but believe me, no problem."

He sure hoped not. When Grimsley burned the photographs, he promised that nothing about the affair would go into Ted's records. "Resigned for personal reasons," was all it would say. The old hypocrisy: the good Rotarian used car dealer sells his lemons to out-of-towners. And was this lemon grateful to be sold!

"So when does the board meet, Dan?"

"Day after tomorrow. I'll give you a call as soon as the meeting's over. You'll still be here?"

"I'm heading back East in the morning, I have a few things to clear up."

"I'm sure. Can you come for dinner tonight?"

"Thanks, Dan, but I'll take a raincheck." It seemed an odd expression to use in this part of the country.

They shook hands firmly in the nurturing sun. For the first time in ages, Ted felt a surge of hope.

Dora drove him to the airport. They sat and talked till the flight was announced, then he grabbed his bag, they both got up, he went to shake her hand—and she stood on her toes and kissed him behind the ear. It sent a quick ripple of heat down his neck. She said, "Thanks for making the trip with me, Ted."

"My pleasure," he said. "It really was."

"When will you be coming back?"

"It all depends."

"Well give me a call when you get in."

"First thing," he said.

As he took his seat, he thought of her dead lover, David; thought of that dream about Brad being cut in half. Apprehensive as exits were pointed out and oxygen masks were demonstrated, he stared at the foreign landscape, the airport's technological bleakness sharp in the brilliant sun. He had landed a job, and thank God for that, but *could* he live out here? Did he have any *choice?* He thought of the discount June could have gotten, what a waste it was to pay full fare, and then with its sickening power the plane began rolling, then lifted off, went up and up, until all he could see was sky.

• • • • •

The Toyota was dead and the mailbox was stuffed with bills. Notices warned of impending phone and electric termination. Ted read them with angry glee. "You thought you had me, you bastards," he said aloud in the cold empty house. "You thought you had me down for the count, but I have a *job!*"

Among the bills and ads he discovered two birthday cards—from the kids. They were regular store-bought items with "Birthday Greetings" and "To Dad On His Birthday"—not the homemade cards he was used to, but still they brought tears to his eyes. They hadn't forgotten about him!

He called Triple A to ask them to start the Toyota, and then, fingers shaking, he dialed the Colonel's house.

He had to see Brad and Kim. These birthday cards, his time with the Schusters' kids made him miss them like mad. He'd visit tomorrow and take them bowling on what was left of the money he'd borrowed from Dora.

Mabel answered the phone and put June on the line. He spoke awkwardly, briefly—it sounded so strange to hear her. "Where *were* you, Ted? I tried to get in touch with you. I've got an apartment, I'll need the furniture. What? You're right, we have a *lot* to talk about. Let's make it at four, the kids will be home by then."

On the drive, no longer bogged down by Dora, he reverted to his usual pace, and arrived in Sellerstown too early; drank coffee in a mall till zero hour. This was the first time he'd been to a mall since he'd split with June. He realized all over again how much he despised them.

Kim answered the door. She looked heavier, softer. He realized how much of her life he had already missed. He thanked her for her birthday card and kissed her on the forehead, then stepped inside.

Mom and Brad weren't home yet, she told him, and Grandpop and Grandmom had gone to the store. He sat with her in the living room and asked her how it was going at school and whether she'd made new friends. The Little Man wanted to run to her and hold her close and hug her hard, but big Ted simply sat there smiling, listening: Her teacher was young and pretty and nice, her school was smaller than the one in Westdale, the Sellerstown kids talked funny but thought *she* talked funny—and Brad came home.

After that horrible plane crash dream it was such a relief to see him alive and whole. He shook Ted's hand like a man, said hi, went into the powder room for a minute, came back and sat opposite Kim. The structure of his face had changed; his cheekbones were higher, his teeth didn't seem as large. School was okay, he said, he was going out for the baseball team, he had made some neat friends. He kept looking down at the floor as he talked, and Ted felt a sudden shame, imagining what was going through Brad's mind.

June dropped her keys in her purse and greeted him cooly, not looking directly at him; asked Kim if she'd seen her blue scarf. Kim said no, and June went to the foyer and hung up her coat; then she too went to the powder room, returned, sat next to Kim on the couch. Ted caught a quick whiff of perfume; she still smelled like Joy.

They talked a little about her job, and Ted felt tight as a drum. With a false cheerful note in his voice he said that he wanted to take them to dinner. "What's a good place? You kids always liked The Pirates' Cove when you were younger, how about The Pirates' Cove?"

Nobody answered. June asked the children to leave for a minute and after they'd gone she said: "Ted, there's something you ought to know. I'm seeing somebody."

His heart took a quick, sick dive. "Oh," he said, and his voice sounded odd in his head. He frowned, saw his hands on his knees; looked up again. "Is it serious?"

"Quite serious. It's someone I've known for years—a high school sweetheart."

"Oh." He looked at his knees again—and a painful congestion swelled in his chest.

"Ted, let me put it to you straight. I'll never forgive you for what you did. I thought for a while I could, but I realize I can't—and I don't feel the same about you anymore. I just don't love you anymore."

He stared at his hands, his knees, the rug, the hurt in his chest immense. And why this moisture in his eyes? Hadn't he known things were damaged beyond repair? Were these tears for the past? For what might have been? For a ruined future with Brad and Kim?

"I've talked it over with both the kids," she said. "You hurt them terribly, Ted. They want to see you, but they also understand my feelings, and—"

"June, listen, I made a mistake." She was blurry, distorted.

She said, "A mistake."

Cursing the breaking sound in his voice: "A horrible mistake."

She looked straight at him. "Murder's a mistake too, Ted."

"June—"

"Ted, I'm sorry, it's how I feel."

"But June—I found a *job*."

"I'm happy for you, Ted. But I could never take you back. Never, under any circumstances."

They agreed to put their lawyers in touch with each other. He agreed to ship the furniture and all her things to Sellerstown and put the house up for sale.

It was time to go. He said, "Do Brad and Kim like the guy?"

She nodded. "Very much."

"I'm glad," he said.

She called them into the room again and he said goodbye. He hugged them both and told them he loved them, and managed to hold back the tears till he got outside.

• • • • •

He got home at five of eight. Dan Jefferson's school board was meeting today, but when? Not till later, no doubt: school boards usually met at night, and in Albuquerque, it was not yet six.

He poured himself a double scotch and drank it gratefully. Perhaps the meeting *had* been held, he thought. Perhaps Dan had already tried to call. Sleep wasn't going to come tonight till he knew for sure the job was his, so, nervous and chilly, he dialed the distant number.

Three rings, then: "Hello?"

"Hi, Dan? Ted Wharton."

A pause. "Hi, Ted."

Not right, Dan's voice not right. Ted said, "I forgot to ask what time the school board meets. I was out today and thought maybe you'd tried to call."

A space: the random noise of wires. "It's not till later, Ted."

Relief. "Yeah, that's what I figured. So you'll call me collect as soon as it's over, okay?"

Another gap, a long one, then, "Ted, I have some bad news."

—And the terror began. "Bad news?"

"Afraid so, Ted. Joe Bishop called me yesterday."

Quick pain in his throat and behind his eyes. "Joe Bishop?" He thought he might faint.

"We used to be tennis partners. We keep in touch. I hadn't heard from him in months and he gave me a call, I said that you'd been here, and well..."

"He told you."

"Yes."

A silence. Dan said, "You're a hell of a teacher, Ted, and I like you a lot, but I can't recommend you to our board. If that story ever got out—and it would—my ass would be grass—and so would yours. Things could really get rough."

Ted thought about what he had told Joe Bishop to do with his vacuum cleaner. The kitchen began to grow dim. Everything of importance was swelling his body: horribly, hotly, stinging.

"You have to understand my position, Ted."

The phone had turned to rubber in Ted's hand; he made his soft mouth work. "I do." It was all he could say.

"Ted, look, I know what a spot you're in, and maybe… Listen, you've tended bar before. I know of a job that's open, it's six nights a week, the pay's not bad with the tips, it's a real nice place. I mean, as an interim thing…"

Ted closed his eyes. "Thanks, Dan."

"Think it over and let me know. I'm sure things can still work out for you here, one way or another."

"Yeah… Right… I'll let you know. And, well…say hi to Gloria."

"I'll do that, Ted. And listen—I'm really sorry, but…I just can't take the chance."

"I realize that. And…thanks again."

"Goodbye, Ted."

"See you, Dan."

He opened his eyes and hung up. With shaking hands he poured a hefty scotch and tossed it down. His heart was huge and aching, and the hurt in his throat splintered into his ringing ears.

He would have to call Frank. He would call his brother Frank, the electrician, and ask for a job. Surely he could take him on until— Until what?

He looked for the number in the little blue book, his fingers dead on the pages. A sickness struck the core of his head and he dropped the book. He stared at it there on the floor.

He was going insane. He was, he was going insane. He had to talk to somebody, *now,* he *had* to, this minute, before he was totally paralyzed. He found the number in his wallet, picked up the phone again, dialed.

It was Richie who answered. Was Dora there? She was, hold on. He did, space whistling in his ears. A shuffle and then her voice. "Hello?" His heart contracted hard.

"Hi, Dora? It's me, it's Ted."

"Ted, hi!"

His face felt weak. "Dora, listen—I won't be coming to Albuquerque."

"What?"

"No, but I'll send you the money I owe you, don't worry about it—as soon as I get a job."

"Oh, *Ted.*"

He told her everything then: about June, Joe Bishop, Dan Jefferson. "That's how it goes, I guess." He was dizzy from fighting the river of fear and pain.

"Oh, Ted, that's a shame, it really is. But listen, I know about something else you might want to consider."

He swallowed. "You do?"

"Al's best friends with the bureau chief of *The Albuquerque Sun.* They need a reporter. Al thinks you'd be perfect."

Astonished, Ted said, "I…really? You really think I have a chance?"

"A *good* chance, Ted. And if for some reason it doesn't work out, there's always printing—or ladies' fashions."

"Oh no, no, Dora, I couldn't do that. Work for Al or Sylvia? That wouldn't be fair."

"Till something else came along."

"Dan told me about a bartending thing. I guess I could always take that."

"Whatever. But I'm sure you'll get the reporter job—if you don't take forever to get here." She paused. "So when are you going to come?"

"But Dora…"

"Ted, listen, I've found an apartment. It's very nice, in a perfect location, it's cheerful as hell, but it does have a problem."

"What's that?" He wanted to keep the conversation going, to never hang up.

"It has two bedrooms. All the smaller apartments were rented. Now what am I going to do with that extra space?"

"You're asking me?"

Another pause. "What I'm getting at, Ted, if I must spell it out, is you'll need a place to stay, and with all the room I have... I mean, since we're both such decadents, since I know the soles of your feet so well, and since you only *really* snored one night..."

"You really mean that, Dora?"

"I kind of like you, Ted."

"Well I kind of like you, too."

"And I promise never to poke your eye again. —So what do you say?"

"Will I have to eat Jewish food?"

A laugh. "No, but you can't make fun of me while I'm eating it, either."

"I won't, I won't."

"Then you'll come?"

"I'll come. I have some stuff to take care of here, but after that, I'll come."

"Ted, that's just great. I'll let Al know you want the job."

"Yes. Yes!"

"Oh, here's some news. Madge Nader, dear soul that she is, called to see how I was, and told me that Armand Dollinger's in big trouble."

"What kind of trouble?"

"It seems the media Review Committee—bless its heart—refused to ban *The Diary of Anne Frank.*"

"*The Diary of Anne Frank?*"

"That's right. So Dollinger got his son to check it out of the library—and burned it."

"Wow."

"The son bragged about it to Terry Blaustein—remember him?—and Blaustein alerted the ACLU."

"Hah!"

"Needless to say, he's finished as school board chairman."

"Fantastic!"

"I thought you'd be pleased."

He laughed. "It's wonderful!"

The line's high hum as she said, "Well, Ted, I'll see you soon. Are you driving or flying?"

"I guess I'll drive. I have few things to bring."

"Okay, I'll look for you. And listen, relax, it's going to be all right."

"I hope so, Dora."

"It will be, Ted."

A pause. "Well, goodnight, Ted—and take care of yourself."

"Goodnight. You take care of yourself too, Dora."

"Goodnight."

He poured himself another scotch, a little one, with water, and went to the family room. The TV's dead eye stared at him. Tomorrow the lawyer, the mover, the realtor.

Eighteen years of marriage down the tubes. Feeling a sudden need for air, he went outside.

Mr. 7-Eleven was out there under his spotlight, smoking his pipe and setting out bags of trash. Invisible in the darkness, Ted watched.

The air was wet, and—at last—held the scent of spring. In the dark Ted saw the row of crocuses against the house—the crocuses that June had planted when Brad and Kim were small. Soon the house would be someone else's house, these flowers would belong to someone else. He breathed the fragrant cool March damp and thought of New Mexico sun.

What a fool he had been. What a perfect suburban fool. And if it had never happened? Would things have gradually gotten better with June? He shrugged and sipped his scotch and thought of Dora. Mr. 7-Eleven looked up at the sky, then went back inside.

Dora and Albuquerque. Another American trap—the New Life. Well, sometimes it actually worked. Ted Wharton, cub reporter? Maybe so. He liked Dora Rosen, and damn it, he'd give it a shot. He'd give it a damn good shot, the best he had.

He held up his glass and toasted the 7-Elevens' spotlight. Good luck, Mr. 7-Eleven. Good luck, June. Good luck, Brad and Kim. And even—hell yes—good luck, Joy and Rod. Life was full of terrific detours and U-turns, you needed every ounce of luck you could get, so good luck to everybody.

The spotlight went out. Ted tilted his head back and swallowed the last of his scotch; then went into the house that belonged to his past and climbed the stairs; used the bathroom; crawled into the chilly king-sized bed.

He was tired, completely wiped out, at peace, fell asleep right away—and dreamed of the time Brad caught that five pound bass.

MATINEE AT THE FLAME

BY CHRISTOPHER FAHY

Signed Limited Hard Cover	500 Editions	$44.95
Trade Paperback	ISBN: 1892950731	$17.95

An elderly junk dealer finds redemption in a defunct burlesque theater. A middle-aged Jewish man discovers the aphrodisiacal powers of a Ku Klux Klan uniform. An annual street carnival provides the venue for legalized murder.

Welcome to the world of Christopher Fahy, a world of fantastical transformation, where the ordinary takes bizarre and macabre twists:

- A druggie wandering in Europe touches a medieval painting and is shockingly changed forever.
- A middle aged bachelor loser becomes a slave to his TV set, which has him carry out its evil plans.
- New dental work turns a cuckold into a vengeful killer.
- A mild-mannered octogenarian comes back from the dead to right the wrongs of his familiar world.
- A greedy businessman is trapped in a life-or-death game played with 1952 baseball cards.
- Frankenstein's monster visits his creator, Mary Shelley, in the dark of a sleepless night with love on his mind.
- A hopeless young factory worker uses her savings to pay for a fantasy tryst with her idol, a dead rock star, and is shattered by the experience.

Christopher Fahy is the author of four horror and suspense novels, *Nightflyer*, *Dream House*, *Eternal Bliss* and *The Lyssa Syndrome*, the medical thriller *Breaking Point* and the erotically charged mainstream novel *Fever 42*. Here, for the first time, are 22 of his strange, disturbing yet often poignant stories collected in one volume, stories that will take you into both haunting shadow and merciless light.

OVERLOOK CONNECTION PRESS
PO Box 1934 • Hiram, GA • 30141
PHONE: 678-567-9777 • FAX: 770-222-6192
EMAIL: overlookcn@aol.com
www.overlookconnection.com